PRAISE F

"Steeped in illusion and ... ...istory of the Luddite Rebellion, ...atural mystery serves ably as both a standalone adventure and the start to a series. Strategically placed steampunk tropes inform but do not overwhelm Elizabeth's headlong quest to find a missing aristocrat sought by the Patent Office, which is fixated on both achieving perfection and eliminating 'unseemly science.' A hazardous border crossing into the permissively corrupt Kingdom of England and Southern Wales provides ample excitement, and a glossary at the novel's conclusion hints enticingly at a much more involved story to come."

Publishers Weekly

"It's all steampunk and circus wonder as we follow the adventures of Elizabeth Barnabas. The double crosses along the way keep the plot tight and fun, and the conclusion sets us up nicely for book two."

The Washington Post

"*The Queen of all Crows* is a smart and entertaining read, among the best of the steampunk subgenre I've read. It continues the story of Elizabeth Barnabus in an alternative history where they take intellectual property protection a little too seriously."

Craig Newmark, founder of Craigslist and Craigconnects

"A tumultuous and utterly wonderful series."

Smorgasbord Fantasia

"I've read all of the books in the Fall of the Gas-Lit Empire series, and I love how inventive the whole series is. Each book has a strong story and fantastic characters. The Map of Unknown Things series takes us outside the main Gas-Lit Empire to other parts of the world that the author has created. I love that these are great adventure stories, but also have a more thoughtful side to them – the worlds we visit are all very different and flawed in very different ways, but inhabited by people who have been shaped by the nature of those worlds. It's very clever, but also very engaging – I find myself completely drawn in, unable to predict what will happen next. I also have a strong sense that there is an overall plan to the whole series – this is building into a fantastic overall tale. Really looking forward to the next instalment!"

Clare Littleford, author of The Quarry

"I absolutely loved *The Queen of All Crows*. It's a gripping alternative history adventure set in an intriguing world. Among the fast-paced plot twists the novel also provides keen insights into power structures, particularly when it comes to gender roles as social constructs. Elizabeth Barnabus is possibly my favourite steampunk main character ever: resourceful, fearless, unusually observant and emotionally intelligent. I was thrilled to follow her to the ends of the world as a reader."

Emmi Itäranta, award-winning author of Memory of Water

"If I had a bowler hat, I'd take it off to the author of this beautifully crafted steampunk novel."

Chris D'Lacey, author of the Last Dragon Chronicles

"Let's get this out of the way: *The Queen of All Crows* is an excellent book, full stop. Duncan has managed to infuse the world of the Gas-Lit Empire, and the character of Elizabeth Barnabus herself, with a new jolt of life, color, and depth. Clear your schedule, because you won't want to stop reading this until you've finished, and then you'll want more."

Eric Scott Fischl, author of The Trials of Solomon Parker

"Elizabeth Barnabus is a uniquely intriguing character who will take readers on a fascinating journey through the strange landscapes of the Gas-Lit Empire. Rod Duncan's storytelling skill brings his fictional world to a mysterious, vibrant life."

Stephen Booth, bestselling author of the Cooper & Fry series

"Rod Duncan's *The Bullet Catcher's Daughter* is a magic box pulsating with energy. Compulsive reading from the get-go, the blend of steampunk alternate history wrapped in the enigma of a chase makes for first-rate entertainment in this finely crafted novel."

Graham Joyce, author of Year of the Ladybird

ROD DUNCAN

The Fugitive and the Vanishing Man

BEING VOLUME THREE *of*
The MAP *of* UNKNOWN THINGS

ANGRY
ROBOT

ANGRY ROBOT
An imprint of Watkins Media Ltd

Unit 11, Shepperton House
89 Shepperton Road
London N1 3DF
UK

angryrobotbooks.com
twitter.com/angryrobotbooks
Please welcome to the stage…

An Angry Robot paperback original, 2020

Cover by Kieryn Tyler
Edited by Eleanor Teasdale, Paul Simpson, Claire Rushbrook
Set in Meridien

ISBN 978 0 85766 844 8
Ebook ISBN 978 0 85766 849 3

Printed and bound in the United Kingdom by TJ International.

9 8 7 6 5 4 3 2 1

THE FUGITIVE &
THE VANISHING MAN

PART ONE

The con artist and the spy, each hiding beneath layers of disguise. Snake-like, they shed their skins, revealing new ones underneath. Thinning themselves by slivers, they wonder, when the last disguise has been sloughed off, if they might vanish even to themselves. And there perhaps find peace.

CHAPTER 1

Standing in the washhouse cubicle below a glassless window, Elizabeth could smell the air from the waterfall thundering outside.

"Hold me," she said, and he did. John Farthing. He enfolded her. She pressed her face into his coat, breathing him instead of the dank air, inhaling the memory of his body, of parting.

Somewhere outside the washhouse, her friends would be looking for her. They'd stepped off the boat together, gone through the ordeal of searches and questioning in that bare border post by the river. Her pistol had been their chief concern: a finely-made thing with the emblem of a leaping hare inlaid in turquoise on the stock. But for all its beauty, it was nothing more than a flintlock. It offended no rule of the Gas-Lit Empire, so at last the guards let them pass and they stepped from the wilds into the Free States of America.

Climbing the long flight of steps up the side of the gorge, she'd looked back and seen the full circle of a rainbow hanging in the air, bright against the darkness of the Niagara's far bank. It was a wonder of the world, the boat captain had said, and now she knew the truth of that. As great a miracle as the miracle of her having lived to see it.

She was halfway up when she saw John Farthing looking down over the railings from the top. Just a glimpse: the silhouette of his head and shoulders. But she knew him. The spark of recognition set a fire in her heart.

Running up stone steps slick with mist from the falls, quickly out of breath, her thighs burned. And then at the top, seeing him looking back at her from the side of the washhouse. He slipped behind it. She went to him, took his hand, led him inside, into one of the cubicles, bolting the door behind them.

The dripping of water in a cistern. That dank waterfall smell.

Having sent word ahead, she'd expected to be met by agents of the Patent Office. But not by John. That was beyond her dreaming. He had crossed the Atlantic to see her. He had come to the border itself.

His fingers kneaded the lines of muscle in her back. He kissed her hair.

"You're thinner," he whispered.

She found herself laughing. "You feel just the same."

She went up on her toes to kiss him, but he angled his face for her lips to find his cheek instead of his mouth. She felt the rub of fine stubble.

"They're going to want to talk to you," he said.

"I know."

"The way they're saying it, they didn't think you'd manage. To risk it all and come back, I mean. With Julia as well."

"And Tinker," she said. "I brought them both. You didn't believe me either."

"I never doubted that you *could*. But storms and tides – they're beyond controlling. Even for you." There was a shudder in his chest, a catch of breath. "You've seen things. Out there in the wilds. Things our spies have never seen." She felt the warmth of his breath through her hair as he spoke, but found herself shivering.

"Please just hold me."

"You've got to listen, Elizabeth. We don't have much time. They're going to tell you to go back. Across the border, I mean. But they don't have the power to force you. They'll say they do. They'll say anything to make it happen. You just need to keep saying no."

"I missed you," she said, hoping he'd say the same, listening for a change in his heartbeat.

There was a shout from outside, Julia calling, trying to find her.

Elizabeth pulled back, to look up at him. "Where do we go?"

"To the hotel. I'll take you."

"Other agents will be there?"

He nodded. "This – your crossing – it had to be quiet. That's why it's only me here to meet you. Your handler. But they have their questions."

Handler. She wished he'd meant it as a joke.

"Elizabeth? Where are you?" Julia was close outside.

Farthing opened the cubicle door. "You'd better go."

So she did.

The sunshine dazzled after the dark of the washroom. Julia seemed relieved to have found her. But when

Farthing stepped out, Julia's expression transformed into a coy smile and she averted her eyes.

They found Tinker, leaning over the railings. Elizabeth had never seen the boy awed by anything before. Or rather, he would usually hide any sign that he might be impressed. But the falls had him gripped. When he glanced back at her, she saw the wonder in his face, as if he was comfortable with the emotion. Strangely, it made him seem older.

"It's time to go," she said, feeling a wave of sadness that she couldn't have explained. She'd done everything she set out to achieve and come back with her loved ones alive. Unharmed. It was a moment to be celebrated. But as they followed John Farthing along the road to the hotel, her feet felt leaden.

"Was your reunion sweet?" Julia whispered.

"Yes," she said, the lie too easy.

"And so will be mine, with Robert."

"Yes," said Elizabeth with more conviction, finding it easier to believe in Julia's happiness than her own.

The hotel was a wide brick building of two storeys, with a balcony running all the way around. She stepped out towards the grand entrance, but Farthing called her back and she found herself following him with the others, down the side until they reached a small black door, unmarked and without a handle. Unlocking it, he ushered them through to a cramped passage and a narrow set of stairs, by which they came to something akin to a drawing room, comfortably furnished but impersonal.

Windows ran the length of one wall. Long net curtains shifted in the breeze.

Two men in grey stood as they entered, one dark-skinned, the other light. Their smiles seemed false. Elizabeth had no doubt they were agents. She and Julia shook hands with each. Tinker went to the window.

"Welcome," said the fair-skinned one.

"Do you need to rest?" asked the other.

She hadn't been able to sleep the night before. But her mind was racing and she knew it would be impossible. "Do you suppose they could bring a pot of tea?"

There were six doors off the drawing room. One led to a bathroom with flushing toilet and hot water on tap. After life in the wilds, such luxuries seemed like a miracle. Four doors led to bedrooms and one gave access to the balcony, blocked off to left and right. When Tinker tried to use it, they called him back.

"It's best no one sees you."

Afterwards Elizabeth couldn't have said which agent had spoken.

The tea things arrived via what seemed to be a small cupboard built into the wall, but which proved to be a dumbwaiter. However, the pot held only hot water. Dry tea leaves rested in a small metal caddy. She sent it all back with instructions:

Please warm the pot. Add two measures of tea leaves. THEN pour in boiling water. Thank you.

In all the months of her travelling beyond the border, she'd thought of this moment – her first cup of tea. She wouldn't allow it to be less than her imagination.

There was no exit but for the flight of steps by which they'd entered, and down which she now saw John Farthing slip away.

"Are you well?" Julia whispered.

"Yes."

"You seem… distressed."

"I'm fine."

"It's not the tea, is it?"

"I am fine!"

Elizabeth had dreamed of many things in the wilderness. But John Farthing had gone and she wanted a cup of tea and if it wasn't made right, she thought she might pick up one of the chairs and hurl it through the window.

With a squeak of pulley wheels and the tinkle of a bell, the dumbwaiter returned. This time it had been done right. She poured through the strainer into a rose-patterned cup. They had sent a small jug, but it contained cream instead of milk, so she sipped it black. It was too hot to taste, but some deep part of her felt the rightness of it.

Tinker must have sensed something because he came to comfort her, put his arms around her shoulders and pressed his forehead into her cheek. That broke the dam of her tears. She ran to the bedroom, slamming the door behind her.

She pretended to sleep, which kept them away for a time. They talked in hushed voices in the other room. Soon she was smelling roasted meat and listening to the clink of crockery. When she did sleep and wake again, it felt as if only a few minutes had passed. Someone was knocking on the door and calling her name. A man's voice. It wasn't John Farthing.

"What is it?"

"Miss Barnabus, we need to talk."

"I'm resting."

"You've been in there six hours."

She looked through the window and saw a streak of red in the darkening sky.

A fresh pot of tea was waiting, cool enough to drink. They'd brought chairs and a writing table to the unused bedroom. She sat facing them. Steam twisted from her cup. The men's faces were hard to read with the window behind them, and the last of the daylight fading.

"What are your names?" she asked.

"Agent McLeod," said the dark-skinned man.

"Agent Winslow," said the other. "We need you to tell us everything." He opened a writing book, unscrewed his fountain pen and dated the top corner in a generous, looping hand. Elizabeth read it upside down.

"Everything? It's too much. There is too much to tell."

"Start from the beginning."

"But where is that?"

"Newfoundland," said Winslow.

McLeod shook his head. "Start before that. The North Atlantic whaling fleet."

Elizabeth's story had started further back even than that, with the loss of Julia as she crossed the Atlantic. The trauma of it had ended her secret affair with John Farthing. It had set her off into the wilds on an impossible mission, to find her friend. She stared at the sunset sky behind the agents, at a streak of dirt on the glass.

"You dressed as a man to disguise yourself," McLeod prompted. "Do you think the sailors of the fleet were duped?"

"Duped?" There was a wrongness to the word. A discordance.

"Taken in," said McLeod.

"They thought me a man, if that's what you mean."

Winslow's pen nib whispered as he wrote.

"Could you tell us how you came to disappear?"

"Our ship was captured."

"And what was your part in the mutiny?"

"There was no mutiny. We were attacked by a submarine boat. It would have drowned us… but…"

The two agents were looking at each other as if embarrassed by her account. Then Winslow said, "The crew survived. They saw what you did, Miss Barnabus. We have testimonies. They all say the same thing. You put a pistol to your captain's head."

"I saved his life."

"Did you not threaten to kill him?"

"They would have shot him dead if I hadn't done that. I stopped them. I saved them all."

Agent McLeod wrote.

"We understand that the pirates were all women. Having captured the ship, they lined you up and assaulted the captain. Whereon you identified yourself as a woman for the first time and asked to join their nation. Is that not correct?"

"You make it sound… bad."

"I'm reporting the facts."

"I played along. But only so I could help the crew."

"Whose crew?"

"Ours! The men!"

"You helped the men over the women – is that your claim?"

"It's the truth," she said, the real truth being too complicated to explain.

"But later you led an attack on the mother ship of the fleet."

"The attack was coming. I risked my life to stop it. If I ever mutinied, it was against the women."

"So you had joined them?"

"I lied to them! I cheated them. I ran from them. They'd kill me now if they were here. And yes, I got myself into the attack. But only so I could rescue my friends."

While Winslow wrote, McLeod nodded, as if her words made sense.

"You were present at the murder of the Fleet Commodore?"

Elizabeth nodded, knowing where they were leading, feeling short of breath.

"Did you kill him?" McLeod asked.

"I tried to stop it."

"But not successfully."

Winslow put down the pen and folded his arms.

"Is that what you want?" she asked. "To try me for mutiny?"

"Murder would be more likely. And since you led the attack on the fleet, it would be treason also."

Would be. There it was: the possibility of an escape from the gallows. John Farthing had said they'd try to get her to go back to Newfoundland. Keep saying no, he'd told her.

He hadn't said anything about this sword, dangling above her head.

"The crew of the ship *Pembroke* survived?" she asked. They'd been locked in a ship's hold the last time she'd seen them. And that ship had been snared in the middle of the battle. Cannons had been firing.

"They survived," said McLeod.

"So the women… the pirates… did they lose their battle?"

The two agents glanced at each other again.

Winslow said, "I'm sorry. I thought you'd know. But you've been away, of course. There was an exchange of prisoners. That's how the crew came back to us. In the battle they lost many ships. But they gained one."

"They captured the Mother Ship?"

Neither man denied it.

If the pirates had captured the floating city of the Mother Ship, it would mean the Gas-Lit Empire was losing control of the North Atlantic.

"How did you escape from the battle, Miss Barnabus?"

"I took a steam launch."

"You stole it," Winslow corrected.

"We escaped from the fight."

"You deserted?"

"We escaped."

"Then why did you flee to Newfoundland? If you were innocent, why not return to the Gas-Lit Empire?"

Winslow had drawn a line in his ledger and was writing a new heading.

"Newfoundland was a mistake," she said. "We thought we'd landed in Nova Scotia but the wind had taken us too far to the north."

"And what did you find there?"

Elizabeth opened her mouth to answer, but then closed it again. What she'd seen was a shift in the balance of power that might change the whole world. New nations were growing in the wilderness beyond the borders of civilisation. It would be wilderness no more. From the chaos of endless war, pockets of order were emerging. And in those far-flung places, weapons were being created that could overthrow even the might of the civilised world.

"Well?" asked McLeod. "What did you see in the wilds?"

She folded her arms and sat back.

"I'm not going to tell you," she said.

CHAPTER 2

From a distance, the castle at Crown Point seemed to be an extension of the basalt cliffs on which it rested. But closer to, and with an eye for detail, the entire history of the fortress might be read from the strata of those stones.

The rough boulders at the base of the wall had once been free-standing: a crude barricade with spaces for cannons to fire down on boats in the Colombia River hundreds of feet below. That had been the start of it, a pirate camp on the plateau, preying on such trade as the wilds could sustain. Then smaller stones had been placed to fill the gaps between the boulders. They'd not been cut to shape. Rather, through careful placing, their natural angles interlocked, creating the first true wall.

By then the camp had grown into something more permanent. They no longer thought of themselves as pirates. Protectors of that section of the river, perhaps. Custodians of a nascent order in the midst of the wild Oregon Territory. For this great service, they levied only a modest tax. And since they now risked just the kind of attack they'd once launched on others, walls were needed all the way around. A castle had begun to emerge.

It was a good business. Wealth accumulated and the walls thickened to contain it. Further out, new wards were needed to protect the storerooms and stables, workshops and marshalling yard. By then the Lords of Crown Point had started to call themselves kings. They could afford the luxury of masons, who cut flat faces on the stones as the walls grew taller. And then, when the only reason for further height was a statement of power, the masons carved gargoyles and grotesque faces to frighten or amaze those who passed below.

At the pinnacle of the castle, with the finest stonework, stood three towers from which flags streamed. The East Tower was the tallest. There, a slim figure stood, dressed in white with a blue scarf rippling behind. Flashes of green and turquoise at her neck were long enamel earrings. Shaped like fish, they danced in the gusting wind.

She had been staring towards the furthest point upriver, sometimes shielding her eyes against the brightness of the sky, sometimes blinking and looking away as if to clear her vision.

Two enforcer guards climbed the final steps to join her. Each carried a rifle with sighting lenses along its barrel.

"He wants you," one of them said. "The king."

She turned to face them. "Where?"

"The Great Hall."

"I thought he was out hunting."

"Great Hall," he said, again.

"Will he want to see me… like this?"

The guard stepped to the balustrade and leaned his gun against the stonework. The other one did a practice aim towards the shingle strands far below, swinging the rifle left and right before resting the gun next to his comrade's.

Reluctant messengers at best, they wouldn't stoop to answer the question. She set off down the stairs, lifting her skirts, revealing glimpses of bare feet, narrow but long.

The stones felt cold in the shade. But she was moving now, almost silent, descending thirty feet to the lower battlements, and then into the castle itself, along a corridor set within the thickness of the wall. Lamps lit the way, though she could have run it with her eyes closed.

The king was supposed to be hunting. He always came back in a good mood after killing some poor creature. Or at least relaxed. At those times, he could be indulgent. But if the hunt had been cancelled or cut short, that would push him the other way. Better perhaps that she did not approach him in that dress, though changing would mean a delay, which would carry its own risk.

A key hung from a plaited cord around her neck. She unlocked the door and stepped into the room. Stripping down, she laid the blue silk scarf and white dress on the bed, then the padded under-cloth. A slim, muscular figure was revealed in the mirror.

Donning trousers and shirt felt like stepping into a different facet of who they were. They sat in front of the mirror, brushing wind knots from dark hair, gathering it back into a queue, tying it in the style of men, with a black ribbon.

Staring at the face for a moment, Edwin unclipped the earrings and started to wipe away the makeup. Leaving a trace could allow for a more androgynous look. The men and women of the court would react to that in different ways. A few would be attracted, some unsettled, some hostile. That ambiguous appearance was the statement of a deep truth. But truth is a luxury for more settled times.

With the last of the makeup gone, Edwin turned his head, checking the reflection one last time, almost ready to appear before the King of Crown Point. Boots were the last to go on. Not something most would notice. And yet they transformed him more than any other external thing. She had arrived in the room with delicate precision. But in leaving, he closed the door with enough force to send echoes reverberating along the stone corridor. Striding away, Edwin planted his feet, landing on the heels instead of placing his toes, rolling shoulders rather than hips, projecting the authority his offices demanded: First Counsellor to the King, Magician of Crown Point.

By the time he reached the final corridor, servants and guards were making room for him to pass. The Great Hall was in disarray. Attendants were righting a table while a serving girl worked on hands and knees, picking fragments of broken china from the floor. The king was pacing, his men giving him plenty of space.

"Where's my damn magician?"

Edwin presented himself. "I'm here, sire."

"What took you so long?"

Half the skill of being a counsellor was knowing when a question wasn't looking for an answer. The king paced. Such force of will as he might have channelled into the hunt was coming out as this evil humour. It would run its course.

Edwin stepped to the fire and crouched, staring into the flames as if they were whispering to him. The king hadn't noticed but some of his men had. Most would be believers, though it was hard to know the degree or the number. He held a hand above the coals, palm down. With his thumb, he flicked open the hollow signet ring, releasing a pinch of powder. Then he began swirling his fingers, as if writing in the air. He could hear them whispering behind him. The king's heavy footfalls had stopped. Edwin began to hum, his mouth creating vowel sounds, like some unearthly language.

The fire began to crackle. He backed away. Green light fringed the flames. The crackling grew louder, became a popping sound that spat green sparks, reaching a crescendo, then fading. The room behind him had become perfectly quiet.

Before turning, he allowed the muscles of his face to go slack, as if from terrible fatigue. All eyes were fixed on him as he staggered to his feet.

"The path behind you is clear," he whispered to the king, quiet enough so all others would need to focus on listening. Though not so quiet that they wouldn't hear. "The path ahead you cannot see. Except for this: the thing that seems now a setback will be your certain road to victory."

He felt the relief rippling through the room. The king managed a smile. He took Edwin's hand and pulled him into an embrace. Then, just as quickly, Edwin had been released and the king was waving to dismiss the others. The Great Hall emptied. The doors closed. They were alone.

"Why must you come to me slathered with perfume, Edwin? Now I stink like a whorehouse. My consort will think…"

Damn, but he'd forgotten about the scent. He bowed his head.

The king paced to the wall. The Great Hall had been decorated in tapestry maps. Not the sort that would be useful for wayfinding. The safe routes across the continent were not the kind of thing to leave in plain view. These maps were broad outlines, more likely to lead astray than to guide. But they still showed the simple arrangement of the continent. In the far west, the castle at Crown Point, commanding the Oregon Territory with its access to the Pacific Ocean. In the far east, Newfoundland, like a fortress, ready to dominate the Atlantic. Between them lay the many nations of North America that belonged to that great alliance, the Gas-Lit Empire. But it was towards the north that Edwin's eyes always strayed: two thousand miles of wilderness between Oregon and Newfoundland, the land through which the messengers would be travelling. If they had set off.

The king kicked a fragment of broken china, sending it tinkling down the hall. "Establish a brother king in Newfoundland, you said. Drive a trade route between the coasts to control both oceans."

"Yes, sire."

"And you have achieved this wonder in the East. But with one issue. The wrong man has become king!"

Edwin noted the word *you*. It had been their joint plan, worked out together.

"You have installed an enemy in the East," the king said.

"He may not be. We don't know yet."

"Don't try to play your burning powder tricks on me, magician. Hollow rings and hollow sayings. Such performances and speeches will sway the men. But don't ever try to use them on me."

Edwin swallowed, ordering his thoughts. "This new king of Newfoundland – he is not the man we hoped for. And it may be that his price will be higher. But he will have a price. There is a deal to be made. Then you'll have the whole route from ocean to ocean."

"And then?"

"And then, my lord, you will tear down the walls of the Gas-Lit Empire."

CHAPTER 3

The Patent Office agents arranged the evening meal on the table: smoked bacon with a sweet potato mash and steamed greens. It had arrived in the dumbwaiter, already arranged on plates, each with a metal cover so that they stacked into a tower. The cutlery was silver and heavy. Tinker wolfed down his portion, licking the plate clean, much to Elizabeth's embarrassment. He then sat unnervingly still, watching the rest of them with a predatory focus.

It was an awkward meal. After her blank refusal to reveal what had happened in Newfoundland, Agents McLeod and Winslow had withdrawn to one of the other bedrooms to consult. If they'd made a decision, she still hadn't been told of it.

While they were out of the way, Elizabeth had taken her chance to talk with the others. Julia had been questioned but revealed nothing. Tinker they hadn't bothered to ask, though his natural mistrust of authority would have kept his mouth shut tighter than an oyster in any case.

When the agents emerged, Winslow headed down the narrow stairs. The little black door closed quietly behind him.

"Can I go for a walk?" she asked McLeod.

He shook his head, seeming embarrassed by her lack of decorum.

"What if I just leave? You wouldn't need to notice."

"It's not a good idea."

His manner was courteous but the gravity with which he spoke gave his words an edge of menace.

"At least let the boy go for a run around."

"I'm sorry."

"Where is John Farthing?"

McLeod smiled that embarrassed smile again. "Rest," he said. "You must be tired."

She was. But rest would not come. Presently Julia came to her room and sat by her on the bed. Tinker followed, closing the door behind him.

"I want to see the waterfall," he said.

"I know."

"They won't let me go."

"Have you tried?"

"The door was locked." He blushed, as though admitting some grave moral failing.

She wanted to hug him, but he was bristling with energy and wouldn't have suffered it, so she hugged Julia instead. "They want to find out what we saw in Newfoundland. So long as we don't tell them, we'll still have something to bargain with."

"How long can they keep us?" Julia asked, distress in her voice.

"All will be well," Elizabeth said, not believing her own words.

"But I am so desperate."

"You'll see your husband soon."

"It can never be soon enough. Never."

"My poor friend."

Julia looked at her hands, as if searching for a speck of dirt. "He won't yet know that I'm alive."

Julia was voicing the very danger that Elizabeth had chosen not to mention. No one knew they had returned from the wilds. These agents of the Patent Office had the powers and resources to make people simply disappear, if that was what they wished.

But the thought of Julia's husband had sparked an idea in Elizabeth's mind. "If he knew… He is a lawyer, after all."

Hope kindled in Julia's eyes. "Could we send a message? Is there a way?"

Elizabeth swung her legs from the bed and stood. "Suppose we could get out. Just for a few minutes. There must be a pigeon loft in a hotel this big. But we have no money."

"Could we put it on the room's account?" Julia asked.

It seemed unlikely.

"Sell the silver," Tinker said.

"To who?"

He shrugged as if to say that finding a buyer for stolen cutlery would be easy. It wouldn't. Every knife, fork and spoon had been stamped with the hotel's insignia. They'd end up in jail if they tried.

"If this was England, we'd be allowed legal representation," Julia said.

But Elizabeth knew better. She had been in the custody of the Patent Office before. Whatever rules a country might have, the Patent Office was above them. The floorboards outside the room creaked. Everyone looked up. They'd been speaking quietly, though Tinker not so much.

"Money first," Elizabeth whispered. "Then we'll find the means of escape. After that we can send a message."

A hand knocked on the door, quiet and precise. Agent McLeod didn't wait for them to answer.

"Are you rested?" he asked, looking in.

"Quite," said Elizabeth, getting up and stepping towards him. Tinker was close behind, as if he'd guessed already what she was about to do.

"I'm distressed," she said to the agent.

He recoiled slightly as if not knowing how to deal with such a statement of emotion.

"I'm sorry."

"But I am distressed!" She opened her arms, as if to display her piteous state or perhaps for him to hug her. The smooth line of his jacket showed a slight bulge on the left side of his chest. It could have been a small gun in a holster or something resting in the inside pocket.

"Shall I send for more tea?" he asked. "Or I could–"

"But I've come halfway around the world! I've faced threats and violence!" She raised the pitch of her voice, making it shrill. "I've returned to civilisation... and now I'm to be locked up?"

"Not necessarily. If you'll just cooperate. We could–"

"...Locked up by the very people I sacrificed everything to help!"

He had taken a halfstep back as she approached. Now she lurched towards him. He looked ready to run, but she'd thrown herself into a stumbling fall. He made to catch her. She grabbed hold of him. One hand on his left shoulder. The other inside his jacket. Not a gun. A wallet. Tinker was waiting for it, bless the boy. As she dropped her arm, she felt him just behind, snatching the wallet from her hand. He pushed on past them, through the doorway, into the drawing room, out of McLeod's eyeline.

The agent lowered Elizabeth to the ground and backed away into the main room, as if remaining near her bed after such closeness might threaten his vow of celibacy. The last thing she saw before putting her head down into a feigned weep was Tinker behind him, stuffing the wallet into grubby trousers.

"I'm so sorry," she wailed.

Julia followed the agent out of the bedroom. "Don't just stand there," she cried. "Order more tea!"

Though Julia had not been brought up in fairgrounds and travelling shows, she'd learned enough from Elizabeth's stories to understand what came next in the dipper's playbook. The mark might realise the strangeness of events. He might feel the lightness of his pocket. Agent McLeod was a quick thinker. His agile mind would need to be kept busy.

He'd just finished writing the order for tea and was ready to send it down in the dumbwaiter, when Julia said, "It needs to be medicinal tea. Ordinary won't do."

"Medicinal?"

"You saw her! And you're responsible."

"But I didn't... And I don't know what–"

"She needs these things," Julia cut in, keeping him off balance. "Get fresh paper and write them down. Quick now!"

Tinker returned to the bedroom and stood against the

wall to the side of the door, out of the agent's sight. He pulled the wallet from his trousers and opened it so that Elizabeth could see the folded banknotes. He pulled out a twenty-dollar bill, crisp as if freshly minted, and seemed set to take out more, but she shook her head. It was a huge sum in any case. They had to leave doubt in his mind. That was the trick. They couldn't let him be certain that he had been robbed.

Tinker opened the other pocket of the wallet and held it for her to look inside.

Julia was still dictating in the outer room. "Aspirin, tonic water, clean flannels, lavender oil…"

Agent McLeod's back was towards the bedroom as he compiled the list.

Elizabeth dipped into the wallet and took out a fold of papers. The first three leaves were receipts. The next was headed *Memo of Entitlement*: a Patent Office warrant of some kind. A letter in John Farthing's handwriting set her heart on an irregular beat: his request to be the one to meet her at the Niagara crossing, formally worded, cold and logical. She ached inside. The last paper was a travel pass.

Tinker looked away as she lifted her skirts and pushed the banknote inside the top of her stocking. The other papers she replaced, then closed his hand around the wallet. "Put it with his things," she whispered.

He stuffed it back inside the waistband of his trousers and slipped from the room. Back on the bed, Elizabeth watched him through the door, stealing across towards the agents' bedroom.

McLeod had finished taking Julia's dictation. He put the note into the dumbwaiter and pulled the rope to send it down to what must be the kitchens below. Elizabeth held her breath. Tinker emerged just as he started to turn.

The whole thing had taken less than two minutes. There was a puzzled look on McLeod's face, as if he was beginning to suspect. Tinker sauntered back to her bedside, looking pleased with himself. He even suffered her embrace.

"Where did you put it?" she whispered into his ear.

"Wardrobe floor."

Though he couldn't write or read and didn't seem to know how to brush his hair or wash his face, the boy was a conspicuous genius.

Elizabeth didn't see the moment when McLeod realised his wallet was missing. But by the time the tea things and medicines arrived, his frown had turned into an angry scowl. He said nothing until Winslow returned. Then the inquisition began.

"I must protest in the strongest terms! You've taken advantage of our trust. And of my instinct to help."

"I don't know what you mean," Elizabeth said.

Julia was standing, looking out of the window. Transparent to the core, she'd not be able to sustain the falsehood.

"Then you're a liar as well as a pickpocket!"

"What am I supposed to have done?"

"I shall have you stripped and searched if you continue with this theatre. And each of your friends!"

Elizabeth stood and spread her arms as if offering herself. "Will you unlace me, or should I do it myself?"

"Have you no shame?"

"Me? Me! You come here and talk of trust. What trust have you given? You accuse me of something – I still don't know what. You threaten to remove my clothes. Is it my naked body you want to see? Is that it? You call me all manner of names. You hold it self-evident that I am a thief. Because of my background. It is you who should feel shame! Tell me what it is you've lost, and I will try to help."

She could feel the racing of her heart, knew her face would be flushed. Good. Let them see the signs and think it anger. Indeed, it partly was.

Agent McLeod opened his mouth but seemed too shocked to speak.

Winslow said, "You've stolen his wallet."

"I assume you mean he's lost his wallet."

"You stumbled against him."

"I half collapsed. He was kind enough to catch me. At least, I thought it kindness. Now he wants me undressed. Did he catch me to feel my body through my clothes?"

She saw the trace of doubt in their faces and felt only slightly guilty for it. Their eyes flicked to each other, as if for confirmation. She closed her own and sat heavily on the bed, feigning exhaustion.

"I've not left this place. You've kept us like prisoners. If the wallet was lost here, it must still be close."

They searched the floor around the doorway first, as if the wallet might have fallen during the scuffle. Then they looked in the folds of the armchair where McLeod had been sitting and on the floor around it. It was Winslow who went to search their twin bedroom and came out only a minute later, his face deep red and the wallet in his hand.

No one could have been more mortified than McLeod.

He was so overcome with distress that he took himself away, out of the hotel.

"Please accept our sincere apologies," Winslow said, his hands clasped in front of him like a schoolboy. "Can we do anything to make amends?"

"You can let us stroll in the grounds."

This made Winslow even more contrite. "That is not in my power."

"Then at least make us comfortable. Bring new clothes. And books for us to read. And paper and pen for writing."

Books were easy. There was a small library in the hotel. Clothes he agreed to in principle, though a tailor could not be brought in, he said, so they would need to be pre-made. "I will look into it," he said. But paper and pen, he could give to her directly. He seemed grateful for the chance to offer at least that token.

Julia was on the second page of her letter before Elizabeth stopped her.

"It is the Avian Post. A few words only. And the pigeon master must transcribe them. So no mention of the Patent Office."

At last they agreed on the message: *My Dearest Robert. I am alive. Please come. Life is nothing without you. Julia*

They folded the twenty-dollar bill inside the sheet of writing paper and around it folded another sheet, with the address and instructions, as if Tinker was merely an errand boy. If he didn't need to speak, there would be no questions about his accent.

Even with his small frame, it was a tight fit. Tinker

climbed up into the dumbwaiter, folding his limbs so that he looked like a dead spider. Then Julia put her hand around the bell to stop it ringing and Elizabeth hauled the rope, sending the compartment and the boy within down through its narrow shaft.

It was two in the morning by the mantel clock. She prayed the kitchen staff would be asleep. The dull tinkle of the bell on the ground floor meant he had arrived. The rope went slack. Now all they could do was wait.

CHAPTER 4

They called it the Room of Cabinets. More properly, it was designated the Workshop of the Magician to the King of Crown Point. Its chief virtues were the locks that kept it secure and a window seat on the north side of the room, overlooking the valley of the Colombia River. It had been his mother's room once. The place where she taught him the arts of conjuring and deception.

"If I teach you to lie, it only makes the truth between us more precious," she'd said, time and time again.

Despite its favourable position in the north wall, it was a lonely corridor from which the Room of Cabinets was accessed. Out of habit, Edwin checked left and right, scrutinising the shadows before turning the door's six brass tumblers, each inscribed with different symbols. They clicked through the combinations until a bolt sprung. Edwin checked along the corridor one final time before scrambling the tumblers again and stepping inside.

No gold was held within. The treasures of the Room of Cabinets were merely secrets. But without secrets, his privilege and safety would be gone. Magician of Crown

Point and First Counsellor to the king were positions of great influence but little direct power. A dangerous combination. The dogs were kept back by the king's indulgence. But if for a moment that favour slipped, Edwin would be torn apart.

He poured himself a glass of red wine then weaved between the cabinets and workbenches to take up his position in the window seat, looking down on the valley. The strands of the river reflected the hills on the far side, a smoky image of blues and greens. That view had once been the entire domain of the Lords of Crown Point. How quickly they had extended their reach. Ambition was one of the few things in the world that lacked discernible limits. But the wider the kingdom spread, the more vassal lords came under its influence, the more complex the politics became.

A raven wheeled over the valley, level with his window, but far above the shingle at the river's edge. Searching for carrion.

If the king achieved his aim, what then? When the King of Crown Point became Lord of the world, he would have no more need of illusions to baffle the minds of his subjects. A few of his counsellors had already lost their belief in magic, though they would never admit to such doubts. Secret conversations were a different matter. If enough of them came to see coloured flames and mind reading acts as simple trickery, disbelief would become the focus of rebellion.

Putting down the glass, half-finished, he walked back through the room, letting his fingers brush the cabinets on either side. The oldest among them were objects of awe, lacquered black with lettering or arcane symbols in blood-red. One had been decorated with closely spaced patterns, which drew the eyes and played with them, seeming to shimmer and jump. He ran his hand over its door, feeling the slight ridges where lines of decoration crossed the smooth surface. Opening the cabinet brought a waft of camphor, a memory of his mother.

Spectacle had been her way. She'd learned her art in the travelling magic shows of England. But in the deadly politics of Crown Point, he had discovered that mundane settings worked better. When an ordinary cupboard vanished a gun, or produced one, magic seemed to be reaching its tendrils into the real world.

Closing the cabinet, he stepped on through the room, deep in thought, hardly seeing his surroundings.

If he could perform a grand illusion without the props of stage magic, it might convince more of the court that his powers were real. That could give him the authority to navigate the present crisis. He knew many tricks. But the greatest illusions required an accomplice: someone who had to know that the marvels were mere trickery. Such knowledge would give them a power over him of life and death. There was no one at Crown Point that he could so trust.

A vanishing act would require just such a helper. Or, if doing it alone, he would be absent at the end, when the trick was revealed, which would undermine its very purpose.

He'd been nursing two possibilities. The first was an ordeal of endurance. Something that would seem not magic, but superhuman. Surviving terrible cold or submersion in the river or a prolonged period without food. Perhaps burial alive. Feats of endurance they would be. Mental and physical. But not to the extent that they appeared. There were ways to take on food while fasting, or air while submerged or buried. There were devices that could allow life to continue in extreme cold. Such illusions would make him seem more like a holy man than a magician. But that might be a protection in itself.

He found himself standing next to a low ottoman made from woven willow: one of his own construction. He'd painted it white, then rubbed all over the surface with a flat stone, leaving it scuffed as if uncared for. The seat, he'd upholstered in green paisley fabric, salvaged from an old curtain. Horse hair showed through one of the moth holes.

Lifting the lid revealed the empty interior. The musty smell came from a layer of soil hidden within the base. That was a sensory detail he had worked out for himself – the illusion of neglect.

He closed the lid and opened it again. This time a flintlock pistol lay in the bottom, the image of a leaping hare inlaid in turquoise in the stock. The balance of it in his hand and its texture were exquisite. The room was full of memories.

The second possibility was more tantalising. He had read about the bullet catch and its dangers. He'd heard accounts of illusionists who'd tried it and failed at the cost of their lives. If all was set up correctly, he could allow a volunteer to fire the gun directly at him. He would then snatch the bullet from the air with his hand. Or, better, catch it with his teeth. That would impress the warriors among the king's court, men who understood what something as small as a bullet could do to human flesh. The implication that he might have supernatural control over weaponry could do no harm. He might offer to cast charms and blessings over the army as it set out to do battle. But only if it outnumbered the expected enemy.

The bullet catch had other virtues. It was loud. It would not be forgotten. And nothing excites an audience more than the possibility that a performer might make a fatal mistake.

But the trickery of the bullet catch did not remove all danger. Who among the audience would step forwards and volunteer to take the shot? It would be all too easy for them to slip an extra bullet into the barrel or substitute their own gun.

Edwin froze. He'd caught a small noise from outside the room, a scuffing of feet perhaps. Carrying the pistol, he slid back the bolts and opened the door.

A man with a pasty complexion stood immediately outside, all his features soft-edged.

"Eavesdropping, Lord Janus?" Edwin asked, mirroring the man's gentle smile.

"I'm no lord. But thank you."

"One day, perhaps."

It was impossible to know if Janus had been annoyed by the reminder of his low birth. Resting the pistol barrel on a forearm, Edwin positioned himself beneath the lintel, occupying the space. "What fair chance brings the pleasure of your company?" he asked.

"The hope of a few words." Janus spoke as if this was the most reasonable request in the world. "This crisis consumes our waking hours. But we who have the king's ear should make the time to speak, in private, don't you think?" He cast his gaze along the corridor, as if to say their conversation would be so much more secure within the Room of Cabinets itself.

"Of what would you speak?" Edwin asked.

"Your plan to install a puppet king in Newfoundland."

"Our king's plan."

"Every plan is the king's plan. But all remember who suggested it. And when it comes to ruin…" The softness of the man's brow could not have sustained a frown of any severity, but his eyes conveyed regret.

"My magic is dedicated to the king," Edwin said. "He understands my loyalty."

"Your magic…" Janus angled his head, looking over Edwin's shoulder. "I sometimes wonder what I might learn from half an hour alone with your mother's boxes. She was very proud of you, you know. Her son. Or daughter?"

"She gave me this," Edwin said, lifting the pistol in a limp grip, letting its aim linger on Janus's chest, as if by accident.

"There's no need for that." Janus pushed the barrel away. "I came with an olive branch."

"Then show it."

"Very well. When Newfoundland rejects your call to arms – and they will – what will happen then? You will lose your place at the king's right hand. I will become First Counsellor. You will be – how should we say – vulnerable? I could protect you."

"Your price?"

"Tell the king that he should follow my advice. No more waiting on the dream of an alliance. War without delay.

Tell him to send the army across the border into the Gas-Lit Empire. Tell him the auguries have revealed themselves, or some such nonsense... I always admire the way you put these things. Tell him the ghosts have change their minds. Tell him you were wrong. Then I promise to protect you."

"My magic wasn't wrong."

Janus rolled his eyes. "Your magic!"

Edwin reached out and snatched a playing card from the air between them, where there had been none before. It made a crisp snap.

Janus blinked, accepted the card, turned it. "If you could really bend the laws of the universe, you'd stop the hearts of our enemies. Perhaps you'd stop mine. But no. You magic up the knave of swords." He tore the card in half. "Your tricks have no power."

"Then why are you whispering?" Edwin asked.

The gentle smile returned to Janus's soft face. "Remember what they did to your mother, when her tricks ran out? She was fully woman. That much they understood. But you – boy, girl, whatever you are – you make their stomachs turn. What will happen to you, do you suppose, when *your* magic is all gone?"

The two halves of the playing card fluttered to the ground in his wake as he walked away.

CHAPTER 5

On the second day after their arrival at the hotel in Niagara, Elizabeth found herself sitting opposite Agent McLeod. Julia was being interrogated by Winslow in another room.

"What is the purpose behind your silence?" McLeod asked.

It was the right question. Rather than asking again about her experiences in Newfoundland, rephrasing to find some more pleasing formulation, or repeating the threats in a louder voice, he had got straight to the heart of the matter. It showed respect for her intelligence. And it hinted at his own.

"You threatened me," she said.

"I stated the facts and offered you help."

"Help against a list of accusations, any one of which would surely send me to the gallows."

"I can't change the facts to suit your sensibilities. Witnesses have told us that all these things occurred."

"Are you offering me help?"

"We might be. If you were to be more cooperative, we would pass that information on to the authorities."

"You *are* the authorities."

He shook his head. "I'm not the one who'd stand judgement. But I could note in my report that you're not our enemy. Not by inclination. That would change things in your trial. It might reverse them altogether."

"You advise me to talk, then?"

"Certainly."

"And who would hand over money before a bargain has been struck?"

He smiled. "A fair point. Though I'd hoped we might skip over all those things as a matter of trust. But you are correct. Very well. What would you like in exchange for your information?"

"Immunity from prosecution for me and my companions. For all the things that happened beyond the borders of the Gas-Lit Empire."

McLeod looked down to the tips of his fingers and frowned. "I think you overestimate your value to us. We already know much of what is happening on Newfoundland. You'd merely be filling in some of the texture. The names of certain individuals, their characters, their interests and weaknesses – as you perceive them."

"What can you offer then?"

"Immunity for the boy."

"He's done nothing wrong."

"He stowed away on a ship of the company fleet. Theft of company property…"

"What did he steal?"

"Food."

"You'd have preferred him to starve?"

"Not at all. I'm merely listing the charges that await him:

stowing away, theft, conspiring with an enemy of the Gas-Lit Empire…"

"What enemy?"

"You, Miss Barnabus."

"But he's a child!"

"The accusations are severe. But as you say, he *is* a child. And led astray. A pardon wouldn't be unreasonable."

"And a pardon for Julia."

"In exchange for your full cooperation, we could discuss that. She didn't go voluntarily into their hands."

"But you will not pardon me?"

"Your problem comes from others. Not I. Not the Patent Office. There are so many witnesses to stand against you. It is hard to imagine you'd not be found guilty. The charges are grievous. But none within our jurisdiction. It's not patent crime you're accused of."

"You have influence, though," she said.

"Limited influence. There is a special hatred in the hearts of the fleet for piracy. I'm sure you understand. The admirals might be coaxed. But further down the chain of command, the sailors wouldn't stomach a pardon."

Elizabeth stood, stepped to the window, looked out through the long net curtain. The grounds outside were empty of people. Lawns and flower beds were not what the guests of the Grand Niagara hotel had come to see.

"Delay won't help you," McLeod said. "Your information is most valuable now. But it will turn. As surely as milk left out in the sun. I'm confident we could guarantee full pardons for your friends if you spoke now. But next week…"

The night before, Tinker had gone to the pigeon master and the message had been sent. It would have arrived in New York already. Robert would be on his way. If he yet lived. Sorrow had consumed him after Julia was lost. Elizabeth had never mentioned it to her friend, but there was a possibility that he'd lacked the willpower to resist his grief.

Turning from the window, she met McLeod's eyes. "Were I to say yes, how long would it take you to have our agreement confirmed?"

"I'm authorised to make such decisions," he said, but a fraction too quickly.

"Nevertheless, if I wanted confirmation from the mouth of someone I trust, as well as in writing, could this all be arranged in the next couple of days?"

"Say the word and I'll have it done," he said. "But you may as well start telling me your story."

"You'd surely think me a fool if I did."

He stood, his chair legs scraping the floor. "If your friends told their stories, you'd have nothing left to bargain with."

She laughed, then. She actually laughed and he seemed offended.

"Go ask Agent Winslow. He'll tell you exactly how much they've revealed. The answer will be nothing."

"These rooms are very pleasant," McLeod said. "This debriefing need not happen in such relaxed surroundings."

"Then move us to some prison. But know that if you do, any trust you've built with me will be gone."

"We have trust?"

"Some. I trust I know what you're trying to do. And I trust you have the best interests of the world in your mind. But I also trust that my information will be of more than passing interest. I know things that you do not know. The fate of the Gas-Lit Empire rests in the balance. I trust that your apparent disinterest is feigned."

"Then what should I trust?" he asked.

"That I do not want the Gas-Lit Empire to fall."

Julia had taken to staring out of the window. When Tinker squeezed himself into the dumbwaiter, she had seemed all excitement. And then, when he returned by the same route, she'd held him and kissed his cheeks and blessed him until he turned beetroot red. But the waiting was devouring her spirit, Elizabeth thought. All the dark possibilities that Julia had not entertained before, now began to haunt her. While the chief danger holding back their reunion had been the possibility of her own death or enslavement, Julia had been her usual happy self. Returning to the land of order had changed that. Perhaps her husband, Robert, had found someone else, or taken sick, or become indifferent. It was all ridiculous but Elizabeth could see the thoughts haunting her friend nonetheless.

"There are hundreds of miles between Niagara and New York," Elizabeth whispered, taking her hand.

"The road is good," Julia said.

"I'd be surprised if he could make it in less than five days. You can come away from the window."

Julia allowed herself to be led back to a chair. "He will come though?"

"Most surely! He will rescue you. You'll see."

"The agents said we're all in trouble. They said you'll hang and I'll be thrown in prison."

"No one is going to hang," Elizabeth said. "You just need

to keep on telling them nothing. That's how we get out of this."

For the afternoon interrogation, the agents swapped around. McLeod took Julia. Elizabeth found herself facing Winslow.

"You've had time to consider our offer," he said.

"I have."

"Will you tell us your story?"

"I will. When immunity has been guaranteed for Julia and Tinker. Full immunity. I want it legally binding."

"This can be done."

"Then... I do agree. On the condition that I can have it set in writing. And on the condition that John Farthing will say it to my face. He's been my liaison with the Patent Office from the start. I do trust him."

"Agreed."

"And you mustn't tell the others what I'm going to do. They must think the immunity is granted to us all."

This seemed to disturb him. "I cannot lie," he said.

"You won't have to," said Elizabeth. "I will do that part myself."

She began the story with something they already knew: the existence of submarine boats, which had disturbed the balance of power in Newfoundland, allowing weapons to be smuggled across the water.

"How were they powered?" Agent Winslow asked, leaning forwards in his chair.

By a kind of steam engine, she told him. He wrote it down, though he didn't seem to believe her. With a submarine boat, the problem was what to do with the exhaust gases. But the fuel of this steam engine was hydrogen. It made no smoke. The product of its burning was water so pure that it could be drunk by the crew.

As she explained the method, the agent's expression of scepticism was replaced by one of wonder. He nodded as he wrote, the story making sense to him. She told him of the wave mills, which captured galvanic energy, the energising of seawater, which created flammable gases, and the iron bottles in which the gases were held under pressure.

When the description was complete, she folded her arms.

The agent waited, pen poised.

"That's all for today," she said.

"We need more. Much more!"

"And you shall have it. Just as soon as you've met your side of the bargain."

"We can have the agreement written for you. But John Farthing has already left. He'll be in New York by now."

"Then you'd better hurry in bringing him back. Before he sets off for London."

The days of their captivity grew long. Agents came and went. But there was always one left to watch over them. Elizabeth took to walking around at night. When the others were sleeping, she opened the door onto the balcony, though it had been forbidden, and stepped out to stand in the moonlight. The air was cold and damp. It made her shiver. But it was worth it, that small disobedience, proving to herself that she had not been broken.

Padding barefoot and silent down the narrow stairs, she investigated the small black door, probing the lock with a piece of stiff wire from the springs of her bed. She had no expectation of being able to pick it. The Patent Office worked with locksmiths of the highest order. Having inserted the end of the wire, she probed, feeling the levers and wards within, knowing it was far beyond her skill.

Back upstairs, she opened the cupboard door and examined the dumbwaiter. Tinker had been able to fold himself double and squeeze inside. But she would never fit. Muffling the bell with one hand, she pulled the rope, sending the compartment down its narrow shaft, into the darkness beyond her sight.

The cold had worked itself into her. Shivering, she returned to bed. This time she slept.

On the morning of the fourth day, Agent McLeod returned from a walk with a new urgency in his step and Elizabeth knew her time was almost gone. Two slices of bacon rested on each breakfast plate, with grilled tomatoes and eggs over easy. Tinker finished his portion and licked it clean as usual. Feeling no appetite, she pushed hers over to him. Instead of wolfing down what she hadn't eaten, he cocked his head and looked at her, eyes questioning. Another sign that he was growing up.

"I'm not hungry," she explained.

Where he put all that food, she never knew, but when it was gone, he looked at her again and took her hand. They would all be pardoned, she'd told him. Now she couldn't hold his gaze. Pulling away, she stepped to the net curtains. The weather had turned mild and the windows had been left open. She inhaled air, scented with the first touch of autumn. A man was walking in the grounds outside. He wore a long, grey coat and a fedora.

It wasn't John Farthing. It couldn't be him.

Behind her, Julia was clearing away the breakfast things. Plates clinked against each other. A door opened and closed. Elizabeth glanced back. McLeod and Winslow had withdrawn to their room.

The man in the grounds was proceeding in bursts and pauses. She couldn't see his face. But he was searching for something. And furtively.

She turned the handle of the forbidden balcony door. The net curtain billowed into the room as she slipped through. The man had stopped and was casting around, as if he'd heard her, though she'd made almost no sound. The sight of him made her draw breath.

It was Robert, Julia's husband. But not as she'd seen him last. He'd been clean-shaven then. Now he wore a beard. Notwithstanding that, his face seemed thinner. He saw her. His haunted eyes widened. She pointed towards the unmarked door below.

Julia and Tinker must have felt the change in her because they were staring as she pushed back through the net curtains. Winslow had caught her entering the room.

"The balcony's forbidden!"

"I'm sorry."

"Why did you do that? You knew the rule."

Before she could answer, a fist began to hammer on the door below.

She followed the agent down the stairs, waiting behind him as he peered through the spy hole. The door shuddered from another series of bangs.

"Who is it?" Winslow hissed.

"Open the door and find out."

"He'll be hauled away for a madman."

"Mad, perhaps. But not a fool. If you don't let him in, he'll come back with the sheriff. If you want to keep this place a secret, I'd suggest you let him in."

"On what grounds can he demand anything?"

"You're holding his wife a prisoner."

There was a rush of fabric and footsteps behind her. She had to hold Julia back while Winslow turned the key. The door burst inwards. Elizabeth found herself pushed against the wall as Julia and Robert forced through into each other's embrace. Both were weeping, unrestrained. Elizabeth looked away from them to Winslow, who'd been squeezed into the corner on the other side.

He glowered at her. "What have you done?"

She found herself unable to speak, for joy perhaps. Or for pain. She couldn't tell which.

CHAPTER 6

A hunting party was a masculine affair in the Oregon Territory. Donning jacket and shirt, Edwin had followed that mode, but instead of trousers, had chosen a riding skirt and side-saddle. A touch of kohl made the eyes seem larger, softer. A bruise of darker tone suggested a hollowness of the cheeks. Not *he* and yet not *she*. Something neither pronoun managed to convey. But something entirely real. *They*.

The king rode at the front with his hunting master, a Salishan marksman. Behind came eight men of the court, including Timon, the king's half-brother. Two more in the hunting party were in the royal succession. It might have been more, but after the first few, any claim to kingship would be disputed anyway. To have so many riding out together was foolhardy. A well-timed ambush could topple the kingdom.

Yet the king had ordered it and they had complied. No questions voiced.

Harnesses jangled and hoofs fell heavy. The clamour was such that any deer within two miles would have gone to ground. The party had been crawling along, slower than the breeze. The mixed scents of horse and cologne would be reaching out ahead of them, alerting any game that happened to be deaf.

Counsellor Janus had kept a polite distance since their encounter outside the Room of Cabinets. He was up front with the rest of the court, laughing at bad jokes. Riding a dappled mare, Edwin preferred to lag behind, closer to the cooks and the baggage mules.

The wide and rolling land above the river gorge bore a scattering of copses. In the distance, Mount Hood stood magnificent against a blue sky. A few patches of snow still remained in gullies on its northern slope. It wouldn't be long before winter set in again. Then the wild north road between Oregon and Newfoundland would freeze. Communications would become dangerous until the spring thaw. After that, mud would be the problem. On a good year there might be eight clear months of travel on the northern trail.

Forming an alliance between the two free kingdoms was only the first step in Edwin's plan. If they could take land from the Gas-Lit Empire to open up a southern road, then trade and communication might continue through the whole year, ocean to ocean. The two kingdoms would become two faces of power, one looking east, the other west.

No one could truly comprehend the vast scale of the Gas-Lit Empire, with all its many nations, its billions of people. Had it been only a question of numbers, what hope could Oregon have had? But the Gas-Lit Empire had chosen to hold back the progress of its science and technology, its weapons little different from how they'd been two hundred years before.

The Founding Fathers of the Gas-Lit Empire had understood that holding back the technologies of destruction would only work if all nations agreed to do the same. Thus, they had frozen themselves into that primitive state, by solemn treaty and through the executive oversight of the International Patent Office. Unable to out-develop each other, and bound in a pact of mutual security, warfare between them had become impractical.

The design had worked, but the order of the Gas-Lit Empire could only continue so long as those tracts of wilderness beyond its borders remained chaotic. That had always been the weakness of the plan, Edwin's mother had told them again and again.

The hunting party had been spread out. But the way now dipped into a wooded ravine, the path narrowing at the lip. Riders bunched up, each man waiting his turn to descend. Janus was there, gesturing others to go before him. Not wanting to risk a conversation with the man, Edwin pulled back on the reins and slowed. The baggage train clanked to a halt behind. Only when the last of the hunters was spurring forwards did they move again. At the edge, Edwin had to duck under a low branch before beginning the short descent. A stream glinted at the bottom. Timon was there waiting, his horse standing in the water, drinking.

"What chance the hunt?" the king's brother asked.

Edwin stopped beside him. "We may be lucky."

"Come on, man, use your powers to help me for once."

"Is there a wager?"

There was always a wager. The culture of gambling had rooted deep at Crown Point.

Timon leaned in close enough to whisper. "Should I lay money on a stag or a boar? I won't bet on nothing. That'd be bad luck in itself."

Prediction was a dangerous game. But so was everything in the court.

"Nothing's guaranteed," Edwin said.

Timon nodded.

"And not a word to anyone that I helped you."

Another nod.

Straightening, Edwin sniffed at the air, eyes closed, as if in meditation, allowing the moment to stretch, to become uncomfortable. The mules in the train were waiting behind, their drivers keeping a respectful distance. After a count of twenty, Edwin whispered, "There will be a deer. Your brother will bring it down from a great distance."

"Then I'll place my bet and thank you," Timon said.

Edwin could have left it at that. But the opportunity was too good to let pass. "There's more. Something... something about this animal will be strange."

Timon's eyes grew wide. "What? And what will it signify?"

"I cannot tell. But when I see it, I will know."

The king's brother had leaned in as they spoke, like a friend or a lover. Then, as if becoming aware that he was too close, Timon pulled back and scowled. "Why do you do this?" He gestured to the skirt.

"I prefer to ride side-saddle."

"You'd be safer dressed as you should be dressed. I'll give you that advice for free."

"Then how would you like me – more fully woman?"

"I don't want you!"

Timon pulled his reins around and splashed away, out of the water. Edwin watched him pricking the stallion into a trot up the far side of the ravine. If the king were to fall and break his neck, then Timon would take the crown. There was some protection for Edwin in that. Timon was a believer. He would look to his magician for guidance. But he was also a man of simple passions, not used to restraining himself. Nor built for long life as a king.

Edwin leaned forwards and patted the dappled mare. It splashed across the water and began carrying them up the path the others had taken. Behind, the mule handlers shouted to their beasts and the whole procession resumed its noisy progress.

By lunchtime there had been no sight of quarry. Nor could anyone have been surprised. They stopped in the shade of some trees while the cooks fanned charcoal fires and began to prepare a feast. For the most part it was cold meats and hot coffee. But there were also fruits and bread and sweet pastries, of which Timon seemed to have a particular fondness. And wine. If an assassin didn't kill the king's brother, then a seizure of the heart surely would.

Edwin palmed a strip of dried salmon and found a rock to sit on away from the others, a place to eat without being seen. Aloofness was part of the role. A magician could not be ordinary. Not on a day of spectacle, as this would surely be. Existing without mortal sustenance, poised between the genders. It would unsettle the others, until they needed a magician. Then all that otherness would make things right.

Facing away from the feast, Edwin discreetly ripped off a sliver of the fish and began to chew. It had been heavily salted. In the afternoon they would need to lag behind again and find a stream to drink from, where the men of the court would not see. Another small sacrifice.

Janus took the opposite approach, trying to appear more like the others, though it was said his father had been a blacksmith. He would choose the same food as them, eat it with them, pretend to enjoy their humour. He would always defer to their decisions, right or wrong. But in secret, he despised them. Edwin had seen that. A man so much more quick-witted than those he bowed to: Janus was the danger, not Timon.

Hearing the approach of soft boots, Edwin slipped the remains of the dried fish into a loose sleeve and brushed away the last crumbs.

"What do you see?"

It was the king himself. Edwin stood, bowed.

"A kingdom without borders."

"How so?"

"It will encompass the globe. You will be ruler of all."

"You're no use to me if you flatter."

"Does a compass flatter?"

"Explain yourself."

"A compass will point towards the North Pole. It isn't flattery. It doesn't say you'll ever reach it. But by pointing, it tells you the direction your next step must take. You wished to rule the globe. It's not a bad thing to remember it from time to time. To keep us pointing in the right direction."

"Clever words might be more dangerous than flattery," the king said. But he was smiling.

Edwin bowed again. "Tell me what you want to achieve, my lord. I'll find the path."

"My father's magician could put on a good show," the king said. "Sparks and entrails. But he wasn't a planner. He wasn't like you. The trouble is, I can't fault your thinking. Forge an alliance with Newfoundland, you said. Put a king in place on that island. Every bit of the plan makes sense. Except now the wrong man sits on the throne in the east and he won't even send an embassy."

"I believe the embassy is on its way," Edwin said, with a certainty he didn't feel.

"Perhaps. Perhaps. But even then, they may refuse our offer. If that happens, I'll be turning to your friend, Mr Janus. He'll be First Counsellor. I'll have no choice. The captains will demand it. We have our army and it needs a fight."

"If we attack any one of these nations of North America, we'll have the full force of the Gas-Lit Empire marching against us. Against you, my lord. Even with our new weapons, it's a war we can't win."

"Janus says we can. He says our victory will be complete. They'll be so shocked by our power that their governments will crumble. The downtrodden will rise up to help us. The oppressors will topple."

It was an old argument, a moment to stay quiet.

A stand of trees in the distance marked out the line of another small ravine. The leaves seemed to shimmer in the breeze. After lunch they would set off towards it, as had been arranged.

"Do you know why Janus is useful to me?" the king asked.

"No, sire."

"Because he disagrees with you. Seeing you at my right hand makes him all the more hungry for my good pleasure. When I listen to your advice, he puts all his soul into thinking up ways in which you might be wrong. And you, my good Edwin, you must focus all your wit on never being wrong. Mr Janus is always waiting. You know what would happen if you slipped. The balance pleases me."

"He threatens me when you're not there," Edwin said.

"You think I don't know that? It's his job. You're like a sword, Edwin. And he is the stone that keeps you sharp for me." The king nodded towards the line of trees, the green of them standing out against the brown of the parched land around. "Just make sure that all today's predictions come true."

Then he was walking back towards his men. Edwin watched as he slapped his gloved hands together. "Are you refreshed, my friends?"

The hunting party cheered. Janus too, pretending to be like all the others. Men were mounting. The servants would clear away and pack the mules. More noise. Even the songbirds had been scared from the trees.

Timon had wheeled his horse and was staring back at Edwin. Not doubtful exactly, but questioning. How much might he have wagered? Edwin mounted, looping a leg over the pommel. A click of the tongue set the dappled mare trotting after the others.

Riding side-saddle was another part of the otherworldly illusion. Men never understood how it could be possible to stay balanced. Emboldened by drink, a young guard had once demanded to try it for himself. He fancied himself a skilled horseman, but had fallen, the saddle being the wrong size for him. It had been made to measure for Edwin though. Another conjuring trick.

The hunting master was pointing towards the line of trees in the distance. He set off at a gallop, with the king riding beside him. The whole court was in pursuit, yet leaving space for their lord to take the glory. Edwin touched the mare's flank with the crop and she broke into a gallop, easing away to the right, away from the dust of hooves, giving a clear view.

And there it was: like destiny, a deer bolting from the tree line, as if it had just scrambled out of the ravine. Clear of cover, it was springing away, a quarter mile distant, far out of range. Yet the king was reaching for his rifle. He raised it, took aim, an impossible shot from the back of a galloping horse. He fired once, twice. He missed, took fresh aim, fired a third shot. The deer twisted in the air and fell.

The men cheered, hardly believing what they'd witnessed. Yet it had happened in front of them. Their blood was up. Anything might be possible. Had they been trained in the ways of the illusionist, it would have seemed different.

Edwin slowed from gallop to canter. The king had reached his fallen quarry. He dismounted, aimed his rifle at the beast's head. There was a puff of smoke, a fraction of a second delay, then a bang. The animal lay still. The king's men were dismounting, clapping him on the back. Such a shot. They would tell of it to their children and their grandchildren.

I was there the day our king brought down a running deer from a galloping horse. They'd say it was a quarter-mile shot. In time it would become a mile.

Edwin pulled back on the reins. Best to arrive late. Let them discover the trick.

They hauled it over to begin the butchery. There were oaths and cries of amazement. Approaching on foot, Edwin could see it too. The animal had fallen showing a brown coat but when they turned it, the other side was revealed as pure white. A freak of nature had divided its colouring left from right, as if it was two different animals somehow brought together. It seemed the king's first bullet had caught it on the hind leg.

Timon looked up from the carcass, his face full of wonder. "Where is the king's magician?" he called.

They parted as Edwin stepped up to the animal.

"What does it mean?" Timon asked.

Edwin squatted, put a hand on the deer's neck, feeling the heat of it. Hidden knowledge should never come easily. Insight had to be a struggle. That way, they would trust it. The animal had taken a bullet to the brain, but its muscles still twitched, as if it had died without noticing and thought itself still running.

The men were breathing heavily. The wind hissed in dry grass. Water trickled in the creek at the bottom of the little ravine. In the distance a hawk cried.

Edwin stood. "I cannot see. Not yet. Show me the entrails."

So they did. Cutting open the belly, spilling the organs and intestines onto the dirt. The trick was the pretence of observation. The random pattern of blood vessels in the viscera, a nodule of yellow fat pressed between finger and thumb, as if its precise texture might reveal the future. It stank, but that was also part of the show.

Edwin stood. "All is clean. All is healthy. There can be no bad omen from this. But to understand – this is not so simple.

There is more than one story to be read here. I see a child."

"Whose child?" the king asked.

"Yours, sire."

A murmur of appreciation whispered through the crowd of men. That was why they all had to be there, the whole damn succession, hunting together, so each of them would witness the miracle with his own eyes.

"Also, there will be a messenger. Someone will come to bring good news."

It was enough. The men were shouting again. The king nodded his approval. Timon's smile was tight, though he cheered with the others. If the king had a son, it would put him and his own son further from the throne.

They parted to let Edwin walk away. They might have wanted a magician to read the omens, but a celebration should be a more wholesome affair. It was time to go and leave the job well done.

But leading the dappled mare away, they heard the sound of following footsteps.

"You've excelled yourself," Janus said. "The king's brother is set to win a small fortune. And all since you spoke to him."

"Did you lose money?"

"A little," said Janus. "But who can complain on a day of such news? A child for our king."

"We all rejoice," Edwin said.

"And only last week I saw you speaking with the king's consort. It must help with the reading of omens to know the truth already."

"Perhaps you might try to read some yourself?" Edwin said. "What would they tell you?"

"I might. But I don't believe in such things…"

They were far enough away from the others that Janus's confession of heresy would not be overheard.

"The king's fame will spread because of this," Edwin said.

Janus nodded. "I'm not such a huntsman as the others. But I am good at looking. I see things they might miss."

"Such as?"

"As the king took his third shot, there was a puff of smoke from the tree line. Did you notice? From just where the poor creature had bolted."

The skin on the back of Edwin's neck tightened. Everyone should have been looking at the deer. That was the way such tricks worked. Misdirection. But somehow, Janus had seen.

"Then do you suspect someone else took the shot?"

"I do."

"And perhaps the deer was released to run into the king's path?"

Janus nodded.

"If you're right, the guilty man must still be down there, in the ravine. Hiding. If you run, you could find him. You could unmask our king as a cheat. Do you think you might be rewarded?"

"You have me wrong," Janus said. "This is only between you and me. I just wanted you to know how much I appreciate your art. And how much I learn from it."

CHAPTER 7

They were seated in the main room of the secret apartment: Elizabeth and six agents of the Patent Office. The windows had been left open and the net curtains billowed. She attempted to time her breathing: four seconds on the inbreath, a pause, eight seconds on the outbreath. It would usually have calmed her heart. Not today.

Five of the six agents were staring at her: McLeod, Winslow and three newcomers who had turned up a few hours before. She folded her arms and unfolded them again, unable to get comfortable.

McLeod had made the introductions. He now sat opposite her, his expression vaguely positive. Encouraging, perhaps. She focused on him, tried to forget that the others were listening. It was impossible. Winslow held his pen poised near the inkwell.

"Oregon," she said, the word sounding breathy. Insubstantial. "Can we start there?"

"You've not been to Oregon," said McLeod.

"I've met a man who has." Strictly speaking she'd met a man who'd met a man. But the story sounded tenuous enough already and she wanted to make them believe her.

"There's a kingdom in the Oregon Territory. That's what I've been told. Their lands reach north as far as the Yukon. There's been no one to challenge them for years."

She paused, giving Winslow a chance to catch up. His pen whispered over the page.

"This is all hearsay," one of the newcomers said.

"It's evidence. You need to understand it if you're to understand what's happened in Newfoundland. Oregon's been building its strength. They've got no Patent Office looking over their shoulder. Nothing to hold them back. They've constructed new weapons. Terrible things. And explosives. All this beyond your gaze."

One of the agents looked away, as if embarrassed by what she'd said. Winslow's pen slipped fast over the paper. She didn't know how he managed to maintain that elegant copperplate. And sitting to his right, on the edge of her eyeline, sat the agent she was trying to not see. If she looked at him, the words would clot in her throat. The speech she'd prepared would dry up.

John Farthing.

She focused on the side of McLeod's dark face, the way the light from the window caught his cheekbone, the pores of his skin. Any small detail to hold her gaze steady.

"They have just the one tract of land?" he asked. "And their population – I assume it must be sparse."

"Perhaps," she said. "I don't know. But they have new weapons. And a new explosive. It is a terrible thing…" An unwanted memory flashed in her mind: bodies and parts of bodies strewn over the ground, smoke clinging to the mud.

"The population in the wilds is small," McLeod said. "Even with these weapons, the danger will be… containable."

She could hear no tightness in his voice, no uncertainty. On the edge of her vision, John Farthing uncrossed his legs and crossed them again.

"They're planning a war," she said. "A great war against all the world. They wish to tear down the Gas-Lit Empire."

"But why?" McLeod spoke with incredulity rather than fear. He was a believer, she thought, radiating calm certitude in the rightness of his cause. But belief can never see itself. It never knows its own limits. Farthing had been the same when she first met him.

"The Gas-Lit Empire has riches," she said.

"Then do these wild peoples wish to plunder?"

"Yes."

Easier to put it that way than to explain the more disturbing truth, that their enemies were believers also. The Patent Office clung to peace and order. The kingdoms of the wilds held to freedom. It was sacred to them. Each side took their enemy's virtues for vices. Water never knows the nature of oil.

"There are other kingdoms in the wilderness," she said. "The floating nation of the Sargasso…"

Winslow stopped writing. He seemed outraged. "A rabble of pirates!"

"Yet they're organised. Don't they now threaten the Atlantic? And there's the kingdom of Patagonia."

"Slavers!"

"There may be other nations we don't yet know. Alone, they're dangerous. But immeasurably more if they can trade and form alliances. Their problem is that the Gas-Lit

Empire controls most of the world. It makes communication difficult for them. Trade, harder still. But if Oregon could make a bridge across the continent – if it could connect to the kingdom of Newfoundland on the other side…"

"They would have both oceans," said Farthing.

He had sat quietly through the meeting. Now the others turned to look, as if surprised to find him still in the room. Elizabeth concentrated on McLeod's face, the wrinkles on his brow. She couldn't tell whether his frown was one of concern or merely confusion. But they needed to be concerned. They needed to be frightened. If she couldn't convince a few agents in one room, how could she expect the nations of the Gas-Lit Empire to wake, to arm themselves against what was coming?

"Should I minute Agent Farthing's comment?" Winslow asked.

"No need," said McLeod. "The witness can speak for herself."

Farthing stared at the floor, as if rebuked.

"Why don't you listen to him?" she asked. "He has it right. While Newfoundland was at war with itself, it was no danger to you. And no use to the other kingdoms of the wilds. So, the king of Oregon smuggled a bomb onto the rock of Newfoundland. I was there. I saw it. Hundreds died. All the warlords were killed except for one. And he is now a king. If Oregon can strike a deal with him… then it'll be just as Farthing says."

"That's a mighty big jump of reasoning, Miss Barnabus."

"You think it can't happen?"

"We've held the peace for almost two centuries."

"Can't you see that things have changed? The dream is

over. In a few years, they'll have the power to invade you. They may have it already."

Some of the agents glanced at each other, as if looking for reassurance. The first cracks of doubt.

"I've made a list of all the weapons I've seen. And all I know of the peoples of Newfoundland and the Sargasso."

She held out a sheaf of papers. No one took it.

"What are you proposing we do?" asked McLeod.

"I'm not proposing anything."

It came to her that these men were so rooted in belief that they couldn't see the truth. The Gas-Lit Empire, the Patent Office: a perfect answer to the problems of the world. If things went wrong, the agents just had to follow the blueprint more perfectly. She'd just told them that the plan itself was flawed, that it had been from the very start.

"If new nations emerge, we'll invite them to join us," Winslow said.

Others nodded.

But McLeod was frowning. "It would mean giving away their weapons."

"It would mean peace," Winslow said. "Prosperity. They would be able to travel in safety, anywhere in the world. They'd trade and become rich. They'd have luxuries, medicines. No one could refuse what we have to offer."

"They want to take those things by force," Elizabeth said.

"Then, what is the answer?"

"Why do you think there is one?"

She met their gaze one by one and all looked away, except for John Farthing.

"I've given you everything," she said. "Our agreement has been witnessed by a lawyer. You'll see to it that Julia and Tinker come to no harm."

"We will," said Farthing.

"And I have one more request. They must know nothing of this till you've taken me wherever it is I'm going. And the boy can't ever know where I've gone, or he'll come looking."

"Agreed," said McLeod.

"Where am I to go?"

"You could walk out of here," McLeod said. "Your lawyer friend has made it abundantly clear that we can't hold you. But if you do, you'll be found and taken into custody. You're a wanted woman. They'll transport you back across the Atlantic in chains. There's a prison cell waiting for you in Liverpool. You'll have your day in court. And then the gallows. But... we could offer you something better."

John Farthing's shoulders sagged. He had warned her of this moment. And now he would think all his fears realised. She hated to see his pain.

"Make your offer," she said.

"Go back to the crossing place. There's a boat captain ready to take you downriver. You'll have to make your own way to Newfoundland. That's beyond our reach. But you have contacts there. From all you've told us, you could even speak to the new king. Convince him to sign the Great Accord. Have Newfoundland join the Gas-Lit Empire, and this conspiracy of rogue nations of which you speak – it will come to nothing."

"The new king won't agree."

"You haven't tried yet."

The more clearly she presented the case, the more desperately they clung to their illusion. So great was their need to believe in the Gas-Lit Empire that they were incapable of seeing its doom.

All but John Farthing, perhaps. His was a different tragedy. He loved her. He trusted her and couldn't dismiss her words. That meant he saw the end of the age approaching. All that he'd worked for would come to ruin. All the sacrifices he'd made would be for nothing in the end. She was crushing him. She hated them for making her do it.

"Will you go back?" McLeod asked.

"I will," she said. It was only half a lie.

Robert had taken Tinker and Julia to see the waterfall again. That had been Elizabeth's idea, to get them out of the apartment. The boy would spend his time staring over the railings while the husband and wife would stare into each other's eyes, no less awestruck. The surprise of reunion had not worn off. Perhaps it never would.

It was dusk by the time they returned: Julia and Robert arm in arm, Tinker striding out before them, a young man in all but stature, a new confidence in his expression.

"Did you give them the information they wanted?" Robert asked, and then turned to McLeod, "Did she?"

"Yes," they answered in chorus.

"Then we're free to go?"

"You are free," McLeod said.

Robert shook the agent's hand and beamed. "We will set off tomorrow. I'll arrange a carriage. New York first. The place is a marvel. You may stay for as long as you wish, Elizabeth. And the boy too. You can stay forever if you will. What you've given me, I'll never be able to repay."

Julia embraced her, then. "We shall be like a family," she said.

But Tinker looked at her and said nothing.

The evening's meal was to be a modest affair, but Robert demanded a celebratory feast, and offered to pay for it, though it seemed the agents had no procedure for accepting his money. Nevertheless, they relented. He compiled a list of courses, with the extravagance of a Londoner. They sent instructions down in the dumbwaiter and presently the food began to arrive: small portions of braised quail followed by a light broth to clear the palate, and then duck, and after a delay, turkey with a sauce made of cranberries, and then fruits and cheeses and coffee. The entire process continued for over two hours, the agents seeming embarrassed by such excess.

When the last of the plates had been cleared away, Elizabeth said, "I should like to walk in the grounds. John Farthing can accompany me."

It seemed that Winslow might object, but Farthing got to his feet and inclined his head in a small bow, which seemed to indicate that he would be honoured so to do. "She will be safe with me," he said.

Hardly believing that they had allowed it, she set off down the stairs to the small black door, which Farthing unlocked. And then she was properly out, for the first time in days. The air was chill. She'd not brought a coat, but would suffer it rather than go back inside and risk a change of mind.

Neither of them spoke as they stepped away. Elizabeth's instinct was to stay underneath the balcony and skirt the building with the agents unable to see from the window above. But John led her out over the grass, in plain sight, his hands clasped behind him. And he was right. They needed to be seen, for his protection. A man sworn to celibacy and a woman who was everything they distrusted.

At the line of trees that marked the edge of the grounds they turned and started off towards the back of the hotel.

"Why did you agree to go?" he said. She could hear the pain in his voice.

"It was the only way I could protect my friends."

"You could have just kept saying nothing. They would have been forced to make a deal. Now they can make you do anything they want. They're sending you out again, across the border. I cannot bear it."

"Can you keep a secret?" she asked.

He laughed. "You told me once that our lives were made from secrets. You were right."

"There's something I didn't tell them. It's not important really. Not for the future of the Gas-Lit Empire. But to me…"

They had reached the corner of the grounds where the land sloped away towards a road below.

"Run," he whispered.

"What?"

"I'll say you gave me the slip. I have money you can take. Get away from here. Hide your identity. Pretend to be a man. They know you can disguise yourself in that way, but it would make it almost impossible for them to track you. America is a big continent. You can lose yourself here."

"They would never believe I got away."

"Suspicion is one thing. Proof quite another."

"You're not as good a liar as you suppose," she said. "They would know what you'd done. What's the punishment for agents who break their vows?"

He didn't answer.

"I could go to Newfoundland," she said. "But I don't believe the new king would do the deal you all hope. Even if he wanted, they're too proud of their independence. Having a king was a big enough step. Submitting to the rule of the Patent Office would be impossible."

"You could hide," he said.

They were behind the hotel now, out of sight of the windows of the apartment, unless one of the other agents had sneaked out to watch. She wanted to take his hand. She loved him. She'd never been so sure of that. She loved him utterly. But she also knew that they could not be together.

She said, "When I was a child – very small – my father taught me to pretend to be my brother. On stage, in front of an audience, I could walk behind one of the disappearing cabinets and when I stepped out again I would look like him instead of me. It was part of my father's great illusion. The Vanishing Man. My brother would be transported from one side of the stage to the other. But really there were the two of us, swapping places.

"Before that – I don't remember it myself, but my father told me – he had performed the bullet catch illusion. He had two pistols, in the same way that he had two children. Twins. The trick involved swapping one for the other. So that when the gun was fired it was not the one the audience had seen loaded. But one day there was an accident. I don't know the details. But one of the men who worked with him was killed. He gave up the bullet catch.

"My mother and brother left when I wasn't quite seven years old. For a time we pretended that my brother was still there. My father dressed me in his clothes and no one could tell the difference. The trick changed. I had to do both parts – my brother's and my own. It seemed easy then.

"When I left, my father gave me one of the pistols. I hadn't seen it for years. It's all I have left of him. You know the gun. You've seen it."

"The turquoise leaping hare," John Farthing said.

She nodded. "When I was on Newfoundland I met a man who'd seen my brother. My brother is in the west. In Oregon. Somehow he's with the people who put a king in Newfoundland."

"How can you be sure?"

"There are three proofs: he had a pistol just like mine, he looked like me, he spoke like me."

"You can't throw your life away on such a chance."

"If my brother was there, my mother might be also."

"Please…"

"If they'd told me to go to Oregon, it would be easy. But they want Newfoundland. I can either do what they say or disappear. If I stay in plain view, they'll give me to the navy and I'll be hanged as a pirate. If I do what they want and go to Newfoundland, nothing good will come of it. Perhaps the king wouldn't kill me. There are plenty around him who might. But in the Oregon Territory – that's where the answer may lie for the Patent Office, for the Gas-Lit Empire. And for me. If I can go there and return, perhaps I'll have enough to bargain with, to save my life."

"You could hide," he said, again, pleading.

"I've spent half my life hiding. I know how to do it. But this is for me as well. I thought I'd lost all my family, that I was the only person like me. I was alone."

"You're not alone," he whispered.

Light from a hotel window caught his cheekbone and she saw that it was wet with tears.

There had been wine with the meal, though Elizabeth drank none of it. Tinker had stolen a glass or two along the way. She hadn't stopped him. Even the agents had taken a sip from time to time. Now, all were asleep.

Standing in the bedroom, she watched the faces of Julia and Tinker, trying to fix them in her memory, peaceful and safe. The boy turned over and sighed. She lifted her bag and her shoes and stepped out in her stockinged feet.

All the agents were bigger than her, but Winslow was closest in size. She slipped into the room he shared. A small wardrobe stood near his bed. She opened it, lifted out his coat and a hat. A hanger ticked quietly, rocking on the rail as she went through the pockets of his jacket and emptied his wallet of banknotes. She had never stolen so much money before. Neither man stirred.

Muffling the bell, she pulled the rope to lower the dumbwaiter a couple of feet. Then placing the bag and coat on the top, she sent it down the rest of the way. She'd thought of this escape route from the start, but quickly dismissed the idea, since the compartment would be too small for her body. But she could perhaps clamber down the shaft itself. It was still a tight fit. Her feet went in first and when she was sitting half-in half-out, she turned over to face the floor. Then she inched backwards, feet searching for holds. There were none. But the rough brick surface gave purchase enough.

When she was at last hanging by her hands, she brought her feet out to press against one wall, forcing her back towards the other. Letting go, she remained suspended. The fabric of her sleeves scratched against the rough brick as she let herself down inch by inch. The blackness was complete. The air felt stuffy. Then her foot found the top of the dumbwaiter. It creaked as she let her weight down onto it.

A thin layer of wood was now all that separated her from the kitchen corridors. Breaking through might have been noisy but she had come prepared. From her pocket she pulled one of the hotel's silver knives. It fitted into the gap between the planks. She pressed down and heard the nails squeak as they pulled free. With one plank out, the others were easy to remove. Letting herself down through the gap she slid out into a narrow corridor, the domain of servants rather than guests.

With her bag in one hand and Agent Winslow's coat over her arm, she set off towards the front of the building, coming at last to a door with no handle, which she pushed through and found herself suddenly standing on thick carpet in a wide space, with the lamps still burning.

Seeing the front desk, she froze. Someone would be on duty and it wouldn't do to be seen leaving. They'd think she was a guest trying to slip away without paying her bill. Explaining to them would be impossible.

She waited and listened. At first there were no sounds beyond the slow ticking of clocks. Then she did hear something: a man's slack snore.

Stepping silently on the thick carpet she slipped through the lobby, casting a glance at the sleeping night clerk behind the counter. Then she pushed open the front door and felt the night air across her face.

CHAPTER 8

The consort was with child and beautifully pale, they said, though sturdy. She stood in the Great Hall, her arm linked with the king's, her gaze lowered from the cheering crowd of courtiers and guards, a faint sheen on her forehead. The most fervent cheer and the loudest clapping came from the king's own brother.

A display of loyalty was in order. But Timon was overdoing it. If the child lived to term it would push him one place further from the throne. Assuming it were a boy. And how could the royal seed do less than sire another stallion? A bowed head of dutiful submission would have been more believable.

For a moment, the consort leaned more heavily on the king's arm. Concern crossed his face as he guided her to a chair. Ladies-in-waiting rushed from the crowd. One touched a handkerchief to the consort's brow, the other wafted with a fan of black and white eagle feathers.

"A toast to the king and all his line," called Timon, raising a glass. "May they live forever."

All followed his lead. But Timon's fervour had been

badly timed. With cups half drained, the consort threw up. Forcefully. Copiously. As befits one who has been practising. Even the warriors in the room seemed shocked.

The ladies-in-waiting helped her away. Two of the courtiers begged leave to go and change their clothes. The king seemed distracted. He waved a hand in dismissal. The hubbub of voices grew to fill the room. Janus had somehow positioned himself next to the king's right arm. Edwin, dressed fully male for the gathering, pushed through the crowd, trying to take back the place that was his by right, but two courtiers were standing in the way and wouldn't yield.

"What does your magician say?" Janus asked the king, his voice loud enough to carry. "Will your heir be healthy?"

Edwin recognised the trap being set for him. With one more push, he shouldered his way between the courtiers and stood before the king.

"Well, magician?" Janus asked.

"I've seen nothing to say otherwise."

All around were listening now.

"Does the consort need doctors?" Janus asked.

"As any woman with child." Damn but Edwin knew he was sounding evasive.

"No special care?"

"For the heir of Crown Point – only the best."

Janus turned back to the king. "The magician should slaughter an ox. Read the entrails. The people need to be reassured."

The king would usually have come to Edwin's aid. After all, it was in both their interests that belief in magic prevailed. But perhaps distracted by the quantity of vomit on the flagstones, he waved a hand as if to say his advisors could decide between themselves.

Janus bowed low. "I'll arrange for the auguries to be read."

People nearby murmured their approval. The king nodded. Triumph flickered in Janus's eye. Few would have caught it, but Edwin felt the jaws of the trap closing.

Woe betide a fortune teller who offers a king any future other than his heart's desire. But the consort might die, even with the best of care. The baby might present side-on. The child could be sickly. Worse still, it could be a girl. That thought brought another bitterness.

"The reading shall be tomorrow," Janus announced. "I'll have an ox sent up from the valley. Bring your knives to the courtyard at noon."

"Not tomorrow," Edwin said, caught off his stride. "It must be a full moon." For a moment he couldn't even think how many days that might buy him.

"The full moon then," said Janus. "You'll do it in a week."

There was a safe way from Crown Point down to the floodplain of the Colombia River. The road cut a straight line for a mile or so across the high plateau before starting its gentle descent. In seven days, the ill-fated ox would follow that path in reverse as it climbed on its last journey. At least it would get a spectacular view.

The quick route was more risky. Just beyond the castle walls the cliff softened into a treacherous gulley, which widened out below. Small trees had somehow managed to root in the scree, holding it together. Between those

slender trunks, ropes had been strung, allowing the brave
or foolhardy a direct route down. Or those with some
particular motive. Still in leaf, the trees allowed for no view,
though it would in any case have been a brave traveller
who lifted their gaze from the next footstep.

Halfway down the steepest section, Edwin stopped
to rest, leaning against a branch which bent under his
weight, but not too much. Wind whispered through the
leaves. Beyond that, he could hear no sound. No audience.

Solitude brought relief, allowing him to touch that
deep loneliness he was obliged to forget while walking the
corridors of the castle. Being First Counsellor to the king
meant trusting none but close family.

He had chosen trousers and boots for the excursion.
Rugged clothes and practical. Though the choice had been
more an instinctive thing, a response to how he felt. The
clamber down would loosen his muscles. The slog back up
would soak him in sweat. Anything to drive the uncertainty
from his thoughts.

*A magician may perform a hundred miracles. But if ever one is
seen to be mere trickery, all that went before will be set to nothing.*
His mother had quoted that line to him, over and over
again. An inheritance from the life of the travelling show.
He could only just remember the rolling roads of England,
being lolled to sleep by the movement of the wagon.

*Never let them choose the time or place of your trick. Nor what
the trick should be.*

Well, he'd be breaking all of those rules in one go. He
would live or die by the consequences. In seven days, the
population of the castle, and many who farmed or fished
beyond, would arrive in the courtyard for a theatre of

blood over which Edwin must preside. He would consult the entrails and pronounce on the future of Crown Point.

A voice drifted up from the valley, thinned by wind and distance. The cry of one boatman to another, Edwin thought. He took hold of the rope and ducked under the tree branch that had taken his weight. Small stones rolled under his heels. A few tumbled away below. He let himself down hand over hand, following the line that branched right towards the edge of the widening gulley. It was the worst route. Most people veered left. This rope hadn't been replaced for many years. Broken strands sprouted like hair from the loosening weave.

It had been spring when he last took that path. Half a year had gone. But there had been so little time.

He branched right again, coming up hard under the sheer rock face where the rope ended, knotted around an exposed root. From there it became a scramble, tree to tree, holding on to the trunks as best he could. He was out of the gulley now, following the line where steep scree met the bottom of the cliff. The trees would still hide him from below, though they had thinned, allowing silver glimpses of river.

He could only see a few paces ahead around the curving slope, so when the rock table came into view, it was a sudden thing, like the flourished reveal of a trick. The slab lay at the base of the cliff, long and narrow as a bed. A pile of smaller stones formed a miniature cairn at one end. He stepped onto it with reverence. A bunch of withered flowers had been tied in place with twine. The petals fell to dust as he pulled them free. He cast the dead stalks to the wind.

He would slaughter the ox. The entrails would tell their

story. The king would present him with a token of thanks. It was always something of more show than substance. Edwin had a chest of such useless gifts. Blunt swords and golden cloaks.

He lay down, curled on his side, his head next to the cairn.

"What should I do, Mother?" he asked, feeling the loneliness bite, immersing himself in the feeling. Voicing the question unblocked his tears. They dripped from his face onto the stone, a validation of loss and suffering. He felt his mind clearing.

He had asked the wrong question. What would Janus do? That was the crux. The king's counsellor was clever and ambitious. When the ox lay dead, what might Janus be willing to sacrifice? It was not uncommon for a woman to die in pregnancy or childbirth. Some miscarried. No one would think it unusual.

There could only be one fortune cast for a king, all others being sedition. Edwin would announce the good news to a great assembly of high and low. He'd tell them that the consort would remain healthy, that the royal heir would be born whole and hearty. There was no other choice. Then Janus would act to make the prediction untrue. How had it come to this, that the fate of a kingdom, the fate of the world, might come to be measured against a scattered pinch of poison?

CHAPTER 9

Elizabeth would have sidestepped into the shadows and made her escape via a drift of bushes that stretched all the way to the road. But the grounds of the Grand Niagara would surely be patrolled by night watchmen. Taking a deep breath, she set out along the path, directly away from the main entrance, in full view, as if choosing to depart before dawn was the most natural thing in the world. Every step of the way, her skin prickled. But she could hear no sound of pursuing footsteps.

At the main gate, she paused to don the agent's coat, which was too long for her, and to button it up. With her hair tucked underneath his hat, she seemed less like a woman. The illusion deepened as she opened her stride into a masculine gait and allowed her shoulders to roll. She didn't know whether the clothes and body language were creating a disguise, or if they had revealed a facet of who she was, or if she was somehow conjuring a memory of her lost brother. Either way, she felt different.

From a distance, she was a man, a tourist, on her way into the small town. Unusual at that time of night. But not vulnerable. Close up it would be another story. Distance was the trick. Not just keeping away from people on the street, but putting miles between herself and the hotel. It was perhaps three in the morning. The agents would wake at six-thirty. She'd timed their routine over the previous days. Julia might wake an hour later. Tinker could get up at any time. She hoped this would be one of those days when he slept in. She'd left cushions underneath the blankets on her bed to make it seem as if she was still asleep. If no one had noticed by eight o'clock, it would be good fortune. Five hours, then, was all she could hope for before they set out to search.

By the time she reached the town of Niagara, dawn had not yet begun to show in the sky. She passed the hotels and guesthouses, the shops and restaurants, always choosing the downward slope until she reached the river itself, the wharfs, jetties and chandlers. It might not have been safe. But Elizabeth had lived among the boat people of England's canals and it felt more like home than anything she had seen in months.

Large boats were moored along the quayside. But she wanted to find something smaller. At last she came to a cluster of single-funnelled steamers with side paddles: little more than engine and cargo hold, no space spared for comfort. Walking closer to the edge, she shifted back to the female gait and allowed her heels to clack more heavily on the stones, loud in the quiet of the night.

She'd passed three boats before someone appeared, the silhouette of a hatless boy sitting up from among a pile of blankets on the deck of a thirty-footer.

"Where's your master?" she whispered.

He made no reply, but scrambled on hands and knees

to a cargo hatch, which he lifted. She couldn't hear the words he spoke down into the belly of the boat, but after no more than a few seconds a man hauled himself out. He seemed fat at first, but spidery legs and arms gave him away. Layer on layer of clothing made most of the girth around his stomach. He clambered up to the quayside and stood blinking at her.

"I need help," she whispered, gripping her pistol hidden within the pocket of Winslow's coat. It wasn't loaded. But if it came to trouble, they wouldn't know. "I need to get away from here. I've got money."

"You're in trouble?"

"They're forcing me to marry," she said, hoping it sounded plausible. Niagara was a place for weddings, after all.

"Who's forcing you?"

"My uncle and aunt."

"You don't love him, then?"

She shook her head. He scratched his.

"I'm an orphan," she said, not knowing if it was true.

He looked her over, as if seeing her for the first time. The man's hat, the oversized coat. He ran his tongue over his lips. He was calculating, sure enough, as was she. What kind of man wraps himself warm in the cargo hold and leaves a boy under a blanket on the deck? Her palm felt sweaty against the pistol stock.

The boat lay low in the water. The cargo hold must be full already. "Where are you bound?" she asked.

"Cleveland."

"Where's that?" She was giving away her ignorance, but needed to know if it was east or west.

His eyes narrowed. "You talk funny. Like a queen or

something. Where's home to you?"

"London. But I'm no queen. My people are shopkeepers."

"Well, Cleveland's two days west of here. But we don't take passengers."

From the boy's glance at his master, she could tell it was a lie.

"I can pay. But you'd have to leave early."

He stroked his chin. "Leaving early would be extra."

"Twenty dollars is all I have."

"That's the very price."

He held out his hand, palm upwards.

She didn't move. "How quick can you get the boiler up to pressure?"

He scratched at his chin, as if beginning to suspect she was more than she seemed. "Three hours."

"Do it in two and I'll pay double."

"You said twenty was all you had."

"And you said you don't take passengers."

A steam engine must be coaxed into life. That's what the boatmen had told her on the North Leicester wharf, where she used to live. Build a roaring blaze right from the start and the joints in the metal will take the strain badly. The trick is to start the fire small. If the water rumbles, slow down.

But forty dollars is forty dollars. Elizabeth didn't know how much boiler repair that might pay for on the waterways of North America. Enough, it seemed. The boat master may have been frowning as he threw coals into the firebox one by one, but he didn't complain.

Elizabeth found a place on the deck, behind the

wheelhouse, out of view from the quayside. The sky began to pale. Her friends would not raise the alarm when they found her gone. They wouldn't need to. As soon as Winslow looked for his coat, he would know.

The boy brought her a tin mug of coffee. It was too bitter to drink, but it warmed her hands. Other crews along the quayside were waking. The sounds of activity echoed from the walls of warehouses.

"What's your boat called?" she asked.

"She's the *Rosy Dawn*," said the boy.

The last bit of firing up the boiler was the quickest. The scrape and crunch of shovelling reverberated through the boat. She could smell the sulphurous tang of coal smoke. Steam began to hiss. The master clambered up from below, his face sheened with sweat and black dust. She put one of the Patent Office's bank-fresh twenty-dollar bills in his hand. He examined it before holding out his hand again.

"You can have the other twenty when we get there," she said.

He nodded his agreement. Too easily, she thought.

The boy threw off the lines from the mooring cleats, hopped aboard and used a boathook to push the prow out towards the river. There was a clank of gears and the paddlewheels began to turn, the noise of the engine building until everything on the boat was rattling. Elizabeth crouched down behind the wheelhouse. A line of buoys marked out the channel. Other boats had been getting up steam, but the *Rosy Dawn* was the first to leave Niagara.

Once the agents figured out that she'd escaped, they'd be sending men to search. Someone would surely ask questions along the quay. The Patent Office was held in low regard by most from the labouring classes, but someone would talk. By ten in the morning they'd have discovered the name of the first boat out and that it had been bound for Cleveland.

When the quay was far enough behind that she wouldn't be seen, she got back to her feet, steadying herself against the wheelhouse. The boat didn't look like much, but it moved at a fair lick.

"What time is it?" she asked.

"Daytime," the master said.

And that was that.

Peering into the hold she could see little, but caught the whiff of food. Her mouth watered. She let herself down into a space stacked with barrels to either side. The boy was crouched in front of the firebox frying eggs on the flat of a shovel. A plate of cooked bacon and a loaf of bread lay to the side. There seemed plenty enough for three so she tore a hunk from the loaf and picked up a strip of hot bacon with her fingers. It was delicious. He watched her eat as if observing some strange creature. There was bacon fat on her chin. She wiped it off with the back of her hand. At that, he smiled. If only the master proved so easy to win over.

Winslow and McLeod would send a message by pigeon to Cleveland. It would arrive long before the *Rosy Dawn* could steam there. That meant agents would be waiting with a description of her, and the warning that she could pass herself as a man.

Little was said as they steamed upriver, but by mid-morning the wide waterway opened out to become what seemed to be an ocean, though they had been travelling upstream. Now there was no current to fight against, but waves pitched the *Rosy Dawn* one way and then the other, growing as the land sank below the horizon. Elizabeth held on for fear of being tipped over the side.

"What is this place?" she asked, shouting against the engine noise.

"Lake Erie," the master said.

She could see no compass in the wheelhouse. He stared resolutely at the horizon ahead. Navigating by the sun, she thought. And presently land came into view once more. As they came closer in, the waves began to subside.

Through the day, she had seen other cargo vessels steaming in each direction. Some great ships raised bow waves big enough to splash over onto the deck of the *Rosy Dawn*.

With the coast close enough to make out individual trees, the master went below, leaving the wheel to the boy. It had been sunny through the morning but Elizabeth's clothes were wet from the spray and the cold was working into her. She stood beside the boy in the small wheelhouse.

"Is he your father?" she asked.

"No."

"How long have you been working for him?"

"Since I turned nine."

"And what is it you usually carry?"

"Stuff," he said.

There was something in the way he said it that marked the evasion as important. Contraband, then. Untaxed spirits perhaps. That would fit with the *Rosy Dawn*. From the outside the boat seemed rusty enough to be leaking from a dozen holes. But they were making seven or eight knots. And though the rattling of fixtures was almost deafening, behind that she could hear an engine running sweetly.

"Where do you put in when it gets dark?"

He glanced back at her but didn't answer.

The sun crawled across the sky. Since meeting the southern coast of Lake Erie they had been steering due west. The master climbed back up to the deck with an apple in his hand. He offered none to her or the boy, but devoured the whole thing, core and pips and all, flicking the stalk over the side. Then he took the wheel.

There was no word of lunch. The boy made more bitter coffee. This time she was thirsty enough to drink. It set her heart racing. Only then did she think of asking for water. Two cups took away the taste of the coffee. At least it had jolted her back to alertness. She didn't trust the master enough to risk sleep.

They knew she'd been carrying forty dollars and was ready to spend it. The master would rightly think she was carrying more. There's no easier place to get rid of a body than in a wide expanse of water.

The master seemed to be looking for some landmark on the coast as the sun dipped below the horizon. The light faded fast. They couldn't continue for long. On some signal that she could not understand, he steered the boat in towards a thicket of trees. It seemed certain that they would run aground, but just in time he pulled the lever to disengage the engine. The paddlewheels began to drag in the water and they suddenly slowed.

The forward anchor was a large stone, drilled through so that a rope could be tied. It was too big for the boy to lift, but he managed to roll it to the edge and push it over. The rope on the deck whipped after it, but only a few coils. It might be shallow enough to wade ashore. The stern anchor was a hunk of iron scrap. Together, they wouldn't have held against a current. But in a quiet inlet on the coast of a lake, they proved easily enough for the job.

"We're more than halfway," the master said, tamping tobacco into a pipe. "The boy will cook up supper."

The gruff demeanour he'd displayed all day had gone. Now he was all smiles. He puffed smoke into the evening air, making a veil between them.

She went below, told the boy to go up top, to give her some privacy. They had a metal bucket in place of a chamber pot. This she used, then lugged it up to empty over the stern, feeling their eyes on her.

Beyond the stones of the shore, the land was thick with scrub and small trees. She could see no lights. The vastness of the country was hard to understand. In England there was hardly a mile but someone would be living there. In America, she might set out on foot and not meet another human being in a week of walking. If she were to slip away in the night, it might not be so easy to find her way back to civilisation.

They released the steam and allowed the fire to die down, but there was enough heat to cook more bacon on the shovel. The bread was stale for their evening meal but softened in the fat. This time the master offered her an apple. The boy seemed content without. As she bit into it, she remembered Tinker and had to blink away the threat of tears. If he'd been with her they could have taken turns to stay awake. Or her dear Julia. But she'd missed one night's sleep already and was having to fight to keep her eyes open.

"Is there a blanket for me?" she asked.

The master nodded and the boy went off to fetch it. While neither of them were looking, she scooped a handful of coal chippings from the bunker.

The blanket smelt of tobacco smoke. She accepted it, then picked her way to the back of the hold where a space had been left, surrounded by stacked barrels. It could only be reached via a narrow gap. There was no way out. But it gave her the best chance of living through the night.

She lay under the blanket, knife and pistol close enough to grab, trying to stay awake for a few minutes more. The boy clambered up through the hatch. The master was pottering about up front, his shoes scraping on the boards. Then the lamp went out, leaving only the dull glow from the firebox.

Moving silently, she uncovered herself and crawled forwards through the narrow gap and started placing the chippings of coal as she retreated back towards the blanket. Once she was covered again, sleep came instantly.

Waking came in a rush. There had been a noise, half in and half out of her dream. Now all she could hear was the rushing of blood in her own head and the whisper of the coarse blanket as she pulled it away to free her arms.

Somewhere close by, a chipping of coal crunched under a boot. She fumbled for the knife and pistol, then propped herself with her back against a barrel. He stepped forwards again. This time she made out the movement, the shift of a darker mass against the dark. He would be a knife man, she thought.

His foot caught another chipping, sending it skittering across the boards. The dark form lowered itself over the place where she had been sleeping. She imagined his knife hand extending, the blade seeking out her flesh. She raised the unloaded pistol and pulled back the hammer. Its click was unmistakable. She heard his intake of breath.

"I could tie you to the anchor," she said. "Leave you on the bottom of the lake. The boy can steer the boat."

"I was sleepwalking," he said.

"Put down the weapon."

There was a soft sound. Not a knife. He started backing away, scattering the coal chips. She groped on the floor for what he had left and found a length of waxed cord tied to a wooden handle at each end. A knife may have many functions but a garrotte has only one. A shiver passed from her neck over her shoulders.

He would not make the same mistake again. She followed him between the barrels then climbed the ladder, lifting the hatch to clamber out on deck. The lake air hit her, cold and damp.

The boy's eyes were wide with fright. Taking his blanket, she gestured with the gun, sending him below to join the master. Then she threaded a rope to stop the hatch opening again and took the blankets into the wheelhouse.

This time she slept deeply, despite the cold. Waking in the thin light of dawn, she walked up and down the deck. And when her muscles had loosened she ran on the spot until the warmth started to flow through her body.

Once she'd released the master, there'd be no going back into the hold. But the bucket was down there with them. So she used the anchor rope for balance and managed to relieve herself over the side. When she was clean and presentable again, she opened the hatch and stood back, holding the pistol so they would see it.

The boy scurried out, with those scared-rabbit eyes. He

walked once around the deck, as if merely taking the air, then dropped himself back through the hatch. She could hear them whispering below. Only then did the master emerge. He nodded towards her, a gesture of greeting, then carried on with his tasks. Just another morning, it seemed, the events of the night not worth the mention.

"Is there a place to stop a few miles before Cleveland?" she asked.

"There is."

Elizabeth lowered her gun and clicked the hammer gently to its rest. "Once you've put me down, I'll give you the rest of your money."

The docking place turned out to be a cluster of factories, canneries and warehouses served by a long jetty. That suited Elizabeth well enough. The boy hopped ashore with her bag. She followed, the pistol resting heavy and reassuring in the pocket of her coat.

She handed over the twenty dollars. Safer to leave the master embarrassed than angry. He stuffed it in his pocket then turned away without a word. The paddle wheels began to turn, slapping the water, and the *Rosy Dawn* chugged off into the lake. It wouldn't be long before they put in at Cleveland. The Patent Office would be waiting. The master might clam up at first, fearing she'd put them onto him. But they'd have the story out of him soon enough. Agents would be swarming toward that jetty before the day was out.

Wooden buildings big as warehouses lined the lakeside. Everything smelled of fish. Five men in blue overalls lounged in the sun next to an open doorway. She caught sight of drying racks within, row after row of them.

One of the men was looking at her. The others followed his gaze. A woman travelling on her own will always be stared at, but she would present a doubly curious sight: oversized coat, over-stuffed bag, charcoal grey trilby. They might be talking about her for weeks. And she was dishevelled after a night sleeping on the deck of the *Rosy Dawn*. But that might work to her advantage. If she could find the right story to tell them.

"Please help me," she said.

One of the men, who seemed older than the others, stood from the crate he'd been sitting on. Fish scales glinted on his overalls and in his grey beard.

"Miss?"

She stepped closer, dropped her voice. "It's my father. My real father, not the one I was brought up by. It's all a secret. And now the secret's out. He's after me!"

The man's brow furrowed. The others gathered around to listen. "Slow down, girl. Who's after you?"

"My real father. I've run away. I think they're going to kill me."

"Who?"

"The Patent Office."

They all recoiled on mention of the name, but only by a few inches.

"Hold on there!" the old man whispered. "How do *they* get into this?"

"My father – the real one – he's a Patent Office agent."

The hint of scandal lit their eyes. Patent Office agents were supposed to be celibate. That didn't stop rumours of carnality. The men leaned in once again, the smell of fish and tobacco smoke overpowering.

"If anyone found out, he'd be hanged," she said.

They nodded as one.

"He'll have me killed to stop the story. They're after me even now. I need clothes to disguise myself. A man's clothes, but smaller than this coat. And a place to change."

The lie worked so well that they refused to take her money. She did persuade them to accept Agent Winslow's coat in exchange, though she warned them that it was stolen and to wait a month before trying to sell it.

Having changed in the privacy of an unused smokehouse, she emerged to great astonishment from the men. So impressed were they by the transformation that each wanted to take her hand. They were tentative, but when she gripped back, as a man would, and shook firmly, they laughed. One even patted her on the shoulder, as he might have another man, though more gently. She slapped him on the back in return, hard enough to make him grin.

The clothes fitted well enough, except for around the waist, which she had to bulk out with a cloth wrapped around next to her skin. The same cloth also flattened down her breasts. The trousers, which they called pants, were canvas and the same blue as the overalls. There was a grey shirt, a dull green jacket and a red cloth to tie around her neck. The hat was not unlike Winslow's fedora, but dark brown leather instead of grey felt, the brim half an inch wider and ragged. She still needed a coat. But that was good, to one manner of thinking. She would find something warm and second-hand in Cleveland. And it was safer that none of these men could give a complete description of how she would come to look.

She'd powdered her hands with a fragment of charred wood, then rubbed her chin to give a suggestion of stubble.

"I wouldn't know you from a boy," the bearded man said. He beamed as if it were the greatest compliment.

She blessed them all, speaking still in a female voice, then walked away with a female gait, until she was around the corner and out of their view. Only then did she allow the greater change to come over her, shifting her balance, leaning into her steps, steering out from the buildings to occupy the middle of the street.

It seemed a down-at-heel industrial town. The few shoppers were working men and women. She strode past a tobacconist's, a dry goods store, a vegetable barrow, a ropemaker's.

After three streets, she called into a gun shop and, using her male voice, bought powder and shot. The man who served her showed displeasure at the crisp, new banknote. But he took it in the end, giving coins and crumpled notes in change. Easier money to spend.

She found a wagon of oil barrels about to set off towards Cleveland. The carter took some of her coins and let her climb into the back. They rattled and jolted along for an hour or so, until the buildings started to grow taller, the streets more crowded. When they reached the back of a queue of carriages and steamcars waiting to turn left, she slipped off the cart and joined the crowds on the sidewalk outside a line of boarding houses.

The Patent Office would track her to the fish drying factory, but no further. She strode around the corner, not looking back, confident that she could not be followed, knowing that the greater danger now lay ahead.

PART TWO

CHAPTER 10

Power was built on belief just as the castle had been built on the rock. The crumbling of either foundation would bring the edifice crashing down.

The first lord – great-grandfather to the king – had used a looted cannon and a quantity of muskets to control Crown Point, extorting goods and food from trappers and traders passing on the Colombia River, hundreds of feet below. His genius had been to take only a tithe. In that way he'd been unlike the other warlords of the wild Oregon Territory. A begrudging order began to settle, so that a man paddling a load of furs downriver might feel a sense of relief on reaching those waters. He knew what he would need to pay. He could allow for it. And if bandits made camp beyond sight of the cannon, the Lord of Crown Point would send out raiding parties to take them down.

But force of arms can only control the land. A nation is built on minds and hearts. It wasn't enough that troublemakers were hunted. The traders also had to believe that it would be done and that their tithe would be spent for justice. The heads of bandits would be raised on spikes above the battlements.

The great-grandfather had started it. But it was his son, the king's great-uncle, who added magic to the mix, using it to fashion a belief in destiny where there had been none before. His magician had been a wild-eyed prophet with unkempt hair, who would fall down into fits, his mouth foaming. In that state, he would rant and rave in the language of spirits, which none present could understand, but which, when he had recovered, he was able to translate. And through those sayings it was discovered that the Lord of Crown Point would become the Lord of the Colombia River for hundreds of miles. He would become a king.

The prophecy proved true. But the magicians who followed, bastard sons and grandsons of the first, were lesser men, falling more easily into alcoholic stupor than visionary fits. So that when Timon found a prophetess sheltering in a tavern, he brought her into the Great Hall of the castle, into the very presence of his brother, the king.

She stood before the throne, her back to the warriors, accountants, armourers, courtiers and brightly dressed women of the royal household, her young son clinging to her skirts.

The king's magician stepped from the crowd and circled her. "This woman is false!" He spat the words.

"But she saved my child," said Timon. "He was dying."

"He would've grown hale without her."

"You didn't see it."

Through all this, the woman who might have been a prophetess had stood looking down at the flagstones, avoiding the pleading eyes of her son.

The King of Crown Point sighed. He could easily have dealt with her in private. But arguments of power held in the public gaze had a way of getting out of control. Doubly so when they concerned matters of faith. If someone had to die, it would be this woman, and that would leave another hungry orphan for him to feed.

"Perhaps Timon's son might have sweated off the fever without help," the king suggested, in a conciliatory tone. "But none are harmed if a little magic helped with the healing."

The court magician stood tall, though this mainly pushed out his beer paunch. "No, sire! I can read her. This woman has no power over life or death."

"What say you?" This the king addressed to the woman, who stood just as tall as his magician, and whose gaze seemed more focused.

"This man is afraid of me," she said.

"She lies."

They'd had their chance to back away. Neither had taken it. "Then we must have a contest," said the king, resigned now.

A murmur of excitement shifted through the court. Everyone was seeing it. A skull would be cracked on the stones. Timon had seemed upset by the woman's chill reception but now he too was licking his lips. His hand dropped to the purse at his belt. A contest meant a wager. And people would lay down good money on the life or death of a magician.

"Well?" asked the king.

The court magician coughed, as if to clear his throat. It failed to quiet the whisper of conversations around the hall: the important business of fixing odds and placing bets. That was the way of things. Gambling was another kind of religion.

The king clapped his hands. That did it. In the silence that followed, the court magician stepped to the centre of the room, turned a full circle, his gaze making the crowd back away. He put both hands on his head and his eyes rolled up in their sockets so that only the whites showed. He began to hum, a single low note, then hunched his shoulders forwards and his voice became suddenly resonant, making an otherworldly drone. The crowd backed away further. His mouth opened and closed making vowel sounds, which might have been some language of spirits. Then he dropped, or perhaps threw himself down, and silence closed in.

The crowd had begun to creep forwards again but stopped dead when he sat, drawing a great howling breath. Overacting.

"She!" He pointed to the woman, her son clinging ever closer. "She has been sent by a demon to deceive you. My lord, I've seen it. In the world of the spirit, I've seen it. Whatever she says has been put in her mouth by an enemy. She would bring great harm."

They were all looking at the woman now, as she prised her child's fingers from her leg and pushed him towards one of the king's mistresses in the crowd, who, seeming to understand, took the boy and held him.

The magician clambered back to his feet, staggering theatrically before finding his balance, whereon he folded his arms and stared hatred at the impostor. She glanced towards the king, who nodded for her to proceed.

"I'm confused," she said. "Is he claiming I have no magic? Or is he saying my magic has evil intent?"

The king's magician seemed not to have expected this question.

"She's weak!" he blurted. "And evil."

"Then, if I prove myself more powerful than you, I will have shown your claim to be false."

The king nodded.

She advanced towards the fireplace, the crowd parting for her, then turned to face them and held up her hands, displaying their emptiness. Reaching two fingers into her narrow cuff, she extracted a small writing tablet, which seemed to be made of ivory. From her other cuff she produced a pencil.

"Can you stop me reading your mind?" she asked the court magician. When he didn't answer, she said: "You must direct your thoughts to a name. Then I will write it down. Use your magic to stop me. If you can."

The magician glanced to the king, as if looking for support.

"Are you scared?" she asked.

"No. But you should be!"

"Are you thinking of a name?"

"I am."

"Then try to keep my mind out from yours."

She held the ivory tablet to her forehead and fixed him with her eyes. Silence pressed down on the room. No one had seen such a competition. The fire crackled, shooting out a spark. As if that had been her cue, the woman shifted the tablet behind her back with one hand and the pencil with the other, and seemed to begin writing. The court magician looked to the crowd, smiling. The woman finished what she was doing and held out the ivory tablet once more, so the blank side showed.

"What name did you think?" she asked.

"You failed," he said, then addressing the room. "She has failed. I thought of no name. I directed my mind elsewhere. If she had a grain of power, she'd know this."

"Then where did you direct your thoughts?"

"To our glorious flag."

"Then what does it show?"

"A blue pentagram," said the king. "A five-pointed star on black cloth."

"What would be the punishment if I failed?" she asked.

"To be thrown from the battlements," said the magician.

"What about my son?"

"He will be thrown before you."

All this time she'd kept the writing tablet in the air above her head, in full view. A cunning observer might have noticed the hint of a tremble in her grip, as her thumb moved over the hidden side. But it was her eyes that held them, wide and staring. She placed the tablet face down on her palm, offering it to her enemy.

"Carry this to your king," she said. "Ask him to show mercy."

Something held the magician back from turning it over. Fear perhaps. He lurched towards the fire, as if to cast it into the flames.

"Cease!" the king shouted. "You will bring it to me."

And so he did, his steps slowing as he approached the throne. It was the king who turned over that sliver of ivory to reveal a pentagram marked in pencil, a shaky line, very much as if it had been written behind the woman's back.

Seeing it, the magician fell onto his knees, crying "Mercy."

But his powers had been beaten by hers.

He gabbled excuses and apologies as they hauled him up the stairs with the king leading and the whole court following in a mass behind. But he had fixed his own punishment with all of them as witness.

His words had run out by the time a cloth bag was pulled over his head. He stopped struggling, went over the battlements limp and without a cry, so that the slack sound of his body hitting the rocks came faint but clear from far below.

The king turned to the woman who had so ably defeated his magician. Her fame would spread. Found in a tavern, she had beaten his own man.

"Will you stay with us?" he asked. He had no choice, really, though there'd never been a woman in such a position of power. First Counsellor and magician to the king.

She bowed. "Yes, sire."

When at last they returned to the hall, her son was released and came running to hold her. She held him, wiped his tears and stroked his hair, saying, "Hush now, Edwin. All is well. We have found our new home."

CHAPTER 11

Elizabeth's boarding house smelled of boiled cabbage from the kitchen and turpentine from the factory next door. Her stolen money would have paid for a room in the best hotel. But she was wearing a poor man's clothes. She could have walked into a tailor's shop and had a smart suit prepared, but that too would have attracted gossip. It came to her, not for the first time, that changing appearance from one class to another was no less troublesome than swapping between genders. Either could be accomplished in secret. But a witness to the act would always feel disquiet.

On her first day in Cleveland, she stayed inside her small room, staring at cracks in the ceiling plaster, listening to conversations through the walls, which seemed little more than cardboard. In the evening she went out, walked a few blocks following her nose, found a street of food vendors with barrows and oil lamps. Such a variety, she had never seen together. Unfamiliar scents of hot oils and spices drifted with steam lit yellow in lamplight. She stopped at a barrow adorned with Chinese writing, didn't know what anything was called so pointed and watched as a mound of rice and meats of different kinds were scooped into a paper cone. Nor did she have the skill of eating with wooden sticks, so bought a spoon as well. The flavours were unfamiliar but delicious. A strange saltiness left her thirsty, so she strolled further down the street to a stall selling bottled beer from buckets of melting ice. Taking her lead from other customers, she drank right there on the roadside.

As the sky darkened, more traders came out and the night market spread. Elizabeth stopped by a clothing stall. All manner of second-hand garments had been arranged on a canvas sheet, patched and darned. She asked if she might try on a coat. It seemed a fawn colour, though it was hard to be sure in the lamplight. It hung to her knees, but had been cut with a long back vent for riding. The sleeves were only an inch too long and, best of all, it had a quilted lining.

The Cleveland air terminus would be watched by the Patent Office. But airships travelling west routinely put down in Vermillion, some forty miles from the city, for fuelling and to take on provisions.

Three days after arriving, Elizabeth found her way to that stopover, bought a ticket and watched the airship approaching. The ground crew were ready. Three other passengers waited. Had they been agents, she thought she would have recognised them. It was a stopover, no more. A field next to the edge of the lake. The engines slowed as it descended, men caught the trailing ropes and made it fast before wheeling out a set of steps. Elizabeth showed her ticket and climbed aboard.

She was surprised to find that she didn't look out of place among the passengers. They were an odd assortment. Some expensively dressed, some in workers' clothes, like hers. Mostly men but a scattering of women. A mixture of races.

She took a seat on the port side.

A white man in a top hat stood pointing out of a starboard cabin window.

"The fuel's brought in by ship," he said. "You can see the jetty. The Vermillion stopover was established thirty-eight years ago by…"

A wrinkle-faced man sitting opposite met Elizabeth's eyes. His cheekbones were high and he had the complexion of a first-nationer. He leaned towards her and whispered, "You should have been with us in Cleveland. He was schooling the captain on the science of air travel. It's going to be a long trip!"

Elizabeth had never mastered the art of male laughter, but she grinned.

The man's name was Conway. Out of habit, she gave hers as Edwin, only thinking afterwards that it was her brother's real name and that when the two-thousand-mile journey was drawing to a close, she would need to learn some other alias. In case he did yet live. She felt a pang of uncertainty mixed with hope. If her brother was there, perhaps too the mother that she'd lost.

The engines roared, drowning out the discourse of the man in the top hat. The ship began to move forwards and tilt back in a steep climb. She watched the land receding below.

"You know why I choose to face backwards?" Conway asked.

She shook her head, expecting him to explain but he did not.

The next stop was Joliet, outside Chicago. As the man in the top hat explained to the carriage, fewer stops would mean carrying more fuel which in turn would mean less passengers and cargo. Though it slowed the journey, it lowered the costs. And lower costs were good for the bottom line.

Not caring to hear an explanation of what the bottom line was, Elizabeth stood and edged between the seats to a rack of newspapers at the back of the carriage. She rotated her shoulders, then stretched out her arms, coaxing her muscles into relaxation. Had she been dressed as a woman, such an exuberant taking up of space would have drawn frowns of disapproval. Selecting a copy of the *Lewiston Morning Tribune*, she returned to her seat.

Lewiston was a border town, the most westerly settlement before the wilds of the Oregon Territory. That meant a military presence. A regiment of border guards were billeted there, protecting the civilised world from what lay beyond. It was the administrative base for the maintenance of many hundreds of miles of border fence. Then there were all the traders who served the military, and the traders who served them.

With the paper spread on her knee, she perused a report of a bar brawl between soldiers and townsfolk. Other articles reported on a parade, and on the replacement of a fifty mile stretch of the border fence being put out to tender. There were a great many adverts, which she skimmed over. But on page five she found a story of particular interest. Bending low over the small type, she read of a woman, known only as Mrs Arthur, and two men, who were said to be her husbands. They had been charged with gold smuggling and found guilty. It was the seventh time they'd been caught and fined. The judge described them as reprobates and recidivists of the first order. It seemed unlikely they would desist, the *Tribune* observed, since the maximum permissible fine was clearly less than the money they were making on each trip back and forth across the fence.

Their crime was to carry factory made goods out of the Gas-Lit Empire into the wilds and return some weeks later with a quantity of gold in the form of dust and small nuggets. Glassware, hand mirrors and brightly coloured linen were apparently popular with the people beyond. The article stated that Mrs Arthur and her husbands lived in a cabin on the north side of Snake River, away from the town.

From the context of the article, it didn't seem that having more than one husband was illegal or surprising, though the writer clearly disapproved. Elizabeth felt an instant liking for the woman. It was also proof that crossing the border was possible and not so dangerous as she might have feared.

Feeling a hand on the newspaper, she looked up. Conway was leaning forwards.

"Did you solve my riddle?" he asked.

"Riddle?" Elizabeth had been absorbed in Mrs Arthur's story. She glanced around the cabin. The man in the top hat was no longer lecturing the entire carriage, but was directing his wisdom towards a much younger woman sitting next to him.

"Why do I sit facing backwards?" Conway prompted.

"I don't know. I'm sorry."

"Then why did you choose to face forwards?"

"The seat was free."

He half smiled, making her think that she'd missed his point.

"I've a question for you," she said. "But it may seem rude."

"I'm not so easily shocked. But ask quietly, if you're shy."

"I'm reading about a woman with two husbands. But I thought the first-nationers did it the other way around – one husband with many wives?"

Conway shrugged. "There are five hundred nations here, they say, though I couldn't name them all. We each have our own ways and customs. But you know, it's often the white folks who come out west so they can live like that. The law won't countenance it in the Free States or the Confederacy. Not all the white race are such good people. And I should warn you, border towns like Lewiston attract the worst of them."

"What makes you think I'm going there?"

"The paper."

"Oh. Yes. You're right."

"What business takes you to the border?" he asked.

"I'm looking for work."

"Are you now?" The raised eyebrow suggested he didn't believe it. "What's your trade?"

"I'm good with my hands," she said, causing him to look at them. Realising the mistake, she stuffed them into her trouser pockets and pushed her knees further apart, in the way that men do.

"Forgive me," he said. "It's a long journey. And you're a puzzle. You're English, right?"

She nodded.

"Most English I see out west are rich boys come to shoot buffalo. Or men with nothing to lose, signing up for the border guard. Escaped prisoners. Men with debts they'll never pay. Sometimes there's a professor who wants to see people like me living in tents and wearing beads, so he can go home and give lectures or write a book. What kind of Englishman are you, Mr Edwin?"

It came to her, then, and so she said it: "You sit facing back so you can see where you've been."

He grinned. "Bravo. Most folks want to think about where they're going. But the only thing you can be sure of in this world comes from facing the other way."

She couldn't tell if he meant it or if he was having fun at her expense, playing a role for a gullible tourist. It felt more like a word game than a gem of folk wisdom.

On the second day, they put down at Sioux Falls to take on a great quantity of packages and provisions. Most of the passengers disembarked. Elizabeth watched through the cabin window as they collected their baggage. One night sleeping upright in a chair had been bad enough. She wished she could be getting off as well.

Having lost most of his audience, the man in the top hat came across the aisle to sit next to Conway. He introduced himself as Colonel Martinshaw and would have lectured them on the divisions of the border regiment if Elizabeth hadn't feigned sleep.

That evening they put down at Billings for a longer stop. They were obliged to disembark while engineers inspected the boilers and carried out routine maintenance. Following Conway's lead, she arranged three chairs in the waiting room and lay down across them, thus managing a couple of hours' sleep.

Travelling on through the night, Elizabeth felt nauseous with fatigue. She woke again with dawn coming up and the sensation of the craft descending. Below lay mile after mile of wooded hills.

"Is this it?" she asked.

Conway put a finger to his lips and leaned forwards. "Don't wake our friend here or he'll relate the history of Post Falls back to its founding. That's where we're about to land."

Martinshaw's head lolled and his eyes were closed. The top hat lay between his feet on the floor.

"I've solved the puzzle," Conway whispered.

"What puzzle?"

"You. We've been two days in the air. Look at the colonel here. His chin's dark with stubble. But you…"

Without thinking, Elizabeth raised a hand to cover her mouth.

"Don't worry," said Conway. "I won't tell your secret."

CHAPTER 12

Some doors must be kicked through. Others will open to a touch. It is the eternal challenge of those who counsel kings to determine which door is which. That and deciding what to wear.

"Enter!"

At the king's command, Edwin slipped through into the observatory. "Sire."

"Oh, it's you." A note of disappointment.

At a wave from the royal hand, a glint from that fat ruby on his finger, the servants were bowing and backing away. Edwin waited until they were quite gone before approaching.

The observatory was an octagonal room with a vaulted roof and glass windows on four sides. The large brass telescope had been angled down as if someone had been watching the boats on the river. Edwin had never seen the king using it. But the observatory was the place in which he seemed most relaxed.

Fully *en femme* today, Edwin curtsied deep and slow. Blue silk from shoulder to ankle, clinging to show curves of hip and waist. A pale-yellow scarf. Earrings that might have been sapphires, but were glass.

"It won't do," the king said.

"What, sire?"

"You're here to beg that I change my mind. About the ox. But I say it won't do. The animal must be killed."

Only two days remained until the full moon, the appointed time for the sacrifice. Preparations had already begun.

"It's my job to offer counsel," Edwin said. "Won't you listen?"

"I can't go back on my word. It's been announced. I know you're squeamish about these things. But there we go. It's done. You'll have to make the best of it."

"Janus set me up."

"Maybe he did. But the people need to be reassured. They need to know what the future will bring. And we haven't had a show like this for years. So he was right, in a way. You're not saying my consort doesn't deserve such a spectacle?"

"I didn't mean that."

"Good! It's what we've always done. Since before your time. Before your mother too. You'd best remember that."

"I only want you to consider the danger."

The king began to circle Edwin. When he was directly behind, he said: "Do you think I treat you differently like this? Is that why you put on a dress? Of all your magic, this is the bit I don't understand."

Edwin felt the king's touch, a finger brushing over the silk from shoulder to arm. There was a hint of pine resin in the air as he passed around to the side. The royal hand took the loose hem of the sleeve and rubbed the silk, like a dressmaker gauging quality.

"I don't always know why I dress one way or the other," Edwin said, though the king had been right. This time it had been deliberate. To be deferential as a man was just as easy. But feminine deference felt somehow different. A different flavour, perhaps. If they'd been meeting in public, it wouldn't have gone well. But in the privacy of the observatory, the curtsy and lowered gaze had often drawn a response that seemed almost paternal.

"Be careful," the king said.

"Of what?"

"Some of the men lust after you. And they hate themselves for it. I don't want to lose another magician."

It was the first time the king had shown such an insight. Edwin wondered why he'd chosen that moment to speak it. Perhaps he'd noticed the way Timon had been staring. There were others, macho men whose eyes would follow the curve of a body sheathed in silk. But the king's brother had never needed to learn restraint like an ordinary soldier.

"It's Janus I'm afraid of," Edwin said. "He hates me."

"I wouldn't call it hate. But he rather loves himself, I'll grant you that. He was here not long ago. I'm surprised you didn't pass on the stairs."

"What did he want?"

"Same as usual: the border is only wire and wood, he says. But he's refined his plans. He wants us to lay explosive charges. Take down three sections of the fence, all in the same moment. One frontal assault directly into Lewiston. Two more units outflanking, north and south. He's drawn a map. We put the automatic guns behind the town. When their men start to run…" The king gestured, the same flick of the hand with which he'd dismissed his servants.

"It's an old plan," Edwin said. "Changing details doesn't make it new."

"He says we should go in on changeover day. That way we'll capture all the men of the garrison. And all the men of the relief garrison. Or kill them. What do you think to that?"

That *was* new. And it was a good idea. If they took the entire border regiment in one go, it would take months for the enemy to regroup.

"But then what?" Edwin asked.

"Ransom them," the king said. "Or kill them. It doesn't matter."

"It does matter!"

"Be careful, Edwin." That warning note.

"I'm sorry, sire. But it's the plan I'm against. Not you. If I can't speak my fears, I'll be of no use. Janus's scheme would work. We'd take Lewiston. With our weapons against theirs, it would be quick. And we could kill all their men. But it's what comes after that should worry you."

The king smiled. "That's why you're so useful to me, my dear Edwin. Janus covets your place on my right hand. He shows your weakness and you show his. So tell me about his plan."

"Where would Janus send your army after Lewiston?"

"Onwards." The king gestured vaguely towards the southeast. "City to city. Staying ahead of the snow. We destroy their means of production, distribution and exchange. Those are his words. He has marked a route. We don't try to hold the land. Not enough men for that. Instead we destroy. Everything. We plunder. We create chaos. Just like the chaos that once ruled here. And we… I… this kingdom…

will spread out into that fertile soil, just as we've always done, since the time of my fathers."

A chill ran over Edwin's skin. The king's words had been animated by the force of vision. An imagined future. Hoped for. It was Janus's future.

"You *will* have all this," Edwin said. "And more."

"Then you agree at last?"

Instead of answering, Edwin said, "Do you know what happened to Napoleon when he marched his army into Russia? His soldiers were veterans, well-trained, seasoned in battle. Nothing could stop them. They advanced from city to city, doing just as Janus says. Destroying. Pillaging. But in the end, Russia was too big. Their supply lines were too long. Most of his army died of cold and disease on the way back home to France."

"We're not attacking Russia."

"We're attacking the Gas-Lit Empire. Russia is only a speck within it. We can throw this continent into chaos. I do agree with that. But how long would it take for your kingdom to grow out into it? How long before we'd be strong enough to farm the land we've harrowed? And most important – how long before we're able to face the armies of the rest of the world? While we push out across America, mile by mile, year by year, they'll be gathering a mighty army from Africa and Europe and Asia and Australia. Before our job is a fraction done, they'll be landing. Our ships will protect the Pacific coast. So they'll land in the east. In their millions. Our guns outmatch theirs. But their forces will outnumber us by thousands to one. Tens of thousands. We could start Janus's war. But we could never win it."

Janus's war. It was a good phrase: one to be used again.

The king's soldiers dying in Janus's war.

The king turned to stare out of the window, resting one hand on the brass barrel of the telescope. Edwin waited. Each time Janus had the king's ear, it seemed that everything needed to be laid out again. And each time it was harder to convince.

"Their losses would be terrible," the king said, perhaps to himself.

"They've sworn to defend their Empire."

"But they're soft. They don't know war. They don't remember it. Not like we do."

"They'd learn. And quickly. They might lose a million men. But there are tens of millions more for them to call up."

"But the shock they'd feel... Janus says it would break them. They'd sue for peace."

"Do *you* believe him?"

Edwin watched as the king pushed open the window glass. A breeze shifted the wall hangings. There was a smell in the air of decaying leaves. Already the trees on the far side of the valley were turning to gold. Soon Mount Hood would be white with snow.

"Janus believes it," the king said. "Is he a fool?"

"Ambition blinds him. Would you risk your kingdom on the toss of a coin?"

"I might."

"But there's no need. If you first control the Atlantic, this whole continent will be yours. And all its people. And all its resources. Within ten years you'll have built a war machine so big that it'll be you invading them. You'll send your forces across the water. Take Australia first. Then Asia. Then march into Europe and Africa. You'll be the king of the whole planet. Greater than Napoleon ever dreamed to be. Greater than Alexander."

"Ten years is a long time," the king said. "But you are a good servant to me."

Edwin knelt. "Then please, sire, will you spare the ox?"

"Not that again! Why should I call it off?"

"If I read the entrails and see health and long life for you and for your child, and if I say it for all to hear…"

"What?" The word had been spoken quietly. But the resonance of the king's voice made it somehow fill the room.

"All Janus will need to do is harm your consort. A sprinkle of poison. I'll be proved wrong. They'll throw me from the battlements. It's what he wants."

"You push too far!"

Edwin didn't know why the king trusted Janus so much. Perhaps it was the blindness of arrogance. "I'm afraid for her. For your child."

"You're afraid for yourself. And your imagination runs away with you." Then louder, as his anger grew: "Janus would never do such a thing! He wouldn't dare!"

"I'm sorry, sire. But I beg you–"

"That is enough!"

The king sighed then, as if weary of the argument. He placed a hand on Edwin's brow and stroked the long dark hair. "Slaughter the ox. Do it for me." The voice was kindly now. That paternal tone again. "Use all your powers and read the future. If the auguries say my child will be healthy and safe, then so it shall be. All will be well. And I will have both of my servants."

There were guards on the stairs and courtiers in the corridors. Some stared as Edwin passed. The observatory was too high in the tower for the king's anger to have been overheard by any of them. Perhaps they were reacting to the shock in Edwin's face, the realisation, for the first time, that for all his collaboration in trickery, the king too believed in magic.

CHAPTER 13

But for the border, Lewiston might have been a scenic town. The Snake River had a certain grandeur cutting a wide curve between low hills. The sky seemed immense, though Elizabeth reasoned that it couldn't be of any different size. On the final descent towards the air terminus, she'd seen a rolling landscape of brown grass with clusters of trees around small creeks.

And the fence.

It cut the land from horizon to horizon, somehow obscene, as if a line had been drawn on a map with a ruler, and that line had then been constructed from wire and wood. Disembarked, and with the bag of her possessions weighing down one arm, she found herself staring at the border. Whilst the town faded away in other directions, to the west it ended abruptly. She saw now that the fence itself was in fact two fences, running a few feet apart, each twice the height of a man. A tangle of barbed wire curled through the space between. A dirt road ran next to the fence for as far as she could see.

"It took twelve years to build. Three hundred and eighty-five workers. Forty-five of them had to be replaced during its construction due to death or serious injury." It was Colonel Martinshaw speaking, the top hat back on his head. "The border regiment carries out general repairs. But from time to time sections need to be renewed. Then we bring in contractors. Keeping the Gas-Lit Empire safe. Noble work."

From one of the bars along the edge of the airfield drifted the sound of a piano, painfully out of tune, and singing, even more so. Groups of men were everywhere along the street front. Off-duty guardsmen, she thought. There were no women, but for a painting of one on the wooden front of another building, lifting her red skirts to show white petticoats and booted feet. The painted smile made Elizabeth shudder.

"Are you here to join the border regiment?" Colonel Martinshaw asked.

"Perhaps," Elizabeth said, relieved when he stepped away towards the porters.

Conway chuckled. "What comes next, do you think? Will we learn about the construction of luggage and the life habits of crocodiles?"

"Can you recommend a boarding house?" Elizabeth asked.

"You might be in trouble there. It's changeover week for the regiment. We've twice the guardsmen as usual. But you can stay with me if you'd like, in exchange for your story. Might be easier in any case, given your secret." This last part, he spoke in a whisper.

"Where do you live?"

He nodded towards the river. "Over the other side."

The oarsman cut a diagonal line against the current.

When they landed, Elizabeth offered to pay, but Conway wouldn't hear of it.

"You're my guest," he said, and placed a coin on the oarsman's palm.

There were a few shacks on the riverside, but beyond the first rise Lewiston began to peter out and the path became little more than a goat track. Conway's hospitality hadn't concerned her at first, but with the last houses left behind, she began to think about her pistol, stowed deep in the bag. The old man seemed too friendly for a border town. Too easily pleasant. And he had seen through her male disguise.

At least she'd put the river between herself and the regiment. And Mrs Arthur would be somewhere near, with her husbands. From the newspaper article it seemed she might be businesswoman enough to entertain a proposition. Elizabeth would offer some of Agent Winslow's money in exchange for information about the Oregon Territory and where best to cross the fence.

"How come you're dressed as a man?" Conway asked, when they were beyond any chance of overhearing.

"I'm running away," she said, allowing her voice to rise to its natural pitch.

"From who?"

"Does it matter?"

"It might."

"From the law, then."

"What did you do?"

"I saved my friends."

"Loyalty's a crime now?"

"Apparently."

The road curved its dusty way around a low ridge. The

bright river was lost. All around lay a brown valley under a blue sky.

"Why Lewiston?" he asked. "Not an easy place for a woman to hide."

"Where would you have gone?"

"It's not me needs hiding. Most folk who come here are concerned with the fence. They come to guard it. Or to cross it. One or the other. You don't look like the guarding type."

The bag bumped against her leg with every other step. She'd packed the pistol right at the bottom, against the chance the porters might rummage her things for valuables. Now she wanted to feel it in her hand. Conway's questioning had become uncomfortably focused.

"Is it far?" she asked.

"Just beyond the next hill."

"Why do you live all the way out here?"

"I don't much like crowds."

She stopped, dropped her bag, as if exhausted.

"That's the other thing that gave you away," he said. "Worker's clothes. But not worker's hands."

"I need something," she said, then unbuckled the bag and delved inside. Her fingers closed around the pistol stock. But Conway had slipped his own hands into his pockets. She caught the outline of something through the fabric of his coat, a straight edge that might have been a short-barrelled handgun. When she stood, she was holding a small pot of whale grease. She dabbed a smear on her lips and put it back. His tension eased. He'd been ready for her.

He was quiet after that, which brought some relief, though she had many questions still in want of answers.

As the track crowned a rise, a house began to emerge in the cleft of the valley ahead, and a small barn next to it. She'd seen no sight of crops growing and the grass would surely be too thin to fatten cattle.

"What does a man who doesn't like crowds do for a living?" she asked.

"Business," he said. "What does a runaway hope to do out west?"

"I haven't decided."

He chuckled. "You can't fool an old man."

"Do many live over this side of the river?" she asked.

"Passing few."

"You know them all, then?"

He looked at her, as if she'd revealed a secret. "Everyone knows everyone."

"I was reading in the newspaper…"

"You're going to ask about Mrs Arthur," he said.

She nodded.

"I saw you reading it."

"Can you introduce me?"

"I can. And I will." He put back his head and called out in a carrying voice: "Mrs Arthur!"

A woman stepped out onto the porch of the house below and waved.

Mrs Arthur was short as a child but there were wrinkles on her face and a grey strand in her hair. Her steely gaze suggested long experience. She sat in a rocking chair as if it was a throne, one arm on each rest. A man stood to either side of her, hands loose, pistols holstered. One seemed hardly older than Elizabeth. The air in the shack smelled of woodsmoke from the stove.

"Why bring her?" Mrs Arthur asked.

"Seems like she's got a story to tell," Conway said. "And on the airship she was asking questions about you."

"Walks like a man. Wouldn't have known but for the voice."

"She can talk like a man too."

"Can she now?" Mrs Arthur sucked her teeth.

Trying to control her panic, Elizabeth snatched a glance around the room. It was a rickety old place for a family of gold smugglers. The window frame would break easily enough if she dived through it. But there was nowhere to go and she'd not be able to outpace their guns.

"Why've you been using my name, girl?"

Elizabeth swallowed. "I want to offer a deal. I'll pay if you show me how to get across the fence."

The men laughed. Mrs Arthur frowned. "You think I can be bought?"

"I think you're a woman of business."

"I can take your money, if you've got any. Bury you where not even the coyotes will look." She snapped her fingers and pointed to Elizabeth's bag on the floor. The younger man was on it in a moment, pulling out clothes, casting them to the boards.

"She's running from something," Conway said.

"What might that be, girl?"

"The law." She needed time to think. To work things out. But everything was coming in a rush.

"She said she broke the law rescuing friends."

It almost sounded as if Conway was on her side. The

young man rummaging her things held up a pair of bloomers. His grin was cut short by a glare from Mrs Arthur.

There was no way out and Elizabeth could think of no lie that might get the old woman to see her differently. She made a decision and was speaking in the same moment: "The Patent Office is after me."

Everyone froze.

"Ach! You've brought us poison," Mrs Arthur said.

Conway held up his hands. "I didn't know. She said the law, that's all."

"They'll come looking," Elizabeth said, pressing on. Everyone was afraid of the Patent Office. But here the name had triggered something more. "If you kill me, they'll find out."

"No they won't," Mrs Arthur hissed. She turned to Conway. "Take her across the fence. Patent Office can't go there. Bury her deep. And her things. Even if it's money. I'll have all trace gone!"

Elizabeth made to run, but Conway's hand shot out and grabbed her arm, his grip tight enough to hurt.

The younger man had stood. Only now she saw that her pistol was in his hand.

"Where did you steal that?" Mrs Arthur demanded.

"I didn't!"

Conway squeezed harder. "Best say the truth."

She twisted her arm but he just shifted his grip.

"It's mine!" she cried.

Mrs Arthur stood and advanced towards her. "You can die slow," she hissed. "Or you can stop your lies."

"My father gave it to me. It's why I need to cross the border."

Conway released her. Mrs Arthur stiffened.

"What did she say her name was?"

"Said it was Edwin."

"And you didn't think to tell? You didn't think to say that first?"

"No, ma'am. Thought it must be a common name in England."

"Will you look at the face on her! And the name. Both together. And then the gun! She's kin to him. Sure as sure. Tell me girl, what are you to the Magician of Crown Point?"

CHAPTER 14

The marvellous deer had been the pet of an old woman, living in a cave far from the beaten track. Others might have thought the patterns of its coat a curiosity: brown to the right-hand side, white to the left. But Edwin's mind, trained in conjuring, had seen the possibility of an illusion. He'd paid the woman with gold: for the animal, and to look after it until it was needed, and to keep it from other people's eyes.

When he explained his plans for the trick, the king had readily agreed. Two servants would be hidden in the wooded gully. One to untether the animal. The other, a marksman, ready to shoot it. The rifle would be mounted on a tripod to guarantee the kill.

All happened to plan.

After it was done, when they were back in the castle, the king had thanked him in private. Such a display of hunting prowess would bring fame, he said. It was a marvellous trick.

It had always been the same with the king and conjuring. He'd been happy to play along with routines of coloured flames and vague prophecies. But after all that, it seemed that he too believed. At least in the magic of auguries. How was it possible for one man to hold two such opposites as true? The thought unsettled Edwin.

The killing of the deer had been witnessed only by those in the van of the hunting party. The second sacrifice would gather an audience of hundreds.

The ox, whose only sin was to have a magnificent set of horns, had been washed and brushed until its coat shone in the thin sunlight. It seemed brighter than anything else in the castle courtyard, brighter than the purple silk that Edwin wore, which had been the ceremonial robe of his mother and the magicians who'd come before her. The ox's horns were of the wide, sweeping kind. Someone had decorated them with jagged lines of black and ochre. Red tassels dangled from the tips, dancing as the beast turned its head to take in its unfamiliar surroundings. The decorations were an inherited tradition, like the robe.

It would be no different from the killing of the deer, he thought. Yet there was something melancholy in the passivity of this great tethered beast. As magician to the king, he advised on the planning of raids. Afterwards he would read lists of the names of the dead, or just the number if things had gone badly. Such actions were needed. Lives to save lives. There was a mathematical logic to it. The death of the ox served no such purpose.

He'd been in the courtyard for over an hour, supervising the building of the pyre, timber stacked layer on layer. The beast had been tethered between it and the platform where the dignitaries would sit. It watched the work as if curious, occasionally dipping its great head to take another mouthful of hay, or looking back at the trickle of arriving spectators, not realising that it was the subject of their attention.

A rope marked out a wide circle on the stones, taking in the pyre, the ox and Edwin himself. Anyone could have stepped across it. But no one did. Even with the pressure of new arrivals pushing in from behind: soldiers, peasants, courtiers, coopers, cooks, children. Some he recognised, but many must have come from beyond the castle.

Animal sacrifice hadn't been part of his mother's world before coming to Oregon. But the previous magician to the king had done it, and the magicians who'd served the Lords of Crown Point before him. The theatre of blood never failed to draw a crowd. His mother had found it useful in the end, and never seemed disquieted. She hid her feelings, he supposed.

The audience was standing five-deep by the time Timon and others in the succession took their places on the platform. The king was the last to arrive, helping his consort to climb the steps. Silence had fallen and all the others stood in respect, until the king was seated.

"Begin!" he said.

Edwin advanced towards the box of ceremonial knives. But before he could select one, Janus stepped into the circle of rope and bowed to his master. He had a confidence about him that made it seem as if his actions were part of the show, agreed and rehearsed beforehand.

"The Magician of Crown Point has been directed to perform this ceremony so the auguries may be read, and the future known."

Janus turned as he spoke, taking in the full circle of the audience, but ignoring Edwin as if he were merely a functionary. He clapped then, as if showing approval for the king's decision. All within the courtyard followed his lead. Even the king himself. The servant who controls the master, Edwin thought. And the ox had been dressed like a king. But then, weren't they all? It was a day for finery.

He selected the largest blade and lifted it above his head. It was long as a machete and gently curved, but not so wide. Somehow he needed to exert his authority over the performance. But before he could speak, Janus began again.

"We all rejoiced at the good tidings. Our king has planted his seed. The royal consort is with child." Again he clapped. The applause from the audience was louder this time, and more immediate. They were learning to follow. The king dipped his head in acknowledgement.

"Are you ready to perform your task, magician?"

Edwin wanted to swear. He would have turned and walked away, but that would have insulted the king. He was taking all the risk, but Janus had found a way to command the glory. If glory there was. And belittling him in the same process.

"I am ready!" he said, acting a confidence he didn't feel, stepping towards the ox, knowing that he was obeying his rival. If he'd been wearing an apron instead of robes, he would have seemed like a butcher, a servant.

Animal sacrifice should be played out, to build anticipation. That's what his mother had told him. This was all going wrong. But by commanding the leading role, Janus might have made himself vulnerable. If Edwin could involve him in the ceremony in some way, the blame of things going wrong might be shared between them. That might protect the consort.

"The question you are called to answer is this," Janus

said. "Is the king's child to be a boy or a girl? Will it be born healthy? And will the consort be healthy also?"

Three questions, for Edwin to get wrong. For a moment, the consort was looking directly at him. He'd heard her throwing up again that morning. One of her eyes was deep red from a small haemorrhage. It gave her a devilish look. And she was holding her belly as if about to throw up again. If she made it through the ceremony, it would be a miracle in itself. Making her watch was another cruelty.

"It is time," Janus said.

Not wanting to seem as if he was obeying, Edwin turned away from the ox and began to walk around the circle, just inside the rope, holding the blade in front of him, showing it to all in the audience. The faster the beat of his heart, the more he forced himself to slow. Small steps. Making the time stretch. Separating the act of killing from Janus's instruction.

Having completed the circuit, he knelt in front of the platform, holding the blade out towards the king on his two hands. He lowered his forehead to the dust. It was an unnatural position and his shoulders ached from it. But he'd practised in the privacy of the Room of Cabinets and knew he could keep it up for a count of fifty.

Somewhere above the castle a raven called. It seemed like an omen in itself. All else was silent. Edwin had counted to forty-five by the time the king spoke.

"Make the sacrifice," he said.

At least now the order was not from Janus. Hoping the shake in his arms wouldn't show, Edwin got to his feet. He stepped to the side of the ox, level with its head. Its eye looked back at him as he wiped the length of the blade across his sleeve. Then he placed the edge to its neck and in one smooth movement, drew it across and in. The ox stumbled but remained standing, seeming more surprised than anything. The stream of blood splashing onto the stones was the only sound. Then the animal's legs gave way and it dropped, first to its knees, then onto its side.

With that first cut, the blood would have stopped flowing to its brain. Edwin knew it. There was no more sight in its eyes. No more feeling in its body. But one of the hind legs kept kicking.

Using the flat of the blade, Edwin anointed his own forehead, then turned to where Janus had been standing, to blood him as well, to implicate him in the magic. But the man had been wise enough to step out of the rope circle. He'd disappeared into the crowd.

Mind whirling, Edwin lay down the blade and took a small knife to the belly of the ox. The tip slipped in easily but cutting towards the tail end was harder work. Sawing through the skin, he extended the cut backwards until the intestines started pushing through under their own pressure. The intake of breath from the crowd sounded like a breeze passing over the land. They would all be leaning forwards, straining to see, but not crossing the rope.

It surprised him how hot the inside of an animal could be. Plunging in his hands felt like immersing them in water heated over a fire. A sharp tug released the organs and viscera, which spilled out onto the dirt, steaming. Though he hated the waste of life, he knew the power of the act. Not to predict the future. But to astound an audience. The spectacle of the familiar being turned inside out. Outside, the beast's fur carried a pattern of browns and cream. But here revealed was a slick wetness of reds, blues and white. Lifting a loop of the intestines pulled out a film of connecting tissue, patterned with veins, like a page on which the creator had written a message, held secret until that moment.

But it must never be easy to read.

His forehead itched with the drying blood. He delved into the carcass again, scooping out a kidney, deep red and lined with yellow fat. The crowd was so quiet now that he could hear the flag rippling in the wind on the topmost turret. He was about to delve within the ox one more time, going for that pattern of three. But just then, a baby started crying somewhere in the castle. It was one of those fortunate things. Never follow a script, his mother had told him. Always watch and listen for something that your audience will consider to be a sign. So he lifted the kidney, using the knife to cut it free. He held it above his head and turned, as if to give each member of the audience a personal view.

At the platform, he prostrated himself again. It might be a lump of meat, but it was also a gift to a king. Cloth brushed against cloth as the crowd shifted, turning their heads or cupping their ears so not to miss anything of what he was about to say.

Clambering back to his feet, he took a breath to speak, but was cut short by the voice of Janus, who had stepped back into the circle behind him.

"What is your pronouncement, magician?"

Oh, but the man was clever. He'd dodged Edwin's one chance to hurt him. And now he had returned to finish the job.

"Good news," Edwin said, hating that he had no other

option, that he was playing a part that Janus had written for him. "The king will have an heir. Healthy and strong."

"Will it be a boy or a girl?" Janus asked, closing the second trap.

"It will be a boy, fit to rule."

"And will the mother be healthy?"

Even though he'd known that a third set of jaws would close, Edwin was surprised by their sharpness. The consort looked down at him from her seat on the platform, fear on her face, mixed with nausea.

"She will be healthy," he said.

A weak smile spread over her face and she relaxed back into her chair.

Edwin placed the kidney on top of the pyre. Then servants carried the other organs to lay alongside it. The wood had been soaked in oil and quickly took the flame. White steam and black smoke rose in a column, swirling near the battlements. The king helped his consort to stand and everyone cheered. Those wearing hats threw them in the air. Edwin had been forgotten. Nor would he be welcome in the celebrations. But Janus had stepped up onto the platform and was congratulating the happy couple.

Edwin watched him. And then, just for a moment, Janus seemed to become aware that he was being observed. Their eyes met. Edwin saw a flicker of a smile, a nod of acknowledgement. There could be no more doubt. It had all happened according to his enemy's plan. Janus would poison the consort. He had six or seven months to arrange it. Unless Edwin could stop him.

CHAPTER 15

"Get in," Conway said from the foxhole.

Elizabeth did, squatting next to him and the bags. Mrs Arthur followed, stepping down with the pigeon basket. They slid the cover over the top – a sheet of corrugated iron covered with sacking and soil. For a moment all was dark and then daylight streamed in through the mirror of a periscope. Mrs Arthur, who had uncovered the viewer, was first to look.

Two days had passed since Elizabeth's unmasking as the sister of Edwin, Magician of Crown Point. Her heart had thrilled with the news that he was alive. And more, he was in some position of significance.

Mrs Arthur hadn't explained beyond that. Nor had her husbands, of which Elizabeth now knew there were at least three, Conway being the eldest. Each new husband was about fifteen years younger than the last. All jumped to her command.

They'd treated Elizabeth well enough, for a prisoner. The food had been simple but filling: corn, or bread, beans and bacon, or sometimes dried fish cooked with wild herbs.

The coffee had been too strong to drink, but there'd been a hand pump outside and no shortage of water. Always one or other of the men had stayed close with a gun.

Her turn came and she looked into the periscope mirror. The hillside sloped away from the foxhole towards the border fences. Turning the angle of view, she saw a patrol of three border guardsmen on horses, picking their way along the road. They seemed in no hurry. It took minutes for them to pass out of view. The pigeon fluttered and cooed in its carrying basket.

"Settle in," Conway said. "We're here till nightfall."

"Is this the way you smuggle?" she asked.

"We don't."

"The newspaper said you were carrying gold back across the border."

He chuckled. "The self-same gold we'd carried on the way out."

"Hush now!" Mrs Arthur warned.

In the darkness, Elizabeth found herself smiling. It was a good trick. Better to be a suspected smuggler than a spy. That was surely what they were – agents of a foreign power, with which her brother had become enmeshed. When Conway spoke of Edwin, it was with a hushed voice. She hoped that was a good sign. Certainly her brother's name seemed to be protecting her.

"Where do you find the gold?"

"Here and there," said Conway. "It's only metal."

"Then what matters to you?"

"Family."

"Honour," said Mrs Arthur. "And land."

"What land?"

"This land. Now, will you hush your questions!"

Conway sat back against the rear wall of the dugout. Mrs Arthur remained kneeling, her back upright. Elizabeth stared out of the periscope. For a time two hawks wheeled in the air over the hills on the other side of the border. Then stillness, the light beginning to fade. The brown earth tinged red as the sun dipped lower.

She'd been thinking about Conway and his travels across the continent, which might be frequent, spying in different cities, gathering information. He would surely be familiar with the wonders of New York. That's where Elizabeth's mind kept drifting: to Julia and Tinker. The Patent Office agents would have had no reason to tell her friends about the deal she'd broken. Julia would think she'd simply abandoned them. But it would be harder still on the boy. He'd have no way to understand such betrayal.

A movement on the hillside below drew her mind back to the present. At first she thought it might be a person emerging from another dugout. But it was an animal. Like a dog. Then the light was too low for her to see.

There had been more patrols through the afternoon. But nothing regular enough to trust. When it was quite dark, Mrs Arthur said, "Off with the roof." She spoke quietly, but it wasn't a whisper.

The cold air outside felt beautifully fresh. Elizabeth hobbled a few steps, stretching out her limbs after the hours of cramped confinement. Cloud covered half the sky, but stars shone from a broad strip overhead. The light seemed enough for Mrs Arthur, who took Elizabeth by the wrist and led her down the slope and along the line of the fence. Conway's footsteps crunched the ground just behind.

"It's here," Mrs Arthur said, tapping one of the posts.

Conway got down on his knees. There was a slack twang of wire on wire and he crawled through. More metallic sounds followed as he parted the scrawl of barbs in the middle.

"Follow him," Mrs Arthur said.

Elizabeth felt the stony ground under her hands as she crawled through.

"How do you hide the break?" she asked, when they and the bags were all together again on the other side.

"There are ways," Mrs Arthur said.

"Tarred paper and gum," said Conway.

"Hush now!"

"She's the magician's sister."

"So she'll understand – some secrets got to be kept!"

"How did they catch you last time?" Elizabeth asked.

"Footprints," said Conway. "But that was meant to be. They were onto us anyway. After we'd dug the new foxhole, we let them find the old one. We've done it before."

"The judge called you recidivists."

Mrs Arthur laughed, the sound crackly from the bottom of her lungs. "We are that," she said. "It's the one thing they got right."

It was slow walking, the ground strewn with small stones. They wouldn't use a light, even after the brow of the last hill had hidden the fence entirely. Once, Elizabeth's foot dropped into a hole and she almost fell, but Mrs Arthur still had her wrist and heaved her back to standing.

She smelled the Snake River before she heard it. They'd been going downhill for some time when the scent of water and damp earth came to her, so different from the arid air of the dusty hills. Then she heard the lapping of ripples. Only when her feet met beach sand did she catch the reflection of starlight from its surface. At last Mrs Arthur let go of her.

"Sit," she said.

Conway rummaged in his pack and put a hunk of bread in her hand. "Eat," he said. "Then sleep if you can. There's a long boat ride ahead."

"What's the Magician of Crown Point to you?" Elizabeth asked.

She heard the stillness as they both stopped what they were doing.

"He's First Counsellor to the king," Conway said.

"He's got the power," said Mrs Arthur. "Did you not know?"

The king's consort lived in an apartment of satin and pastel shades. Edwin would have liked to dress to match. But in that world of handmaids, friends, cooks and dressers there was not a sinew of masculinity. However fully the feminine persona was felt, however perfect the dress and movement, Edwin would always be seen as an outsider.

Instead he went the other way, donning a pair of heavy boots to emphasise the difference. Having knocked briskly, he stood to attention and waited. Presently the door opened and a doe-eyed maid peered out.

"I need to speak to the consort," he said, his voice deep, his tone abrupt.

The consort had positioned herself in front of the window, so that anyone presenting themselves would need to squint. Coloured silks hung around, defusing the light to some extent. Threads of smoke rose from incense burners to either side of the divan on which she sat.

"Ma'am," he said, bowing.

"Bad news?" she asked.

He couldn't quite make out her expression.

"Why should there be?"

"Trouble follows you. Are we to be attacked? Or is it a plague this time? Bears? Mosquitos?"

"No, ma'am."

"Then what?"

"I need to speak with you alone."

He heard her sigh, as if that was confirmation. "Bad news clings to you, magician."

But she signalled to her handmaids nonetheless, and to others in the room, who curtsied towards him before slipping away to rooms further into the apartment. Two women remained. Chaperones. One sat to either side of the divan, facing outwards so as not to look directly. But they were listening. One of them he trusted. The other, a young girl with copper coloured hair, was in the pay of Janus.

He clasped his hands behind his back to stop any fidgeting giving away his anxiety.

What he wanted to ask was whether she thought she might yet have been poisoned. What he said was: "How are you feeling?"

"If I eat, I'm sick. If I don't eat, I'm sick. It's a miracle my belly grows, for it's getting no food. And I have spots." She touched the side of her nose.

It was a pimple, he thought. "Is the baby well, do you think?"

"I've felt no kick from him. How can I know?"

"That joy will come," Edwin said, soothing.

"You said I'd be well, magician. But I feel so bad, I want to die."

Inside, his panic was growing. How could he know the difference between morning sickness and a slow poison? "This is the way of things for those with child," he said. "The sicker you feel, the better the baby is faring."

"How can you be sure?" There was a sting in her question. Fear, perhaps. Giving birth might be more dangerous than going into battle.

"It's what the midwives say."

"Wearing a dress doesn't make you a woman," she said.

That took him aback. "I... I don't claim to be."

The chaperones hadn't moved, but he could sense their tension. "You're right," he said. "You're right. But I still want the best for you."

"You've no need worry. The ox told you I'd be well. And the baby." Now the catch in her voice sounded more like anger than fear.

"Do you not believe the augury?"

"What does it matter what I believe? I'm the consort. I'm only a woman."

"It matters to me."

"Ah, yes. It would. I can see that." She tilted her head, but he couldn't read her expression against the daylight streaming in from outside. Silk hangings shifted in the breeze. The smell of autumn, always stronger.

"Would your chaperones still be able to do their job from the other side of the room?" he asked.

The girl with the copper hair gave herself away with a sideways flick of the eyes.

"I think they might."

Both young women got to their feet. The consort waved them away. When they had retreated to the far corner of the room, Edwin got down on one knee, bringing himself closer to the divan, closer to her ear.

"Sometimes we must work to help the auguries," he whispered. "They say you will be safe. But–"

"Why did you send my maids away?"

"The girl… Please don't look at her, ma'am. Janus pays her."

"How do you know?"

"He's not the only one with spies."

The consort leaned closer. Her voice was little more than a breath. "Should I get rid of her?"

"If you did, he'd only place another."

"How do you know he hasn't already?"

"I don't." He frowned. "If you were to fall sick…"

"I am sick!"

"I mean, if you were to lose the baby, I'd be thrown from the battlements."

"Like your mother."

He clenched his jaw till his teeth ached.

"I'm sorry," she said.

"If you lost the baby, I would be killed. And if that happened, Janus would become First Counsellor. It's what he wants above all things…"

"What are you saying?"

"Please be careful what you eat. And if your health should take a sudden change, please send word to me. You may not like me. But we are in each other's care."

CHAPTER 16

The canoe had been pushed in among a tangle of dead bushes and covered in brush, so that even standing close, it was impossible to see. Mrs Arthur supervised as they hauled it to the water.

Elizabeth had lived for years in and among boats, on the waterways of England and on the Atlantic Ocean. But she'd not experienced travel by canoe. The first surprise was the quiet. Paddles slipped through the surface of the water, clean and silent as knives. She scanned the hills on either side, fearing bands of warriors. But the country was empty and vast.

Dip and pull. Dip and pull. The cry of a hawk circling in the distance. Hills of brown grass. Dip and pull. Elizabeth's mind drifted. Somewhere ahead, was her brother.

She thought of the bow top wagon she'd lived in as a child. It'd had a name: something like *vargo* or *vardo*. She couldn't quite remember. At night she'd lain in a nest of blankets in the back, the rolling motion lulling her towards sleep. Another child lying next to her. Holding his hand. The sound of her father at the front humming a travelling tune. A woman's voice joining his in harmony: the same woman who tucked them in at night. The smell of her skin. The softness of her kiss. There had been a mother once. Elizabeth had dreamed it. She knew she had dreamed it. But before the dreams it had been a memory. And before the memory, it had been real.

That she must have had a mother was a biological truth. She'd lived with the knowledge of it for as long as she could remember. Strangely, she didn't think she'd asked her father about it. She'd pondered it for sure. But more in terms of how the other children in the travelling show must have felt with a real mother in their lives instead of the knowledge that one had carried her.

There had been a brother. Then there was not. There had been a great illusion, which they did together on the stage. The Vanishing Man, the daybills had said. Yet they'd been children. Then there was only her and she'd played both parts. She was sister and brother and the audience never knew. It was a pretend game. The great secret between herself and her father. Riding at the front of the wagon she would sometimes be Elizabeth, sometimes Edwin. Even some in the travelling show didn't know. One child but two personas.

Dip and pull. Dip and pull. Navigating between sand shoals. Rocks slipping past under the surface, green-grey, big enough to rip a hole in the fragile hull. The pigeon fluttered in the carrying basket. They eased towards the right bank, following such current as the great, slack river could show.

It seemed strange that she could remember learning the hand movements of the quick-change act, but not the day her brother left. Releasing the side of the canoe, she twisted her hand in that almost-dance, unclipping imaginary fastenings, fleet as the fingers of a musician.

"Your spells won't work over water," Mrs Arthur said, the first words she'd spoken in hours.

Elizabeth looked back and was about to protest that she hadn't been making magic, that she couldn't. Mrs Arthur shifted her oar, so that it cut against the water, turning the boat. Her gaze gave nothing away. But her words already had.

Elizabeth put on a smile. "You're taking me to see my brother. I wouldn't do anything to harm you."

Mrs Arthur nodded. "Can you keep us hidden?"

The first rule of deception is to tell what others already believe. So Elizabeth said, "Not over water."

"But at the camp tonight?"

"It would help if I knew who we're hiding from."

"Spies."

"Aren't you spies?"

"We are."

"Spies of the King of Crown Point?" Elizabeth had picked up the title from their conversations.

"Not all the king's servants want the same thing," Conway said.

"What does my brother want?"

"Do you not know?"

They'd come in close to the bank and sand was scraping the bottom. Conway stepped into the shallows and the boat lifted. He pulled the prow forwards until they grounded properly. Then Elizabeth got out to help and together they hauled the canoe up onto the beach. When Mrs Arthur stepped out, it was onto dry sand.

A few yards of beach led to brittle grass and then to a low scarp of dark rock. Conway guided them into a crevice, which widened inwards to an enclosed space. The remains of an old campfire proved that it had been used before. Looking up, Elizabeth could see a circle of sky.

"Are we safe to light a fire?" Conway asked.

Elizabeth longed for the comfort of one and with the rocks all around they would not be seen. So she mimed the unclipping of fastenings, as she had done before and had been taken as magic. Conway and Mrs Arthur watched her fingers dance.

"A small fire will be safe," she said, at last.

Dry branches caught easily and made little smoke. Conway did the cooking, fetching water from the river, resting the coffee pot in the embers. Soon he had beans and chillies and bacon simmering and the smell of it was making Elizabeth's stomach grumble.

"Show me some magic," Mrs Arthur said.

Elizabeth regarded her across the fire. She could easily palm a small object, making it seem to disappear. But it was impossible to know how they'd react. That one word "magic" meant different things to different people.

"What would you like to see?"

Conway glanced to his wife, as if for permission, then said to Elizabeth, "Can you summon animals?"

Mrs Arthur scowled. "It'd be more useful if she told us what dangers we'll see tomorrow."

No luck there, Elizabeth thought. She lay back on the ground and looked up at the sky, which was losing its brightness. "I haven't seen my brother for years," she said.

"How many?"

"We were small."

"Was it your mother taught you magic?"

"It was my father."

"He also had the power?"

"Yes," she said, trying to keep her voice level.

"Then you have the power from both sides," Conway said. There was awe in his voice.

Elizabeth felt the stirring excitement in the beat of her heart. These strangers knew of her family. They knew parts of her history that she'd lost. But to ask about her mother directly would reveal her own ignorance.

A flicker of movement caught her eye. A small bird had alighted on the rim of rock above her. If they'd been in England, she'd have called it a wren. It flitted across the circle of sky and landed again, angling its head to look into a joint in the rock. Hunting for insects perhaps. The others hadn't seen it. Elizabeth looked away from it and sat, making her movement gentle, hoping the bird wouldn't be alarmed.

"Are there many animals in this land?" she asked.

"If you know where to look," said Conway. "Coyotes, mountain lions, bears, lynx…"

"Eagles," said Mrs Arthur. "Hawks, grouse, songbirds."

"Songbirds," Elizabeth echoed the word. She nodded and closed her eyes. She raised her hand and made her fingers dance. Then she looked up, as if aware of something for the first time, feeling them follow her gaze. The wren fluttered across the gap of sky. It chirped for the first time. There's no accounting for luck, but the wise conjurer grabs it when she can.

Conway kissed his knuckles and crossed himself. Twice. Mrs Arthur nodded, as if such miracles were commonplace. But there was something new in her eyes, which might have been respect or fear.

Elizabeth woke in grey light to see the dark outline of Mrs Arthur bending over the pigeon basket. Then the woman was slipping out through the rocks and away. When she returned, Elizabeth pretended to be asleep. But later, when the bedrolls had all been packed away and the Arthurs were getting the boat ready, she checked the wicker basket and found it empty. A message had been sent.

CHAPTER 17

Edwin was jolted from a dream by the rattle of the door handle and a feeling of panic. His first awareness was the knowledge of the room and the blankets, then a realisation that he had fallen asleep in his clothes.

The corridor lantern was spent. Or someone had snuffed it out. Either way, the spy hole showed only black.

"Who is it?" he whispered.

"Pentecost," came a voice.

He slid the bolts, opened the door, felt the brush of the air on his face as the assistant to the Pigeon Master slipped inside.

The pigeon loft of the castle was as much a place of intrigue and politics as the Great Hall or the king's bedchamber. Its master was a wealthy man and difficult to bribe. Not so Pentecost, the assistant.

Edwin couldn't see the man's face in the dark. Nor would Pentecost be able to see how he was dressed. But a masculine pitch of voice would form the image.

"What news?"

"A bird came in late," Pentecost said. "The bell didn't ring. No one saw."

"Who found it?"

"That'd be me. It has your mark on it."

"Did anyone see you coming here?"

"No... sir."

Edwin caught that hesitation before the pronoun. It was a sign of respect that the man had cared to think about it. Edwin found himself smiling in the darkness. Illiteracy was another of Pentecost's virtues. Another reason to trust him. But he knew how to recognise the mark of each person in the castle and many beyond it. Edwin's own mark was the leaping hare, copied from his mother's pistol.

"You did well," he said. "How would you like your payment?"

"Please keep it for me, sir. Same as always."

For all his lack of letters, Pentecost had clear thoughts in his head. Holding no money, his corruption would never be proved. Edwin wondered how many accounts the man had stored up. Perhaps he would not be so poor when all that was counted. One day he'd surely cash in those hidden riches. Then there'd be no more sight of him.

He touched Pentecost's shoulder in the dark and felt him flinch. Finding the man's hand, he opened the fingers and took the tiny glass vial.

When he was alone again and Pentecost's footsteps in the corridor had receded beyond hearing, Edwin struck his steel and lit a lamp. The wax bung at the top of the message vial seemed pristine, though it was impossible to know for sure that it hadn't been tampered with. The sender's mark was a triangle with a line cutting through it. That was Mrs Arthur or one of her husbands. The wax also bore the leaping hare, so it would in any case have come to Edwin in the morning. But this way, there would be no record in the ledger of the pigeon loft. No one would know that a message had been received.

He crumbled the seal and dropped the fragments of wax into the lamp flame, making it spit and sputter. The paper slipped easily from the tube. Uncurled and unfolded, it made a scrap smaller than the palm of his hand. The ink was reddish brown, the letters small and precise.

We bring one who carries your face, your gun, your powers, your name, your blood. Come to the East Cairn after midnight in three days.

There could be no sleep after such news.

First there was confusion: reading the message over and over again. *Your face, your gun, your powers, your name, your blood.* His mother. It had to be his mother. He couldn't get past that ridiculous thought. The gun had been hers. But she was dead. He'd seen it. Not the death itself, but her last look at him before they'd pulled the sack down over her face. She hadn't screamed as they dragged her to the battlements. In his mind, he saw her go over the edge. Again.

Then, in the last watch of the night, the thought of Elizabeth came to him. She was him and he was her. But in the past they had been sometimes two people as well as one. Then, the *she* of them both had been called Elizabeth. The *he* had been Edwin. It had been a game. It had been real. It had been secret. Almost memory. Almost dream.

The *she* of him. The *he* of her.

That set the tripping beat of his heart, set its power and its weakness. He wanted to jump up. He wanted to climb the walls of the castle, or fall down in an almost faint. He wanted to be not alone. The impossibility, becoming possible, that there might be someone else, someone out there who was more fully *she*. That they would not be alone.

It was that otherness, that separation, which Edwin had felt through all their life. Being different. Others might look and see a slim man wearing feminine silk and think the oddness was centred in that mismatch: the taboo of crossing genders, or mixing them. But the otherness was something apart from that. Something real. To slip silk around his body was merely to give it form, so that it could be seen, to say *I am not the one you think me to be*.

And yet there was a dream from before. A bed of blankets in the back of the wagon, the rocking and jolting of the road, another warmth, another body in the same nest. A sister. Elizabeth had been her name. Or maybe it was their name. For sometimes they were each other. There had been stage lights and cigar smoke and heat underneath the canvas roof and behind the glare of the lights, row on row of men and women, the country people who came to see them perform.

The ringmaster, wearing a sequinned jacket, burgundy red, and top hat, addressing the glare-hidden audience, describing the Vanishing Man as if it were a display of supernatural magic. The boy would disappear from one cabinet, cross via the ether to the other side of the stage and materialise in the other cabinet. He would carry a playing card signed by one of the audience, as proof that it was not an identical twin.

So strange how the minds of audiences work. They believe they are being convinced by one thing, when in reality their minds have been swayed by another. To pass a signed card in secret so that it came to be in the other cabinet: this was trivial. Yet, when the child emerged, impossibly in the wrong place, it was that card that proved the laws of nature had been warped.

Connecting the dream world of half-memory with the life he knew was something hard to think about. A dark space lay between. A void from which no memories would come.

There had been that before-time of wagons and the warmth of a sister. Then there was the after-time, the real world, riding on horses next to his mother. Travelling always west. There had been an ocean crossing. Seasickness. Throwing up over the side of the steamer. Then the sights and smells of New York. A new life and a new continent. Performing tricks. Telling stories. Selling medicine.

For a time their mother had been an eye doctor, though the miracle cure had been mostly a tincture made from tea leaves. They had crossed the Free States, crossed the First Nations then ventured out into the wilds of the Oregon Territory.

In the Gas-Lit Empire, conjuring had given them the means of earning money. Audiences had believed and yet at the same time known the magic for trickery. They had willingly given up their critical faculty in exchange for entertainment. But in the wilds it was different. Outside the Gas-Lit Empire their audiences not only believed them capable of the supernatural. They also approached in secret after the shows to ask for special blessings to be made. Or as often, curses. They wanted amulets to protect them from grizzly bears or bullets or whatever it was that most frightened them.

And they most particularly wanted to know the future.

It was that which won them their place of influence in the castle at Crown Point. Two right predictions proved the difference between starvation and the ear of the king. First, a trapper asked when the salmon would run, for they were late that year. Edwin's mother had said "next week" and taken his money. It was no risk. They would be long gone by the time the trapper found the prediction false. But a month later they came upon that same trapper in a bar in one of the small settlements by the coast. They'd been ready to slip away, but the man was all smiles. He told everyone in the room of the marvel she'd performed. "This woman made the salmon come," he said.

How slippery that distinction, between making a prediction and them thinking the thing had been made to happen. All the patrons of that bar had been pleased to buy them drinks and food. All had some question of the future to be answered. Edwin's mother had been cautious. She'd known not to trust her luck again, for every promise is a seed thrown to the wind, which might come up as vine or briar. Only one prediction did she risk, and that because of the weight of the purse laid on the table in front of her.

"My son is sick," the man said.

She turned his hands to read the lines on his palms, then stared into his eyes so closely that it seemed she was reading the strands of colour in his irises. Long after he had blushed and looked away, she carried on examining him. Then she nodded.

"Your boy will live," she said.

They stole away in the night.

"What if he dies?" Edwin had asked.

"We'll be long gone."

But that man, too, found them again. It was the following spring when they came upon him on the road, travelling with a dozen guards. They could not have escaped. She whispered in Edwin's ear, "When they take me, you must run. It's me they'll want."

The man dismounted, his face full of emotion. Edwin thought he might rip her from the saddle. Instead he knelt and kissed her foot in the stirrup. The boy, his son, had seemed to be on the road to death until she had ordered his recovery. Then all had changed.

"My name is Timon," he'd said. "You must come with me. My brother is the king. He will want to meet with you."

Elizabeth and the Arthurs had been paddling down the river since dawn, that same hypnotic rhythm, Conway in the front. Neither of them spoke to her, contented it seemed with the sound of ripples and wind.

But with the sun reaching its highest point, something changed. There had been a growing alertness in her travelling companions – or captors. She still wasn't sure how to think of them. Then, a whispered conversation in a language she didn't understand. Through the morning she'd seen signs of people in that vast wilderness: cabins on the valley sides, smoke rising, small boats on the river, fish drying on racks.

Conway had paddled them close in under the left bank, though the waters moved more slowly there. Quite suddenly, he gave two deep pulls, and they were heading in towards a sandy beach.

"What do we do now?" Elizabeth asked, when the canoe had been pulled up into the bushes and covered with brushwood.

No answer came, so she said, "Tell me about the King of Crown Point."

"He's brought peace to these lands," Conway said. Mrs Arthur gave him a warning look, but he carried on. "When I was a boy, I lived out here. There was always killing. Warlords. Reivers. Every man with a sword might call himself king. I lost two brothers to men who were kings, in their own minds. And my parents, I guess. Though I never saw that. I came back from a hunting trip and they were gone."

He squatted by the water to wash his hands and face. Mrs Arthur had stalked away and was standing with her back to them some distance off. The smoke from her tobacco pipe drifted in the breeze.

There were so many questions that Elizabeth wanted to ask. How did one woman have three husbands? Why did Conway put up with her displeasure? If they did not smuggle gold, what paid for their spying? They seemed poor. So why did they risk so much for the King of Crown Point? Yet sometimes more can be learned by staying quiet.

Conway scooped water into his mouth and spat it out. He stood and stretched. When he turned to face her again he was smiling. "It always feels like coming home. I don't miss it when I'm away. But when I get back here… I don't know. I just feel more alive."

"Why don't you stay here then?"

"I will. One day. But there's work to be done before that."

He seemed to be examining her with renewed intensity.

She wanted to look away, but there was a clue in this, as well. Somehow, she was important to him.

"When will you make your home here?"

"When the King of Crown Point has no more need of us in Lewiston."

"Will that ever happen?"

"It will," he said, nodding with the kind of certainty she had seen only in religious converts.

"You'll see soon enough," he said. "Now don't get me in more trouble than I'm in already." He flicked his eyes in the direction of Mrs Arthur, who was glowering at them, puffing fiercely on her pipe.

They wouldn't light a fire. That was another clue. Elizabeth chewed on a strip of salted fish which left her mouth so dried out that she had to swallow two full cups of water to get it down. When she tried to wander off along the riverbank, they called her back. They no longer threatened her. But in that unknown land she would have been helpless as a baby.

Towards dusk, Conway began to gather up their things. He dropped her bag in front of her. "You'll need your coat and a change of clothes. But everything else – you must leave it in the canoe. We've a long walk tonight."

When her bag had been mostly emptied, he showed her how to tie ropes as straps so that it could be carried on her back. Then he took her pistol from his deep coat pocket and offered it.

"Thank you," she said, as she took it back.

By the time she had it stowed and was ready to walk, Mrs

Arthur had brushed the beach sand clear of their footprints. They set off along a barely discernible path between the scrubby bushes. It might have been an animal track. At first the sky was brighter than the ground in front of her and she found herself stumbling. Then stars began to show and the moon rose from behind the mountains. She took to listening for the rhythm of Conway's footfalls up ahead. Whenever he broke step, she knew some small obstacle would be in the path. Mrs Arthur walked so quietly that from time to time Elizabeth found herself looking back to check that the woman hadn't been left behind.

Sometimes they followed dry river gullies, crowded with small trees. At other times the way took them over hillsides of scrub. But always they climbed. Then – they must have been walking for several hours because the moon had started to sink – they reached a cairn of rocks, which had been built around a wooden flag post.

The air was dry, the only sound the rippling of cloth in the wind. Conway and Mrs Arthur put down their bags. Elizabeth did the same. Her feet were sore from walking and the ropes had rubbed her shoulders raw.

"What is this place?" she asked.

"The East Cairn," Mrs Arthur said. "It's where we'll meet him."

"Who?"

But the woman had turned and was peering into the darkness. Then Elizabeth heard it also, the scrunch of loose stones under a boot. A figure stood there under the moonlight. He must have been hiding behind the bushes to watch their approach. He stepped forwards, took off his wide-brimmed hat, uncovering his face from shadow.

Conway and Mrs Arthur bowed. Elizabeth stared, not understanding what she was seeing, though it was clear enough as he approached. She reached her hand to touch his face, and he did the same to her. It was like her own face, yet not quite. The chin more sturdy, the nose a fraction more prominent.

"Edwin," she said, not as a question, but simply to voice his name.

"Elizabeth?"

She had known it was true already. But when they held each other and she found herself inhaling the scent of him, she knew all over again that she was no longer alone in the world.

"Where is our father?" he asked.

"I'm sorry," she said. "He's gone. Dead. But where is our mother?"

At which, he wept.

PART THREE

CHAPTER 18

A generous road approached the castle, curving gently across the plateau. It had been built wide enough for two men to ride abreast in comfort, or four men to march in close formation. The outer wall had no moat or ditch – nothing to slow the charge of an attacking army. If the forces of the Gas-Lit Empire did ever cross the border into the Oregon Territory, they could march right up to the stones, but few would survive the last hundred yards. Loopholes to either side of the main gate looked out on that spread of exposed land. The automatic guns of Crown Point would cut through the ranks of its enemies like scythes through long grass.

The second way into the castle was via a narrow sally port on the east wall, a few yards from the cliffs. It had been built small and deep, so that a broad-shouldered man would need to sidestep in order to pass and a lone defender might hold it against a horde.

But walls work in other ways. A castle may hold its residents inside just as surely as it keeps attackers out. And whoever controls the gates may keep a record of all those who pass.

Getting Elizabeth into the castle proved easier than Edwin had feared. One of the guards who should have been at the sally port was away at the latrine. The other one was uncertain. He seemed relieved, himself, when Edwin ordered him to turn around and face the wall. The fact that someone had arrived in the night would be reported, since the guard was on Janus's payroll. But Edwin made sure that the Arthurs were spotted by another informant before they left on their long journey back to Lewiston: a passing glimpse near the front gate. Their arrival would be the story in the end. It would unsettle Janus.

Elizabeth: he still couldn't get used to the idea of having a sister. She stepped across the room touching the lacquered cabinets, tracing designs and edges with her fingers, just as he would have done, eyes wide. She seemed unable to speak.

"My mother's things," he said. Then, adjusting: "Our mother's things."

"Where did you bury her?" she asked. "What I mean is, I'd like to visit her grave. To leave flowers. Or say something. I don't know what. All these years, I put her out of my mind. I never prayed for her."

"Do you believe in that? In praying?"

"No. Or, I don't know. It just feels as if I should do something. To say goodbye."

"There isn't a grave," he said. "I'm sorry."

"Then tell me how she died."

"We can talk about it tomorrow," he said. "You should rest."

"Tell me now."

He felt her eyes on him. There was something of his

mother in the intensity of that gaze.

"They threw her from the battlements," he said.

Elizabeth's hand went to cover her mouth.

"I'm sorry," he said, feeling as if he'd slapped her.

"Why did they do it?"

"She'd made a prophecy. It didn't come true. And then… grudges build up when you're First Counsellor. Someone found an old law that said a failed magician had to die." It was hard enough to think these words, let alone speak them. "Afterwards… I would have made a grave. I would have…" His eyes stung as the tears began to roll. "The king gave the order. To kill her. And for me not to go to her. It was a test.

"I would have gone anyway. I could have chanced my luck – out there. But she… Mother… she'd made me promise that if it ever happened, I'd take over from where she'd left off. That I'd finish her work. So when the king asked me to be his new magician, I had to do it. I knelt – in front of the man who killed her. I felt his hand on top of my head. And heard him telling everyone I was the new magician, even though I was just a boy."

"What happened to the body?" Elizabeth asked, a look of horror on her face, as if she'd guessed already.

"I couldn't leave the castle without being seen. If I'd have done it, they'd have known I'd disobeyed the king. You don't understand what it's like in a place like this. They were jealous of my position. If they found an excuse, it would have been me dead as well. I begged to go. For six months the king wouldn't let me."

A tear dripped from his chin. Elizabeth looked away. His sister.

"Do you blame me?" he asked.

She didn't answer. Her mouth hung slack.

"Maybe I could have gone out before. I don't know. But she'd made me promise to not do anything to risk my position. When the king said I could go out – it was spring by then – the first thing I did was climb down under the cliffs. But when I got there, all I could find were a few shreds of cloth. From the coat she'd been wearing. There are animals out there. Even the birds will strip a body down to its bones."

"Then, where are the bones?"

He shook his head. "They must have been carried off. I searched. You've got to believe I searched."

"Then, can you be certain?" Elizabeth asked. "Did you see her going over the edge?"

"Yes." He said it quickly, to get the word out of his mouth. Without thinking whether it was true.

"I'm sorry," she said. "But I had to ask. How old were we, when you left?"

"Seven," he said. And then, though he felt stupid for asking, "Are we twins?"

"I think so." She opened the cabinet in front of her, "I remember this."

"You can't," he said.

Elizabeth reached inside and pressed the catch, releasing the false panel. It had been quite hidden. She ducked her head and stepped into the compartment. He watched as she squeezed herself into the secret space.

"We must have been so small," she said.

"How did you know where to find the catch?"

"I told you," she said. "This is from the Circus of Mysteries. When we were children. Don't you remember? The show was our life."

"But we left with nothing – Mother and me. She only built this after we got to the castle."

He saw his sister's eyes flick around the room and alight on the second cabinet, the twin of the first. "There." She pointed. "One for each side of the stage. One for each of us."

He shook his head, trying to clear the confusion. "Perhaps it's easier for you to remember. You stayed on with the circus. We were thrown out."

"Thrown?"

"Yes."

"You left!" Elizabeth's voice sounded brittle. "She left! She abandoned me. You were the one she wanted."

"Is that what he told you – Father?"

"I remember him weeping," she said.

Feeling his legs weaken, Edwin dropped himself into the window seat. Elizabeth had turned very pale, as if she'd felt it in the same moment: the story of who they were becoming insubstantial. A sudden vertigo, as if the stones under their feet were heaving, cracking to reveal a yawning void. He'd hoped she might complete his story. Instead she was tearing it up.

"Our mother never wept," he said.

"Then it's like I told you. She was the one to leave."

"No. She never showed her sadness. Crying just wasn't her way. Not for anything. But I could see the hurt in her. She used to stare away into the distance, out of this window, as if she was longing for someone. You, I think. I watched her when she didn't know I was there. You were the daughter he stole from her. You were the child she really wanted."

"You were the one she chose to take!"

Elizabeth closed the door of the lacquered cabinet and turned her back on it, as if she couldn't bear to look at it anymore. "How many years have you been here?" she asked.

"Thirteen."

"And when... How long ago did she die?" There was a break in her voice, as if she was battling to hide her emotions.

"Five years ago. I've been the magician since."

"Then she lived two years longer than our father. He died in a debtor's prison."

She stepped towards him and seemed about to sit beside him in the window. He held out his hand to warn her back.

"Someone might be looking up from the valley. I'm sorry. It's unlikely, I know. But you can't be seen."

"Why not?"

"There are enemies. If they knew I had family..." He couldn't finish the sentence. The enormity of that one word had taken his breath: family. "You're going to have to stay here in this room. For now. I'll bring food as often as I can. And water. And blankets. There's a few bottles of good red wine in that chest." He pointed.

"I'll need a chamber pot," she said. "Or a bucket. Or something."

He felt himself blushing. "I didn't think of that. Trouble is, there are so many spies around the castle and half of them are watching me. If I leave this room with... well, a bucket and go to empty it... They're going to know I'm hiding someone here."

"Where would you empty it?" she asked.

"There's a latrine two floors down."

"The people watching… will they follow you when you leave here?"

"Most certainly."

"Then I could empty it myself. Once you're gone. If you tell me where."

"What if someone sees you?"

She smiled then, for the first time, and he found himself smiling back at her, though he didn't know why.

"Bring me a set of clothes," she said. "Something that people will recognise as yours. I can make it so they'll think that I am you. At least from a distance."

"What if they come closer?"

"We're the children of bullet catchers. Mother and Father. If we can't find a way to make this illusion work, then we don't deserve our heritage."

From the place the Arthurs had hidden their boat to the castle must have been twenty miles: rough ground and most of it a climb. They'd trekked all through the night with no rest. Now Elizabeth felt the tiredness of that journey, all the way through to her bones. But still she could not sleep.

Edwin had left her alone, locking the door behind him. She doubled over a rug and laid down. But towering over her on either side were her mother's cabinets. She got up and opened one. The smell of mothballs brought back a memory from the Circus of Mysteries: playing games with her brother in the baggage wagon, opening chests and dressing in over-sized costumes, pulling faces, laughing at each other as if they were laughing at themselves in a mirror, pretending to be the strong man, the fortune teller, the ringmaster, pretending to be the people their mother and father pretended to be. In the glow of the Drummond Lights no one was who they really were.

The camphor had clung to them after those dressing up games. Not that they could smell it by then. But their mother could. She'd gathered them in, one in each arm and pressed her face to their hair, then held them at arm's length.

"Have you been rummaging?" she asked.

They shook their heads. It wasn't allowed.

"The truth!" she said. "We never lie to each other."

So they'd owned up and she'd kissed them. Him first, it seemed, and longest.

Elizabeth would have trusted the memory, but this strange reunion with her lost brother had thrown everything into doubt.

She couldn't remember her father building large props for the show. That would make sense if her mother had been the engineer.

Elizabeth moved on to another piece of stage furniture – a lacquered box on trestles, little bigger than a coffin. Walking around it, she found herself touching the hand and foot holes. On stage, her father had placed a woman in just such a box and sawn her in half, only to put her back together again. Curious that her mother had reconstructed it, down to the precise arrangement of markings. Elizabeth didn't believe those symbols held magic power. And yet here they were, reproduced in fastidious detail, as if their mother had been recreating her lost life out of timber and paint.

Sitting on an old ottoman of woven willow, Elizabeth surveyed the room, trying to clear her mind, trying to see it as if it were all completely new to her, to see what was really there instead of seeing what the conjuror intended her to see. A wooden floor and ceiling. Stone walls. One window set deep with a seat before it. An abundance of functional lamps hanging from beams, all unlit. A work bench with saws, drills, planes, chisels, a spirit level, protractors, parallel rulers.

Fresh sawdust lay around it. Yet he'd said their mother had died five years before. And there were other signs of recent work. A quantity of timber stacked nearby, planks, posts and boards, all of different sizes. Two bundles of fine willow.

Standing, she turned to look at the ottoman. She'd thought it old, but age was easy to fake. She opened it. Instead of camphor, she smelled dank air. But the wooden frame inside had been dovetailed together in just the manner of the vanishing cabinet. The saw marks on the wood were crisp and sharp. She closed the lid, felt along the edge and found a hidden catch. This time when she opened it, she felt the change in weight as panels shifted inside. But when it was opened, the cavity was still empty. If something secret had once been stored there, it had gone.

She began to examine other furniture of no consequence. Some items proved just as they seemed, or at least she was unable to find any deeper secret. But one chest had a false side panel, concealing a ring of iron keys. This she replaced, taking care to leave it as it had been, shy to have her activities discovered. Even by him.

Then she sat at his writing desk. Some drawers wouldn't open. She could have tried the bunch of keys, but locked was somehow different from hidden. It would have seemed more a breach of trust. Three drawers opened, containing paper, pens, candles, sealing wax, a set of fine pencils, paint brushes, a jar of varnish and fine glass tubes of the kind used for sending messages by avian post. Pulling the drawers out, she felt inside each cavity. In one she found a line of three buttons. Pressing them made a faint click but did nothing else. She tried again, pressing in a different order, and then again whereon a small panel sprang out from the side of the desk.

A book toppled out. She opened the cover and found vellum pages within, dirty with age, the text written in a looping hand.

There was once a line marked out by God,
through which were divided Heaven and Hell.
And thus was chaos banished from the world.
The Devil created lawyers to make amends.
They argued the thickness of the line
until there was room enough within it for all the sins of
*   men to fit.*
And all the sins of women too.

It was a verse she'd heard spoken to her father by the ringmaster of another travelling show. Don't trust governments and laws. That had been his argument. And like so many stage magicians before, he'd turned to a verse from the Bullet Catcher's Handbook to close the conversation.

Her father loved other verses more, and had the whole book memorised. Though she'd never seen him with a copy in his hand. Perhaps this had been his book, stolen away by their mother when she left.

The sound of footsteps in the corridor outside had her fumbling to replace it in the desk and the panel that had hidden it. She stood, feeling guilty, stepped away, then returned to shove the chair back underneath.

It seemed impossible that the ox sacrifice had been only one day before. Gods! But he'd never known so little time bring so much change. He'd seen no one in the corridor outside the Room of Cabinets. But he'd stopped halfway down the spiral stair and caught the sound of footsteps before whoever was following had frozen.

He'd gone to his bedroom first, collected clothes for Elizabeth, bundled them to hide what they were, then set off again towards the timber store. He had no need of timber, but it would confuse the story, when reported back. They might think he was gathering construction supplies. Then he was off again. Courtyard. Small red door. Servants' passageway. Back stairs. Main corridor. Spiral stairs. Stop.

This time the following footsteps continued, getting closer. Edwin wanted to grab for his knife, but his hands were full. Caught by indecision he lost a second. A figure scrambled around the turn and into view. A woman wearing a patterned cotton dress. He shifted his feet back from the fighting stance.

"Clara," he whispered. "You should be with the consort. Is she still throwing up?"

A nod. "Twice this morning."

"She needs to keep something down."

"I'd be with her, sir. But it's the king. He's there now. They're talking about food."

"You came to tell me that?"

Clara nodded. "I thought you'd want to know."

"Yes. You did well."

"And there's a doctor with her too."

A doctor. Not *the* doctor. Edwin had been alert, ready for danger. But that word kicked his heart into double time.

"Who?"

"It's not anyone I've seen before," she said. "Mr Janus brought him."

Edwin tried to keep the panic from his voice. "You must go back. Go now. If you love your mistress, stop her taking any medicine. Throw it from the window if you must."

"But the king–"

"Do it. Do it now."

Her eyes widened. She turned and ran off back down the stairs. She did love her mistress. Of that he felt sure. They'd been girls together. The consort was the pretty one. The king had plucked her early and would have moved on to others, but she'd wits as well as looks. She'd insinuated her way from a place in his bed to a seat by the throne. In doing so, she'd rescued her childhood friend from the kitchens. Clara was now her maid. Clara would protect the consort from this new doctor's potions. For now. But Edwin needed to be there himself. And in short order.

He ran, up the stairs, back to the Room of Cabinets. Gods, but the world was turning too fast.

Elizabeth was standing next to his mother's writing desk.

He threw down the bundle and undid the ties to reveal the things he'd selected for her. He'd chosen all masculine clothes. Dressed in that way people were less likely to challenge her. Only as she lifted a dark blue shirt to her chest did it occur to him that he might have been unconsciously trying to make her different from their mother.

"They'll fit," she said. "But you're taller by a couple of inches."

"It's not going to matter."

"We could work on my boots. A few layers added to the soles. We have your workshop. If you could get me some leather of the right grade–"

"No one's going to see!" He knew he was being unreasonable. "Look. I'm sorry. But everything's turning too quickly. I can't stay."

She frowned, stepped towards the window seat.

"Don't," he said.

But she seated herself in it anyway. "It doesn't matter. From down there, they're going to think that I'm you. So long as we're not seen together."

There was a defiant look in her eye, which even more reminded him of the mother he had lost. "We need to talk," she said.

"It can't be now. There are things happening. Big things. And dangerous. But I'll be back as soon as I can."

"Do those big things involve the Gas-Lit Empire?"

He'd been about to walk away, but that stopped him. "Was that a guess?"

"Partly."

"Look, Elizabeth, there's no time to explain. But you chose the wrong day to come. Everything is in the balance. My life. And yours now. Though it's not your battle, you'll be caught up in it."

He began to turn again, to leave.

"Does your battle involve Newfoundland?" she asked.

He froze. "Who told you that? Only the king's advisors should know!"

"The king of Newfoundland knows. And I was there. I was with him. That's where I learned that you might still be alive. It's no coincidence I came looking for you right now. And if you think the future of the Gas-Lit Empire isn't my battle, then you're wrong."

CHAPTER 19

Mind reeling, Edwin dashed away along the corridor. He would need to get his own people in place around the consort. And quickly. There was no telling how soon Janus might make his move.

He took the first flight of stairs down to ground level, then set off the wrong way. Deliberately. His pattern of movements would be watched and analysed by Janus and others. Returning continually to the Room of Cabinets might already have aroused their suspicions. Thus, he would confuse them. It meant a detour, counter-clockwise around the castle, through the storerooms, the kitchens.

Never trust coincidences, his mother had said. And yet hadn't he done just that? He should have asked why his long-lost sister had chosen this very moment to seek him out, crossing the border from the Gas-Lit Empire just as the army of the king was preparing to cross it in the other direction.

He skirted the servants' quarters, which had been built up against the south wall, then the guardhouse. Turning back towards the keep, he entered the Great Hall and finally the royal apartments. The guards at the doorway parted for him.

The king stood at the window, his back to the room, fists on hips. The consort was reclining on the divan, a woman of the court sitting to each side. Clara waited by the wall, ready for any errand her mistress might order. And Janus stood in the very centre of the woven carpet. But it was the stranger standing with him that took Edwin's eye: a hunched figure wearing a black skull cap.

Edwin coughed and all but Clara turned to look at him. Only the consort seemed pleased by his arrival. Her right eye was still deep red, but it looked less devilish when she smiled.

"I wondered how long it would take you to get here," the king said.

Edwin bowed. "I happened to be passing."

Janus's eyes flicked around the room as if searching for the informant. "Our audience is finished," he said, too quickly. He surely hadn't wanted Edwin to find out about the meeting.

Edwin bowed again, this time towards Janus, underlining the man's presumption of authority. The king's frown deepened. He strode across the room, then back, gesturing for one of the ladies-in-waiting to get up.

He took her place on the divan. "You prophesied health," he said. "Only yesterday you said it. But this morning she's... she's bled." He gestured to the consort's lap, but angled himself away from her, as if wanting her to leave.

Panic knotted in Edwin's stomach. It was happening too soon. He'd had no time to put precautions in place. If Janus had poisoned her already, all hope was gone.

"I'm... That is... was there much blood?"

The consort's chest and neck flushed red with embarrassment but her face remained waxy and pale. She shook her head, eyes cast down.

"What's to become of my child?" the king demanded.

"Only a few spots," said the consort. "It's normal enough."

"All will be well," Edwin said: the only possible answer. He glanced at Janus. But if the man had already done this terrible thing, there was no sign to be read from his face.

"We shouldn't worry," said Janus. "The magician has prophesied health."

"Will the change of diet help?" asked the king.

"Yes, sire," said the man in the skull cap, his voice crackling with age.

Edwin looked from face to face, searching for explanation.

"Doctor Winnowbrooke, this is my First Counsellor," said the king. "Edwin, this is Dr Winnowbrooke. He's prescribed meats and fruit for the consort."

"Venison and goat," the doctor explained. "With berries, fresh and dried. It is the natural diet, which we stray from at peril to our health."

"Who will prepare it?"

"Doctor Winnowbrooke has cured many this way," Janus said.

"He is a cook also?"

The doctor nodded. "Food and medicine are one and the same."

Edwin's mind was churning. When food becomes medicine, the patient cannot refuse to eat. And with Janus's man in charge, they would have complete control. The poisoning could happen at any time, or be spread over many weeks. They could choose their moment to manipulate the politics of the castle. But at least it meant that the poisoning hadn't happened already.

"Good," said the king. "That's agreed, then. Now, I only need you to agree on..." He glanced at Doctor Winnowbrooke and seemed to change his mind about what he'd been about to say. That was a good sign. He didn't completely trust the man to hear of war plans. "...to agree on our matter of state. I put up with the both of you because you're good at what you do. But now you're like two stags, with your antlers locked. We can't go forward and we can't go back. It won't do. Do you hear me?"

Edwin saw Janus bowing, so did the same. Then he stepped into the middle of the carpet, shoulder to shoulder with his rival. They were like schoolboys lined up in front of the master.

"You are right, my lord," Janus said. "We are locked. And no progress for months now, as we wait for your magician's plan to mature. So may I suggest a time limit. Give him some more days to work it out, and if he has still failed by then–"

"We have not failed," Edwin said. "Diplomacy takes time."

The king grunted. "He's right. You may not have failed but we're no closer to success. But then, don't think I can't see what you're trying to do, Mr Janus. A few days is too little. We must give him more than that."

"You are wise and kind," Janus said. "But once the snows have come, there'll be no way for a delegation to travel. Not until spring."

"Till the snow, then," the king said. "When Mount Hood is covered white, and no word from..." He gestured towards the east, towards Newfoundland. "Then we'll follow Mr Janus's plan. Am I fair?"

"You are, sire," Janus said, quickly.

Edwin nodded.

The king beamed. "Good. You are brothers again. Tomorrow I'll go hunting."

Janus and the doctor started backing away towards the door. That was when the idea came to Edwin: simple yet elegant.

"Sire?"

"What now?"

"I'm grateful to Mr Janus for bringing this doctor."

"Good. Good." A touch of impatience.

"But I'm concerned that we may be missing out on all the benefits of his knowledge."

"How so?"

Out of the corner of his eye, Edwin caught Janus's frown of confusion.

"Doctor Winnowbrooke said that her diet should be meats like venison. And fruits. Is that so?"

"It is our natural food," the old man replied.

"So it is the food best conducive to health?"

"Indeed so."

"Then all other diets may bring illness?"

"Yes. This is the knowledge of the ancients."

"In which case, I cannot allow you to prepare food for the consort–"

"What is this madness?" Janus cut in.

Edwin had put on a frown, that he hoped would be taken as concern. "...I cannot allow it without my king also benefitting from the same good health. Doctor Winnowbrooke must prepare enough food for him also. And... if I may say, for all the others in line to the throne."

The king was frowning again, but this time from thought not displeasure. Slowly at first, his head began to nod. Then he stood and extended his hand to Edwin. "This is why I love my counsellors. You see things that others miss. It shall be so. We shall all eat the same. And you too, my faithful servants. I will not see you deprived. The consort will not be alone at her table."

He flicked his hand in dismissal. The red gem in his ring glinted.

In the corridor, Edwin was setting off to march away, but Janus grabbed his arm above the elbow, fingers digging in.

"I know you're keeping the Arthurs up there," he hissed. "In that room of yours. But all your plots will be exposed."

The kernel of an illusion must never be where and when the trick is seen. Edwin's trick had been in two parts. First he had revealed the Arthurs, fleetingly, as if by mistake, hurrying them between buildings. Then he had got them away from the castle without any of Janus's spies knowing. This had been expensive rather than difficult. Mrs Arthur and Conway would already be paddling back up the Snake River towards Lewiston.

But it hadn't been until Janus's giveaway accusation that he'd realised how well the trick had worked. Nor how powerful it might be. He now had easy means to keep Elizabeth fed without more questions being asked.

He slipped into the kitchens, furtive, but with the intention of being seen. He had no idea what his sister liked to eat, so picked to his own tastes: two cold sausages, two apples, half a loaf of bread, butter wrapped in paper.

Also two wooden bowls. Two was the number. Both the Arthurs had to eat, at least in Janus's mind.

Having bundled everything into a cloth and tied the top, he set off. But through the door and just out of view, he stopped. He only had to wait a couple of seconds before one of the kitchen boys scampered away across the courtyard. What was the price of such a morsel of information, Edwin wondered.

His own money came from a stipend, which the king gave to all his advisors. At one time it had been paid in hack silver. But coins were now being struck at Crown Point, with the profile of the king on one side and the image of the castle on the other. His allowance was enough to cover the cost of food, clothing and to put a little aside for retirement. But not enough for all the bribery it took to remain in the precarious position of counsellor. Janus sold influence to make up the difference. Edwin sold charms and talismans. At least Janus's customers got something more than jewellery.

Edwin followed the same circuitous path back towards the Room of Cabinets. Not to hide his destination this time, but to pretend to hide it. He saw no one watching on the way. But that didn't mean much.

When he opened the door, Elizabeth was standing, waiting. The sight of her made his heart constrict. His sister, who had been in Newfoundland. His sister who had seen the new king in the east.

Left alone in the Room of Cabinets, Elizabeth had wanted to run. Or to have someone to fight. Any tangible action would have done. She opened the one window, inhaled lungfuls of autumn air, trying to clear her head. She'd crossed into the wilds seeking a helper in the form of her lost family. Instead, she'd found... The truth was, she still didn't know what she had found. All she felt sure about was that she yearned for movement. She paced from one end of the room to the other. She ran on the spot. But even without boots, her footfalls reverberated on the floorboards. Her presence was supposed to be secret.

Then the door tumblers turned and he was back: her brother, the source of her consternation. She could smell the food even before he'd unwrapped it. Grabbing the bread from his hand, she tore off a mouthful, following it with a bite of sausage, surprised at the hunger she found in herself.

"When did you last eat?"

After she'd managed to swallow, she said, "Don't know. I lost track. It must have been... yesterday. I've had some of your wine but it goes to my head."

"I'll bring water next time."

"Soon. Please."

She was aware of him examining her as she ate. There were depths of strangeness in him that she couldn't fathom. And how strange she must seem to him.

"Tell me about Newfoundland," he said. "Why were you there? Or how? I need to know everything."

"It was an accident. A bad one. Our boat washed up there and we had to hide or we'd have been made slaves. But that's where I learned about you. I met a man who'd seen you in the Yukon. I showed him my pistol. He recognised it... So here I am."

"What man?"

"His name was Elias. He worked making explosives."

Recognition sparked in Edwin's face. He nodded slowly.

Elizabeth had been eating too fast. Or perhaps it was the tension his questions had made in her. But suddenly her stomach felt too full and it was hard to swallow. She placed the bread back on the paper it had been wrapped in.

"What about the new king of Newfoundland?" Edwin asked. "What's he like?"

"He's a man with an army. Not the worst of that kind. He said he'd be fair to the people – which is what all tyrants say. But then he stopped his men from looting. And he asked his old enemies to be advisors – so he was giving them power. I'd say he's got clear thoughts in his head. As for goodness and badness, I don't know."

"His age?"

"Hard to say. Seventy perhaps? Stiff in his movement. But no other sign of bad health."

Edwin stepped between the cabinets and dropped himself into the window seat.

"You look as tired as I feel," she said, following. This time she didn't attempt to sit next to him, but stood with folded arms.

"Everything's in turmoil in the castle," he said. "There's a lot to explain. And I don't have much time."

She made herself hold his gaze. "What was our mother's name?"

He blinked, as if startled by the question. "Ellyza," he said. "I thought you knew."

"Ellyza. Like…" Elizabeth's stomach constricted.

"She named you after herself."

The strength had gone out of her legs. "I… I didn't know."

"I can see her face in yours," he said. As if his words might make her feel better, instead of worse. As if all the thoughts she'd held about the woman who'd abandoned her weren't now at war.

"You did see her die?" she asked.

"You asked me that already! Don't you know it hurts me to think of it?"

She did, but still wanted to know every detail, every sensation. She yearned for a share of that grief he carried, which should have been her birthright.

"I'm sorry," he said. "It's been a long few days. For both of us. But I have to know about the king of Newfoundland: will he be sending an ambassador? Will he make an alliance? Everything hangs on that."

"How should I know?" she asked, terribly weary.

"You can't," he said, this mystery, her brother. "But you've been there. You can guess better than me."

"Can I sit?"

He got up, sidestepped out of view of the window. She took the seat, closed her eyes, thought, regathered her energy.

"He's sure to have advisors telling him to make an alliance," she said. "And some telling him he shouldn't. He's a new king. He won't want to cross any of them. But there's no danger in talking. So yes – he will send someone. I'm sure of that."

"Will they agree?"

"To what?"

"To an alliance. Combining the forces of Oregon and Newfoundland. One nation to hold each ocean."

"What happens if they do?"

"There's going to be a war, Elizabeth. One way or the other. But with this alliance it'll be done more quickly. Fewer lives will be lost."

"Isn't it about who wins?" she asked.

"The Gas-Lit Empire has to fall," he said. "It's an abomination."

She felt a vertiginous lurch, a twist of her stomach, as if the castle might tip her out of the window behind her back.

"You'd bring chaos to the world?"

"Don't tell me you're on their side?" he said.

And Elizabeth looked away.

CHAPTER 20

Elizabeth woke, with no sense of time having passed, though it was night and had been day when she lay herself down. Sloughing off the blankets, she felt her way between her mother's cabinets to the window and looked out towards the hills on the far side of the Columbia River.

The Oregon Territory had a different beauty at night. She could see less of its fertility but more of its grandeur, the topography carved out in black and silver. Her mother would have known nothing of the place when she set out from the counties of southern England. Yet she had left. An argument can only drive a person so far. To have crossed the world, she must have been impelled by a stronger force. Thinking of her brother's antipathy for the Gas-Lit Empire, Elizabeth shivered.

At first the Room of Cabinets had seemed to be a refuge. But with this argument – Edwin wishing the destruction of the order she had grown up with – it had taken on a different aspect.

She rummaged through the pile of clothes he'd left for her. The moonlight was too thin to see by, so she struck her flint and lit the lamp, keeping the wick low enough to give shape to the clothes, but not colour. The trousers were loose around her. The belt kept them up, but emphasised the femininity of her figure. She chose a coarse-woven shirt, the material prickly over her bare arms. A long coat over the top hid her waist and did away with the need to bind flat her breasts. There would be scant chance of meeting anyone in the castle corridors in the early hours of the morning. But her heart beat heavily all the same as she slipped out and locked the room behind her.

On bringing the bucket, he'd made her memorise a route to the nearest latrine. That was when he'd thought he couldn't do the emptying. But his enemies now believed the Arthurs were staying in the room. Edwin could empty the bucket himself and there would be no need for her to risk stepping through the door.

Yet she was doing just that. She'd thought of leaving the bucket behind. The task did give her a kind of purpose. Not quite a justification for the risk. But at least a direction to go in. Julia would have called her choice foolish. But Julia had a direct way of thinking about the world and could divide logic from emotion, something Elizabeth had always found difficult. Tinker, on the other hand, would have been out and exploring with no regard for risk. She missed them both, so terribly.

In the morning, the empty bucket would reveal to her brother what she had done. He might see the needless risk as a betrayal. But she would feel more a traitor if she tried to hide this nocturnal walk.

Carrying the oil lantern in one hand and the bucket in the other, she stepped away down the corridor, keeping up the gait of a man, but placing her feet lightly all the same. That made it harder to think herself into the role. If she did meet anyone, she trusted that they would get out of her way.

The second staircase on the right. Turning right on the corridor one floor below. Then down again: the first set of stairs this time. Turn left. Twenty paces. The door to the latrine should have been on her right. But her legs were shorter than his. Another two paces, and there it was.

She emptied the pail down the sluice hole then pumped water into it and emptied that as well. The job was half done. Her heart had slowed. But as she set out again for the return journey, she felt the tension coming back to her. On the way there she'd been almost silent, but flushing water down the chute might have alerted someone.

Passageway. Staircase. Passageway. Climbing once more, aware that she was rushing in a manner that Edwin would not have done. Her footsteps were quiet enough. But she could hear them. And so might others.

The second staircase. Shadows swinging more wildly than the lantern in her hand. She wanted to put out the flame, to be hidden by darkness. But that would be wrong. If she did come across anyone, they must see her well enough to recognise her brother.

At the top, she waited, listening, trying to think her heart into beating more slowly, though that had the opposite effect. There had been a sound. It could have been someone snoring in a room or a dog growling outside in the courtyard. She waited, breathing deeply, then stepped out onto the final passageway leading to the Room of Cabinets.

"Who goes there?"

It was a tentative challenge, spoken softly. Elizabeth turned, held up her lantern, careful to leave some of the light on her own face, though it made it harder for her to see.

A man stood in the corridor facing her. Not a guard. And not one of the grand people of the castle. He shuffled towards her.

"Edwin," she said, using the resonance of her chest to lower the voice, hoping he would leave. When he didn't move, she added, "Magician to the king."

Instead of backing away, the man approached, small steps and hesitant. He angled his head as if trying to see, then raised a hand to shield his eyes from the lantern light.

"Are you well?" he asked.

So the man was on speaking terms with her brother.

"Sick in the stomach," she said, for he had glanced at the bucket.

"It's me," he said. "Do you not know me? Were you sleepwalking?"

"I... I was sick." He was too close. She lowered the lantern, casting her face into shadow. "Why are you about at this hour?"

"On your business," he said.

"Perhaps I *was* sleepwalking," she said, trying to cover the strangeness that he was clearly feeling. And yet, her identity did not seem to be a question in his mind.

"There's been another message," he said. "It came in two hours ago, but I haven't been able to get away. A bird flew in just after midnight. I couldn't see the wax. My master read the message and threw the pieces into the fire.

He should have written it in the ledger. But he didn't. He burned the paper. When he left, I followed. But he doubled back on himself and I had to run."

Elizabeth's mind was reeling with all the new information. The man was one of Edwin's spies, that was clear. A worker in the pigeon loft. "What direction did he go?" she asked.

At that the man's shoulders dropped and she caught a sigh of released tension. She'd clearly got her question right. Beyond how she looked and dressed and moved, it was the way her mind was working that had made this man accept her.

"My master was on the way to the South Staircase." This was voiced in an even quieter whisper, as if it carried great meaning.

"What did you do?"

"I cut across the courtyard." She could hear the smile in his voice. "Took the door next to the kitchens. Then I was up the serving passage and waiting out of sight when he came past."

It would have meant something to Edwin. The man was assuming she'd understand.

"Tell me everything," she said.

"Well, that's the thing. I did hear them talk – some of it. And it'd be worth you knowing what they said."

"I'll pay what I usually pay."

"I'm not saying you won't. But times'r troubled. More than usual, I mean. And I'm thinking that I'll be wanting the silver in my hand this time. Just in case. The wind's changing. I can feel it."

"How much do you need?" she asked.

"Just what I'm owed for my years of serving you. And serving your mother before that."

It sounded like a large sum. She had no idea if Edwin would have easy access to so much silver. "It might take me a few days to get it all together," she said.

"But you do have it?"

"Yes. Of course. You can trust me."

"And you'll help me get it out of the castle?"

"Yes." Her words were surely storing up trouble for Edwin. "Now tell me what you heard."

His voice had seemed that of a middle-aged man. But now he giggled in the manner of a child. "What I heard. Oh yes. Mr Janus says to my master, what is it? And my master says, I've got news just in. And Mr Janus, he says it better be good. *Or I'll make you suffer for waking me.* He says it just like that. Sharp-tongued. And my master says it'll be worth a fortune to him and that the usual price's doubled. After a quiet, I hear Mister Janus counting out coins until there's enough. Then my master says he's had word from someone called Bartholomew and his gang. Says they found a boat hidden by the Snake River. They waited to see who would come to get it. Turns out it was Mrs Arthur and one of her men. Bartholomew's gang grabbed them and knocked out a few teeth. They held them over a fire till they talked."

Elizabeth felt nausea rising up from her stomach. "What did Mrs Arthur tell them?"

"That a new magician's come to Crown Point. A powerful one. And he's hidden right here in the castle."

CHAPTER 21

Breakfast with the consort on the last day of October. The redness of her eye had faded. So had her nausea. With every mouthful of dried fruits she swallowed, the king's face beamed more brightly, though he hadn't touched his own food. Timon had heaped cold meats onto a plate and was chewing with purpose. Janus had taken the middle way: a little bit from every platter, trying to show solidarity with everyone.

Having seen Janus swallow, Edwin put a morsel in his own mouth.

He'd read once of a killer who had accustomed himself to small but increasing doses of strychnine, then served up a meal laced with it. He and his family sat down to eat. All were gripped by the poison. Only he survived, his body having learned to cope. And the courts found him innocent of the crime, for the maids had seen him eat it, and it was held that no sane person would poison himself.

Janus was sane, Edwin thought. It was a coldness of the soul that set him apart and made him so dangerous. But he was not the type to undergo personal rigours. Many the bullet catcher who'd starved himself or lain on a bed of nails or walked across hot coals for the sake of an illusion. Janus had been cut from a different cloth.

"The snows aren't yet come," the king said, gesturing from Edwin to Janus with a strip of meat. "And the sky's set fair."

Janus did his usual shallow bow of submission to the king's will. But Edwin found little comfort in the weather. The northern side of Mount Hood still bore white strands from the previous winter. One good storm could lay a full blanket and that would be it. It would come in the next six weeks. Sooner or later.

"How many magicians can there be in the castle?" Janus asked, his words slipped into a lull in the conversation around the morning room. It caught Edwin mid-swallow and he had to battle not to cough the food up again.

The king seemed displeased by the question. "Why ask this?"

"I've heard rumours, my lord. Another magician wandering in the hills."

"Let him wander. We have our Edwin. That's enough."

"But if another magician did set foot in the castle?"

"I'm well pleased with this one."

"They'd fight," said Timon, his mouth half-full. "That's what happens. We'd throw the loser from the battlements."

This displeased the king even more. "There will be no fight!" And then to Edwin: "There is no other magician. Is there?"

Now it was Edwin's turn to make that little bow of submission: "I know of none." The lie came smooth and easy.

When the king pushed his plate away, the meal was over for all of them. Janus did his solemn act while the royals were leaving. Half-monk, half-advisor he seemed. Edwin tried not to let any emotions show. Somehow the obsequious little creep had found out about Elizabeth. It was the only explanation.

He was about to follow the others from the room but Janus grabbed his arm. "Nice try, magician," he whispered.

"I don't know what you mean!" Gods, but his protest sounded hollow.

"You lied. To the king." Janus's teeth seemed unnaturally white when he smiled. "What would happen if he found out... when he finds out... I imagine being thrown from the battlements will become your fondest wish."

"Go to hell!" Edwin snapped back, knowing his anger was a confession, unable to hold his tongue. He wrenched free, stalked away, not caring what others would think.

Climbing the stairs his mind was reeling. He could hire actors to play the part of an embassy from Newfoundland. No one knew what the real embassy would look like or how they would be dressed. He could reveal the extent of Janus's corruption, if there was only proof. He could poison the man. Or push him from the battlements in the night. But each new idea was a fantasy conjured by anger.

Outside the Room of Cabinets, he took a moment to compose himself. It wouldn't help for her to see him in such a state. He had thought that with her arrival he would at last have someone to confide in. But somehow, she had come to be a secret in herself. And a person to keep secrets from.

She was standing, tensed, as if expecting some danger to

enter instead of him. Or perhaps she'd had a premonition of what he was preparing to say. But before he could begin, she said:

"They know the Arthurs have gone."

"How? Who?"

"Is there a man in the castle called Janus?"

He caught the tremor in her voice.

"There is."

"I went out last night. I'm sorry. I couldn't bear to be here anymore. I met a man from the pigeon loft. He thought I was you."

Edwin listened as she told her story. He hadn't heard of the Bartholomew gang before. Not by name. Though there'd been accounts of bandits in the hills, waylaying messengers. Always to his disadvantage.

In return, he told her of the things Janus had just said in the morning room. It felt good to be open with her. Though she wished to protect the Gas-Lit Empire and he wished it gone. It came to him that they might be able to help each other in some way. Perhaps if they ran away together, all would be well. The two of them against the world, watching the old age collapse. They might find somewhere to shelter.

He paced almost to the window, then back. "If Janus knows about you, it's only a matter of time before he persuades the king's men to search in here."

She was shaking her head. "He doesn't know about me. He only thinks you're hiding *another magician*."

"I am hiding another magician."

"If they come and search, they'll be looking for a man," she said.

"Man. Woman. What does that even mean to us?"

"It means the Arthurs didn't tell them everything. It means they don't know the magician is your own sister. I can walk out of this room and they'll think I am you. They can search all they like and they won't find me."

"You can't pass in full daylight," he said. "Not if they're close."

"I could with the right misdirection."

His heart kicked with the possibility in her words. "I can't let them search. It's what Janus has wanted to do for years. There's too much in here to prove I'm using trickery."

"Then invite your king to come. Choose your own time, so Janus will be away."

She was right. If he hadn't been so panicked, he would have thought of it himself.

"I could bring him in for a demonstration of some new magic."

She was nodding. Smiling. It was a beautiful sight. He found himself smiling back.

"Have them look in all the cabinets and boxes," she said. "Say it's part of the trick. Then, later, when Janus asks for the room to be searched, they'll say there's no need."

"But what trick can I show that they haven't seen before?"

"Have they seen the Vanishing Man?"

Timon was fighting with a crowd of soldiers in the practice yard. Sword and shield. The old way. The honourable way. He was good, but his opponents were polite enough to set on him one at a time. And perhaps they didn't swing with such intent, or grip their hilts so hard. One by one, he sent their weapons flying, giving them a smack or two with the flat of his sword as a parting gift. Bruises to remind them of the cost of courtesy.

Janus stood a distance off, watching, his hands clasped before him. And Edwin stood back further still, in the shadow behind a wall buttress. Not hidden, but not moving either. Unnoticed.

When the last of the mock enemies had been disarmed, Timon took off his helm and punched the air with a fist. But for all the bravado, his face was sheened in sweat and more purple than red. The soldiers were queuing up to shake his hand. He turned from them and took a few steps away. Catching his breath, Edwin thought. Janus must have seen it too, for he didn't approach until the after-fight formalities had been done and a servant was unlacing Timon's leathers.

"Well fought, my lord."

Instead of speaking his answer, Timon made a vague circular gesture with his hand. Still not trusting his breath, it seemed.

"If you're done with the yard, we'll be needing to test the Mark Three."

"We're done."

Janus signalled towards the open doors of the metalwork shop and three technicians emerged. Two carried the barrel of a gun so fat that it was a wonder they could lift it between them. The third moved ahead with a stout tripod, which he set up in the middle of the yard. Between them they assembled the machine, then hurried back to heft out a box of ammunition.

Edwin knew the theory of how it worked. But the fact

of this new weapon still amazed him. The bullets, complete with the charge needed to fire them, were sewn into a long belt of canvas, so that they would feed naturally into the gun, once it started to devour them.

"Would you do the honours?" Janus asked.

Timon got stiffly to his knees. He swivelled the barrel to aim at the bank of straw bales and unfired clay bricks, which were used for target practice. Then he looked up, as if seeking approval. Janus nodded. The king's brother took sight. Then it began: shots firing so fast they couldn't be counted, dust flying at the other end of the yard, straw bursting from disintegrating bales. The belt of bullets juddered from the box as if with a life of its own.

So much noise. So little smoke. So complete a destruction.

Timon seemed unable to stop, his arms shaking with the machine's recoil. The gun mounting was juddering back, the aim becoming wilder. Bullets were slamming into the ground, the castle wall, Timon losing his battle to control it. Someone would die if he kept on. And then, as suddenly as it had started, it was over.

The entire belt of bullets had been consumed. Metal cartridges lay strewn around. But still Timon knelt, as if his hands had been welded to the infernal machine. Even Janus seemed shocked.

"It didn't jam," shouted one of the technicians, who'd been standing near it and must have been half deafened. "It didn't jam!" His voice echoed off the stone walls.

As dust cleared from around the target wall, the scale of destruction began to reveal itself. Edwin looked up and saw faces at every window. Fear in some, hope in others. But all of them wide-eyed.

The king arrived, then. Without ceremony, most likely drawn by the noise. Edwin was quick to step out of the nook he'd been watching from and was following close behind when the king stepped up to the gun and reached out, as if to touch it. Panic gripped the faces of the technicians.

"It'll be burning hot, sire," Edwin said, getting in before Janus could react.

"Thank you. Yes. Of course."

Then he was off again, towards the ruins of the straw bales.

"We're still working on the stand," one of the technicians said.

"What's wrong with it?"

"The recoil. It's too strong. It sends off the aim."

There'd always been a few pockmarks in the wall at this end of the yard. Stray shots from raw recruits. But after this assault, it looked as if a team of men with hammers had been attacking it all day. The worst damage was behind the hay bales. The bullets had gone clean through and demolished the bricks of unfired clay that were supposed to protect the stonework. Most had turned to dust.

Edwin's mouth felt gritty. Timon hawked and spat.

"When will it be ready?" asked the king.

"The Mark Three is ready now," said the technician. "You just have to pull the trigger in shorter bursts. Easier to control that way. But we'll have it more stable. And the Mark Four is going to be more than twice as fast."

"We'll rule the world!"

"You will, sire," Edwin said, getting in quick again. But it was a bad situation. Any monarch in possession of a new weapon wants a chance to use it in battle. And quickly. That would make Janus's plan seem even more attractive.

"I've had news of bandits," Edwin said. "Up the river. Twenty miles. Hiding out in the hills. You could send rangers to flush them out. Drive them towards the gun."

The king glanced to his other advisor.

"Not a good idea," Janus said. "If bandits were there, they'll be long gone by now. And we don't want this weapon to be seen. Not before we use it in a real battle."

"Why is it the two of you will never agree?"

"I have a better idea, my lord," said Janus. "I told you this morning of a wandering magician. We thought he wouldn't come to the castle. But now I hear he's used his magic to do just that. If he's found, you could use this gun to execute him. Right here."

"That would seem brutal," Edwin said. "Too cruel."

"It would send a message," said Janus.

The king sighed. "Very well. Search if you must."

CHAPTER 22

Edwin bowed with a sweep of the hand so deep that his sleeve almost brushed the floor: a theatrical move that might have worked on a big stage. "My lord, would you care to inspect the cabinet?" He opened its door, revealing the interior, lined in black velvet.

"Too much!" Elizabeth said.

"I'd do it different if the king were really here."

She'd persuaded her brother to try a new variation on the Vanishing Man, which she'd worked out while alone in the room. But he was doing it wrong, not taking it seriously.

"Start again," she said. "Properly this time."

"I feel stupid." But he closed the cabinet, setting it up for another run. "I've not practiced in front of anyone. Not since our mother died."

"Then let me," Elizabeth said, getting up. "It'd be me doing the vanishing anyway. Your king wouldn't look at us so closely till the reveal. But after that, he's going to be asking questions. I might not know how to answer. And he's going to look close at whichever one of us is un-vanished. So that's got to be you."

She stepped to the door, then proceeded across the room as if she'd just entered. "This is it," she said to an imaginary king, putting on Edwin's masculine voice, patting the side of the cabinet, stepping round it as if it were strange to her. When she reached the front again she clicked it open, reaching a hand inside to pat the interior walls, like someone exploring the space, though in reality it was to give the impression of depth.

"This is new magic," she said. "New to me. My mother made it years ago but I've only just found its secret."

Stepping inside, she pulled the door closed, plunging herself into absolute darkness. But she knew how to find the catch and open the inner panel. It was a tight fit, but the panel closed silently, sealing her in. "Please stand back!" she called out the words. "Please stand back. Please…"

"…Stand back." She heard her brother finishing the sentence outside, his voice muffled by layers of wood and lacquer. "Please stand back."

The voice was the trick. As she softened hers, fading it out, he would begin to speak from the hidden compartment of the other cabinet. To their small audience, standing close, it would seem to be a single voice, which would shift through the air, crossing empty space, alighting in the cabinet from which he'd then emerge.

But when she stepped out again, he was wearing a frown.

"It won't work," he said.

"But it's brilliant."

"The idea is. But your voice is too crackly. Like I'd sound if I had a cold. They would notice."

"We can practise," she said. "I can practise. As many times as will make it work."

But now he'd said it, she knew he was right, and felt ridiculous to have not seen it for herself. To achieve the pitch of a male voice, she used a resonance from deeper in her throat, but that gave her words a husky edge.

She sat on the ottoman and sighed. "I'm sorry. I've wasted our time."

He shook his head, though he still looked troubled. "I'm glad to have done it: the misdirection, the cabinets, it's giving me flashes of memory. This was our mother's great illusion. The Vanishing Man."

"It was our father's illusion," she said.

"But Mother built the cabinets."

Feeling doubly stupid, she said, "I always thought it was his because he was the one on stage with us."

"Isn't that just like men?" Edwin said. "Taking the applause for what they didn't make."

"I never thought about who'd built it," she said. "I guess we'll never know who thought it up in the first place. Shall we say that it belonged to all of us – the family business?"

He nodded. "I can live with that. It feels so strange though. They used to tell us what to do. But now they're gone and we're working out new settings."

He came to sit beside her on the ottoman.

"What happened to them?" she asked. "And don't tell me he threw her out. I knew the man. He would never have done that."

"He told you she abandoned you?" Edwin asked.

"Not in words. It was a feeling I had."

"Well, I knew her. And it can't have been that way."

"Did they just stop loving each other?"

He paused before answering. "I don't think so."

All this time they'd been sitting straighter, becoming more rigid, as if the conflict between their parents was reaching through to them from that lost generation. But now Edwin lent forwards and covered his face with his hands.

"If they'd stopped loving each other, it would have been easy," he said. "She might have set up her own show. Toured the market towns of England. But... he... your father..."

"Yours too."

"...Yes. You're right. I've got to start thinking of him that way. *Our* father. *Our* mother. Politics came between them. That's the truth. He was going to turn informant. He was going to go to the Patent Office, give the names of everyone in the Union of Agitators. He was going to..."

Elizabeth turned to face him straight on. She could hear her heart in her ears. "I know nothing of this... union. Tell me what it was."

"We worked for freedom. As the Circus of Mysteries moved from village to village, we carried messages between the agitators. Father was part of it too. Did he not tell you? But then he turned... that is, he took against us."

"How come you knew all this and I didn't?" she asked.

"Mother told me. Afterwards. When we were heading out west. It's the reason we had to leave."

Elizabeth took her brother's shoulders in her hands. "What were they agitating against? What freedom did they want?"

"Freedom from the tyranny of the Gas-Lit Empire. Freedom from the Patent Office. Freedom to be..."

The sentence was never finished. Edwin scrambled to

his feet. He was looking past her to the bolted door of the room. And then she caught it too: the sound that had alarmed him, footsteps in the passageway outside. They weren't nearly ready to deal with a search. They weren't even dressed the same, so no trickery would be possible.

The footsteps had stopped. Elizabeth lifted the lid of the ottoman. There'd be just room enough to curl herself into it, though anyone looking might think it too small to hold a person.

A fist knocked on the door.

She climbed inside, knelt, breathing out as she folded herself down, lowering the lid. It wasn't as dark as the cabinet. Cracks of light showed up the joins in the wood panels. The smell of dank earth made her want to gag. She forced her stomach muscles to go slack.

Faintly, she heard the door opening.

Then Edwin's voice, surprised. "My lady?"

A woman replied, "May we enter?"

A hesitation. Then her brother's reply: "Yes. Of course."

The door closed again. Footsteps approached: two women to judge by the sound, one delicate like the hooves of a deer, one heavier and with a slight unevenness of gait. Edwin had spoken of the consort. There was surely no other woman in the court that he'd invite into that room. A shadow crossed the cracks in the wood near Elizabeth's face.

Then a creaking. Someone was sitting on the ottoman. It would be her brother, she thought, preventing them from looking inside. But then the woman's voice came again, very close above her.

"You've always been kind to me," the woman said.

"Thank you."

"And I've done my best to give you protection."

"We've looked after each other, my lady."

"That's why I'm here. You've been hiding yourself away. I don't know what it is you do in this room."

"Magic," he said.

"Yes… well… you should spend more time at court. There's more people to win over than just the king and Mr Janus."

"Who?"

"Timon. Zanar. The Master of Horse. And… well… no one notices, but I also have thoughts in my head. Just as much as any of the men. More than some. And yet all I'm seen to be is this…"

She would be touching her belly, Elizabeth thought. The pregnancy that so dominated the hopes of the castle.

"I understand." Edwin's voice had taken on a softer lilt.

"You do not! You weren't born a girl. You don't know how they've always looked at me – like I was a pot waiting to be filled. And now here it is. He's done his work and this thing's growing inside me. And there's nothing I can do or say that will make me any more than a kitchen pot."

Elizabeth's legs were folded so tight that her toes had started to go numb. She wanted to move. She wanted to breathe away from that ill-smelling dankness. The ottoman creaked. The shadows shifted across the cracks of light. The consort had stood.

"Why did you come here?" Her brother's voice. Quiet now. Her words would have hurt him.

"Climb the tower," she said. "Look east. See the mountain."

Then footsteps. The clack of the door bolts. The door closing.

She waited, though her limbs were screaming at her to move. A sudden light as the lid of the ottoman opened above.

She tried to lift herself, but her left leg was numb to the thigh. She stumbled and would have fallen, but he caught her. As he helped her out, she leaned against him, allowing herself to feel the comfort of that small physical contact. He was trembling.

"What was that about?" she asked.

"The mountain... Mount Hood... Wait here..."

Edwin walked, though his heart was pumping blood enough for him to have sprinted the passage all the way to the tower and climbed the stairs three at a time. But to run would have been to reveal his weakness. His fear.

The consort had chosen to come to him. That was the thing he should hold onto. But his mind was snared in the sting of her insults. Her mockery.

"She came to me." He whispered the words. "She gave a warning." However much she might despise him, that proved she was still on his side.

Half a turn around the spiral of the stairs, beyond view of the passageway, he allowed himself to accelerate. Narrow windows came in succession, one to a turn. Then two to a turn as he climbed clear of the battlements, ascending the tower. Views opened to north and south, but not to the east. His thighs were burning with the effort of the climb. Another turn. Then another. There was daylight above, and moss in cracks between the stones.

Two lookouts would be stationed at the top. They'd think him deranged if he blundered up there red faced and gasping. He should stop. He knew it. He should get his breath under control. A few seconds would make no difference, but his feet carried him on.

The wind caught his hair as he emerged, cold and from the north. He was dimly aware of the lookouts staring at him as he staggered to the eastern parapet.

One narrow strip of blue sky lay between the distant hills and a slab of grey cloud above. In shadow, the land seemed almost purple. Behind those hills reared the peak of Mount Hood: a triangle bathed in sunlight. A snow storm must have passed in the night. The king of mountains bore its blanket of white from slope to slope.

CHAPTER 23

Janus was not in the Great Hall, nor the consort's apartments, nor the Morning Room. He was not in the Marshalling Yard. In the workshops Edwin found three technicians bolting a heavy steel leg to a bulky contraption of some kind. It took him a moment to recognise it as a gun mount, upside down. It had to be several times the weight of the one they'd been using with the Mark Three.

He waited till they had it securely in place, then asked, "Have you seen Mr Janus?"

One of them, who had a dark grease smear down his forearm, said, "He's hunting."

"Janus hunting?" It seemed unlikely.

"Not like that," said the technician. "A man sneaked into the castle. Another magician. Mr Janus is going to have him. And then…" He patted the gun mount.

The others nodded, faces grave.

Edwin found a window that he could look out from unobserved. Janus stood in the open below, hands clasped behind him, the soft clay of his face showing the mildest of frowns. From inside the stables came the sounds of men working: the clank of tools and buckets, the scrape and thud of hay bales being dragged and turned.

Janus possessed a dangerous mix of patience and clear thought. He had begun his search in a place where he knew the forbidden magician would not be found. He would continue in that manner, no doubt placing a guard in each building as it was cleared. It would be a huge task to search the entire sprawl of buildings that made up the castle. But whilst it was going on, Janus would have command of the garrison. He'd also be able to leave informants everywhere. In a few days, he'd be able to track Edwin's movements throughout the castle. Only when every other hiding place had been searched would he turn to the Room of Cabinets.

Edwin cast his mind around the wings and buildings of the castle, trying to work out how long it might take for the job to be done. Four days. Three perhaps. He would need to be ready before that time, in any case.

One thing was good, though. With his focus on the stables, Janus had yet to realise that snow now blanketed the slopes of Mount Hood. It might win another few hours of grace.

Back in the Room of Cabinets, he explained the new dangers to his sister. She sat on the wicker ottoman, listening while he paced, trying to contain the energy of his panic.

She asked, "How long before he hears about the snow?"

"Not long."

"And how many days will it take to get the army ready?"

"Four or less. The preparation's been done for weeks.

And the planning. They need only muster."

"Then you still have that time. And the days till his search reaches us."

"It's not enough. The embassy from Newfoundland…"

"They *will* be travelling," she said, her voice level, her expression earnest. "Of course they will. They knew the snows would come. They would have set out early enough in the year to make the journey. Talk costs nothing for a new king. He's wise enough to know that."

"What if they've been waylaid?" he asked. It was the thought that had been gnawing at him since he heard of the Bartholomew gang. If Janus had men out there, they'd surely be looking for a party of Newfies on the road, ready to cut them down.

"They're warriors," Elizabeth said. "I've been there, remember? I've seen them. Born and raised for battle. They'll get through."

But her eyes were on the floor, her face grim. He waited, watching her turmoil, wanting to go and sit next to her, to comfort her, but holding himself back, just as she'd been doing. They were dancers, he thought. Each the mirror of the other, as they must have been in the womb. But their mother had set the steps for them. And their father. Now they circled. When Elizabeth stepped right, he stepped left. And if they closed for a moment, it was always to pull away again.

When Elizabeth raised her eyes, he guessed what was coming.

"If you succeed," she said, "then the Gas-Lit Empire will fall."

"It's what our mother wanted."

"But not our father."

"The Gas-Lit Empire has held us back for centuries."

"It's given us peace," she said. "Through all that time. It's stopped new weapons being made."

"Do you really call it peace? Servitude, I'd say. It's not just the machines that have been held back. They've stopped everything. All through history, there's been change. New ideas. New ways of dressing. New understanding about what it means to be a woman or a man, married or single. Politics, art, philosophy, sex – everything changes. But two hundred years ago, a handful of men in a room somewhere – men, yes – take it on themselves to decide for the rest of us that progress is going to stop."

"They did it for our sakes," his sister said, sounding oh-so-reasonable. "If they hadn't held things back, there would have been a race to make new weapons. The moment the powers fell out of balance, there would have been war. Do you really want those unseemly sciences?"

"We were never given the choice. They made their decision. They imposed their design on the world." His words were coming sharp, now. "And if they were so set on peace, how come they used force of arms to make the other nations join? They did it for power. That's the truth. Their own power!"

In the silence that followed, he knew he'd vented too much anger. Elizabeth's eyes were wide with shock. But the stress had been building up in him for months. Seeing the mountain now covered in snow had cracked his mask. Bitterness was flooding out of him.

"The Gas-Lit Empire isn't a thing," she said. "Don't you know that? It's an idea. There never was an emperor. Nor a single government. No great army. And it wasn't just a few men in a room. The nations agreed. More nations joined, because they understood what peace might bring them. It's been almost two hundred years and there's been no bloodshed in the civilised world."

"The *civilised world*?" Her words tasted bitter as he spoke them. "What's so civilised about being bound up with laws? You can't even design a machine without their agents swooping in. They police your thoughts."

"They don't throw people from battlements!" she snapped back.

That stung him. And it seemed to have stung her to say it. She put a hand over her mouth, as if to stop more words from spilling out.

He put his own hands up between them, calling a halt to the battle. Or dance. Or whatever it was.

"I'm sorry," she said. "I'm sorry. But the way we think… It's so different. It's like we're talking about two different worlds. Perhaps if our parents had stayed together…"

"They didn't."

"But if they had, wouldn't we be able to see both sides? You'd have been taught about the Great Accord, about everything it's achieved."

"I know about it already," he said. "And the Patent Office. I know the history of the whole thing. Our mother taught me. I know that peace has a cost."

"Then is it war you want?"

"No. Never! But peace should come from inside." He put a hand to his chest, over his heart. "If it must be forced on us, then it's no peace at all. Do you deny that the International Patent Office exists?"

"Why should I?"

"Or that it has spies and agents in great number? And it has prisons, yes?"

"As must any system of law."

"Then they must have lawyers also? And constables. And jailers."

"I suppose."

"How many jails have they built?"

"I don't know."

"How many people have they locked away?"

"Doesn't your king have prisons?" she asked.

"As we have criminals, yes. But how many do the Patent Office execute in one year? And that isn't even a fraction of the cost. They've got into your minds. They've tied up your thoughts."

Elizabeth got stiffly to her feet and stepped away towards the window as if she'd had enough. There was no point to the argument. He knew it too. It was damaging the fragile connections that held them together. It could serve no good purpose. But halfway across the room, she wheeled and started back towards him. "Tell me of your prisons," she said.

His mouth felt dry. "Murderers must be punished."

"You lock up no others? Are there no criminals of thought?"

He couldn't hold her gaze. Those dark eyes staring so intently at him, reading him just as surely as he was reading her. How could they have so much in common and yet find themselves set against each other?

"We have only one," he said, knowing he must sound like a hypocrite.

"What was his crime?"

"Her crime," Edwin said. "She doesn't believe in magic."

"Nor does Janus. Nor do you or I."

"But she... well, she wouldn't keep quiet about it. It's a kind of madness. She stood in the castle courtyard and told her views to everyone who would listen. And people did listen. That's the problem. The king would let her leave if she'd just retract. It's her choice."

"I'd like to meet her," Elizabeth said. "What's her name?"

"Mary Brackenstow. But you wouldn't like to meet her. Believe me."

"You're judging the Gas-Lit Empire by its prisons," she said. "It seems only fair I turn the mirror on you."

"Don't joke. She's stubborn and dangerous. Mule stubborn. So there she sits. Not recanting. Trying to die so she can become some sort of martyr saint. It's an illness. But none of this makes any difference. It's out of our hands. The snows have come to Mount Hood. The army will march. I will lose my place by the king's side. Janus will have the whip hand."

And yet, there was something in his sister's face that said otherwise. All through their argument, she'd seemed as conflicted as he had felt. But now he saw a tinge of guilt in her eyes.

"What aren't you telling me?"

"We can't stop them searching the castle. But I do know how to stop the army marching." She said it so quietly that at first he thought he'd misheard.

"How?"

"The king needs to believe the embassy is on its way. If someone sent you a message saying they've been seen on the road, then wouldn't the king delay?"

"He might. But who would send it?"

"You. Send it to yourself. Who knows if a pigeon's flown a hundred miles or if you've just released it from the window. Write the message as if it's come from one of your spies out there. They can say the embassy will soon arrive."

The idea was so simple. He couldn't decide whether it was brilliant or stupidly naive.

"If the embassy never comes, the king will know he's been tricked."

"They'll come," she said.

"Why are you helping me?"

She said, "I don't know." And then, "You're my brother. How could I think it and not tell you?"

She was right. Of course she was. They could disagree. But they had to be honest.

"I told you about Mary Brackenstow," he said. "If you look out from this window, you'll see where she's kept. Just look down. I hate what we're doing to her."

A truth for a truth. If they started with that, they might build trust. And then, who knew? Perhaps a way to agree.

When he was gone, Elizabeth found herself crying. She had escaped from the agents of the Patent Office, leaving Julia and Tinker. She ached to be so far from them. And leaving John Farthing as well: the man who had allowed her to love herself – or at least one facet of who she was – in a way that no one ever had before. She felt incomplete without him. She had travelled thousands of miles in deep disguise, illegally crossed the border, abandoning the safety of the Gas-Lit Empire. All this to be reunited with her brother.

But how cruel the fates: to find the missing part of her life so set against her present will. Elizabeth caught herself thinking that perhaps she'd forgotten her mother on purpose, to banish the memory of her parents' conflict. For years she'd assumed her mother had abandoned her. But now, illogically, it felt the other way about. And how terrible the irony, that reunion with her brother had summoned that old argument, bringing it back to life.

She loved this man, Edwin, though they were strangers. She'd felt it from the first moment she saw him approaching the cairn. Even though he was little more than a silhouette against the stars. It was as if a secret part of her mind had always known that something was missing and he perfectly fitted that void.

Stepping to the window, she knelt on the seat and eased open the glass. Chill air breathed into the room, more winter than autumn. With the window swung out to its maximum there was just enough gap to squeeze her shoulders through. Stretching, she managed to get her head clear of the wall.

A vertiginous expanse opened below her: dressed stone from the window all the way down to rough stone and the natural rock, then far below, a steep slope towards the first green, which were such scrawny trees as could find root in the loose scree. And then at last to the valley floor.

But there was something else. Away to the right-hand side, above the cliff: a line of weather-worn slats projecting from the castle wall. For a moment she couldn't make sense of what she was seeing. Then it resolved into a precarious walkway. Below it, five structures clung improbably to the stones: shacks roofed with shingles. The scale was hard to figure in the midst of that vertical landscape, but they were small, she thought.

A cruel jail, exposed to the wind, with the freedom of a death-leap to tempt the prisoners. She pulled her head back in, feeling revulsion for the king who had built it. Edwin had told her where to look, but only after she had been fully honest with him. They had reached an impasse in their argument, as their parents must have done. How much more it hurt as the barriers between them dropped away.

She'd wanted to keep her idea hidden from him. That's what enemies do. But even though they were on different sides, each turn of their argument revealed more truths. And at last it had been impossible to hold in the bitterness of secrecy. She'd spat it from her mouth, hating what she was doing, only wanting the distance to disappear between them.

From the writing desk, he'd taken a fine pen and a leaf of paper so thin it was translucent, then written out the fake message in block capitals, disguising his hand. She'd watched him roll the paper tight, slip it into a glass tube and seal it. He'd then heated a pin in the lamp flame and pressed a design into the sealing wax.

Then he was on his way, eager to put her plan into action, to fool his king and buy a few more days. All to the end of destroying the very world Elizabeth wished to protect. She could not stop him heading off to the pigeon loft with the fake message, but she might find some other way to act.

Her mind kept returning to Mary Brackenstow. If the woman's ideas were so dangerous that she had to be kept prisoner, might they not be worth learning? In that moment, Elizabeth resolved. When night fell, she would find her way down to those precarious cells.

CHAPTER 24

Edwin slipped the glass message tube between the stitches of the hem of his loose sleeve. It was barely an inch in length, thin and hollow as the leg bone of a bird. If he were searched, if it were found, all his plans would unravel. He wouldn't survive the aftermath. Nor would his sister.

"Good morning, magician."

"Good morning," he replied to the ladies of the court, as they passed in the passageway.

He could hear them giggling behind him. Perhaps he looked guilty. But it wouldn't be found. He stifled the intrusive thought, repeating the obvious truth: it wouldn't be found, it wouldn't be found.

"Good morning."

It was a cook this time. He nodded to acknowledge the man. Being magician put Edwin outside the normal class structures of the castle. Or perhaps it was their assumptions about his gender. Though he was the king's closest counsellor, no one saw him as above them in rank. Nor below. Strangeness had put him off to the side, unclassifiable.

He was passing the royal apartments now. Other than the kitchens it was the busiest part of the castle at breakfast time. He received more greetings and nods as he went. His clothing would not be unsettling them today. He'd been dressing fully male since Elizabeth arrived. Somehow it felt easier to face her that way. But people still stared.

The pigeon loft had been built above the royal apartments, in its own tower, with its own spiral staircase. He was glad to step into the quiet of it, away from the smells of cooked meats. Even the dank air felt comforting. It offered a spiral climb all the way to the loft, with no doors or side passages. No ambiguity. A half dozen people must have seen him leaving the passageway. Reports of his movements would be passed on. Soon enough someone would find an excuse to follow. But for now, the master of the loft was away at breakfast.

Round and round he climbed. Clear of the keep, the windows were no longer glazed. The wind moaned softly in the throat of each narrow slit, so it wasn't until the final turn that he caught the cooing of the pigeons. The loft was a circular room, though the floor-to-ceiling cages around the walls made the central space into an octagon. At the crude table in the middle sat Pentecost, who his sister had spoken to on her night-time excursion. The big ledger lay open in front of him, as if he'd been reading, though he was illiterate. Dark sand trickled through the hourglass.

"I need your help," Edwin said.

Pentecost got to his feet. "You've brought my payment?"

Edwin held out a coin. The man looked but made no move to take it.

"And the rest? I told you I needed it. All my silver."

"You want it brought here? What if you were found with it?"

"Nothing's safe," the man said. "Nothing's safe these days."

Edwin pocketed the coin again, wondering what such a man could have to fear. "Tell me when and where. I'll bring your silver."

Pentecost's face crinkled with thought. "Next week. Wednesday midnight. At the East Cairn."

"And then you'll be leaving us?"

"Maybe. Maybe not."

"But for now you're here." Edwin worked the message tube out between the stitches of his sleeve and placed it on the table.

Pentecost bent to examine the marks on the wax seal then straightened again.

"I want you to give it to the master and say it's just come in."

Pentecost shook his head. "I've never cheated. Least, not like that. If it were found out…" He dropped his voice to a whisper. "How many saw you coming here?"

"Give it to him later, then," Edwin said. "In the evening. Then no one'll think to connect it to me. You'll be safe."

The wind gusted, making the flaps of the pigeon doors clatter. The birds fluttered and shifted, seeming unsettled by the sound. Edwin caught a whiff of ammonia from the soiled straw at the bottom of the cages.

"I can't lie to him," Pentecost said. "He sees through me. I can't tell him it came in like that when it didn't."

"Then put it on a pigeon. I'll release it later. You won't need to say anything."

Pentecost scratched his arm, his eyes flicking from bird to bird in the cages, as if searching for one in particular.

"And I can have my silver? All of it?"

"Next week. By the cairn. Just like you said."

Pentecost unclipped a hatch in one of the cages. None of the birds tried to get away as he reached inside. Their heads bobbed as if his hand were merely another pigeon, even when he gathered one from its perch.

"There you go, my beauty," he whispered. Then, to Edwin: "She flew in two nights back. Got a leg ring, so she's owned. But not one of ours. They do that sometimes – strangers. Been mostly roosting in one of the boxes since. Only come out this morning. Master won't have seen her. He won't know her. You're lucky."

Edwin watched him closing up the cage again. Lucky wasn't what he felt. But he handed over the message tube and watched Pentecost work one-handed, deftly clipping it into the carrier ring. Edwin took the bird from him. Her tiny body seemed warmer than the room. He'd handled white doves before, in the magic show. They'd been a shade smaller, but the pigeon sat in his hands just the same.

"If it's a stranger to the loft, won't it just fly away?"

"She's been fed here," Pentecost said. "Chance is, she'll come back."

"Chance? Then it could take the message somewhere else entirely?"

Pentecost shrugged.

"Can't we just leave it in the cage?"

"Best it flies in. Best the master hears the bell himself. That way I don't get to tell no lies."

As if conjured by its mention, a tiny bell did then chime, and a hatchway clattered. Pentecost turned his attention to the cages, where a bird was fluttering in.

"There are so many of them," Edwin said. "Surely he'd not notice if we just left it there."

"He'd notice." Pentecost opened the cage door a crack and extracted the newcomer. It took only a second for him to remove the glass message tube from the ring on its leg and put the bird back inside. He glanced at the wax seal and then placed the tube on the open ledger, resting in the centre crease.

"Who's that one for?"

"Not you."

The hourglass was spent. Pentecost flicked it to clear the final grains, then turned it and scored a pen mark in the ledger. "You'd better go," he said, and seemed about to say something more, but instead put a finger to his lips and cocked his head, like one of his birds, listening.

Then Edwin heard it too: the faint padding of slippers, the laboured breath of a fat man climbing the stairs. The master was returning. Pentecost's eyes opened wide with panic. He jabbed his finger towards the bird in Edwin's hand. Edwin's first instinct was to lunge for one of the cage doors. But there wouldn't be time. So he tucked it into his loose sleeve, wishing immediately after that he had chosen a pocket.

The master heaved himself up the final steps and into the room. He wore a red garment, which could have been a dressing gown. His face and neck were red to match. He stood for a moment, catching his breath, his eyes swivelling from Edwin to Pentecost and back.

"Good morning, magician," he said, suspicious.

"Good morning, Pigeon Master."

"You were missed at breakfast."

Edwin bowed. "It is a day of fasting," he said, making up an excuse on the spot.

"Ah yes. The duties of a magician. To what do I owe the honour of your visit?"

He cast this question towards Pentecost. But Edwin managed to speak first.

"As ever, I watch for omens."

"Omens of what?"

It should all have been so simple. But lies have a way of multiplying. "I saw this morning a dark bird circling the East Tower," Edwin said. "Three times it passed, flying counter-clockwise."

"What does it signify?"

"It… wouldn't be right for me to say."

The pigeon in his sleeve shifted, as if trying to push its way back into the light. Edwin folded his arms, bringing it next to his body, hoping its movement hadn't been seen.

"What has the omen to do with us?"

The bird in the sleeve was struggling. He eased his arms closer to his body, trying to stifle the movement. To press any harder might kill it.

"Have you seen any strange signs?" Edwin asked.

The Pigeon Master and his assistant both shook their heads. It was enough. He could leave with that. One turn down the stairs and he'd be beyond their view. He could release the pressure on the bird.

Then the bell chimed again, a clear small sound, and the birds in the cage fluttered with the arrival of a newcomer. Perhaps he was lucky after all. Before anyone else could move, he stepped to the cage door, opened it and reached inside, just as Pentecost had done. But the pigeons reacted differently, flapping their wings to get away from him. The bird in his sleeve struggled free.

The fat hand of the master pushed him aside. "Stop!" he said. "It's not your place, magician."

"I'm sorry. I thought I could help."

"Look at the state you put them in!"

Over the master's shoulder, Pentecost's face showed panic.

The master clicked his tongue and made a cooing noise. The fluttering subsided. In a slow movement that seemed too graceful for his size, he reached into the cage and scooped a bird from one of the perches. Edwin couldn't see if it was the one he'd just released or the one whose arrival had rung the bell. The master's rounded back was towards him. Then, with a click of the cage door, it was over. A tiny glass tube lay in a fold of the fat hand. The hand closed and the Pigeon Master set off, back down the stairs.

"Why did you do that?" Pentecost hissed.

Edwin grabbed him by the shoulders. "Which bird was it he took?"

"I didn't see! You were both in the way."

"Then which still remains with a message on its leg?"

Neither pigeon was in sight.

"You've scared it into one of the boxes," Pentecost grumbled. "I'll just–"

Edwin cut in: "Get it out, whichever it is!" Then he set off down the steps, treading lightly, slowing when he heard the Pigeon Master's laboured breathing below, keeping just out of sight. Five steps before the passageway entrance, he stopped, counted to twenty, giving the man a chance to get clear. But also getting his breathing and panic back under control.

Stepping out into the light, he almost collided with a line of kitchen boys, carrying away the empty breakfast platters. They jumped aside on seeing him.

"Sorry, magician," said the front one, then they all ran, laughing.

The morning room was empty. Edwin followed the sound of voices through to the Great Hall, where the king was standing facing the fire, hands clasped behind him. The Master at Arms was by his side, and two captains, with swords at their belts. Janus saw him, approached.

"The snow is here," he said.

Edwin yearned for words that would shake the man. He could think of none. Or to strike him across the face. Anything to take that bland smile from his lips.

Instead he waited, keeping his gaze towards the king.

The Pigeon Master seemed lost in such a formal setting, still wearing his red dressing gown and slippers, easing his weight from foot to foot, his palm outstretched, waiting for the tiny glass tube to be taken from him. He made a polite cough.

"A message, sire."

The king turned, then, and saw them. Janus bowed first, damn his eyes. Edwin found himself following. Again. The king beckoned. This time Edwin was a step ahead and took his place at the royal right hand.

The king took the message tube.

Edwin angled his head, trying to read the seal, willing it to be the mark he had forged with a heated pin.

"It's from the Yakima garrison, sire," the Pigeon Master said, simpering.

Edwin felt sick. It had been the wrong bird: the new

arrival rather than the one with the fake message. The risk had been for nothing. He would need to do it all again. Or trust the bird to fly to the loft that wasn't its true home. The captains and the Master at Arms had stood more stiffly to attention as the king broke the seal and cast the wax into the fire.

"We're mustering," the king said to him. "I'm sorry, Edwin. You tried your best. But now you must make room."

Edwin's mind felt numb. One of the captains had to ease him away by the arm so that Janus could step in next to the royal shoulder: the position of the First Counsellor. From there, the man would work to bring about his downfall. It surely wouldn't take long.

A roll of grey paper slipped from the message tube, flattening out to a rectangle smaller than the king's palm. The writing was fine and regular but Edwin, standing now away to the side, couldn't bring it to focus.

The king read silently, frowning, then passed the paper to the Master at Arms, whose grey eyebrows arched.

"It seems I've been too hasty," the king rumbled. "The embassy from Newfoundland arrived in Yakima late last night. The garrison gave them beds. They'll be here in six days."

"The snow came first!" Janus said, his voice just too shrill.

"And yet now we have word…"

"Talk costs nothing, sire," Edwin said.

Only when the king started to nod did he begin to breathe again.

PART FOUR

CHAPTER 25

Everyone who knew the significance of the embassy had been on edge for days. Those who didn't know, seemed to pick up the tension. A practice fight in the marshalling yard turned vicious. A blow with a blunted sword shattered a soldier's thumb. Healing would take months and in the meantime he'd be no use as a fighter. The Master at Arms lost his temper and had the other man beaten. Then Timon berated the Master at Arms in a voice so loud that all the castle garrison must have heard.

The king had slipped into a sullen mood. Logic must have told him that Edwin's plan was the better. But he had an army ready to fight. And Janus's plan would have allowed him to do just that: a quick strike at Lewiston, the swift pleasure of the conqueror, the adoration of the men. The weather had turned squally, making a hunt impractical, so he paced in his apartments drinking too much wine.

The one bright note for Edwin was the new workload, which suddenly fell on the garrison. Riders were sent out to check the road for bandits. Wagons of fresh food needed escort on their journey up from the south. Everything had to be made immaculate for the visitors. There were simply no men left free and Janus's search of the castle had to be postponed for a few days.

The embassy was making good time along the road from Yakima. The day of their expected arrival dawned and the kitchens set to work preparing a feast. Edwin suspected hot baths might be more to their liking, after months in the saddle. By noon, the entire court were dressed in their finery. Timon wore armour, which he loved to do, but which was too heavy to be carried around all day. Janus chose a black suit and boots. The consort was the lucky one, her pregnancy gave the perfect excuse to stay out of the way.

The hours of the afternoon wore on. Timon pretended to not be bothered by the weight of steel pushing down on his shoulders. His sharpness with the servants gave him away. Janus seemed the least troubled. He stood or sat to the side of every conversation, seldom noticed except by Edwin, speaking only when questioned, answering briefly, listening to everything, his face a mask of patience.

By late afternoon, Timon was sweating. He'd drunk too much of the red wine. And eaten too many of the small cakes the kitchen staff kept putting in front of him. One of the captains helped him away. When he returned half an hour later, all knew better than to ask where the armour had gone.

In the hour before dusk, Edwin had all the candle lanterns emptied from the storerooms and loaded onto a wagon. He gave instructions that one be placed by the roadside every fifty paces, starting at the castle gates. If the embassy got within a mile or so, the lights might encourage them to keep riding. Then they could feast through the night. It would make for a sweeter beginning.

But when it had grown full-dark and cold food was being carried back to the kitchens, Janus met his eye and smiled.

"Better luck tomorrow, magician."

Instead of answering, Edwin wheeled and set off after the line of kitchen boys. He caught up with them in the main passage.

"Wait!"

They didn't want to, of course. They must have been dreaming of a feast of their own. So he ordered them again.

"Follow me."

Having led them to the gates, he had them load the feast onto the cart, which had not long returned from placing the lanterns. Then he ordered the carter to turn around and head off back into the night.

If there'd been a moon, the candles would have been too dim to be seen. But clouds had blotted out most of the sky and so the curve of the road was marked out in dots of light.

"Can't see nothing," the carter grumbled, though Edwin never heard him miss a step.

It was slow going. He'd counted off only twelve lanterns when heavy footsteps sounded behind, catching up. Too heavy for Janus, Edwin thought, though his fingers sought out the hilt of his knife, just in case.

"Who goes there?" he called.

"I'm brother to the king, damn you!"

Edwin relaxed. "Lord Timon. What can we do for you?"

"You're off to find them, then? The embassy?"

"If we can."

"Why?"

"So they won't go hungry tonight."

"You'll be feeding bandits, more like! Pray you're carrying enough venison, or they'll make you the second course."

"Bandits wouldn't dare. Not so close to the castle."

Timon grunted rather than answer. The cart had begun to roll forwards again. Edwin set off after it and Timon followed, stumbling.

"How do you see, blast it all!"

"Put your hand on the side of the cart," Edwin said. "It makes for an easier walk."

Edwin felt Timon's hand linger on his shoulder. Then he had passed and taken up a position just in front. By the light of the next lantern, Edwin saw that the king's brother had followed his advice.

"Better," Timon said. "And I'd thought you were seeing with magic."

"Not tonight."

Edwin had lost count of the lanterns. He glanced back but the road had dipped down, putting the castle out of view. At the next light, he caught an impression of low trees on either side. As they picked their way forwards, their shadows leapt ahead of them.

"How far does it go?" Timon asked, his voice quieter now.

"Perhaps a mile. We only had so many candles."

"And at the end?"

"We turn back."

"Damn but we're going slow."

Ahead, the dots of light marked a low climb. But there was something else. At the top of the rise, the trees were visible from time to time, as if one of the lamps was brightening and fading. Halfway up, he caught the scent of wood smoke. Timon must have smelled it too. Metal whispered as the king's brother unsheathed his sword. If it were the embassy, drawn steel would make for a bad start. If it were a bandit camp, it might get them killed. One sword could be worse than none, but there was no point telling that to Timon.

The carter had slowed as they approached the top.

"Wait here," Edwin whispered, then set off. The trees and undergrowth at the brow of the ridge were picked out by the wavering light of a campfire behind it. A small one: newly lit to judge by its inconstancy. He could hear men's voices, but not clearly enough to pick out an accent. Instinct told him to draw his knife and crawl over the last few yards. Logic told him not to. He stood tall, walked forwards, giving a twist to each footfall making the grit of the road scrunch under his boots. The bright light of the fire below exposed him, though he'd be a shadow to those sitting around it. They had to hear his approach, to have warning.

A twig cracked behind him and a blade pricked him in the back. He raised his hands, but slowly.

"State your business." The voice was a man's, sounding part-Irish, part-American: the accent of Newfoundland.

"My name is Edwin. I'm counsellor to the King of Crown Point. And I bring food to our good friends."

The sword point withdrew. Only then did Edwin's heart begin to slow.

There were twelve of them around the fire. Thirteen counting the watchman who'd poked Edwin in the back.

The mood became less prickly once the cart had rolled into the light, revealing the feast.

"Your names?" the eldest among them demanded, a stout man with a grey beard.

Edwin got in first: "May I present Timon, brother to our king."

"Where are your guards?"

"We need none. The king's law is unchallenged." The lie came unplanned. But Edwin felt pleased with it. They'd not seen Timon's sword. He'd had the sense to slip it back into its scabbard before stepping into the light.

"I'm Brandt of the Shanks clan," the bearded one said. Then he bowed towards Timon. Edwin began to breathe more easily.

The mood brightened as the men took their places around the fire. Timon and Brandt sat shoulder to shoulder as the others unloaded the food and laid it out on the ground. The Newfoundlanders received the meat as a polite gift, but their eyes widened when they saw the fruit: baskets of fresh apples and pears, jars of apricots and bitter cherries.

Edwin tried to take the place on Brandt's left side, but one of the Newfoundland warriors sat there first. And then another of them was sitting on Timon's right. By the time Edwin squeezed himself in, he was a quarter of the circle around from the men of power and finding it hard to hear their conversation. Half of it was impossible to lipread, since the king's brother kept a leg of turkey hovering in front of his mouth.

But for all Timon's lack of subtlety, the feast seemed to be doing its work. The apples were half gone already and the men were passing round a jar of apricots. Sugar syrup dripped as they fished out slices with the tips of their knives.

The jar went left around the circle from Brandt to a man with a ginger beard, to a laughing youth with a clean-shaven face. Then it skipped one place and carried on around, each man taking a portion of the sweet fruit, until it reached Edwin, who passed it on without eating, being too busy trying to hear the conversation between Brandt and Timon.

When the feast was done, the men rolled out blankets on the ground and set themselves down to sleep. Places had also been set for Timon, Edwin and the carter.

"Why didn't you follow the lantern trail?" Edwin asked of the man with the ginger beard, whose name was, unimaginatively, Red.

Red glanced in the direction of his leader before answering. "Thought we'd best not sneak up on a castle last thing at night."

Edwin nodded and said goodnight. But as he lay down and pulled the blanket over his shoulder, it came to him that Red's reasoning made no sense. Lights had been laid. They must have known a welcome was waiting. They could have arrived to a feast. Instead they were choosing their own time. They would march into the castle with the dawn, mud-stained from the road. Brusque and to-the-point: that is how they intended to begin the negotiations. Not with food and wine.

He had been trying too hard. He saw that now. Janus's hostility to any deal had been pushing him in the other direction. He needed the deal to succeed at any cost. But Brandt of the Shanks Clan had clearer thoughts in his head. Better to be the party who seemed ambivalent to the deal on the table.

The sounds of wine-heavy sleep soon surrounded him. Slack breath and snores. Two guards had been set to watch. But cloud had made the night sky dark. After the fire had died down, Edwin could barely make out the shape of his own hand before his face.

The men of power were sleeping next to the embers. His place had been at the edge of the camp. When he pulled back the blanket and began to crawl away, feeling the ground rather than seeing it, there was no one lying between him and the road. The trick was all in the first fifty paces. Beyond that, he'd be able to stand. The sound of unsteady feet scuffing the ground would not carry back to the guards. When the embassy woke in the morning, he would simply have disappeared. A touch of rudeness there. And of mystery. If Brandt had decided to play it cool he need must follow.

At the top of the ridge, he saw the line of lamps. Guessing one of the guards would be near, he crawled on down the other side, the gravel and dirt digging into his knees and palms. He had no way of gauging the time, but guessed an hour must have passed since leaving, before he dared stand. And then to walk half-blind the mile back to the castle. He tapped on the small postern gate. The spy hole cover slid across and a light shone out.

When the door opened, Edwin put a finger to his lips. "There could be silver for you," he whispered. "Unless people hear that I came in this way."

The guard licked his lips. "Don't reckon no one'll find out."

CHAPTER 26

Though isolated in the Room of Cabinets, Elizabeth had been able to sense the expectation gripping the castle. The passageway outside would normally have been quiet. But three times during the afternoon, she'd heard footsteps hurrying past. And there were other noises, a distant banging as if some carpentry project were underway, and on the edge of audibility, a low hum of activity and voices. Then, as the evening drew on, all became unnaturally still. Unable to bear the suspense, she took the risk of venturing from her hiding place in the Room of Cabinets. Through a corridor window she looked down on the castle courtyard. Torches burned, even though it was not full dark, and soldiers of the castle garrison waited.

Edwin did not return all that day. This she had expected. He had said as much. And he had left her food and water enough to last two full days. It was to be the time of his triumph. The coming together of the strands of a plot long planned. But now it seemed the embassy must have been slow on the road. Her brother's triumph would have to wait.

Night fell. She slept fitfully. When she woke again, the silence was complete. She rose, wrapped a binding cloth to flatten her breasts and fill out her waist. Then she pinned up her hair and darkened her chin, to give the suggestion of stubble.

Among the clothes that he'd left for her, were two sets almost identical: navy blue canvas trousers and jackets of lighter blue. One of these she'd adjusted for better fit, taking in the trouser legs and cuffs. None of the white shirts were entirely a match, but she'd unpicked the ruff front from one and added the French cuffs from another to make a pair that could not be easily told apart. Both wearing the same outfit lowered the risk.

Usually she would have been confident about her voice. But it had been more than twenty-four hours since she had spoken: that to her brother. First she hummed to make warmth and resonant depth. Then she spoke, deepening the pitch until she could feel the top of her chest vibrating.

It was perhaps three in the morning when she felt ready to step out of the Room of Cabinets once more.

She had seen jails in England: brick buildings with high, windowless walls, inmates crowded together in exercise yards. To visit a cell required an escort along dark corridors. The wardens carried great rings of keys at their belts. Above ground or below, they had always felt subterranean, the air dank and stale.

The kings of Crown Point had followed a different track. Instead of trying to hack an underground chamber from the basalt on which the castle stood, they had strapped their cells to the outside wall, above the cliffs. No dank air for these prisoners, though pity the one who suffered from vertigo.

Edwin had sketched her a map of the castle, which she'd spent hours committing to memory. But he hadn't marked the entrance to the jail. Looking down on them from above, she'd counted the windows in the North Wall and worked out that it had to be two floors below. It was some distance to the right of the Room of Cabinets. Sixty yards, perhaps.

The passageways of the castle were empty and silent. Approaching the place where the doorway should be, she began to plant her heels, allowing the footsteps to echo. But still the guard's eyes were closed.

No chair had been left for him. He had propped himself in the alcove of the doorway, feet wedged against one side, back resting against the other, head lolling towards a shoulder. Asleep but standing.

"Well?" she demanded, pleased by the menacing reverberation of her voice in the stone passageway.

He woke with a start, seeing the king's magician, or thinking he did, and panicked to attention. Not waiting for him to offer an excuse she barked: "Open the door! I need to speak to Mary Brackenstow."

Relief showed on his face as he reached for the keys at his belt.

The wind hit her as he opened the door. She stepped through a short passage, the thickness of the North Wall, and out onto a small wooden platform, which creaked under her feet. The stairs that took her down were little more than staves embedded in the stonework. There was no rail to stop her toppling over the edge, but a chain had been strung over the rock surface. With one hand on that she stepped precariously down towards the cells. They had been spaced far enough apart to make conversation between them difficult. Elizabeth's path took her over the top of each.

Moonlight fell on the opposite side of the valley, but the cliff and castle walls cast a great shadow, so that Elizabeth had to feel her way and only knew at the last moment that she had reached the end of the walkway. Looking down between the slats, she could just make out the cell.

"Mary? Mary Brackenstow?"

For a moment there was silence then she heard a creaking sound, as if someone was moving around below her.

"Who is it?"

The accent was European. French, perhaps.

"Edwin Barnabus. I'm here to question you." She felt foolish in the silence that followed. "How long have you been here?"

"Questions, I'll answer," said Mary. "But not taunts. You know how long you've kept me."

It was a stupid mistake. Elizabeth bit her lip, then said, "I'm sorry."

"Even enemies should respect each other."

"Yes. I agree. So, please help me to respect you."

"How?"

"You could be released tomorrow. You only need to recant what you said before. It's only words."

"Does your conscience bother you, Edwin?"

"Always."

"Well," she said, "at least that's some kind of respect. I do thank you for not sleeping so well while you keep me here."

Elizabeth sat herself down on the wooden slats of the walkway, her back to the stones, one hand still above her, holding the safety chain. "Why won't you say the words?" she asked. "Tell the king that you believe in magic and he would let you go. You could leave this awful place."

There was a long silence after that. A swirl of wind rose up next to the rock face, tugging at Elizabeth's clothes.

Then Mary said, "You've kept me here for six months because of my words. You must think they're important. I have nothing else. How could I give them away?"

"It's not your words that matter," Elizabeth said. "It's the meaning behind them. Words are just sounds. You can make those sounds without ever changing what you believe."

"It almost seems as if you're begging me."

"Would that help?"

"How could it? If words are only sounds, your begging would mean no more than the howl of the wind. But if you really want to understand, answer me this: do you believe in peace?"

"I do."

"Then tell me how it may come about."

The woman was mad, according to Edwin. But that didn't square with the way she was speaking.

"In the Gas-Lit Empire they've had centuries of peace," Elizabeth said.

"But peace is more than the absence of war. Do you think that a deeper peace might come to be? Something more than the Long Quiet?"

Elizabeth thought on this. In some part of her mind it felt as if she did believe it. But perhaps that was only because she found the alternative too desperate to be entertained. "I would like it to be so," she said.

"And in this time of peace that is to come, who would make the rules?"

"Kings, I suppose." Elizabeth knew that the tone of her voice would give her away. The uncertainty. The rising inflection.

"Kings like the one who cast your mother from the battlements?"

A drop of rain landed on the exposed skin of Elizabeth's hand. Just the one, but there would be more. She could smell it in the air. The stars overhead were being blotted out by cloud.

"Tell me your answer," Mary said.

"I cannot."

"Whisper it, if you will. Confess the truth."

"I cannot."

"And yet you want me to speak an outright lie in front of that same king – in front of his courtiers. Perhaps words are important to you after all."

"Now it's you teasing me," Elizabeth said.

"Do you want my respect?"

"I should like it."

"Is that why you come to see me at the dead of night? So none of the king's men will know of your visit?"

"It is."

"Then if you won't do anything else, take my hand."

There was a clattering sound of wooden slats moving against each other, the shingles of the roof of Mary's cell, Elizabeth supposed, though she could see nothing. She got onto her knees, put her face to a gap between the planks on which she'd been sitting. In the dark she saw a shifting of pale skin, a hand reaching up towards her.

"Take it," Mary said.

But to give her hand would have been to give the secret of her identity. Her fingers and wrists were too slender to belong to a man. With senses heightened by darkness, Mary Brackenstow would know the wrongness of the grip.

Gloved, Elizabeth might have risked it. "I can't," she said. And then: "I must go, before someone comes looking."

As she felt her way back along the walkway, holding the chain, she heard Mary's voice calling after her, "Why are you lying to me?"

The guard had the door open for her and stood to attention as she approached. Desperate to get out of his view, she turned left in the corridor instead of right, bringing her quickly to the corner of the passage. Her eyes were stinging. She screwed them closed, trying to force the tears away, not understanding how a prisoner had so unsettled her emotions. It was not Mary Brackenstow, she thought. It was the isolation and the argument with Edwin and the loss of a mother she hardly remembered, a bereavement long overdue.

She pinched the skin between her thumb and finger, the sharpness of her nails forcing her thoughts back into focus.

In near-darkness, every corridor and spiral stairway looked the same as all the others. She began climbing, hoping to go up two floors, but found her way blocked after one. She turned right, which seemed to her like north. But when the passageway reached its corner, the turn was in the wrong direction. Disorientated, she stepped to a window. A glance outside would fix her bearings.

"State your name!"

The voice brought her up short. A man emerged from the deeper darkness of a doorway.

"Edwin," she said.

The man stepped closer, as if unconvinced. "It's my orders. I've got to ask what you're doing here."

"Whose orders?"

"Mr Janus."

She sharpened her voice. "Why does Mr Janus want to know?"

"I'm sorry… sir. It's the search. For the other magician, I mean. We've started up again. And I'm set to watch that he doesn't sneak past."

"How many days more will you be searching?"

"We'll have it done in two. But… I've got to ask it again… What is your business, Mr Edwin?"

"I'm keeping watch," she said. "I'm keeping watch, like you."

CHAPTER 27

Brandt Shanks, the leader of the embassy, had been given an apartment in the main keep of the castle. Red and four more of the party were sharing the adjoining room, though it was smaller. The remaining Newfoundlanders took bunks in the garrison building. All this according to Edwin's instructions. He had stayed back whilst the arrangements were being made, out of sight but watching as best he could.

Brandt refused the offer of a breakfast feast. Also the offer to postpone negotiations until the next day. Having ordered coffee and salted oatmeal, the Newfoundlanders ate in their quarters.

"He said they didn't ride across America just to feast and get fat," one of the kitchen boys reported, his eyes widening as he said it, as if not believing he was being allowed to speak such words to the king's magician.

"Who said this?"

"The top man."

"And who did he speak it to?"

The boy leaned closer and whispered, "To Lord Timon!"

Edwin put a newly minted copper with the face of the

king onto the outstretched palm. "Good lad. Keep your ears open."

"They're eating the oatmeal like they're starved," said the boy, hopefully, then seeing that no more money was coming, he turned on his heel and scurried away to join a line of other kitchen workers carrying empty bowls.

Edwin had dressed fully male again. He couldn't remember a time when he'd gone so long constrained. If he let the embassy see who he really was, the apparent strangeness might work to his advantage. But different people would react in different ways. Foreigners were in any case unpredictable. The way his sister had told it, the people of Newfoundland were a warrior cult. Strength of arms meant status to them. Any perceived weakness or difference might be a barrier to the negotiations.

He could manage for another few days. Clothes were only an outer expression, after all. Yet the difference between what he was inside and what others could see had begun to feel like a physical weight. He longed to lay it down.

At ten in the morning, according to the castle clock, the king took his place on the throne in the Great Hall. The servants had been at their work early and a good blaze already crackled in the fireplace. Timon had seated himself close to it. Janus stood just behind the king's brother's chair, far enough from the action to show a moral distance. Close enough to read every nuance of the negotiations. As First Counsellor, Edwin had taken his place immediately to the right of the throne, angled so he could see the king's expression.

The king himself was the last to sit. Then the room fell into an awkward silence. A messenger had gone to fetch the embassy. Yet no one came.

Now, it seemed that the air was too hot. Edwin became aware of sweat on his brow and upper lip. Most of the courtiers were looking at their feet or gazing at the ceiling. But some of the younger ones were staring at him. The consort too. The king's expression hadn't changed, but Edwin knew the man well enough to read his impatience. He half-turned and Edwin leaned in to hear his words. But all that came from the royal lips was a sigh. Twice this happened.

"Should I send someone else?" Edwin whispered at last.

The king seemed set to agree, but on that moment a guard hurried in and gave a vigorous nod. Then Edwin heard the sound of booted feet outside. They weren't keeping step, but it was the sound of an army nonetheless: men advancing towards conflict.

Brandt Shanks led them into the hall. Senior members of his party followed: Red and the others who'd been sitting close to their captain around the campfire. Edwin still didn't know their names. Chairs had been set out for them at the front of the room, level with the king, but placed at an angle so that all could see each other without turning. The angles implied a deliberate ambiguity of status.

Brandt had achieved the same as on the previous night, Edwin thought. Then he'd held back from attending the planned feast. Now he had made them just late enough to fray tempers, but not to the point of insult.

Edwin kept his gaze fixed forwards, listening to the scrape and shuffle as they took their seats.

"You are welcome to my hall," the king said, in a ringing tone.

"Thank you," Brandt replied. "And for sending food last night. Though it wasn't needed. We'd managed well enough for two thousand miles. One more day wouldn't have starved us."

"It was my pleasure," said the king, who had had nothing to do with it.

"The company of your brother was also welcome," Brandt said. "But who is the man standing next to you?"

"This is Edwin, my First Counsellor."

"The same Edwin who left an empty bed for us to find this morning."

It wasn't a question. Edwin kept himself still and erect, facing the end wall as before.

"Edwin is a magician," the king said. "He disappears and appears where he will."

"We have conjurors in the east. And jugglers too. Makers of entertainments."

"A different kind of magic," the king said. "It was Edwin's foresight to invite you here. He sees the future."

"Then is our future set? Do we poor souls from the east have no choice?"

Edwin became aware of the king's glance towards him, and a growing irritation.

"If I may speak, sire?" Without waiting for an answer, Edwin turned towards the embassy, making a low bow, but no smile. "To see the future is akin to predicting the weather. We may say that August will be hot and January cold. Yet the wind is unconstrained. It blows where it will. Your king will decide whatever he will decide. All I can say is this – the unseen forces that direct our lives are in flux. If we align ourselves with this change, then great things may be achieved."

"What things?"

"Wealth beyond the dreams of men. Power over all the world."

"Power for who?"

"For Newfoundland and for Oregon."

"And what would you do with this power if you had it in your hands?"

Edwin almost answered but caught himself.

"Well?" An insolent tone had crept into Brandt's voice. He was pushing too far. One of his embassy leaned close and whispered something. Edwin tried to remember where that man had been sitting at the campfire. The knuckles of the king's hands had started to whiten as he gripped the arms of the throne.

"Kings use their power as they will," Edwin said. "Whether that be only such power as would fill a drinking cup, or enough to over-flood this great continent. Your king may take this offer, or refuse it, as is his right. Then he would never need to decide what might be done with his portion."

"How did you disappear last night?" Brandt asked.

"He's a magician," said the king again. "It's what he does."

The man who had been whispering in Brandt's ear now turned and spoke: "There's no such thing as magic."

He was a thin man with a prominent aquiline nose.

"Who are you?" the king asked.

"My name is Gilad." There was no bow.

He had been there at the campfire, Edwin thought, but not sitting with the men of power.

The king stood. His patience exhausted it seemed. "Gilad, is it? Well, boy, there may be no magic in Newfoundland.

But there is in Oregon. It has swept my enemies away. And it will sweep away all those who stand against me!"

As the king stalked out, with Timon and the consort close behind, other members of the court seemed less certain. But when Janus strode out after the royal party, it was the signal for everyone else to follow. Damn but the man had found a way to lead once more.

Brandt stood and strode from the room by a different door, followed by his men. Gilad was the last in line, though it was his rudeness that had broken the king's patience.

"It's a long way to ride," Edwin said. "Two thousand miles."

Gilad turned in the doorway, paused, stepped back in. It was just the two of them remaining. "A long ride," he agreed.

"Will you be leaving today, do you think, for your journey back?"

"We'll do whatever my master decides."

"What would your king in Newfoundland say if you just turned around and rode home?"

"Oh, we'd tell him we tried, but the mighty king of Oregon demanded we submit to his rule. Or something like that. We'd make a good story of it. He'd reward us for our saddle sores."

"You'd lie?"

"As would you, *magician*. There is no magic, as you know well. So don't you accuse me of lying in that high tone."

Their conversation had become hushed as it became more dangerous.

"What do you want?" Edwin whispered.

"It's not what I want that you need to worry about."

"It's your rudeness that stopped us."

"You look but you don't see. Tell me, magician, do all in this castle agree? Do all want this alliance?"

Edwin didn't answer.

Gilad nodded. "Then why should it be different in Newfoundland?"

"Who should I be worried about?" Edwin asked.

"Red. He hates the new ways. Any overlord is bad enough for him. But you want to make our king into an emperor."

"Do you agree with Red?"

"I don't know, for myself. But you say change is coming. Perhaps it is."

"Does Red like to hunt?" Edwin asked.

Gilad cocked his head, as if puzzled. "He does."

"Then stay another day or two. Killing something might soften his heart. There are deer to be had."

The other man smiled, as if appreciating some morsel of new knowledge. Or seeing a joke deeper than Edwin's intended irony. He dipped his head, then stepped away. Unlike the others in the party, his footsteps were so light that Edwin could barely hear them.

Climbing the stairs, Edwin felt a sudden hollowness. His future had become welded to the negotiations. Janus would be doing his best to sour the king's mood, pointing out the numerous clear insults to their hospitality, with a few imagined ones thrown in. That's where Edwin should be: by the king's side, protecting the royal ear from poison.

But danger was approaching from so many directions that he couldn't begin to think through the map of what might happen. Foreboding pressed down on him, like a dead weight.

Halfway up, he stopped, held his breath, counted to twenty, listening. Those spiral staircases built within the thickness of the castle walls had a way of carrying sound, making distant things feel close. But all he could hear was the clanking of pans in the castle kitchens and far off, the call of a hawk.

At the top of the stairs he stopped again. This time, he caught the sound of fabric against stone. It had come from an alcove further along the passageway. Janus often paid a man to stand there, but not a spy of great quality. Sometimes he breathed so loud that Edwin could hear him from that alone.

At the door to the Room of Cabinets, he turned the tumblers, making them click through the symbols his mother had designed. He expected his sister to be standing, waiting as before. But when he found her, she was curled up on the floor with two blankets over her and a third rolled up to make a pillow.

It was the first time he'd seen her sleeping. No. That couldn't be right. They had slept together as children. For a moment he allowed himself to imagine running away with her. They could escape the castle, travel only at night, walk their way out into the wilderness, find a place to live quietly, away from politics. A shack in the hills. But it wouldn't do. The storm that was coming would sweep the world, one way or another. There was no hiding to be done.

He crouched, put a hand on his sister's shoulder, feeling her warmth. His own shoulders were thicker, broader. And yet dressed in identical clothes to him, those differences seemed to vanish.

She stirred. It seemed a shame to be waking her.

"What's happening?" she asked, her voice thick with sleep.

"Nothing. I just need to talk."

She sat up. "What time is it?"

"Still morning."

"I thought you'd be gone all day." She blinked, as if bringing her eyes to focus.

"I need to talk," he said again.

There was no time to get the stove hot, so he lit a spirit lamp on the bench and set the coffee pot over it. At the other side of the room, Elizabeth was washing her face. When she returned, all sign of sleep had gone.

"Tell me everything," she said.

He narrated the events of the morning, remembering more details as he went, all the way up to the disaster in the Great Hall. As he spoke the pot began to rumble. She poured herself a cup and cradled it in her hands, breathing the steam but not sipping until he had finished. Then she did drink, pulling a face as she swallowed.

"I'll never get the taste for coffee," she said.

"What should I do?" he asked. "What should we do?"

She shook her head. "It will be wrong, whatever it is. You tried to be welcoming and friendly. The Newfies took it as a sign of weakness. That's what you're telling me. But when you acted formal, they chose to take it as an insult. They're looking for an excuse to turn around and ride home. They've made the middle ground narrow as a tightrope. Even if you found the right tone, your enemies could simply push a little one way or the other. You'd fall from your balance. I'm sorry."

He got up, fetched a pewter mug and poured from the pot. The coffee made his heart speed. All that his sister had told him was true. He could have worked it out for himself. But it had been helpful nonetheless: the process of speaking it out and having her confirm his fears.

"What of you?" he asked. "Don't you want me to fail?"

She took another swallow, her face screwing. It seemed wrong that she should have such different taste from him.

"I want Oregon and Newfoundland both to join the Gas-Lit Empire," she said.

"That will never happen."

"Why not?"

"The king has an army. He has guns and explosives. They can't not be used."

"Then thousands will die."

"Yes," he said, though the truth was worse. The deaths would be numbered in millions. "The king will have his war."

"What if he were to die?" This she asked in a whisper.

"His brother would become king. Timon. Not a man of subtlety. Janus's advice would be more to his taste. They both want to launch their war before winter sets in. They'd work their way south, ahead of the snows. I've seen the plans. City by city. They'd lay waste to the continent. So much ruin."

There was a long silence after that. She drank more of the coffee, as if the act were some kind of penance. When the cup was empty, she handed it back to him.

"I can't count the dead like this. Numbers in a mathematical equation. I can't understand even one of them."

"No one can," he said. "There'll be millions, either way. No one can weigh that. You have to turn it around. Think of the lives saved. If my plan leaves one million dead and Janus's plan kills twenty million–"

"If," she said, cutting in. "You can't know any of this."

"But if no one does this calculation... Do you not see the danger?"

She sighed. "What does Gilad want?"

"That's what I don't know. He was the rudest one. But he stayed back to speak to me afterwards. He must have had a reason for that. He could have just marched out with the others."

"I wish I could meet him. Or do anything, really. I hate the waiting. Does he believe in magic, do you think? Gilad, I mean."

"No. On that point he was set."

She frowned.

"What is it?"

"I just thought to ask... What would happen if Janus were to die?"

"The killer would be thrown from the battlements," Edwin said.

After he was gone, Elizabeth couldn't get back to sleep. The coffee had made her heart race. Their exchange had made it worse. She prowled the room, pacing at first, then searching her mother's furniture again, as if each piece might contain a secret that could make the world right.

That was what they were supposed to do, mothers: make things right. The woman she remembered holding her as a small child had filled that role. Warmth and food and soothing words, the soft pad of a thumb wiping away tears. Full lips placed gently to kiss away the sting of every bruise and scrape. Their mother had been the soother of hurts, the dispeller of arguments. How many times had they been enfolded together in that one embrace?

Seeing her lost brother had shaken free memories of their shared childhood. At first the images had been indistinct. But with every day they were coming at her brighter and sharper. Some she could not have touched for many years. Now they flowed unbidden. In her mind, she caught a glimpse of rose-printed cotton and knew it was a blouse her mother used to wear.

"Never fight each other," their mother had said. "It must be us together. Always. Together we are strong."

Elizabeth could almost remember the scent of her. But when she tried to recall it, all she got was that sense of warmth and the softness of her mother's chest.

She pulled out the drawers of the writing desk, stacked them on the ground, lay down to reach inside the cavity, knocking on panels. She turned chairs and caskets upside down. It was a kind of madness. She had searched every part of the room already. Solitude and powerlessness had been gnawing at her for days. Her only agency had been to talk with a man who looked so like her that they might be mistaken, yet who thought so differently.

And to creep out at night.

The thoughts were tumbling in her head. She'd asked him if he'd seen their mother die. There'd been something wrong in the way he'd answered. A lack of sincerity. Then the second time she'd asked, he'd brushed the question away.

She had reached the tool bench, now, pulling every chisel and saw from its slot. Every setsquare, ruler and pencil. She wasn't even trying to hide the evidence of her search. Let him know. The chaos of the room would convey her feelings better than any words.

She turned over the stack of timber, spilled bolts of canvas, threw paint brushes onto the floor. She unspooled rope from a drum, casting it haphazardly behind her, hardly noticing the noise she'd been making.

And then to find herself standing in the midst of her own chaos, panting and sweating despite the cold air. And crying. For a long time, she stared at the destruction before stooping to right a work stool. She gathered the chisels and slotted them back, each into its place. Then, turn by turn she coiled the rope. But this, she did not replace.

CHAPTER 28

Even the hands of a king may be bound by law. If a crime is not worthy of death, a king cannot order an execution without being thought a tyrant. Thus the need for prisons, which can sometimes do the job of an executioner.

On this second midnight visit, the guard was awake and standing in the corridor, lamp in hand, as if he'd been waiting for her. Or, rather, for Edwin. On seeing his light, Elizabeth opened her stride into that masculine gait and occupied the centre of the passageway with all the entitlement that she could muster.

This time, he had the key ready, as if he'd been expecting her, and the deference had gone from his gaze. She was glad she didn't need to speak. The click of the lock turning echoed around the stones.

The wind hit her face as he opened the door: the scent of winter in the air. On stepping out, she looked up at the battlements. In such darkness, she couldn't make out the window of the Room of Cabinets. The castle's shadow would never let the moonlight touch that desolate place, she thought. Nor the sun. How cold it must be. How many prisoners survived a winter in one of those prison shacks?

Letting the chain slip through her fingers she stepped along the walkway, feeling for the planks with her feet. The moon was lighting the other side of the Colombia River Valley, turning the hills to silver. The beauty of it felt sharp as a knife.

"Mary? Mary Brackenstow?"

"Did you think I might have run away?" The voice from below had a crackle to it that had not been there the previous day. As if the prisoner was suffering from a sore throat.

"You might have been asleep."

"Daytime is for sleeping. If I slept at night... Well, I'd be afraid there might be no waking to follow."

"So you do want to live?"

"I do."

"But not enough to lie to the king? You just have to say a few words. Tell him you believe in his magic. Tell him he'll be victorious."

"If you've nothing more to offer, you may as well go back into the warm."

"I've something," Elizabeth said.

Feeling inside the coat, she brought out a chicken leg, wrapped in paper. She'd remembered to wear gloves this time. Kneeling, she slipped her arm between the planks of the walkway. It seemed impossible that Mary could have seen what she was doing, so deep were the shadows, yet the shingles slid and she felt a hand taking the roasted meat.

Elizabeth sat with her back against the rock wall, listening for any sound that might suggest it was being eaten. All she could hear was the wind. At last she said:

"What makes the lie impossible to say?"

"The truth's too important."

"Why?"

"The world needs peace. We can't build that by lying."

"Is building peace your job?"

"Yes."

Elizabeth could hear no doubt in Mary's voice. Perhaps this was the madness that her brother had spoken of. He must have had just such a conversation. But who is the greater fool, the madwoman or the ones who go to argue with her?

"If you die of cold out here, you'll be leaving your job unfinished."

"Peace will come. Killing me won't stop it. Yet while I'm here, it's my job."

"How do you claim to know the future?"

There was a longer pause before Mary answered. "Order is more powerful than disorder. Peace is more powerful than war. It will gather what forces it needs: me, you perhaps, others. It will surely come."

"Not me."

"Are you so sure?"

"Sure enough. I don't believe what you're saying. It takes fifteen years to raise a child. Twenty years. It's never done. But I've seen hundreds killed. I've seen bodies maimed. Children and old men. A single bomb can do that. So much order destroyed in an instant."

The image of severed limbs lying on the smoking ground flashed in her mind again, bright and vivid as the day it happened. She breathed deeply trying to banish the nausea that followed.

"I'm sorry," Mary said.

"Don't be sorry for me."

"But I am. No one should see such things. I can understand why believing is difficult for you. But think of this – I've lived in the Gas-Lit Empire. I was born there. When I first came to the wilds, that's all I found. Savagery and lawlessness. But all it takes is one small pocket of order for peace to take root. Yes, there are battles. And there are bombs. But in fifty years, in one hundred years, progress will always push forwards. Order will be established. Isn't that what history teaches us? Families become tribes. Tribes create cities. Cities become nations. Nations group together. And one day – it will come – the world will be united."

"You believe this?"

"I do."

"Then go to the king and tell him. This is the same thing that he believes. He wants to make the whole world into his kingdom. At peace."

In the cell below, suspended above that sheer drop, Mary laughed. It was an incongruous sound, joyful as a bubbling stream. Then she coughed, with a crackle that sounded bad. "I'm sorry," she said. "I don't mean to be disrespectful. But the king's dream is just the same as the dream of every other king. None of them can achieve it. And even if such an empire could be built, it would just as quickly tear itself apart."

"You contradict yourself," Elizabeth said. "A moment ago you told me it was inevitable and now you say the opposite."

"They are different things. The order that I am talking about will grow from the ground upwards. It will happen because people believe it will happen."

"Then it will not happen. People do not believe."

"I do. Others will. You cannot lock up an idea."

"What others? Name one of them."

"The king. He already believes. Otherwise why would he be so afraid of me that I have to be kept away from all other people, suspended over this chasm? Could I be so dangerous if what I'm saying were impossible? And I think you believe it too."

"I've told you I don't. I can't. Not after what I've seen."

"But you'd like to. Tell me this, do you believe in anything?"

"Loyalty," Elizabeth said.

"To who?"

"My friends."

"Do you believe that you can protect your friends and help them?"

"Yes!"

"Even though they might fall ill, or be attacked, or taken prisoner, or any one of a thousand things that you can't do anything to stop?"

"I know it's not logical," Elizabeth said. "But I have to think that I can protect them. Otherwise I'd just give up. And that would be the worse for them and for me."

"Then we're not so different. It's believing that makes us strong. It gives us a chance to make it happen. The only difference between us is that you've drawn the circle around yourself and your friends. But I've drawn it around the whole world."

"There's another difference. You're locked in a cell down there. I'm walking free."

"But which of us will make the greatest change?" Mary Brackenstow asked.

"You can't protect the whole world," Elizabeth said.

"If you really believed that, you'd be asleep in a warm bed. But here you are, come with gifts."

"I was trying to be kind."

"Well, thank you for that, magician. How many times is it you've come to me, asking these same questions?"

Elizabeth got to her feet, with a queasy sense that she might have given away too much. "Why do you ask?"

"If I had no power, you wouldn't keep coming back. It's eight times, by the way, if you'd lost count."

"I won't be coming again," Elizabeth said.

She felt her way back along the planks, her hand slipping over the chain links. On the way out, the guard nodded, as if to say that he would see her again on the following night. She told herself that he was wrong. Mary Brackenstow's dreams made no sense. She might as well have tied two sticks together with twine and called it a palace. Yet somehow a splinter of those dreams had caught under Elizabeth's skin.

The corridors were silent. Once out of sight of the guard, she turned down the wick of the lamp and closed the shutter, picking her way through the deepest of the shadows, one hand trailing the stones of the wall. She was becoming a ghost, her real self invisible even when she was seen.

Perhaps it was to prove to herself that she had the power of choice, or perhaps to drive Mary's words from her mind, but she took the stairs down to the courtyard, then followed the memory of the map her brother had sketched, entered the buildings again, climbed to the corridor in which Janus had his room. His door would be the third from the turn. She stood in shadow, staring at it. The man was Edwin's enemy. But also the enemy of his plans to overthrow the Gas-Lit Empire. She listened, trying to hear something beyond the distant moan of the wind over the battlements. A man breathing, perhaps.

There was nothing.

At the door of the Room of Cabinets she un-shuttered her lantern and clicked over the tumblers. But as soon as the door opened a crack, she knew something was wrong. A bar of light shone out.

"Where were you?" Edwin asked. He seemed almost frightened.

"Walking," she said. And then, angry with herself for feeling so guilty, "Why are you here?"

"It's my life you're risking as well!"

"You want to be safe from me?"

"I want us both to be safe!"

"Then show me how to get out of the castle. I'll walk back to the Gas-Lit Empire. You can be safe from me!" She knew he was right. But that just made her angrier. With herself. With him.

"I don't want you to go," he said.

"I was alone all day. I can't live like this. I have to do something."

"What did you do?"

"I talked to your prisoner. What of it?"

"She's mad, Elizabeth."

"You talked to her! How many times was that?"

"What does it matter?"

"It was six times!"

They were staring each other down.

"What are we doing?" he asked.

The fatigue hit Elizabeth as her anger drained away. She unclenched her fists and rubbed her face. "I'm sorry," she said.

Edwin sat himself on the floor, back resting against the wall. He seemed just as spent.

Elizabeth stepped to her bed roll and lay down, looking up at the ceiling. "I know I've been stupid."

"It's not your fault. I'd be the same if I were locked in here."

"Can you talk to me about the embassy? Consult with me. Give me something to think about that's outside this room."

So he did, describing the people to her again, the things they'd said, the way they'd acted, the way he thought of Brandt and Red and Gilad.

A memory was tickling somewhere at the back of her mind.

"Why are you frowning?" her brother asked.

"I'm trying to think where I heard that name – Gilad." Then it came to her. She sat up, clutching her knees. "I think he's the grandson of Patron Calvary – as was. But now, grandson to the king of Newfoundland."

CHAPTER 29

The king had fallen into a foul mood and brooded through breakfast, cutting at his meat as if it were the flesh of a Newfie. Timon pronounced himself ready to challenge Brandt to single combat. For each insult, he would leave a separate scar. There had been nineteen of those, he said, as though counting were something he ever did. Janus was the mathematician, always keeping track, tallying deaths and bushels of grain with equal concern.

"I will mark him!" Timon growled again. No one but Janus was listening. "I'll send them back knowing the edge of my sword."

"What was the meaning of yesterday's performance?" the king asked. "We invite these people to our hall so they can insult us?"

"It won't happen again, sire," Edwin replied.

"It cannot."

"Their culture is different."

"So different that we can never trust them."

"Trust may come."

"How?"

"Through actions. Not words. Yet words will be the start of it."

"I won't have them in my hall," the king growled. "Not again."

"You're wise, sire."

"Then you agree we send them back?"

"Let them stay a few days more. Command me to talk with them. In private. If an agreement is possible, I'll find it. If not, at least we'll know it for sure."

"I don't like it." This the king said in a lowered voice, leaning in closer.

"You won't need to talk with them," Edwin whispered back. "Not unless they see reason. And then it would be in good spirits – to celebrate."

"What might you say to them that could make a difference?"

"If I could show them the Mark Three, they'd come to understand the power we're offering. It could be the very thing to sway them."

The king chewed, his frown deep. "Shall we hear what your friend says on the matter? Mr Janus?"

"Sire?"

On the opposite side of the table, Janus turned his soft, attentive face towards the king, as if becoming aware of the conversation for the first time. Edwin's stomach clenched.

"My magician would give our guests a demonstration of the Mark Three. What do you say?"

"It would be… unwise."

"Might it not win them over?"

"Could anything do that? You are magnanimous, sire. But after their insults yesterday, such an act would be seen as weak. As if you were begging. They would leave with knowledge of our weapons. They would surely make copies."

The king turned back to Edwin. "His words make sense."

"They couldn't copy from merely looking."

"Perhaps," Janus said. "And yet how many times have you told us of their skill in arms?"

Edwin could feel the argument slipping from him. "To use a sword isn't the same skill as to design a gun."

But the king's frown had changed from concentration to fatigue. He was done with them. "You will not show them the Mark Three," he sighed. "Is that clear?"

Edwin bowed, defeated.

"Nor the other guns," Janus cut in. "And I must be there with him when he negotiates."

Edwin's heart tripped. His rival was overreaching again. "The king may wish me to go alone..." he said.

"You must be watched."

"Enough, Mr Janus!" The king's patience snapped. He pushed his plate away and stood. "My magician will talk with them alone." Then he turned to wag his finger at Edwin. "But you will not show them my arsenal. And you will not claim to speak with my authority. Remember what happened to your mother!"

The men of the embassy had gathered in Brandt's apartment, most standing, arms folded. Their breakfast plates lay stacked on the table. Edwin knocked on the open door and waited, only stepping across the threshold when Brandt himself had beckoned.

"Have you brought more food?"

Edwin shook his head.

"Then you're here to beg on behalf of your king?"

"No."

"Is it a conjuring trick you want to show us?"

"Would that help?"

Edwin caught the hint of a smile on Gilad's face. But only for a moment and then he was wearing a scowl again like the rest of them.

"It would not help!" Red growled from his place next to Brandt's shoulder. "Fairy tales are fit for children. Fact is the realm of men. Do you deny it?"

It was a question Edwin had no intention of answering. "Are your quarters satisfactory?"

Brandt nodded. "Thank you. Yes."

"If you leave in the next few days, you might be able to make it back home before the passes are blocked."

"You want this?"

Edwin shrugged. "I'm sorry we weren't able to negotiate. But it is done."

Brandt's head tilted, as if he was trying to find a new angle. "Is that what you came to tell us?"

"I was going to suggest a hunt. But so little time… Perhaps I could at least show you some more of the castle? It would give you more to tell your king when you make your report. I couldn't take all of you. But…" he let the offer hang in the air.

Brandt stood. Red stepped forwards, also a skinny man, whose name Edwin didn't know. If he hadn't been watching, Edwin might have missed Gilad, slipping in behind them. Just those four followed from the apartment. They hadn't needed to consult and there had been no question from the others. It felt like a clue of sorts. He would think on it later.

Edwin turned right in the passageway and led them away from the grand rooms of state. "We won't go to the royal apartments," he said. "After yesterday, you might not be received so well." He kept his voice light, as if sharing a joke.

Red picked up the humour and smiled. But the skinny man frowned, as if this were bad news.

"What's your name?" Edwin asked.

"Tomo," said the man.

A servant's doorway led to the courtyard. Red and Brandt looked up at the castle walls as they crossed the open space, as if they were connoisseurs of such fortifications.

"Here's where your food comes from."

Kitchen staff stood to attention as Edwin led the party inside and between the preparation tables. A hog was roasting next to the fire and the air smelt acrid with burned fat. Then they were out and immediately in through the door of the garrison. He kept up a brisk pace, as if they wouldn't care overmuch about what they saw. Though he could see the mental effort in their expressions, the conscious noting of details. The size of the kitchen was a clue to the numerical strength of the castle. The number of beds in the garrison, the thickness of the outside walls. From the number of steps in the spiral stair, they'd be able to work out the height of the east tower. The view from the top was breathtaking as ever, but he gave them little time to take it in. Then they were down again, and through the south wall to the outer ward.

He wasn't permitted to show them the automatic guns. But they could walk around the perimeter of the marshalling yard. "This is where the garrison makes their practice," he said, moving quickly. "And where new weapons are tested."

Here and there, faces sneaked a look down on them from high windows.

"What is this?" Brandt asked, gesturing to the ruined mud bricks and hay bales.

"It's to protect the stonework."

"From what?"

"From... I..." Edwin made himself frown then turned half away.

They were staring at the pockmarked stonework. Fresh chippings from the stone wall lay scattered around, remnants of the last onslaught from the automatic gun. It was Red who seemed most troubled by the sight. Tomo crouched to pick up a fragment of basalt, its edges sharp. After each test firing, servants gathered what remained of the bullets to be melted down and recast. But some they had missed. Tomo picked a deformed lump from the mess of ruined mud bricks. He weighed it in his hand before standing. Out of the corner of Edwin's vision, he saw the man slip it into his sleeve.

"What did this?"

"I'm sorry," Edwin said. "I'm not allowed to speak about it."

"It was a weapon?" Tomo asked.

It was one of those moments when silence did better work than any words that Edwin might have spoken.

The men were quieter on the way back. Edwin slowed his walk, allowing them time with their thoughts. At the door to Brandt's rooms, he stood aside to let them pass. But Gilad tarried in the passageway.

"I have a hunger for apples," he said.

"Then should we return to the kitchen?"

"If you don't mind."

Edwin did not.

Brandt had appeared to be the one in whose hands the final decision would rest. And Red was an enemy of the deal. That seemed clear. Conversely, Tomo leaned in Edwin's direction. But knowing that Gilad was the grandson of the king of Newfoundland changed everything. Young and arrogant, he'd used insolence as a tool, controlling the disastrous meeting of the morning. Yet he'd hung back afterwards to let slip clues. It was not apples he had a hunger for, Edwin thought. Gilad was the key.

They slowed as they crossed the courtyard.

"It is a beautiful castle," Gilad said.

"Thank you."

"Beautiful but useless."

That insulting tone was back. They had come to a halt halfway to the kitchens. None of the servants were in earshot.

"Why useless?"

"You have walls to hide behind but no enemies left to attack them."

"You mistake them," Edwin said. "Everything above fifteen feet was built for show. It's sculpture not defence."

They both stared up to the battlements and the towers.

Gilad sighed. "If it were you and me, we'd have an agreement signed already."

Edwin searched the man's face for signs of insincerity. "What would we agree?"

"I don't know. We'd find something. But it's not up to us, is it?"

"What do you want to happen?"

"What I want doesn't matter. Nor what you want. All we need to think about is what's possible. The rest…" Gilad turned up his hands, "…the rest is only dreams."

"This castle was built on dreams."

"It's too solid for that. Dreams vanish in the morning."

"But don't you know, I'm a magician? I can make things happen."

Now it was Gilad examining him, with a half-smile, as if it might have been a joke.

"What deal would you like?" Edwin asked.

"I should like peace between us. And trade. And some of your new weapons."

"It's hard to trade when there's such difficult country between us. But if we could take land further south, the road would be open year-round."

"You're talking war, not trade."

"One thing leads to the other."

"It's a war we couldn't win. We'd be crushed."

"Not with our weapons."

Gilad shook his head. "I'd like those apples," he said.

So they walked again, side by side, to the kitchens. Then to one of the storerooms behind it. Edwin pulled a sacking cover off a barrel, revealing red apples packed in straw. He picked one for himself and one for Gilad. The skin was cool and waxy to the touch.

"They're fresh in from Newberg," he said.

Gilad took a bite. The sound was as crisp as if it had been fresh-picked. "My gods, but that's a fine thing," he said, when it was swallowed.

"Apples might get bruised on the journey. But cider travels well enough," Edwin said. "When there's a road."

"Nice thought. But it'll take more than apples to have Newfoundland go to war."

"What, then?"

"Something written. Get the easy parts down first. Peace and goodwill between brother kings. That sort of thing. Then something about trade. We've not much to offer. Whale oil, perhaps. And whalebone. You can send us that cider in return. When the road is open. It doesn't matter what the trade is. It's a symbol."

"And weapons?"

"Those we'd be happy to receive."

"In exchange for helping in our war?"

"You call it 'helping'. Red would call it 'pricking a sleeping giant'. You want us to attack the Gas-Lit Empire. Why would we choose such an action?"

"Because you believe you'd win."

Gilad nodded. "Red knows what battle is like. You tell him he's going to fight and he's going to look at the land. He's going to count his enemies. I don't even know how many men he's killed. But he won't step into a fight if he thinks it can't be won. That's why he's still alive. For the rock of Newfoundland to take on the entire world…"

"With our weapons," Edwin said.

"Weapons you won't show."

They stepped away from the barrel and out of the storeroom. Edwin wasn't sure if he or Gilad had begun the walk back, or if they had each decided to set off in the same moment.

"Why are you helping me?" he asked.

"Perhaps it was that wall you showed us. Such ruin! You might have had servants do it with hammers for all I know. But even if it was a trick, it was a clever one."

"I'll bring paper and pens this afternoon," Edwin said.

"We'll find words that don't offend your people or mine. Writing them down won't hurt."

Gilad smiled. "Signing them might."

Elated, Edwin climbed the spiral stairs. At last he had something hopeful to bring to his sister. Though she was set on defending the Gas-Lit Empire, her fate had become tangled with the politics of Oregon. If his own place were secure, he would be able to protect her.

But as he approached the top, he caught a murmur of men's voices. He peered around the edge and saw the king standing before the Room of Cabinets, together with Janus and two guards. One was on his knees in front of the door, turning the tumblers of the lock.

Edwin stepped out into full view. "May I help you?"

"Ah," the king said. "Where were you?"

"The marshalling yard." Janus would have known that full-well.

"We couldn't find you and… Well, the room must be searched like any other."

The guard stopped working the tumblers and stood, not meeting Edwin's eyes.

"This room is private."

Janus said, "We can't make special cases."

"It's my room!" Edwin snapped. Knowing his mistake a fraction too late.

The king's face darkened. "Whose room is it?"

"I'm sorry, sire. Everything is yours."

"Then open it, sir! Open it now!"

CHAPTER 30

Elizabeth listened to the voices outside. With her ear to the door, every word became clear. She'd studied the tumblers of the lock and knew the number of permutations. Unless they'd been given the combination, it might take days to crack. Nor could they easily gain access by force. The door had been made of thick oak and banded with iron. The king might think twice before using explosives against his own castle.

But then she heard her brother's voice and her heart lurched inside her chest. Edwin couldn't refuse his king.

She stepped to the ottoman. It had hidden her before. But it would be one of the first places they'd look. Even the cabinets would give up their secrets. There was nowhere in the room they wouldn't find her. Then all would be revealed: her presence, Edwin's duplicity, the trickery of a conjuror. If they called her a spy, she'd be locked in one of the cells, waiting for winter to freeze her. If they called her a magician, she'd be thrown from the battlements. Either way, it would be the end for both of them.

Even a low chance was better than none. She threw a travelling cloak over her shoulders, pulled the hood low. With her right hand she took a chisel and with her left hand dipped into the pot of chalks on the workbench.

The door tumblers were turning. She lunged for the corner of the room, putting herself where the opening door would hide her. As she flattened herself to the wall, she drew the chalk across her face, feeling the dust of it sticking to her cold sweat. Warpaint, of a kind. Not a disguise. Rather, a distraction, in case they did glimpse her face, to stop them catching the similarity between brother and sister.

The door opened. Just in time she raised a hand to stop it slamming into her forehead. Booted feet marched into the room. Four men, she thought. Or five. She was holding the door handle now, to stop it swinging back.

"It must be me to search!" That was her brother's voice.

"I'll do it," came another, soft as putty. That would be Janus.

"You will work together." The third voice carried irritation. A man who expected his words to be obeyed. The king. "Start in that corner."

The footsteps and voices moved deeper into the room, further from the door. There was a grating sound, something heavy being dragged over floorboards.

"It's delicate," Edwin cried.

Elizabeth took a deep breath, readying herself, then sidestepped from her hiding place, took in the guardsmen and the others. All had their backs towards her. But as she lurched for the open doorway, one of the guards turned, saw her, shouted.

She ran. Full tilt. Along the corridor. She was slinging herself down the first flight of stairs when they burst from the room behind her. She couldn't outrun them. Down one flight, taking three steps at a time, then four, stumbling out into another passageway, sprinting. Startled servants dived out of her way.

She was in the next spiral stairway before the chasing guardsmen were out in the corridor. They wouldn't know which direction she'd gone, but the scattered servants would point the way. It might have won her a second or two.

She was approaching the jail, now. The guard standing by the door seemed unsure. But he let her pass. She'd turned the corner when a whistle started blowing somewhere in the castle. Then other whistles joined in, calling their shrill alarm. Guards would be closing and barring both of the castle's gates. She ducked into a doorway and found another spiral staircase. This time she climbed, slowing to a walk, trying to drag enough breath into her lungs. The whistling subsided. But now everyone would be on their guard. She emerged into a familiar passageway. Janus's rooms were just ahead.

The handle of his door wouldn't turn. It was locked, of course. The corridor was still empty. She backed up and launched herself, lifting her foot to kick at the last moment. Wood splintered in the frame, but the door held firm. The echoes died.

They'd be on her any moment. She tried the door next to Janus's room and blessed the saints when it opened to her touch. Pulling off the cloak, she wiped it across her face, scrubbing away the chalk. Then she bundled it tight and flung it through the window. She needed a mirror. But that is the reason for practice. The thousand repetitions, all in preparation for the one time when there is no chance to check.

Changing back to appear like Edwin had taken perhaps fifteen seconds. She opened the door, stepped out. The corridor was still empty but footfalls were approaching at a run. She stood tall as they rounded the corner: the king and two guardsmen, with Janus just behind. And at the very back, her brother.

He saw her. And she saw him. He turned and disappeared back around the corner, just as recognition was showing in the king's eyes. And confusion. He looked behind himself as if searching for Edwin at the back of his party.

She strode out towards them, emphasising the male gait. "He's been here," she said. "He must have gone into Janus's room."

"How did you get here?" the king asked.

"Back there," she gestured vaguely behind them. "I turned and came the other way, trying to cut him off."

Janus stared hatred at her. "You were with us!" he said, stepping closer.

Misdirection. The art had been so drummed into her as a child that it was second nature. She turned to the door and pointed: "Look!"

They did. Even Janus. The doorframe was cracked where she'd tried to kick it in. "I heard him slamming it," she said.

The king pointed to the lock. "Open it!"

One of the guards tried. Failed.

The king turned to Janus. "Do it."

Janus shook his head. "If it's locked, he can't have got in."

"You said he's a magician," Elizabeth offered. "He got through the walls of the castle. He even got into the Room of Cabinets."

Janus's eyes flicked from place to place, seeking escape. Out came the key. He turned it in the lock and seemed about to open the door himself. But one of the guardsmen pushed him out of the way and entered first, pistol drawn.

The room seemed comfortable rather than luxurious. Muted colours but fine quality. A wide bed. Yet not conspicuously wide. Two cupboards. A chest of drawers. The air smelled faintly of sandalwood. Three strongboxes along one wall, each banded with iron. A small brass padlock hung from the central one.

"There's no one here," said Janus. "I told you."

The king pointed to the floor. One of the guardsmen got down on his knees to look under the bed, sword at the ready. The other opened the cupboards and swung his arm around between hanging clothes. Elizabeth considered the window. It could have been just big enough for someone to climb through. She opened it, got her head out and looked directly down to the walkway that led to the cells, fixed precariously to the wall below. And there was the cloak she'd thrown: caught on a plank, the wind tugging it into a flag.

"I know how he escaped," she said.

For Edwin – the real Edwin – the panic of the search and the chase had given way to an awful dread. Seeing his sister outside Janus's room, he knew it was over. They were both going to die. For a fraction of a second, he'd stood, dumbly, expecting to be seized. It was instinct rather than thought that saved him: the backward step, then one to the side, putting him around the corner of the corridor and out of sight. In the seconds that followed, he couldn't understand why no one had come after him. He listened to their voices and footsteps moving away.

No one would be fooled by Elizabeth's poor impression of his voice. They would hear the burr of resonance coming from her chest rather than her throat. They would see the narrowness of her chin. He clenched his teeth, waiting for the inevitable shout of discovery.

None came.

The illusion of context had saved them: the one illusion that should never work, but always did. He had been expecting to see her. Fearing it. So that is what he saw. The king, Janus and the guards were seeking someone else. It blinded their eyes. He had seen her made up to look like him. They had tried to match their voices and failed. But they had taken to wearing identical clothes and it was the king's first viewing.

The noise of the search party was suddenly muffled. With the corner in shadow, he risked a look, saw the empty passageway and the open door of Janus's room. His sister had somehow changed a disaster into a victory. The search of the Room of Cabinets had become a probing of Janus's own property.

She would want to be away from them. And he needed to move. Every moment that they were both abroad would add to the risk.

As he crept back up the stairs, he wondered what they might have achieved if they were fully on the same side.

For these few days, circumstance was allowing them to fight together. It was easier to think on that and forget the bigger truth. They'd nailed their colours to the masts of different ships. At the end, one of them would lose. For all her quietness, his sister's brilliance would make her a formidable enemy. The thought of it was too disquieting to hold.

When they first gave chase, Edwin had pulled closed the door of the Room of Cabinets behind him. But now standing in front of it again, he could not remember scrambling the tumblers. He put his ear to it and listened. Nothing. He gripped the handle. It turned. He must have left the room unlocked. The door opened, silent and smooth. He stood under the lintel, taking in the stillness. The scents of other people still hung in the air. One of his mother's cabinets had been pulled away from the wall.

The stress and surprise had made him forget to lock up. *Mistakes always cost in the end*: his mother's words. He stooped, pulled the knife from his boot and advanced into the room. There was no one behind the door. Nor inside the ottoman. He tipped each of the cabinets an inch, feeling their lack of body weight. Treading lightly, he looked under the workbench, around the back of each item of furniture.

A scratching sound made him spin around, knife blade extended, pointing towards the door, which was swinging inwards. Elizabeth slipped through the gap. His sister. The relief hit him unprepared and his eyes prickled with the threat of tears.

"That was… extraordinary," he said.

She closed her eyes and teardrops ran. "I almost didn't make it."

"But you did. And now… they won't need to search this room again. Leading them to Janus – that was inspired."

"It was an accident," she said. "I was looking for a room to hide. They'd never check in there. That's what I thought. But that door… there's no way I was getting through it."

He listened as she told him about the cloak, smiling as the story developed.

"The king was angry," she said.

"But that helps us! Janus won't be able to use this same attack again."

"I think he was angry with both of you," Elizabeth said. "As if he could feel something had happened, but didn't know what."

CHAPTER 31

On the dawn of the third day following the arrival of the embassy, which was the first day after the search of the Room of Cabinets, a hunting party assembled in the castle courtyard.

The king had been unwilling at first. Petulant. "I'll not go with them!" he'd said.

It was the arrogance of the embassy that had cut him, an injury he'd since rubbed raw. Helped by Janus, no doubt.

"We'll be a small party," Edwin said.

He didn't need to spell out the implication, that if the Newfies played the same insulting game, there'd be few to see it, and none that would talk about it afterwards. The king's emotions might be childish, but he understood the way things worked.

The horses stamped. Their breath made fog in the cold air. Edwin looked up to the towers, already touched by the morning sun. Good weather for a ride. The gates opened and the king led the way with Brandt just behind: the correct order for anyone who happened to be watching. Then came Red and Tomo, followed by two of the king's guards. Trusted men, who would keep their mouths closed. Edwin set off next to Gilad, bringing up the rear. There was no Timon to get in the way. And no Janus. Whatever mischief the Second Counsellor might get up to would have to wait till their return. For now, Edwin had gathered all the people he needed.

A small party. That was how the king liked to hunt: moving fast, no train of mules clanking and clopping behind. No ceremony. And no need of trickery to provide a kill. Some of the stiffness and irritation he'd been carrying seemed to drop away from him as they put the castle behind. Once over the first rise with even the towers out of view, they could have been anywhere. Brandt too seemed more at ease. How strange that the prospect of shooting a defenceless animal could bring such men together.

Red and Tomo were more pensive. But with Elizabeth's revelation, this made perfect sense. She had unlocked the puzzle of the embassy. Each of the men had been sent with a different purpose. Brandt was the figurehead, a kind of diplomatic misdirection, drawing attention away from where the real decisions would be made. Red, fiercely independent and a natural sceptic, was there to argue the treaty out of existence. Doubtless he represented a faction in Newfoundland's turbulent politics. Tomo would speak for the other side. He was outward-looking, facing the future, hopeful of the opportunities that change might bring. He would argue for an agreement to be forged. If Red and Tomo could be made to agree, so would their people back home. But it was Gilad who held the real authority. Edwin saw that now. It would have been on his word that the embassy delayed its arrival. Grandson to the king of Newfoundland, he was the ringmaster. It was he who'd sabotaged the first meeting. How strange it had seemed when he'd spoken to Edwin afterwards and offered helpful advice. Only now did that make sense. He had created the argument to watch its ebb and flow. One side or other would win. And he would be the judge of it. On his word, an agreement would be signed. Or not. The more Edwin thought of it, the deeper his admiration for the king of Newfoundland. And for Gilad.

"What will they kill, do you suppose?" Gilad asked.

"Hopefully not each other," Edwin said. And then, "What is your wish for the future?"

"Why should my wishes matter?"

"Wishes are all we have. They matter more than anything. But if you won't speak of that, tell me of your family."

Gilad glanced at him, suspicious. "I have a mother, a father, two sisters. Much like any family. What of you? They say your mother was killed."

Edwin didn't let the sting of that remark show in his face or voice. "We were from England," he said. "Poor folk. We moved from place to place."

"Yet here you are. Magician to a king. Whatever that means."

"Like all titles, it means nothing. And everything. But you and I – there's something the same about us. We both stay at the back of the hunting party."

"Why is that?" Gilad asked.

"So we can keep watch on the others who ride ahead."

The King and Brandt had spurred their horses into a gallop, much to the alarm of the two guards who were struggling to catch up. The dust began to settle. Edwin watched the rest of the party riding away.

"Will we find them again?" Gilad asked.

"It'll be easy enough. There is a wooded ravine a couple of miles from here. It's kept stocked with game. That's where the king will lead them."

"Not a real hunt then? Not wild animals?"

"Almost real. Let them enjoy themselves. Think of it as a performance. Like diplomacy."

Edwin glanced over to see if Gilad would react. But the man's expression gave little away. They rode on in silence after that. It was a kind of agreement, Edwin thought.

Coming to a stand of trees and a fork in the path, they headed left, down into a ravine, then followed the flow of a laughing brook. He could see the footprints of birds in the mud, but no horse tracks. He hadn't expected any. The guards would have warned the king from this particular shortcut. Such ravines offered hiding places to robbers. Not that anyone would have dared waylay the king so close to Crown Point.

A flock of small birds flitted through the tree branches above them, chirping as they went.

"Beautiful country," Gilad said.

"It is."

"You have more trees than Newfoundland. More plants. More of everything. Except for fish and seaweed."

"Seaweed?"

"You can eat it. It'll keep you healthy when you can't get greens and fruit. That's what you've got to understand about the Rock. The hard life makes for hard people. In a fight, we're the ones you want with you."

"I'll remember that."

They had slowed to a stop in the shade, with the smell and sound of water.

"There's something about you I can't figure," Gilad said.

"How so?"

"I don't know what it is. You just seem different – the way you look at people, your seat in the saddle, the way you picked those apples from the barrel, everything. It's all so precise. Like you've learned it or something."

Gilad's clarity of vision was astounding. Edwin knew it now more surely than ever. A formidable opponent. The temptation to tell him the truth felt overwhelming. *You're right. I'm not this person that I'm pretending to be. I'm not those movements. I'm not these clothes.* He looked away, trying to control himself. His hand had clenched to a fist around the reins.

"Don't take offence," Gilad said. "I didn't mean anything by it."

Still not trusting himself to meet the man's gaze, Edwin nodded. "None taken," he said.

Three shots rang out as they were climbing the other side of the ravine. Not close. It was another mile before they found the king and the rest of the party, dismounted next to the body of a deer. There was no strange patterning on the deer this time. Nothing remarkable about it, except that when viewed close, all such animals are remarkable.

The king and Brandt were exchanging hip flasks,

congratulating each other. Even Red and Tomo seemed more relaxed.

"We thought we'd lost you," the king said. "You missed the fun."

"They both shot at once," Tomo explained. "And look…" He pointed to the animal's neck, to the two entry wounds, only a few inches apart.

Edwin kept back and watched as Gilad crouched down and laid his hand on the animal. It hadn't been a trick this time. Mere chance that they'd both hit in the same moment, and so close. But Brandt and the king had been bound together by the shared experience, the extreme unlikeliness of the twin shot. Even Gilad seemed to be moved: a man who had dismissed magic and fortune telling as trickery.

While Brandt and the king strode off to drink and talk, the guards gutted the deer and skinned it. One set to work butchering out the backstraps while the other built a fire and soon the smell of roasting venison and the smoke of burning fat was drifting in the breeze. Tomo and Red had been quiet. Edwin went to sit with them.

"Enjoying your day?" he asked.

"The meat smells good," Tomo said.

Even Red managed to smile.

"I've been thinking," Edwin said. "You may not want to be part of our war with the Gas-Lit Empire. But we can still have an agreement signed. Something about peace between our kingdoms."

Red nodded, enthusiastic. "We can do that."

"There's no harm in writing it," Edwin said. "And we can write more. Something about trade."

"And the military alliance?" Tomo asked.

"We can write that too. Just the words. So we know exactly what we'd be talking about."

Red frowned. "I don't see why that's needed."

"Writing it isn't the same as agreeing," said Tomo.

"It just means we know what we'd be rejecting or accepting," said Edwin.

They were both looking at Red now.

"I guess it could do no harm," he said, though he still seemed troubled. "Nothing's agreed until it's signed."

Edwin stood. The Newfoundlanders did the same. He offered his hand and they shook it. Not a contract exactly. An agreement to not agree. Not yet. The wash of relief was so intense that he felt like crying.

Then the guards-turned-cooks were calling and handing out skewers of meat, scorched on the outside but still pink in the very middle. He couldn't remember a more delicious feast.

CHAPTER 32

The prison guard stepped from the doorway alcove as she approached, the ring of keys already in his hand. His direct gaze ran from her hat to the bulky cloak, all the way down to her boots. On her first visit, when she found him sleeping, it was he who had been discomforted. The second time, he'd stood taller. Now she caught insolence in his eyes. As if he'd glimpsed the secret of her unseemly fascination for the prisoner, Mary Brackenstow, and was calculating where such currency might be spent.

With a clanking of the bolt, he opened the door, letting in the north wind. She welcomed its tug at her hair and clothes. The iron chain burned cold under her hand as she stepped out along the platform. The planks felt slippery. It was too dark to see whether they had caught a frost or if it was merely dew.

The previous afternoon, she'd pushed open the window of the Room of Cabinets, craned her neck out to look down and across the castle wall to the line of small cells suspended below the walkway. Had it been on the level, she could have estimated the distances with ease. But something about the verticality of that stony expanse played tricks on the mind. At first she thought the height of the cliff might be more than four hundred feet, which would have been too much. Then she guessed the length of the castle wall, and in her mind turned that length by ninety degrees until it became a height. This gave her a more possible answer.

But now, in the dark, the void below her felt limitless. If she slipped, she might fall forever with the wind rushing around her ears. She might freeze to death before ever reaching the end of it. Or if she jumped.

"I knew you'd come to visit me again." Mary's voice sounded warm, as if she was smiling.

"Then you were right."

"That's the way of it," Mary said. "Once you've seen a spark from the truth, you have to keep coming back."

Elizabeth lay down the burden she'd been secretly carrying under her cloak and sat herself next to it, her back resting on the stones. "I haven't seen anything," she said. "I just don't want you to die."

"Last time you brought me food. It was a kindness you didn't need to show."

"You're welcome."

"I only wish I could see you. So I've someone to picture in my head when we talk."

Elizabeth repeated Mary's words in her mind. The suggestion that she hadn't seen Edwin before seemed wrong.

"I'm only here to ask questions," she said.

"That's precious also. The talk means more to me than the food."

"Last time you said you wanted the whole world to be like a single country."

"No," Mary said. "Those are your words. I'm telling you that the world *is* a single country. Right now."

"But there are hundreds of kings. Hundreds of countries. Each with different forms of government."

"So you say."

"Can you deny it?"

"Show me a line where one country ends and another begins."

"The map has many."

"But a map of the earth is just a piece of paper. And every king has his own, with lines in different places. If they were real, you could show me one marked on the ground."

"I crossed one of them to get here," Elizabeth said. "So did you, if you came from the Gas-Lit Empire. Two fences with barbed wire in between. Do you not remember?"

"That?" The sound of laughter came up from below, incongruous. "That fence will rot and rust. It is only the border because people believe it's a border."

"You don't?"

"The world is one country. That's the truth. And that's the real reason the king put me in here. Not because I don't believe in magic tricks. It's because I don't believe your prophecies. He isn't going to rule the world."

Mary's was a particular kind of madness. For every question an answer had already been prepared. Perfectly rational. Elaborate. Through all those hours of confinement, she must have been planning this conversation. Yet it made no sense in the real world. Elizabeth felt herself half crazy for entertaining the idea.

"Would there not be chaos if people stopped believing in their kings and their countries?"

"Maybe so. If it came about like that."

"Millions might die."

"It could happen."

"Then how can you wish so many deaths on the world?"

"I wish them not," said Mary. And again, "I wish them not."

"The king wants to conquer all the other nations. Fewer men might die that way than with what you're planning. Doesn't that make you worse than him?"

"There have always been wars," Mary said. "And if you follow his way, there always will be. Say he builds his empire till it goes on forever. What then?"

"Then the world would have one king. Just like you say you want."

"No. I say it is one country. And the people will decide who rules them. But even if your king does manage all the things you say, how long would his empire last? In time, there'd be revolutions and splinters. New kings breaking it up from the inside. In fifty years, a hundred, you'd have maps with borders all over again."

"You can't make anything happen sitting in this cell."

"I made you come here," Mary said.

"No. I came to save you," Elizabeth's voice had dropped to a whisper. If she could only prove the woman wrong, she might put it out of her mind. "You say a border isn't real because you don't believe in it."

"I do."

"And you say the world is one country because you do believe in that."

"Yes."

"There are more people who believe in borders."

"But my belief is stronger. Once you've understood it,

you can't un-know it. That's why it can only grow and spread. This way sees all people as equal. Wherever they were born. Men and women. All races."

"Pleasant words," said Elizabeth. "But without swords and guns, none of that would happen."

"I have none," said Mary. "I never will. Yet your king is afraid. Not of weapons, I think. Words are more powerful in the end. I thought you were an intelligent man, Edwin, with your conjuring and your fortune telling. But if you can't see that the dreams of a poor woman, who owns nothing but the clothes she wears, can be more powerful than the army of a king – then you're less than I thought."

"I don't want you to die," Elizabeth said.

"The king won't be moved," said Mary. "And he will have his way. This winter will kill me, sure enough. You need not blame yourself. Your part in it is vanishing small."

Elizabeth had thought it through a dozen times or more and come to no conclusion. She still didn't understand why Mary's words had pushed her. But they had. The decision was made.

"I have something for you."

"Another chicken leg?"

"Something else. For you to keep. But not to use till I say."

"Now you have me curious."

"Can you agree to keep it secret?"

"Without knowing what it is?"

"Please."

The wooden shingles shifted below, as Mary opened a hole in the roof of her cell. "I can't lie for you," she said. "But neither would I tell."

In the dark Elizabeth felt for the rope, which she'd brought hidden under her cloak. Coiled, it would be too fat for the hole in the cell roof. Unwrapping the end, she began to thread it through between the planks of the walkway. She felt the moment when Mary grasped the end, the sudden tautness where it had been slack before. And she heard a breath of surprise. Then it began to slip over Elizabeth's hands, as Mary pulled it through.

"Why are you giving this to me?"

"Can you hide it?"

"There's no need. They lower down the food and water. No one ever sees this place. They never see me."

"If you use it to escape, they'll know I was the one who gave it to you. Hold it there, for now. I'll tell you when it's time."

"Why are you putting your life in my hands?"

"I don't know," Elizabeth said. "I don't know. It's just something I feel."

"Bless you," said Mary Brackenstow.

When the real Edwin stepped into the Room of Cabinets, he expected to find Elizabeth sitting up amid her blankets. That would be the usual way. She was a light sleeper. Only once had he found his sister curled up, eyes closed. But the room was silent. The absence of her breathing registered on some unconscious level. He shivered, lifted his lamp, stepped further, found her nest of blankets empty and cold.

Finding her gone made a panicky feeling in the base of his stomach. Uneasy possibilities flashed through his mind. He might meet her on his way back down. Someone else might see them together. She might have run away, just like his mother had done all those years before.

He was being irrational. The chances of such an event were small, manageable, no different from the other dangers he faced. And, in some ways, this was better. She didn't need to see what he was about to do.

In the corner of the room furthest from the door, he knelt and set to work on one of the screws that held down a floorboard. Then, with the tip of the screwdriver, he levered the end of the board until there was enough of it exposed to get a grip with his fingers. With that laid to one side, he could reach into the narrow darkness of the hole and extract a small ledger and a crock of coins.

The first quarter of the book was filled with his mother's handwriting. Columns for dates, names of people, incremental amounts of money, and a running total for each person. The names were not their actual names, rather a code. The maid to the consort was recorded as Stella, though her real name was Clara. But it was the pigeon master's assistant that Edwin needed to check. He was recorded as Lion, though his real name was Pentecost.

In the time when Edwin's mother was magician to the king, Pentecost had emerged as a useful source of information. But in her last two years, his help had become invaluable. Edwin flicked through the ledger to the place where his own handwriting took over. Then on, through the years of his own tenure. The last pages, he leafed through one by one. The total was an eye-watering sum. Yet it had been earned. Two hundred and sixty-eight times, Pentacost had come with information or done some other service.

Edwin began counting the coins into piles of twenty. The man was illiterate. It seemed unlikely that he would himself have kept such careful tally. And yet, he was charged with scoring off each hour. Five vertical scratches of the pen, then a diagonal scratch through the group, making a bunch of six hours. Four of those bunches would make a day. Though there were clocks in the castle, events in the pigeon loft had ever been gauged by the falling of sand.

From the crock Edwin counted thirteen piles of twenty silver coins. Then eight more. The whole treasure he dropped into a cloth bag, which he then tied closed.

He'd chosen simple weapons: a knife that fitted into a hidden sheath within his boot and his mother's flintlock pistol, which rested in a deep outer pocket of his coat. The touch of it gave comfort. The purse of coins, he tied to his belt. It would stop him running, but it seemed the best way to hide it.

For all his fears, he met no one on the way down to the small gate. One of the guards was sleeping. The other watched his approach with hooded eyes. Edwin put a finger to his lips and the man nodded.

"Has anyone else passed this way?" Edwin whispered.

The guard shook his head then unlocked the door and opened it. Edwin doused his lamp and left it hanging on a hook on the wall.

East Cairn had once marked the limit of Crown Point. Or, rather, the limit of the order it could impose. It lay a mere two miles from the castle. Beyond that, bandits had once been able to operate. The piling of those rocks into a heap had been an act of conquest, a statement that all the lands within would be defended. At the time, no one could have guessed how far this new ambition might spread. All the land north up to the Yukon River was now under their control. And all the land south as far as the great Redwood forests. There were still bandits. But they knew they lived on borrowed time.

Edwin picked his way along the track more from memory than from sight. From time to time he stumbled, and felt the heavy weight of the purse swing back against his leg. Then, over the last half-mile, the clouds cleared and a sliver of moon lit the way, so that he could see the East Cairn ahead of him. And, as he drew closer, the figure of a man standing next to it. Even in the dark, Edwin knew that it was Pentecost. And knew that the man was anxious.

They acknowledged each other with a nod, then as if it had been prearranged, stepped away together into a thicket and crouched low.

"Did you bring it?" Pentecost whispered.

Edwin tapped the purse through his coat, making the coins clink against each other. "When did you leave the castle and by which route?"

"Yesterday. The main gate. They think I'm visiting my mother. I told them she's sick."

Edwin began to relax. He unbuttoned his coat, produced the purse, which Pentecost took. The man seemed surprised by the weight of it, as if it was more than he'd expected.

"Don't bring it back to the castle," Edwin said. "If they found you with it…"

"I got a secret place," said Pentecost.

"Will there be bribes from other men to add to that?"

In the dark it was impossible to see the man's reaction. "There may be," he said.

"I won't be asking who. Don't worry."

Pentecost's shoulders eased down. "You've always been the best of them," he said.

"You're collecting all your earnings now?"

A nod.

"Be careful. It might be that some of them thought you'd never collect. They might not have put the money aside. You asking for it… It might cause trouble."

"Thank you, Mr Edwin. But they've all of them agreed."

As Edwin picked his way back along the path, climbing by stages towards the castle, he wondered who those people might be: the other clients of Pentecost.

CHAPTER 33

The placing of words on paper had never felt so much like a dance. The circling began with the opening line. The scribe dipped his pen and Edwin spoke.

"We the kings and representatives of the peoples of Oregon and Newfoundland…"

Red slapped his hand down on the table making the lid of the ink pot rattle. "It should be the other way. Newfoundland and Oregon."

"On what grounds?"

"Alphabetical," Tomo said, reasonably.

Edwin imagined the king's reaction to that wording and knew it wouldn't work. Newfoundland was the smaller. It had less people, less wealth and more primitive armaments. It would be the junior partner in the alliance, except in its position: holding the eastern seaboard, while Oregon held the west. In that one way, they would be equal.

"How about this," he said: "We the kings and representatives of these two peoples…"

The Newfoundlanders glanced to each other before nodding. Edwin hoped they couldn't see his tension. They'd still have to figure whose signature went top at the end of the document. But that would be a fight for another day.

"…affirm our present and future peace…"

"That should be brotherhood," said Red.

That implication of equality again. But Edwin could at least tell the king that Newfoundland was the younger sibling. "…affirm our present and future brotherhood and commit ourselves to lasting peace…"

By the end of the opening paragraph, the scribe had filled two sheets of notepaper, mostly with lines that had been struck through and re-written. How much worse it could have been with Janus present. But on the ride back from the hunt, Edwin had begged the king's indulgence.

"Order Janus away," he'd said.

The king's curt nod had given him hope. But he couldn't expect more than a day's grace.

The council room was airless and overwarm. The skin of Edwin's forehead felt sticky with sweat. He was aware of a disagreeable smell of body odour. Not only from himself.

From every page, they were salvaging a few lines at most. The hours were creeping, yet passing too fast for Edwin. The light in the window faded. He called for a second scribe and a second table. They split into two working parties. Red and Gilad began drafting the trade agreement, which they would surely write as a wish-list of Oregon produce. Meanwhile Edwin and Tomo worked on the war alliance, which would be a wish-list of Oregon's military ambitions.

Red and Gilad finished their work first and came to look over Edwin and Tomo's shoulders. Red set about arguing against every line they'd already drafted. All progress stopped.

"We should eat," Edwin said.

At least they could agree on that.

It was a meal of bread and cold meats. Edwin had whispered to the steward to keep refilling their glasses with the best wine that Oregon's vineyards could offer. Red and Tomo made the most of it. Gilad wetted his mouth, but little more. Edwin had the impression of a man keeping count, as he was. Both of them would stay sober. And both would be able to judge the drunkenness of the others. It seemed odd that Gilad did nothing to stop his comrades.

"It doesn't matter what we write," Edwin said. "Nothing's agreed unless it's signed."

"I'm too tired to carry on," Red complained. Tomo nodded.

Edwin pictured Janus, pacing like a caged animal, waiting for his chance to get into the council room. "Let's at least finish a draft," he said. "Then we'll deserve our sleep. Tomorrow we can edit."

It was Gilad who swung it. He stood, clapped his friends on the back. "It won't take more than half an hour. If we dig in our spurs."

The writing went faster after that. In the warmth of the council room, with a fire crackling in the hearth, Red's eyes drooped. Tomo was little better by the end, head tipping forwards then jerking awake, while Edwin and Gilad transcribed the whole thing into a final neat copy.

The two kingdoms would be like brothers. Newfoundland would receive all it wanted in trade and the new weapons. Oregon would have its eastern ally and a war that they could win together. So said the agreement.

It meant nothing, of course. With signatures and seals attached, it would mean fractionally more. Even then it could hold no more weight than a child's promise, which might be discarded on a whim. No sanction had been stated. Only honour, that most slippery of laws. Like all such insubstantial things, it would become real only after time and tests had proved it.

Red snored. Tomo slept silently. When Edwin had finished writing, he showed the copy to Gilad, who read through it line by line.

"Congratulations," he said, handing it back.

"Will you advise it's signed?" Edwin asked.

"Only if they can agree."

Edwin followed his gaze to where the others were slumped. Tomo had wedged a cushion in between his head and the wing back of the chair. Red's chin rested on his chest. He would wake with a sore neck.

"If they do agree?"

"They would bring their factions with them. All would be possible."

"I'd like to know what you want to happen."

"What would it matter? I can only do what is possible."

"Then why have you helped me?"

Gilad frowned. "They say that fools befriend each other because no one else will. It's the same with kingdoms. Why would my king shake hands with yours if Oregon was ruled by idiots? I don't know what you are, Edwin. But a fool you're not. You've earned your chance."

Edwin folded the paper down and slipped it into an inside pocket. "Thank you."

As he was turning to go, Gilad said, "Red and his

faction won't agree straight off, just so you know. Next year, perhaps. Or the year after. It'll take time for them to change their minds. Or a miracle."

The chill air outside the council room sharpened Edwin's mind. He wondered what Gilad had meant by that last remark. It almost seemed as if the man had been asking for a demonstration of magical power. More likely, he was angling to see the Mark Three in action.

The lamps had been hung too far apart. Pools of shadow dotted the passageway. Catching a movement in one of them, away to the right, Edwin turned left and hurried to the nearest doorway. Then he cut back and climbed a spiral stairway, up two flights. Along the corridor and around the corner. Another short flight of steps. But with only a few paces to go, Janus stepped out to block his way, dressed for the cold.

"You can't keep me out forever," he said.

"How long have you been waiting?" Edwin asked, meaning in the corridor.

"A lifetime," said Janus. He was holding one hand within the folds of his coat.

Edwin tensed, shifting his weight, ready to jump back. "It doesn't need to be like this – fighting at every turn."

"That's easy for you to think, from the king's right hand."

"What if we were equal? We could help each other. Take the best from each of our plans."

"Equals?"

"I'd yield my place."

"Nature allows for no equality."

"We could try."

A slow smile grew on Janus's soft face. "You know you're

going to fail, Edwin. Else you'd never have made such an offer. When the embassy rides home with no agreement – and they will – I'll take your place by the king's side."

Edwin flinched as Janus's hand withdrew from his coat. But it was empty.

"Did you think I was going to shoot you?"

"Perhaps."

"You have me wrong. I have others do that kind of work." Janus leaned closer, dropped his voice to a whisper. "I heard the other magician in that room of yours, pacing, pacing. Should have been quieter when you were away."

Edwin felt the fear curdling his stomach. "Think of my offer," he said, trying to keep his voice steady. "For the good of the kingdom."

Janus laughed, a soft, wet sound. "Don't insult me with the greater good. This was never that." And then, as he turned to go, "What would you say to a bullet in the head?"

At the door, Edwin listened to silence and pictured his sister lying on the floor in a spreading pool of blood. His hands were trembling so badly that he could hardly turn the tumblers of the lock.

The door swung open. And there she stood, ten feet back, face grim, pistol levelled. Seeing him, she lowered her arm.

"I was listening," she said. "I heard it all."

Elizabeth could not bear to be alone. She begged him to stay, even though there wasn't enough bedding for them both.

"We can share," she said, spreading out a blanket on the floorboards.

He lay himself down on the edge of it, facing the stove. And she lay with her back towards his. The other blankets covered them, keeping in their warmth. They had each travelled far, in many ways. But somehow they always seemed to be reaching back towards that lost childhood, nestled together in the back of a wagon in the Circus of Mysteries.

CHAPTER 34

Elizabeth woke in the dark to the squeak of the stove door opening. Her brother had squatted to feed twigs into the remains of last night's fire. The embers cast an orange glow over the side of his face. Then yellow flame blossomed and the kindling crackled. She watched as he began arranging larger sticks on top of the pile.

In sleep, it had seemed they were close again, but glimpsed in the flame light, his face had become a mask once more.

"We're both acting parts," she said.

He turned. "It's hard not to." And then, "I didn't mean to wake you. I'm sorry."

She'd shared things with this stranger, her brother. Things she'd told no one before. Not Julia or Tinker. Nor even Farthing. Some of it she'd hardly been aware of herself, as if her feelings had needed forming into words before she could fully see them. But through all those confidences, a barrier had remained.

"The sun will be up soon," he said, then set off towards the door. "I've something to do."

"What about me?"

"Please wait."

From frustration, she hissed towards his back, "Do I have a choice?"

Then she was alone. Again.

In truth she did have choices. None of them she liked. She knew enough now to be able to escape from the castle: a treacherous climb down that thin rope with Mary Brackenstow. The rivers would guide them. Food would be the problem. She could fashion a barbed hook, find something to bait it with, trail it in the water. But lighting a fire would be too great a risk. They would need to eat the fish raw, drink river water, stay alive. She could get them back to the border, to Lewiston.

But what then? She would be returning as she left, accompanied by a mad woman and rumours of a treaty. Even if she risked waiting to see the thing signed, she'd be offering the Patent Office little more than her beliefs and asking for her life in exchange. A bargain written in smoke. They would surely refuse, just as they had at the start.

She thought again of Julia and Tinker. Being away from them had been a kind of bereavement. And her dear John Farthing. The idea that she might never see them again was more than she could bear to hold. Through her hours alone, she had tried to keep it from her mind. But it took such strength to hold the thought at bay, and she did not think she could sustain the discipline for much longer.

Grey light showed in the window. She got up, began to pace. In the prison that was the Room of Cabinets, she'd walked the path from wall to wall so many times, it seemed a wonder the floorboards hadn't been worn away.

What if she were to stay and her brother's plans came to grief? If the embassy were to return to Newfoundland leaving the document unsigned, Edwin's life would be in danger. He'd told her that his fate and the negotiations were tangled. Having overheard Janus's threats, she knew it for herself.

She imagined her brother abandoning Crown Point, returning with her to the Gas-Lit Empire. She could take him to the agents of the Patent Office. Edwin knew the full inventory of the forces of Oregon: troop numbers and divisions, their bases and supply dumps, the capacity and weaknesses of their new weapons, the place and method of manufacture of each item. Such a hoard of knowledge would surely be enough for the Patent Office to spare her life.

Kneeling in the window seat, she looked out over the valley, which was still in shadow, though sunlight had reached the high peaks. In all her travels she had never seen a place more beautiful than Oregon. It was hard to imagine Edwin abandoning it and returning to the gentle hills of England, but harder still to think that he could betray all his ideals. To bargain for her life, he would be handing over the means of destruction of everything he'd worked for. And everything their mother had worked for. If he did it, he might never forgive himself.

Sunlight crept its way down the slopes of the hills. The sky brightened from grey to blue. When the tumblers clicked in the door lock, she realised she'd been drifting in her thoughts. Weaving back between the cabinets, she set to greet him, but stopped dead.

Edwin's hair was still tied back in a queue, but the eyes had been adorned like a woman's, dark lines of kohl making them seem larger. Trousers had changed to khaki riding skirt but the shirt and jacket were of the male fashion. Edwin seemed uncertain standing in front of her. Shy, almost.

"Well?"

At first, she could think of nothing to say. "I'm… sorry."

"For what?"

"Staring. It's just… I don't know. This… half and half…"

"I often go about like this."

"They see you then?" she asked. "In between?"

"Yes. I wanted you to know. I'm sorry, but I don't know why I kept it from you before."

She felt a sense of recognition. "It's almost like I knew."

"What about you?" Edwin asked. "When we were children, we sometimes dressed as boys. Sometimes as girls. And now, here you are dressed as a man. But you also go as a woman. How do you choose which way to dress?"

"There are places where I need to appear like a man," she said. "And places where I need to be a woman. It's not me who chooses. It's rules that other people set – who can do what and where, man or woman. It's a disguise, I suppose. Both ways perhaps."

Edwin nodded. "I'm happy for you," they said. But a shadow of disappointment had crossed their face. "If it was left to you… might you choose to be like this? Like me?"

It was a question she'd been asked before in a different form. One of the Sargasso pirates had wanted to know if she would choose masculine or feminine clothes. At the time she'd said she'd wear a dress, though she hadn't been certain. But here there was a third option. An ambiguity.

"Do others at Crown Point dress this way?"

"No."

"But they don't mind you doing it?"

"Some do. Some don't. Prejudice takes time to wash away. What would they say in London?"

She didn't want to tell him that it would be impossible in England to appear that way, ambiguously poised between genders. She imagined the laughter and shouts of outrage they'd face. A crowd of jeering men and women. A mob, shouting all the louder to drown out their own uncertainties. But to admit it would feel like a betrayal of her father's choice. And her own. Somehow she'd become a bad apologist for the Gas-Lit Empire, the grudging defender of a lesser evil.

Edwin nodded, as if her silence had proved him right.

"I'm glad you can do this," she said. And then, perhaps to change the subject because of her own uncertainty: "What will happen if your meetings fail, if the Newfoundlanders won't sign your agreement?"

"I'll show them some marvel. I'll make them believe. They'll agree in the end. They must."

"But if they don't... might you come away with me?"

She knew by his face that he'd thought of it already: the impossibility of his helping the Gas-Lit empire, juxtaposed against the impossibility of life continuing if his agreement was not signed.

"You've asked me to think things I don't want to think," she said. "I've done it. And I'm helping you. Please now do the same for me. If your plans fall to ruin, will you come with me? Back east. We can escape together. If you agree to that, I will help you do all you wish. We will devise a conjuring trick, an illusion grand enough to persuade them of your power. I'll give it all my ability."

"You'd gamble with the fate of the world?" Edwin asked.

"We've been doing that from the start. This is about us. It's about finding a way to live."

"Then I agree," he said.

The trick had to be a demonstration of magic, with no possible explanation based on chance. It would be witnessed by all the members of the delegation in the same moment. And then, in the stunned aftermath, with their understanding of the immutable laws of nature in flux, a prophecy would be presented: a prediction of inevitable victory should the alliance be formed.

"It could be the bullet catch," Edwin said.

They had placed the two pistols side by side on the workbench. The inlaid turquoise seemed identical. Not just the outline of the leaping hare: the marvel of it was revealed in Edwin's magnifying lens, the pattern of filaments and mottled imperfections in the precious stone. One could not be told from the other. Two thin slices must have been cut from the same lump, a fraction of an inch separating them in the rock. And though the two pistols had been taken to opposite ends of the Earth, now here they were united again, lying together, the miracle of their similarity revealed.

"Don't worry about how the trick might be performed," Elizabeth said. "Think of what effect you would like to show."

"Fire coming out of my hands…"

"We could do that."

"…and consuming Janus!"

"I'm trying to be serious!" she said, but Edwin was smiling at her and she could not remain severe.

"I'm sorry. But this is a grim business. If we can't laugh, then what are we even trying to save?"

"Perhaps we could vanish him," she said, now smiling herself.

"To make him vanish would amaze them. But they would applaud when we made him reappear. Which I would rather not happen!"

"Then let us change Janus into you. Or have you transport yourself from one place to another."

Elizabeth laid her hand on one of their mother's cabinets. Somehow their conversation had strayed to the grand illusion of that shared past. On the stage, a child would be seen entering one of the cabinets. A moment and a flash of gunpowder later, they would emerge from the cabinet on the opposite side of the stage, carrying some unique token: a playing card, a watch, a pistol, to prove it was the same child.

Sometimes it was Edwin who disappeared and Elizabeth who appeared. Sometimes the other way around. Either of them could play boy or girl. Each knew both parts.

"Where do we perform the trick?" she asked.

"There is to be a grand feast before the embassy departs. That is the place. All must see it. A shared experience, so that none of them can afterwards doubt their memory."

"It will seem odd, don't you think – to have cabinets there?"

Edwin stared at the bare wall, as if looking through it. "Our cabinets must seem to be something else," they said.

"The more they belong in that setting, the more impossible the illusion will seem."

"Then shall one of us burst from a giant pie?" she asked, meaning it as a joke.

"Not a pie. The kitchens would need to help. And no one else can know. But it could be a container of food. The Newfies love to eat fresh fruit. We could have a chest of apples and pears set before them."

Elizabeth pictured it in her mind. It would seem the most natural thing in the world. A generous gift for the embassy. It could sit before them through the meal. Then the king's magician would announce a demonstration of his power. In some way he would disappear. A fraction of a second later – just enough for their minds to be able to understand the vanishing – the fruit would begin to shift and spill. The same magician would eme Drge before their eyes.

"I must be the one to appear," Edwin said.

She understood the reason. After the miracle would come the prophecy and the treaty document. Even if she could be schooled in the politics and know everything to say, it would be hard to argue for a treaty that she wanted to fail.

"You can leave the feast to fetch a gift for them," she said. "Then I return in your guise, with servants carrying a cask of fruit, which is laid before them. You're going to be cramped in a small space. How long can you last? We're not as small as we used to be."

"I'll manage as long as it takes."

"But how shall I disappear?" she asked.

"In fire and thunder," Edwin said, smiling. "You will vanish in fire and thunder. I will show you how."

CHAPTER 35

When Elizabeth had applied the makeup to darken her chin, giving the suggestion of stubble to match her brother, she stood at arm's length from him and took her turn with the hand glass. They were not so similar, she thought. His nose was bigger, and his chin. He was taller by a couple of inches and broader in the shoulder. It seemed impossible that anyone had mistaken her for him. Yet they had. As with so many illusions, it worked through confidence and context.

And shadows, she thought. Under the full sun, a sceptical eye might see the truth.

"You'll only be talking with guards," he said. "And that'll be in a dark passageway. When the door opens, try to be turned away from them. That's when you'll have full daylight on you. And don't look back."

"I'll be fine," she said, silently telling herself that it was excitement stirring her heart, not fear. She'd be outside the castle for the first time since she arrived. If they let her through.

"Half an hour," he said. "Then I follow. But through the front gate."

Day transformed the castle. Small windows let in light, painting the stones with a warmer tint. The light faded around the turn of the spiral, greying until the next window came into view. So much detail she had missed on her night walks.

The corridors were no longer dank with the cold night air, but carrying the hints of smells: food and perfume and body odour and woodsmoke and more things she couldn't quite name but which left a feeling in her nonetheless.

Then there were people: three young men decked out in kitchen aprons. *Make them get out of your way*, her brother had said. So she did, opening her stride.

"G'morning magician," they chorused.

She pushed through, brushing a shoulder against one. Striding away, she caught their hushed laughter.

Edwin had told her the route, made her repeat the list of turns and stairs, directing her through those passageways used by servants.

And spies.

"What brings you here?"

Janus's voice, close and quiet, made her wheel. He emerged from something that might have been a storeroom. She couldn't read the soft features of his face. The man she least wanted to meet. She took half a step to the side, putting the light of the window behind her, hoping the shadow on her face would be deep enough.

"Did I startle you?" he asked.

"Yes."

The curve of his mouth suggested a smile. "What brings you to the west range?"

"Why do you ask?"

"Concern?" He spoke the word as if it was unfamiliar.

"I'm going somewhere," she said.

"Indeed. Well, the First Counsellor has his work, I suppose. But what of the negotiations? You and your new friends, huddled in that room for hours. The way the scribes tell it, you're giving away all our gold and goods."

"It's only writing. We've given nothing."

"And nor have they."

"But they will."

"We should make a wager of it," Janus said. "You say the agreement will be signed. I say not. Will you take my bet?"

"No," she said, just wanting to get away.

But Janus flinched. Anger showed on his face, real and unhidden. "You go too far! I will see you die, magician," he hissed. "And then I will piss on your corpse. Just like I pissed on your mother's."

Elizabeth walked on in a daze of shock, unable to understand the feelings that were surging, not understanding the full meaning of what she'd heard, glad of the darkness, for there were no windows on that stretch of passage. She wasn't in full control. She did know that.

Then the sally port was ahead. One of the guards raised a lamp. She put up a hand to shield her eyes.

"I'm going for a walk," she said, as she'd been trained, but sounding too shrill.

"Why?" asked the guard with the lantern.

"That's my business!"

He didn't like it. But he nodded to the other one, who stepped into the narrow way, which was the thickness of the wall, and drew back the bolts to open the door. Daylight streamed in. As he sidestepped back, he was looking directly at her.

"Out of my way!" Turmoil gave her words force.

"I'm sorry," he said, averting his gaze. "No offence."

She was through. The daylight and cold air sharpened her. She had to get away, had to trust her brother's instructions.

One path turned to run under the castle wall, heading for the front. The other, easy to miss, cut off at an angle, over the lip of the plateau. She set off along it, counted her paces, reached one hundred and twenty before finding the thicket of black hawthorn. She sidestepped as he'd instructed, ducked down and crawled under the branches into a little hollow. The hiding place had been invisible from outside.

She had no means for measuring time, and no will to bring it into focus. It passed nonetheless. Clouds moved over then cleared again. The leaves of the hawthorn shivered in the wind. A flock of small birds flitted through the branches where there had been none before. Then just as quickly they were gone.

Footsteps approached. She knew them for her brother's. A moment later he was crawling through into the hollow, a small leather bag in his hand, his eyes wide with excitement. But seeing her, he frowned.

"What's wrong?" he asked.

"Janus was there."

She told him what had happened: the fencing with words, the abrupt switch to hatred. As she spoke, his expression changed from concern to fear. She'd been going to tell him everything, but when she came to those hateful parting words, she stopped.

"What then?" Edwin asked.

"He said he wants us dead."

"He wants me dead, you mean."

"Yes. I'm sorry."

He had found the secret hollow whilst still a child. The gate guards hadn't minded the child of the magician scampering out to play. So long as it was in sight of the castle. There were other hiding places out there, but none so perfect. For a time it became a den, garrisoned by toy soldiers. One day, he would tell his sister about those happy times.

From the leather bag he pulled a thin coat, which fitted over her clothes as a kind of disguise. A skullcap completed the transformation. He watched as she tucked her hair out of sight. Anyone who happened to be looking up from the valley would see two individuals picking their way under the cliffs. Not one man magically duplicated.

Leaving the bag, he crawled out from underneath the hawthorn. Elizabeth followed on behind, along the track to the top of the gulley.

She didn't understand the taboo against refusing a wager. At Crown Point, such an act would be understood as an insult, cowardice or both. There was so much she didn't know. He would never have thought to tell her such a thing. It seemed common knowledge. Had there been witnesses, the damage would have been more severe. Janus might still whisper it around. But that would be dangerous for him.

Edwin stopped at the top of the gulley and looked down

the scree slope. "Take the rope," he said, showing her how to hold it. "Always keep one hand gripping. I'll go first. It starts steep but don't worry. It'll get shallower as we go."

Hand over hand, tree by tree, they began the descent, following the main rope at first. Then branching towards the gulley wall along the frayed line. It seemed to have deteriorated in the short time since his last visit. He could feel the stretch of it. Loose strands twisted, trying to unravel under their combined weight.

Resting against the final tree, he glanced back. She was keeping up, a grim expression on her face. Had it been another person, he would have thought them scared. But not his sister. It was another emotion, he thought, the looming encounter with the place their mother died.

Digging in his heels, he scrambled to the base of the cliff. She followed, matching his steps. Then they were picking their way around under that wall of basalt, hidden from view by the trees. At the stone, he looked back. The last of the colour had drained from her face. It seemed as if she might be sick.

He had to be honest with her. "I told you our mother went over the edge. And I did see someone go over. But I didn't have her in my sight all the time. Not for every second. So... what I mean to say is, if she'd been in on it, they could have made a switch."

"They didn't," Elizabeth said, with certainty heavy as the stone itself. "She *is* dead."

"Shall I let you... pay your respects?"

"No," she said. "Our mother isn't here."

How many times had he lain on that slab and wept? But Elizabeth didn't even bend to touch it. He realised then, and it took him aback, how much of their mother he could see in her eyes.

When Edwin had told her that they would need to leave the castle to practise the flash bomb, her thoughts had jumped to this spot. If they were going to risk it anyway, why not come to the place her mother died? Her mother's memorial was shielded from view, he'd said. From one side by the trees and from the other side by the cliff itself. They would think the bang a rifle shot. There were enough of those. It would be perfect.

She'd thought that being there would allow her to touch her sadness, perhaps to wallow in grief. But Janus had cheated her of that. Descending the slope, she had felt only anger. And here, at the memorial Edwin had so carefully arranged, she felt anger still.

Edwin put the flash bomb in her hand. It looked like a ball of putty with a metal ring attached. She closed her fingers around it to test the size, found it firmer than it looked.

"The thing is not to panic," he said. "Pull the ring clean out, drop it straight down, take a half-step back with your eyes closed. It won't bounce. It won't roll."

He made her mime the actions just as their father would have done. Or their mother. Again and again. *By repetition do the hands of the clock move slow.* And then, when she could do it flawlessly and without thought, he stood back. To give her room.

"Do it," he said.

So she did.

Pull.

Drop.

Half-step back.

Even through closed eyes, she saw the world turn white with the brightness of the flash.

CHAPTER 36

For the benefit of the embassy, Edwin was once again clothed in the fashion of the men of Crown Point. But he no longer needed to hide his nature from Elizabeth. The barriers were falling away between them. He felt empowered.

In the morning room, he greeted the king and the consort, then took his place at table and began to load his plate with slices of apple and venison.

"You've got your appetite back," said the consort.

"He's a magician," said the king. "Some days he fasts."

Edwin nodded, though she'd been right. He'd hardly noticed it himself, but the stress had been stopping him from eating. Now, his hunger made every morsel delicious.

Janus entered, bowed to the king, to Timon, to the consort, then sat. That bland smile gave nothing away. It seemed impossible that only a few hours before he'd been threatening torture.

"I hear you have your agreement written," Janus said.

"It will be the king's agreement," Edwin said. "Should he wish it."

All were staring at him.

"And if I don't wish it?" asked the king.

"Then I will throw it in the fire."

"Then I shall read it. But why the long face, Mr Janus?"

Janus's brow was indeed folded into a frown. "It is not agreed yet, sire, by either side."

The king's face darkened. It seemed he would respond, but the Master at Arms stepped into the room, face grave. "A body's been found," he said. "A mile from here."

Edwin was suddenly alert.

"Who?" asked the king.

"A working man, to judge by the clothes."

It would be bandits, Edwin thought. Yet so close to Crown Point.

The king clearly had the same idea. He scowled. "How dare they!"

"The body was left in the track. No sign they tried to hide it."

"Which track?" the king asked.

"Just off the east road. Halfway to the Cairn."

Edwin's mouth had turned dry. "How's the man not known?"

"Oh, he may yet be," said the Master at Arms. "But not by his face. He's been lying there through one day and one night at least. The crows have been at him. And there was... damage."

Edwin had seen the Master at Arms describe battles where scores of men had died. His unease in making this report seemed wrong. Edwin's stomach tightened. "Was anything found with the body?"

"A worker's knife. A key. Tinder box, steel, a length of twine, a handful of grain..."

"What kind of grain?" Edwin asked.

The Master at Arms shrugged. "Didn't see it myself."

"How was the grain carried?"

"A pocket. Sewn into the poor man's coat."

"Where's the body now?"

"I sent men with a handcart. Give it an hour and they'll be back. Then you can see for yourself."

The king was peering at Edwin. "You have a thought on who it might be?"

Edwin answered with a shake of the head, not trusting himself to lie in a level voice. "If you'll give me leave, sire. I'd like to see the body where it lies."

The king gestured his assent, suspicious it seemed.

Edwin marched from the room, breaking into a run only once he was clear of the royal apartments. The guards at the gate stood back to let him pass.

He had argued with Janus over the lives of millions. No doubt the man might order an army to attack. But somehow, it was hard to imagine that pasty-faced counsellor getting his own hands wet. *Please don't let it be Pentecost,* he thought. *Please don't let it be him.* But in another part of his mind, he already knew and was ashamed that his care was more for what the death might mean than for the snuffing out of the life of a man who had helped him so much over the years. And his mother before him.

He caught up with the soldiers and the handcart, walked behind them until his breath was less ragged, and then took over the lead. Two more of the castle's garrison had been left to guard the corpse. The feet were the only part of it visible.

"Show me," Edwin told them.

One stooped and half pulled back the cloak that had been covering it, revealing the back of the body, but keeping the front covered.

It was Pentecost, though Edwin wouldn't have known without the context of place and time. A lumpen man with steely grey hair, whose fat hands had been so gentle in gathering pigeons from their cages. How often had he dipped inside his coat and flourished a few grains of wheat or corn to scatter as treats.

"Show me the rest," he said.

The guard didn't like it, but didn't complain. He stood back and dropped the cloak away from the body.

A trickle of blood had seeped from a coin-sized wound in the steel grey hair. An entry wound, Edwin thought, and then remembered Janus's threat: *a bullet in the head.* Taking a breath to steady himself, he stepped to the other side of the body, looked then retched. The bullet must have fragmented on its way through. Little wonder no one had been able to recognise the pigeon master's assistant. Everyone thought he was visiting his sick mother, in any case. Who would think that such a mass of flesh and shattered bone had once been the face of gentle Pentecost?

But his identity would soon be revealed. Then the king would send out trackers. The pigeon loft was a place of politics, after all. The secrets of the kingdom passed through it. With the ground dry and dusty, there wasn't much that Edwin could see, beyond a chaos of prints from garrison boots. But not so long before, he had walked on beyond that point to their night time meeting.

"Has anyone gone further up the track?" he asked.

The guards said no.

"Then take the body back to the castle. I'm going to scout around the cairn."

As he walked away, he wished that he had the skill to read the ground like the king's hunting master. But with every pace, he allowed his feet to scuff away any evidence that he, or the killer, might have left behind.

A wintery breeze rattled the branches of scrub trees on either side of the path. He shivered, trying not to think of that ruined face. At the cairn, he knelt, getting his head low. It seemed the wind had done his work for him, scouring the dust of traces.

"Looking for something?"

The voice made Edwin scramble back to his feet. Janus had crept close without him hearing. The man wore an easy smile. They were quite alone.

Edwin tried not to let his panic show. "What are you doing here?"

"Watching you. Were you checking for footprints?"

"I… I was."

"And do you think this might be something to do with it?"

Janus held out a bag, which Edwin found himself accepting. It was his own, once filled with silver. Now empty.

"Do you know it?" Janus asked, the soft clay of his face impossible to read. "I found it caught in the scrub." He gestured back along the path.

Edwin had passed that way and not seen it.

They were standing close enough that either could have reached out with a knife and stabbed the other. Edwin tried not to blink, though his eyes were stinging.

"Why do you hate me?" he asked.

"How little you understand," Janus said. "You and your

mother. She was the same – always missing the subtext. You want to know where the hate came from? It was bequeathed to me. There! I've given you something for free. I wouldn't want you to die without knowing."

Edwin could think of only one person who might be able and willing to tell him the answer. His feet took him to her door, and into that room of pastel silks. The consort must have sensed the turmoil in his thoughts, because she dismissed her ladies-in-waiting and stepped with him to the window furthest from any ears that might hear.

"Who was Janus's mother?" he whispered.

"The blacksmith's wife. Why is it you ask?"

"I thought… I don't know. It's something he said to me."

She sighed, as if disappointed with a child who won't learn their lesson. "You didn't ask about his father."

"The blacksmith."

She put a hand on her belly. "All can see when a woman carries a child. But a man can sow his seed in any bed and be gone by morning."

"Not the blacksmith?"

She nodded as if encouraging him to take the final step. Only then did he understand.

"The old magician…"

"Yes," she said. "The father of your enemy is the man your mother had killed."

PART FIVE

CHAPTER 37

On the morning of the final day before the embassy departed, a rainstorm blew in to lash the window glass. So dark was the cloud that an hour after the sun should have risen, lamps were being lit again around the castle. A bad omen, for those who believed in such things. If the squall continued, the farewell feast would be held in the Great Hall instead of the courtyard. That would mean a hundred or so fewer revellers to witness the illusion. But worse, Elizabeth's vanishing would need to be re-designed.

In the courtyard, she would be able to back up to one of the doorways and under cover of the flash, slip away into an empty passage. But servants would be using all the passages outside the Great Hall. Unless some task could be devised to send them all back to the kitchens.

"The rain will stop," Edwin said, peering out of the window, not believing it himself but wanting to make their task seem less impossible. There was work to be done and the weather they could not control.

Ever since he'd finalised the words of the agreement, Elizabeth had been transcribing them onto parchment. A painstaking process. One copy for the King of Crown Point. One copy for the King of Newfoundland to sign: this Edwin would keep with him as he lay waiting in the crate. And one copy, the twin of Edwin's, for Elizabeth to be holding when she vanished. The size of her handwriting had to be constant. The number of lines and the position of the text on the page. Bent over the workbench, she kept her back so still as to seem like a statue. But whenever he looked over her shoulder, he saw the pen moving in her hand.

His own task was to finish the crate in which he would conceal himself. It had been one of his mother's unfinished props. She'd prepared the outside surfaces with that distinctive lacquer, and would have added arcane symbols in red had she lived to complete it. But plain black worked far better for this illusion.

He had taken out the lowest plank on the rear wall and added a hinge, so that it would swing out on the pressing of a secret catch. The hole was just big enough for him to crawl inside. Above that hidden space, a rectangle of cotton formed a thin barrier. Strong enough, he hoped, to carry the weight of apples and pears that would rest on top.

As he was hammering in the last small nail, she came over to inspect.

"Are you done?" she asked.

He stood back and surveyed his work. "I still see a dozen flaws."

"Well, it looks perfect to me," she said. "I was never taught all this – the building of stage props."

At the workbench, he examined the twin parchments, which she'd left side by side. She'd chosen sheets with similar patterns of imperfections. And the placing of the text was marvellously similar.

Standing next to him, she frowned. "They're quite different."

"I couldn't have done it half so well," he said. "And they'll never be seen together. Except by us."

Flipping back the lid of the ink pot, she dipped the pen and placed a matching spot on the right-hand margin of each parchment. Then she wiped them away with her thumb, leaving a smudge on each sheet.

"That's better," she said.

And it was.

Elizabeth had to hide when the servants came to carry away the crate. He'd covered the whole thing in sacking, to stop them looking inside and seeing its secrets. They bumped it on the inner pillar of the spiral stairs. Following behind, he found himself clenching his teeth. If by accident they pressed in the wrong place, the hidden door would fall free. They knocked it again on the frame of the door leading out into the courtyard. And one more time in the kitchen on the corner of a table on which great piles of vegetables were being diced.

By the time they reached the small storeroom, he felt sick with tension. Having thanked the men and dismissed them, he leaned his back against the closed door, and steadied his breathing.

The barrels of fruit were already waiting: pears and two varieties of apple. He locked the door, stripped off the sacking and examined the crate for damage. Two of the knocks had chipped lacquer from the corners. The third, the kitchen table, he thought, had left a small dent in the middle of a surface. But the catch worked and the door still sat flush. He began placing the first layer of fruit inside, resting it on the cotton barrier, alert for any sound of tearing cloth as he filled it almost to the top. When it was done, he stood back. It looked better than he had imagined. The fruit was beautiful: colour and sheer abundance drawing the eye.

He began to allow himself to think that it might work. They would perform this apparent miracle. Everyone would feel the power of it. Even the most sceptical. After that, he would make his prophecy: power and wealth for Newfoundland if the alliance was made. He would unfold the parchment. Red would at last agree. Gilad would nod. And Brandt would sign.

The rain had stopped and sunlight slanted down over the courtyard walls. The puddles had already started to dry. He stood, taking in the beauty of it all.

A dazzling clarity surrounds the conjurer when everything that can be controlled has been controlled. It is the awareness of detail, which is the sum of all the planning and preparation that has gone before. As Edwin walked across the courtyard, he could feel the texture of the flagstones under his every step. The men and women setting out tables seemed to move with unnatural slowness, whilst he could take everything in with a single glance.

They stood facing each other, he and his sister, dressed in their identical clothes: navy blue canvas trousers, white shirts, jackets of lighter blue. She had trimmed his hair so to more perfectly match the length of her own, then tied it back in the masculine fashion. Each of them wore a brown bowler hat.

Looking at themselves in the hand glass, she had pointed out a slight difference in complexion. Despite her time on fogbound Newfoundland, Elizabeth's cheeks showed touches of apple-blush. Powdering both their faces made them more similar. But it was the final detail that completed the illusion.

"This might hurt," she said.

That proved an understatement. With her little finger, she dabbed a drop of soapy water into the corner of his left eye. The sting of it made him suck air through his teeth.

Through his one good eye, he watched her do the same to herself and double over in pain. But when the tears had stopped running and they looked at themselves again, he understood the genius of her idea. She'd performed the same trick as with the parchment. Each of them now bore one red and weepy eye. Anyone looking at them would be too conscious of that unsightly blemish to think of the finer points of their complexion.

"How long will it last?"

"Long enough," she said.

She held up her pistol in one hand and a copy of the agreement in the other. He matched the move, except that her pistol was loaded. Those objects would be the convincer. She would be holding them when she fired a shot in the air and disappeared in a pyrotechnic flash. He would be holding them when he emerged. Who would doubt that they were one and the same?

The flintlocks seemed more ceremonial than practical.

They could be worn from the belt and upset no one at the feast.

"This is it then," he said, meaning the last moment for them to be alone together before they performed the Vanishing Man.

"We're ready," she said.

She'd agreed to help him to this point. But for everything that lay beyond, their hopes fell in different directions.

"Good luck," he said, not understanding how he could mean it whilst yearning for his own plans to succeed. Yet somehow he did. It was a kind of love.

The upper corridors were empty, but expectant voices bubbled up through windows from the courtyard below. Descending the stairs, the sounds and smells became more vivid: roasting meats and spices, conversation and laughter. The ordinary people cared nothing for negotiations and treaties. But tonight they would feast and drink. Tomorrow could care for itself.

Outside the royal apartments, the Master at Arms was in full flow, relating a tale of military prowess, to judge by the sweep of his sword arm. His audience, two ladies-in-waiting, giggled, hands before mouths. On seeing Edwin, the Master at Arms broke off to stare.

"God's blood, magician! But what have you done to your eye?"

"An accident."

They'd fashioned a story, Edwin and Elizabeth, a magical experiment gone wrong. But the Master at Arms asked for no more explanation. Pulling an expression of disgust, he looked away, as did the ladies-in-waiting.

"What will the Newfies think of you?" said one.

"They'll say you're a devil," said the other.

It was working like a dream.

In the courtyard, the fire was in its first blaze, sending up flames half again the height of a man. The servants had to turn their faces away from it as they passed carrying serving trays and wine butts. Janus was nowhere to be seen. Nor at first could he see anyone from the embassy. Then a hand touched him lightly on the shoulder and he turned to see Gilad next to him.

"Light-footed, as always," Edwin said.

Gilad examined him. "You, my friend, should get to a doctor."

He seemed genuinely concerned about the eye. Given a chance, they might even grow to be friends, Edwin thought.

"It was an accident," he said. "It'll heal."

Gilad seemed not so sure.

On the far side of the courtyard a bottle slipped from a servant's grip and smashed on the flagstones. The kitchen boys laughed. The overseer shouted.

"You've done well," Gilad said. "Getting the words of an agreement."

"With your help."

"I'm sorry you'll not see it signed."

"I might yet."

"We're leaving tomorrow."

"Then I still have a few hours."

Gilad laughed. "I like the way you think. But next year perhaps. Or you could come back with us to the Rock. Talk to my king face-to-face."

"Perhaps," said Edwin.

Gilad nodded a respectful farewell and headed back towards Brandt's apartment. Through the whole conversation, he'd not once dropped his gaze. Edwin had the queasy sensation that the man had been seeing him in the way that a conjuror sees another: storing away each detail for later.

The fire was falling in on itself, forming its bed of embers. The lower benches were already filling with castle workers and their families, with farmers and traders from beyond the walls. But if he ran, Edwin thought he could get to the Room of Cabinets, warn his sister and be back in the courtyard in time. With enough light, Gilad would surely see through her disguise. When the time came, she would have to stay away from him.

But as he stepped inside, he came up against a rush of servants moving in the other direction, getting out of the way. Timon, the king and the consort were approaching, shoulder to shoulder. Edwin backed up to the wall to let them pass, but the king saw him and stopped.

"My faithful magician!" the king's voice boomed. "This is your day. I'll have no slinking in the shadows." He put an arm over Edwin's shoulder, like a brother, then dropped his voice. "All will be done this night. One way or another. I want you to promise that you'll give Mr Janus your loyalty too, if he becomes First Counsellor. Will you do that?"

"Yes, sire. I promise."

"Good! Good! But what has happened to your eye?"

"An accident."

"Never mind, then," said the king.

Edwin found himself being pulled along, back into the courtyard, up onto the raised platform, just as Brandt was emerging on the other side, followed by the other twelve men of the embassy.

The room had been a wonder to Elizabeth when she first arrived in the castle. Its objects with their familiar-yet-strange textures and scents had each been the door to a lost memory. It had taken only a few hours for her to understand that the room would be her prison. How quickly those objects of wonder had become ordinary.

But now, with everything prepared, she felt a pang of impending loss and stepped back to open one of the cabinets. That camphor smell: the last trace of her mother. With no remains and no grave, part of her mind had been carrying a hope. Perhaps denial was a kind of grieving. But there had been perfect sincerity in Janus's cruel words. All doubt was gone, replaced by another kind of grief.

She closed the cabinet, took one final look around the room, then stepped out to meet her fate, whatever that would be, not expecting to return.

Two floors down, she found a window alcove from which she could spy on the throng of people and lights below. But for a square around the fire, the whole courtyard had been filled with long tables. The lower classes were seated to the right. The more well-to-do to the left. And at the far left, on a raised platform, sat the dignitaries. It was her first time seeing most of them, but from Edwin's descriptions she could name them all.

The king sat in the middle. To one side sat the consort, Red, the Master at Arms, Tomo and the Hunting Master. To the other side sat Brandt, Timon, Gilad, Edwin and

Janus. When the time came, her brother would make his excuses and head to the storeroom where the lacquered crate lay waiting. From that moment he would disappear and Elizabeth could take the risk of being seen. She would enter the kitchens by a back door, order help in carrying the gift back to the embassy, then lead the way.

It was that most risky thing: a performance without a dress rehearsal.

From her shadowed lookout, she watched the feast. They'd be eating tenderloin and soft white bread on the high table, gritty crust and beef shin stew away to the right. But whether they were drinking fine Oregon wine or strong dark beer, the effect would be the same. The din of chatter and eating increased. Tipsy, they'd be less likely to see through the trick. But if they drank too much, they wouldn't see the full marvel of it, nor believe their memories when they sobered up the following day.

The noise of the feast became louder. Here and there groups of men and women were standing to toast each other. One reveller tried to clamber up on a bench and ended up sprawled on the table.

Elizabeth missed the moment when her brother left his seat. But when she looked back, he was weaving between the benches, on his way to the kitchens. As he stepped through the doorway to leave the courtyard, she began to count in her head, trying to keep slow and regular, though her heart had begun to speed. When her count reached sixty, she set off. Along the corridor. Around the corner. Then down one flight of steps. The upper stories had been deserted. But here at ground level, servants were hurrying about. She was following the same path that Edwin would have walked a minute before. Any of these people might have seen him. The trick was not to hide, to occupy the centre of each passageway. Into the kitchens, the heat and smells suddenly intense. Striding between preparation tables. Then to stop, turn, summon up all her bravery, trusting that masculine voice, long practised.

"I need four of you to help carry. Men not boys."

Three were there in the kitchen. They beckoned a fourth from outside, then set off following her, along a path she'd memorised from Edwin's description. Second exit from the end of the kitchen. Short passage. Third storeroom on the left.

She began to open the door, but froze. Edwin stood immediately inside waving his hands in warning. Slamming it closed again, she wheeled to face the kitchen servants, mustered all her authority, pointed back the way they'd come.

"Wait over there."

They obeyed. Hesitant. Casting questioning looks to each other.

Opening the door a crack, she slipped inside.

"You should be in the crate!" she hissed.

"It's Gilad," he whispered. "You can't let him get too close. He'll see the difference between us."

Something scuffed against the outside of the door. The servants, trying to listen. She jabbed her finger towards the crate. Edwin nodded. He took her hand, placed it on his forehead, his eyes not leaving hers, as if he had some premonition, or had guessed her plans and knew that he would never see her again. When he pulled his hand away, the weight of the tragedy hit her.

"I love you, my brother," she whispered.

For a moment he smiled. Then he was down on his knees, opening the secret hatch at the bottom of the crate. As he tried to worm his way inside, it seemed they might have made a mistake, that the space would be too small. But then he twisted his back, bringing his shoulders level with the ground. The fruit at the top of the crate shifted and heaved as he pushed himself inside. His legs disappeared. Then he brought his hand around to close the panel, completing the illusion.

The servants scrambled back as she opened the door. And when she beckoned them in, they looked around, wide-eyed, as if expecting to see another person. So they had overheard something. But then, nothing was too strange for the Magician of Crown Point. Remembering the Arthurs, she made her hands dance in the air, miming the undoing of corset stays. The servants were trembling with fear by the time she gave the order:

"Pick up the crate. And be gentle. It is a gift for the guests of our king!"

CHAPTER 38

She led them back through the kitchen and then out into the noise of the courtyard. A man and a woman were standing on one of the tables near the corner, singing a duet. As Elizabeth led her strange procession between the tables, they broke off their song. The chatter died down all around.

"What is this?" the king asked, a half-smile playing over his face, as if he thought it might be a joke that he hadn't quite seen through.

Elizabeth had the men place the crate on the end of one of the long tables, closest to the king. "A gift for our friends from the west. Apples and pears from Oregon."

"Thank you," said Brandt. His face was flushed from the wine.

Elizabeth bowed towards Brandt and then, deeper, towards the king. The noise of chatter began again behind her. Her rush of panic was subsiding. The first task was over.

But now she had another problem: to move away from the crate, to stop the minds of the audience resting on it. The actual trick and reveal should always be separated by as much time and space as possible. But going back to her brother's seat would put her directly between Gilad and Janus, the man who might see through the disguise and the man who wanted her dead. Some shadow lay over that end of the table, but not enough to trust.

Two of the kitchen servants were still waiting to be dismissed. "The fire's getting low," she said. "Throw on more wood."

She made her way between the king's platform and the ends of the long tables, as if she were Edwin returning to his seat. Gilad was beckoning. She waved to him, a vague gesture, a suggestion that she would be there presently. But she was slowing to a stop. One of the revellers blew a stream of tobacco smoke towards her face then laughed.

"Shorry, magician."

She could smell foot odour. The chatter had become a din.

Then the kitchen servants were back, carrying armfuls of split logs, tossing them into the middle of the pile of embers. Sparks leapt into the night air. Those sitting closest to the fire wouldn't thank her. New yellow flames licked from the logs, growing taller as she watched, brightening. Quickly brighter than the lamps and torches around the courtyard. But further away, the shadows deepened. It would have to be enough.

"We thought we'd lost you," Gilad said, when she lowered herself into her brother's seat.

"The duties of a magician," she replied.

"If only magic were real," he said, laughter in his voice.

"You shouldn't tease him," Janus said, from the end of the high table. "It's a precarious job."

"How so?" Gilad asked, speaking across her.

"A magician is only as good as his last prophecy. Fail and fall. That's the way with magicians. They always do in the end. One mistake and they're thrown from the top of the castle. Like your mother, Edwin. I can still remember the sound she made when she hit the rocks."

Elizabeth's hands had bunched into fists, as if through a will of their own.

"Edwin is too clever for that to happen," Gilad said. There was still a smile in his voice, as if such banter was not dangerous.

"He's not as clever as he thinks," Janus said.

It wasn't just rudeness. Elizabeth could feel a dangerous game at play, but didn't know the rules. Even with the shadows, coming back to her brother's place had been a mistake. It was too soon to perform the trick, but she had to get away and let Edwin take over.

She stood. "Excuse me."

"You can't be leaving already," Gilad said.

"I'm sorry."

She stepped down from the platform, made her way back towards the crate. Her brother wouldn't be expecting her so soon. But when he heard her speak, he'd understand. He'd be ready to reveal himself.

As she reached the crate, a hand tried to grab her arm from behind. She twisted free and wheeled to discover that Janus had followed her. Gilad was there too.

"Running away?" Janus asked.

Elizabeth was aware of the king and Brandt watching from the high table.

"This isn't a night for argument," Gilad said.

Janus wouldn't be stopped. "This magician refused my wager. Did you not know? He is a coward and a cheat. If his magic were so strong that he knows the future, then he'd take my bet."

All talk on the high table had stopped.

Timon's face showed alarm. "You turned down a wager?"

Janus nodded. "The magician said our guests would sign the agreement. I said they would not. I challenged him to put money behind his words. But he refused."

Edwin would know what to do. And him so close, he would be hearing every word. Anything she said might be the end of them both.

"He's lying," she said. There'd been no witnesses, after all.

"Lying?" asked the king. He seemed angry. But there was no way back.

She nodded, feeling the tension and the hush rippling out from person to person. Quiet fell in the courtyard. A hint of pleasure flickered across Janus's face.

"I demand satisfaction," he said.

The king closed his eyes. His cheek muscle twitched. "This does not please me," he growled.

From somewhere Janus had found a handgun. He placed it on the table before the king.

"Yours too," said Timon, his face grave.

She unholstered her flintlock and put it down.

"Are you both resolved?" asked the king.

"I am," said Janus, taking up his gun.

When she didn't at first answer, Timon hissed at her, "You've got to say it!"

So she did. "I am." And found herself reaching to take

her pistol, as if her hand had been animated by someone else's will.

The wood of the handle felt warm, the turquoise cool. For a moment the barrel pointed directly at Janus's chest. Then she realized what she was doing and angled it down at the flagstones.

"If you must do this thing, then do it quickly," said the king.

"How?"

"Walk away," said Timon. "Then turn and fire. Simple as that."

Her thoughts were spinning. Janus was not a fighter, Edwin had said. He calculated everything. He took no risks. Yet he seemed too certain of himself. Unless there was a trick.

"Choose your ground," said the king.

Everyone was staring at her. She had to think. The crate rested at the end of a long trestle table, running directly away from the king, ending near the far wall of the courtyard, a doorway lay immediately beyond. She clambered up.

Timon stood. "What the hell are you doing?"

"I'm doing what the king asked. I'm choosing my ground."

She took a step away from the dais, away from the crate, feeling the flex of the tabletop underneath her weight. It took a few moments for the people sitting on either side to understand what was happening. Then they were getting to their feet and scrambling clear. Elizabeth stepped over wine goblets and between platters. She glanced over her shoulder to see the king, the consort and the embassy moving away to either side. Only Timon remained, grim excitement in his eyes as he pointed to the table. Janus climbed up. They were both of them above the throng now. Janus still wore that half-smile, as if every choice she made was playing further nto his plans. Something was very wrong.

The side of her foot caught against a cup and sent red wine spilling into the white tablecloth. Her gun had been in its holster through the feast. No one could have tampered with it. Her thoughts were coming too fast to hold on to. She was halfway down the length of the table already. Even if they'd been marksmen, the chances of hitting with handguns would be low at that distance. They would each fire a shot. They would each miss. Janus would have earned nothing but the displeasure of the king.

Then a memory flashed in her mind: the story Edwin had told of another miraculous shot, the king bringing down a deer from the back of a galloping horse. A second shooter, armed with a long rifle. Windows dotted the wall behind the platform. When she reached the end of the table and turned to face her enemy, a second gun would surely be aiming at her chest.

Lying cramped in stuffy darkness, Edwin had been listening to the sounds of the feast, aware that his toes were slowly going numb. He wasn't sure if he'd be able to move his leg when the time came. In his mind, he rehearsed each action. The twist. The upward push. Breaking through the cloth. Standing. It could not seem like a struggle. If his leg didn't obey, he might need to grab the sides of the chest for support. Torchlight would be blinding after the dark of his hiding place. He couldn't let it show.

Then he heard his sister's voice returning. And Janus. In horror, he listened to the argument, to Janus's challenge. Elizabeth didn't understand what was coming: the demand for satisfaction.

The table juddered. He felt footsteps vibrating through the crate, tried to picture the scene in his mind, to understand what she was doing. The vibration of her footsteps receded as she picked her way down the table. Then he saw it – in his mind's eye – a dark entranceway at the very end, where she was heading. Her gun was loaded. His was not. That was the illusion they'd planned. She had the flash bomb in her pocket. It could still work.

He began flexing his toes, tensing his leg muscle and relaxing it again, trying to get blood to circulate, trying not to shift the crate or its contents.

The back of Elizabeth's head itched as she imagined a hidden shooter taking aim. She slipped her left hand into her pocket and withdrew the flash bomb, keeping it concealed in her fist. Once the ring was pulled, she would have half a second.

Pull. Drop. Eyes closed. Half a step back.

There would be no misdirection this time. Indeed, she was the misdirection for Janus's second shooter. Would Edwin even understand what she was going to do?

Five paces remained to the end of the table. The courtyard had fallen completely silent. She had to make noise to stop them hearing the fall of the flash bomb. Bringing back a foot she kicked a metal goblet, sending it clattering onto the flagstones.

Four paces. Nothing to kick.

Three paces. With the side of her foot she pushed a metal plate over the edge.

Two paces. Trying to fix in her mind the dark entranceway just beyond the table end.

Pulling the ring from the bomb. Dropping it. Stepping over it. Turning. Seeing Janus facing her, raising his pistol. And in the last moment it seemed she did catch the crisp line of a gun barrel in a window.

Eyes closed.

Detonation.

The world turned white. She let herself fall back, twisting as she dropped. The ground hit her hard on the shoulder, knocked the breath from her, but she was scrambling away, blind, towards the memory of the shadows.

Hearing the bang, Edwin launched himself upwards, using the barrel of the pistol to force through the thin cotton. The sudden weight of fruit pressing down on him was more than he'd expected. He pushed himself onto one knee, raised his gun hand, felt the chill air of the courtyard as he broke through.

Suddenly there was light and the smell of cooked food. And air. He tried to stand, but the muscles of his left leg felt like clay. With his free hand he gripped the side of the crate and pushed himself up. A woman screamed. It was the consort, in front of him, not behind. He was facing the wrong way. Disorientated, he whipped around, bringing his gun to aim at the back of Janus's head.

There had been noise, the sounds of surprise. Gasps,

oaths. But as Edwin's senses cleared, he began to take in the whole scene.

Janus had been holding out his own gun, aiming along the length of the long table. Aiming at nothing. Slowly his hand dropped. He turned. Edwin saw recognition in his eyes. And torment. It was a terrible thing.

"Do you yield?"

Janus shook his head, though it seemed not a response to the challenge, but to some internal conflict. His head snapped back to look towards the end of the table, where Elizabeth must have been standing moments before.

"Do you yield?" Edwin asked again.

"How did you do that?" It was a whisper. Then, again louder, "How did you do that?"

"He's the Magician of Crown Point," said Timon, approaching.

There was something frightened and brittle in Janus's expression. The man who had believed in only the powers of the physical world. He had witnessed a thing beyond explanation. He looked down to the spilled fruit on the table, then to the gun in Edwin's right hand, and to the parchment in his left.

"No," he said.

"No you don't yield?" Timon asked.

"It's a trick. It has to be a trick."

"That was no trick," said Brandt. "I'd never thought to see such a thing."

"Now you believe in magic?" Timon asked.

"No," said Brandt. "It is some strange science. One we've not yet learned."

Edwin held up the parchment for all to see. "There

are many powers you haven't seen. Will you not be our partners?"

Gilad glanced towards Red, who seemed too shocked to speak.

Edwin handed the document down and watched as Brandt unfolded it on the table and bent close, as if to check that no words had been changed through its transportation.

Edwin wanted to speak, to give them one more push towards signing. But he kept his mouth closed. They had done enough.

Of the three hundred people in the courtyard, no one beyond the high table had spoken a word. Edwin glanced around, and saw them staring, many open-mouthed. It was going to work. For the first time he felt certain. What a trick it must have been. He wished he could have seen it for himself. It was greater than all the grand illusions his mother had described. She would have been proud. And their father. For the first time that he could remember, he wished his father were there.

They'd scattered. Lowborn and lord, it made no difference. As Elizabeth advanced down the long table, gun in hand, they'd scrambled away. By the time she reached the end there'd been no one within ten paces on either side.

Then the flash. Even through closed eyelids, the detonation had been brilliant. A purple sun still floated in her vision. Anyone looking directly at her when it went off would have been blinded. She'd thrown herself back, then scrambled over the flagstones into the shadow of the entrance. Or, into the memory of it. She still couldn't see.

There she'd remained, hiding through stillness, not daring to draw her legs further into the passageway until her vision had cleared enough to be sure that she lay beyond the corner and out of direct view.

Her shoulder throbbed from the fall and her cheeks smarted from the flash bomb. The stink of burned hair clung to her. She felt queasy with it. The hubbub of voices had disappeared, as if everyone in the courtyard had vanished in the same moment as the explosion. All that remained was a thin hiss of tinnitus.

She got to her feet, back pressed against the wall, then inched towards the edge of dressed stone.

Edwin was standing on the table at the far end, facing away from her. Everyone else was staring at him.

Her first feeling was amazement. And triumph. They'd done it. Not as planned. But better than they could have imagined. Anyone watching would have thought Edwin had been forced into the situation. The flash. The vanishing act. The magical reappearance. It all came from someone else's will.

Staring at her brother in the distance felt eerily like catching sight of herself in a mirror. In front of him the king and Brandt were bending over something on the table. Immediately behind Edwin, Janus had crouched, head bent, face covered by one hand, as if in mourning. She scanned the dark windows behind and above the high table, searching for another glimpse of that gun barrel.

CHAPTER 39

At first Elizabeth walked slowly, to be quiet. Then she ducked into an alcove, unlaced her boots, and set off at a run, with one in each hand. Even the kitchen staff were at the feast, now. The passageways were empty and silent. At the turn of the corridor she set off up the stairs, climbing two flights, then out and along another passage, heading north this time.

She'd seen a gun barrel in one of the windows. Or thought she had. The fraction of a second before the flash had seemed so vivid. But in memory it felt unreal. She'd been looking for a shooter. Perhaps the window had been empty and her mind had filled in the blank.

Approaching the north wall of the castle, she slowed, stopping at the turn of the passageway. To listen. To wait.

Little time had passed since the vanishing. Yet the crowd in the courtyard had begun to make noise again. A low hubbub. The sound of excitement. The story being re-told. At first she could hear nothing else. Then a metallic click echoed in the passageway: the mechanism of a gun, crisp and clear.

Relying on the blackness to hide her, she stepped around the corner. There were no lamps. But five splashes of light marked out five tall windows, each most of the height of the passageway. In the fourth splash of light she saw the silhouette of a figure, standing, gun raised to shoulder, the long barrel angled steeply down into the courtyard. Whoever was in his sights, they were close to the north wall. That meant the platform. The high table. The king, the consort, the embassy. And Edwin. The last remnant of her family.

Elizabeth shifted both of her boots to one hand and raised her pistol with the other. She began to advance, silent and with purpose. The figure shifted aim a fraction, readying to take a shot. She had passed through the light of two windows unseen, but as she stepped through the third, the shooter flinched and jumped back. They were both in shadow now.

"Who goes there?"

A man's voice, further to the right than she'd imagined. She shifted her aim, sidestepped to the left, bringing her shoulder to the wall. If she fired, it would bring guards running. She'd be captured. The trick would be uncovered. If she ran, the shooter might finish his work.

"Who is it?" he asked again.

She adjusted her aim. To the left this time. He was on the move, as silent as her. The calm of his voice chilled her. Her own blood was pumping so hard that she could hear the thud of her heart. She lowered herself to the ground, trying to get under his aim, but the sleeve of her jacket brushed against the stones. A rasping whisper.

His footsteps rushed at her. Something hard jabbed into her side: the muzzle of his gun.

"Get up," he said. That same calm voice. "Let's have a look at you. And you can leave that pistol on the floor."

She did as he said, clambering back to her feet, the gun barrel never shifting from her kidney. Then a shove, sending her into the splash of light next to the window. She heard the catch of his breath.

"Turn," he whispered.

She did. Slowly. Facing him. A wiry figure. With the light of the window directly behind, she couldn't see his expression. But she heard the gasp as he saw her: the very image of the man he'd been aiming at a moment before. His shoulder twitched. The barrel of his long gun wavered.

"Impossible." He hissed the word. His head turned, as if he was about to look behind him, through the tall window, down into the courtyard.

There would be no better chance to act.

She lunged, twisting so her shoulder caught him in the chest. He tripped backwards, towards the window, toppling, set to fall through. But in the last moment he twisted his long gun around so it caught the stones on either side. She could see his face now in the light of the torches. A man she'd never seen before, his surprise twisting to anger. He began to heave his centre of gravity back towards standing. She ducked, grabbed one of his ankles, lifted. The long barrel scraped the wall as it twisted free. Then he was falling, and the rifle with him. She heard the impact as he hit the ground and a split second later, a gunshot.

The vanishing act had shaken them: the king, the men of the embassy, perhaps Janus most of all. The only one who seemed unmoved was the consort, who had believed in his magic from the start. Edwin had been standing on the table since the miracle, watching the king and Brandt as they examined the agreement. He wanted to tell them to sign. But this apple would only fall when it was ripe.

They'd unfolded the parchment on the high table and were bent over it, reading line by line. Others in the courtyard had begun to whisper, the volume of their voices growing as they gave confidence to each other.

Edwin could feel the atmosphere changing from wonder to excitement. If he left it much longer he might not even be heard. He took a deep breath and began: "There are two paths before you. One path leads to our separation. The Gas-Lit Empire will grow outwards into the free wilds. In time we'll be cut off from each other. There won't be a battle. Just a slow decline. At last we'll be begging to join them. Or our children will."

Everyone on the high table was looking up at him now. Brandt seemed troubled, as if disturbed by a thought that he might agree. Everything rested on the next few words.

"Is that a prophecy?" Gilad asked.

That had been the plan: to claim mystical knowledge. But meeting Gilad's eyes, he changed his mind. "No. This is the science of reason." Afterwards, he would wonder why he'd said those words.

"Then what does reason say about the other path?"

"It's harder to read," Edwin said. "If we make this alliance, you will have our newest guns. You will control the eastern seaboard. We will launch our war against the nations of North America."

"The outcome?"

"Together we take the continent. Probably."

Red got to his feet. "And the first path? Is that certain?"

"Nothing is certain."

Gilad and Tomo were looking at Red, whose thoughts seemed in turmoil. He shook his head. He tugged at his beard.

But whatever he had been about to say was cut short by the crash of something heavy landing behind the high table. A body. A gunshot reverberated around the courtyard. Gilad cried out in pain.

Then everyone was moving. The king jumped to shield his consort. Brandt dived on the man who had fallen. Timon drew a knife. Gilad staggered back, clutching a bloody hand to his chest.

Edwin felt the table shifting under his feet and turned to see Janus in the act of clambering down. There was fear in his face. Terror. On instinct, Edwin grabbed his arm, hauling him back.

With Brandt's body in the way, he couldn't see the face of the fallen man. A sniper rifle lay next to him. The impact must have triggered the shot. Gilad had taken the random bullet. Grandson to the king of Newfoundland.

Janus was thrashing his arm, trying to get away. But other hands were helping now, a gang of revellers holding him, his struggle to escape the only instruction they needed.

Edwin left them to it, jumped to the high table, clambered down on the other side. He ignored the shooter. It could have been anyone. A paid assassin. Gilad was all that mattered. His hand was still clutched to his body, blood-soaked clothes seeming black in the yellow torchlight. If he died, there could be no alliance.

Others were pressed close around him.

"Hold it up," one of them shouted.

Then Gilad was swearing, raising his arm, and Edwin saw that the wound was in the hand itself, not the body. All the blood had come from there. He would live.

The assassin did have one more part to play. Edwin recognised the face, but vaguely. He'd been one of the castle garrison a year before, a man by the name of Bartholomew who had gone missing. Brandt had him pinned, though he couldn't have escaped in any case. He'd fallen badly, the unnatural twist of his leg spoke of shattered bones. But it was his words, not his injuries that proved fatal.

"It was Janus made me do it," he said, which was enough of a confession to seal his death.

The king picked up the long rifle. Brandt stepped back. Edwin looked away and didn't see the shot. Then it was Janus's turn. Everyone remembered his demand for satisfaction, so uncharacteristic. Everyone could see the assassin's long gun with its telescopic sights, and the window he had fallen from. Timon took hold of Janus's arm and dragged him before the king, who gave a nod. The revellers had become a mob. Edwin watched them surge forwards, pushing his enemy ahead of them, driving him not towards the battlements, but to the marshalling yard. He did not want to follow, but had no choice. He needed to be with the men of power.

In the yard, the crowd parted for them. Janus was revealed, standing in front of the ruined straw bales. No one had tied him. But there was nowhere for him to run. A wall of bodies and faces cut off any possibility of his escape.

And there stood the means of death: the Mark Four

automatic gun on its reinforced mount, a technician slotting in the end of an ammunition belt.

A hush and stillness spread through the crowd. Janus was shaking his head, as if denying some point of argument. He wiped his brow and blinked.

No one had taken the controls of the gun. The king looked to Timon, who avoided his brother's gaze. Then to the technician, who suddenly seemed to realise what was expected of him. The man's expression fell to horror, but he knelt all the same. He gripped the gun, his finger hovering over the trigger, glanced back to the king with a pleading expression. But the king's nod was a command he could not ignore.

The gun roared. The ammunition belt leapt into life. Straw bales to the left of Janus exploded into dust. As the technician began to pull his aim around, Edwin closed his eyes. The barking roar of the gun went on and on. Then stopped, the silence somehow more dreadful than the noise had been.

Later that night, Red agreed to the treaty and it was signed. Edwin never knew if it had been the Vanishing Man that had persuaded him, or the brutal demonstration of the new gun. Either way, he had achieved his goals and Janus was gone. It should have been a moment for celebration but he felt sick. He thought of his family: his parents divided, their argument bequeathed to him and Elizabeth. He had won, true enough, but could not be glad of it. Nor could he forget the image of his fallen enemy, broken and pathetic, revealed by the settling of the dust.

CHAPTER 40

The prison guard sat with his back to the wall. One hand rested on an earthenware jug, the other cradled a wine glass. His eyes did not open as Elizabeth approached. She looked to the keys at his belt, then to the door he guarded. His breathing sounded slack, but she didn't trust his sleep.

"What are you doing, man?" she growled, the masculine rumble tickling the very back of her throat. She poked him with the toe of her boot and his eyes snapped open.

"Get up, you fool. The king would have you whipped."

He scrambled to his feet, panic in his face, wine glass still clutched in his hand.

"I was awake. I'm sorry. Please…"

"Unlock the door!"

His hands were shaking. The keys jangled like a tambourine. The door opened and a cold wind blew in, tugging at her clothes and hair. She stepped through and then turned to face him.

"It's a feast night. So I won't report your drunkenness."

There wasn't enough light to see his expression, but she

could hear the relief and gratitude in his voice. "Thank you, sir. Thank you. It won't happen again."

"Lock the door behind me," she said. "And never speak of the magic I am about to do."

She saw his head nodding. He wouldn't understand until the morning. And then, perhaps a night of sleep and wine would make him doubt his own memory.

She made her way out along the wooden slats of the walkway, letting the cold chain links run through her hand. At the end, she crouched and whispered, "Are you awake?"

Mary's voice came up to her: "Always."

"I need to come down."

There was no questioning from below. Just a scraping of wooden shingles. Elizabeth reached down between the slats and felt the outline of a hole in the roof of the cell. It would be big enough for her to drop through. But to reach it, she would have to let herself over the edge and somehow get her feet and legs back underneath the walkway.

"If I start to slip..."

"I'll hold you," Mary whispered.

The planks of the walkway had been weathered smooth. Elizabeth lay flat, her feet projecting out over the void, then inched backwards until her hips reached the edge. She felt her balance shifting. Clinging on with her hands, her feet scrabbled under the walkway, trying to find contact, slipping against the sloping roof. Worming backwards again, arms straining to keep hold, she swung her legs under and felt a hand close around one ankle. Then her other ankle was gripped and she was sliding back. She fell the last few feet, her back landing heavily on the roof shingles, but her legs were inside, and then her hips. She dropped down to land on a floor of planks, in the darkness of the cell.

"Welcome," Mary whispered.

All Elizabeth could do was pant, catching her breath, feeling her heartbeat beginning to slow.

"You're not Edwin," Mary said.

"When did you know?"

"The second time you came here. You have the voice. But the things you were asking… They weren't like him."

"Do you have the rope?" Elizabeth asked.

"I do. But who are you?"

"My name is Elizabeth."

"That's not what I meant. Who are you really? What happened to Edwin?"

"He is still in the castle. And he's still the magician. I am…" She faltered. "I am no one."

"That's not true."

The wind gusted, rattling the roof. In the darkness, Elizabeth heard Mary getting to her feet and replacing the missing shingles.

"Will you come with me?" Elizabeth asked.

"You're going down the rope?"

"Yes."

"Escaping?"

"Yes."

"If I go missing, they'll come after us."

"We'll travel at night."

"If you go alone, no one will follow. And if I went with you, I'd only be giving the king what he wants."

Elizabeth said: "If you die in this cell, what will it achieve?"

"I don't know. But then, I could never have guessed that you'd be here like this. You're going to go out into the world and you're going to tell other people what I've told you. The world is going to change."

There was the warmth of a smile in Mary's voice.

The wind slackened. Elizabeth found herself listening to near-silence.

"You're his sister," Mary said.

"How did you know?"

"You're so similar. Yet different. Let me hold your hand."

The skin of Mary's fingers was rough, her grip firm. "Remember me," she said.

"If I live, I will never be able to forget."

The cell had been bolted to the wall by four iron brackets. Onto one of these, Elizabeth tied the end of the rope. Mary unlatched a section of the end wall and swung it inwards. The rope dropped into the blackness. There were no more farewells. Elizabeth let herself over the side, keeping her body close to the rope and gripping it with her feet, she began letting herself down, hand over hand.

The wind gusted again, blowing her against the rock. The further she went, the more the rope stretched to her movement. Then the cliff began to slope outwards, so that she could find footholds. Two times she stopped to rest her arms. She couldn't see the ground, but at last heard the wind in the tree tops. She was among the branches when her feet slipped off the end of the rope. She dropped, landed on loose scree, began to slide down the steep slope, but came up hard against the slim trunk of a sapling.

She heard the rope falling before feeling it. It landed in loops all around her. Mary had cast off from above.

The next morning, the king stood with his magician at the top of the highest tower, looking east towards the mountain, its edge lit by the rising sun. The feasting had gone on all night.

"Your fight has cost me a counsellor," he said.

Edwin bowed in that way that Janus had once done, a suggestion of agreement, but yet not. "I've gained you the whole of Newfoundland," he said. "A king for a counsellor. It's not a bad exchange."

The king's frown deepened. He had seemed uneasy since the grand illusion: a darkening of his brow whenever he glanced in Edwin's direction. It must have been comfortable to think that magic could tell the future and that tricks could manipulate the minds of lesser men. But the Vanishing Man had been too perfect. It had upset the balance between them. Edwin had gone from being a useful tool to something more powerful. A rival, perhaps. The king's unease would only grow.

"It was a trick," Edwin said, too quietly for the guards on the stairs below to overhear.

The king stared at him. Shook his head. "I saw the impossible."

"But you didn't see what you thought you saw."

Clouds hung heavy in the northern sky, making the water of the river dark. After the treaty had been signed, he'd slipped away, run back up the stairs to tell Elizabeth he had won. The room was empty. He asked the gate guards. They told him that no one had passed. After that he searched the room again, and found the rope missing.

Somewhere out there she was struggling back towards Lewiston, carrying the third copy of the treaty document. If she made it across the border, the forces of the Gas-Lit Empire would learn of their plans. He remembered what she'd said: *I can't weigh a single life, let alone a hundred million.*

All he had to do was tell the king. Hunters would be sent out. They'd get her back and stop that parchment getting into the hands of the enemy.

"How did you do it?" the king asked.

"I built the crate of fruit just like one of my mother's cabinets. And there was a flash bomb to blind the audience for long enough."

"But how could you have gone from one end of the courtyard to the other so quickly?"

Edwin remembered the warmth of his sister's touch. "Did you not see the sweat on my face when I emerged?" he asked.

The king shook his head.

"I scrambled back underneath the trestle tables, then up through a trick hatchway in the bottom of the crate. I had longer than you think."

Some of the tension drained from the king's face. He sighed. "When you tell me how your tricks are done, they seem... so much less. And yet you fooled our guests. I will need a new counsellor, Edwin. More than one perhaps. People who disagree with you. Yours can't be the only voice in my ear."

"Yes, sire. It is the best way."

At that the king smiled, and more warmly than Edwin

could remember. "I should have trusted you," he said. "History has proved you faithful."

Edwin knelt. The king's hand rested on his head, a royal blessing.

When he stood, the king held him by the shoulders and looked straight into his eyes. "We have much to do, and little time. Are you ready for the challenge?"

Edwin said, "I am."

CHAPTER 41

Wars are won in battles. But also in those battles never fought. The historians of the End, those people who would study the great collapse of the Gas-Lit Empire, would point to this as the moment that divided time. The event that the future-casters of the Patent Office feared had come to pass. The Americas were being cut off from the rest of the world. Change had become inevitable, but its outcome could not be predicted. It was the greatest unknown in the Map of Unknown Things.

As for Elizabeth, she walked until she came to the Columbia River, then found a thicket to sleep in through the day. At nightfall she set out again, walking always against the flow. In this way she reached the mouth of the Snake River. Her food ran out after four days. Beyond that, she walked hungry, and would soon have died but for a trader's camp where she stole two loaves of bread.

The vastness of that great country seeped into her, a kind of delirium, awe mixed with fatigue and hunger. The river always flowing on her left. The brown hills reaching up to the sky on her right. When she turned her head, the horizon swam.

When the loaves had been eaten, she chewed grasses and leaves from the scrubby bushes next to the river, trying to fool her body with the illusion that it was still being fed. It could have been the wrong river. She might have been walking into an endless wilderness. But one day she saw an insubstantial line cutting across the world. Wooden posts and barbed wire. It would seem more substantial on a map. She remembered the words of Mary Brackenstow.

There was no way to find the place where the Arthurs had made the crossing. So she walked along the fence, on the wrong side, so to speak, until she came to a small gully where the wire didn't quite reach the ground. With her last strength, she lifted it and crawled underneath, hardly feeling the barbs raking against her shoulders.

Some feelings are too complex to be rendered into words, but tears are enough to express them. So she lay down and wept for all the tragedy she'd seen, and the loss, and for the chaos that was to come. One piece of her own history had been completed. A void that she'd not previously been aware of had been filled. And on this foundation she felt somehow stronger.

In the dust next to a mile marker she dug a hole, scooping it out with her hands until it was deep enough to feel moisture below. Then she laid the parchment in the bottom and back-filled it, flattening the earth until all that remained was a darker patch, which grew pale as it dried in the wind. Then there was nothing but the marker stone itself. Twenty-three miles to Lewiston.

Later, it may have been the next day, though afterwards she couldn't remember the sky becoming dark, a wagon came rolling along that track. Two outriders found her first, men dressed in the dark blue of the border regiment. They took her up, laid her in the back of the wagon, gave her water and food. This is how she returned to Lewiston.

None of them recognised her, though there were wanted posters on the wall of the guardhouse. It was a bad likeness. She could have stepped out from that place and disappeared from history. Instead she pointed to the poster and pointed to herself, still too weak to express herself in any other way. Then they understood.

Patent Office agents arrived within the hour and took her into custody. It took two more days before she was strong enough for questioning to begin. After the first session, she asked after Mrs Arthur. No one could tell her anything. But two days later, as she was being escorted to the air terminus, one of the agents said that he had checked it out. No one had seen Mrs Arthur or Conway for several weeks. As they escorted her onto the airship, hands cuffed, she found herself weeping once again.

In New York, the agents tried to threaten the story out of her, as they'd done in Niagara. But Julia and Tinker were free already. The Patent Office had nothing left to bargain with except her own life, which they'd already said they could not protect, and which she despaired of saving.

In response to every question she replied: "I will talk to John Farthing."

After three days they moved her from comfortable accommodation to a bare concrete cell. Three times a day they brought food and water. Otherwise she was left alone.

But on the fifth day, the door opened and Farthing stepped inside. His cheeks had hollowed since she last saw him. He covered the spy hole with one hand, holding her with his free arm. She clung to him, as she had in the washroom above the falls.

"You're thinner," she whispered.

"You're just the same," said he.

She breathed in his scent and felt a wave of warmth pass through her body, as if every vessel and capillary had dilated in the same moment.

"I've done it," she said.

"What have you done?"

"I know their plans. I know what they're doing. In Newfoundland. And in Oregon."

"I'm supposed to ask you to talk. I'm supposed to say that you'll be hanged as a mutineer if you don't."

"They'll still hang me if I do," she said.

"I know."

She felt the sag in his body as the truth of what she was saying took hold of him. "They've offered me no deal. They say it's not in their control, and in any case my words aren't so precious to them. The sailors – they're demanding my death. Once I've told my story, the Patent Office will hand me over."

"Elizabeth – you're so much stronger than me. I don't think I can take this anymore." He struggled free from her embrace, still covering the spy hole, and from his pocket drew a small glass vial of pale green liquid. "There's enough in here for both of us. It's painless, they tell me. Once I crack the seal, I'll drink half. The rest is yours."

"The Patent Office wants to know the things I've seen," she said. "And I want to tell them. But I can give them more than words. If they had something they could hold in their hands, something to place before the governments of the Gas-Lit Empire…"

"It's the Navy that will kill you. It will be a hanging. In public. Oh, my darling. Oh, my Elizabeth."

She took the vial from him. "I will die sure enough. And so will you. But not for nothing. There may be a deal to be done. If your masters had hard evidence in their hands, they might persuade the governments to act. And to do it now – before it's too late. You must take a message for me. And trust me."

It seemed that he did, for they kissed then. More like true lovers than they'd ever been. Not just with the passion of their first kisses. But also with the knowledge of each other and themselves that all the trials and separation had given them.

CHAPTER 42

FUGITIVE MUTINEER DEAD

Elizabeth Barnabus, fugitive mutineer from the Battle of the Grand Banks, recently recaptured by agents of the International Patent Office in New York, was yesterday discovered unconscious in her cell. Despite valiant efforts to resuscitate her, doctors arriving half an hour later pronounced her deceased. According to constabulary sources, no third-party is being sought in connection with the death.

This brings to a close the remarkable scandal of Miss Barnabus who, having been uncovered masquerading as a sailor on the whaling ship Pembroke, *joined forces with a band of female pirates, took part in the imprisonment and cruel treatment of the crew and later led the attack on the mother ship of the North Atlantic fleet, which resulted in its capture.*

— FROM *THE TIMES OF LONDON*

At about the same time as the newspaper article was being read on the other side of the world, in an anonymous office on Fifth Avenue, John Farthing and the five most senior Patent Office agents in North America were sitting down to a meeting. The seventh man at the table, a recording secretary, had written the date and the names of all present. Now he waited, face impassive, pen poised.

There was a soft rapping on the door.

"Come," said the most senior agent.

A young man with dark hair stepped inside. John Farthing stood, the others following his lead. Only when the newcomer was sitting did they retake their places.

"Thank you for coming," said the senior agent.

The recording secretary transcribed the words, but then looked up, confused. "What name shall I give?" he asked.

The newcomer smiled at him. "I'm Elizabeth Barnabus." The feminine voice was at odds with the masculine face. The recording secretary squinted, his eyes widening in surprise.

The senior agent held up his hand. "That name is left behind, my dear. Even our records will show that Elizabeth Barnabus is dead. The circle of people who can connect your past life to your new identity must be confined to those in this room."

"Did you go to the border fence?" she asked.

The senior agent removed the lid of the box, revealing a folded parchment. "All was as you said. Twenty-three miles north of Lewiston, buried in front of the distance marker."

"I know about the Map of Unknown Things," said the woman who used to be Elizabeth. "I know that it shows those moments beyond which your future-casters can't see. And I know that America being cut off from the Gas-Lit Empire is the thing you've feared beyond all others. This document tells you that they know it too. Your enemies in Oregon and

Newfoundland have worked out the same truth. For you it is the threat of change. For them it is an opportunity. If they first strangle this continent, they'll be able to wage war against the rest of the world. I don't know if there's anything that you can do to stop them. But if you act quickly…"

The senior agent nodded. "Perhaps," he said. "Perhaps the Gas-Lit Empire will fall. But with this, we may be able to change the manner of its falling. And shape whatever it is that will come after. There's much to do. And little time. We've read your report. You've given us much. Now, according to our agreement, you can walk free and start your new life."

Elizabeth looked from face to face around the table. She still couldn't quite think of herself by her new name. It would come with practice. It seemed she'd learned her own true history only to have to cover it up again.

The world was changing. Perhaps she could find a hiding place somewhere that would be free from the storm that was coming. It would have to be far from the cities. They would surely be consumed. She could grow her own food. Raise some animals. And keep a gun ready, in case the battle came to her. But she'd seen too much on her journeys to trust in that idea. The war, if it came, would be terrible. New weapons were ready to tear apart all order and grace. The people she loved would be caught up in it. Julia and Tinker. And John Farthing.

For a moment, she met his gaze across the table and felt her heart constrict. To walk away would mean never seeing him again. It was a price too high.

"I would rather help you," she said. "With my new identity, could I not work within the Patent Office, instead of against it?"

"I'd hoped you might say that," the senior agent said. "We have much to do. And little time."

The safe house was a damp, single-roomed apartment with peeling wallpaper. Its one window looked out on the wall of another building, almost close enough to touch. The corridors and stairway were narrow. But no one asked any questions. She guessed the other denizens of the building had their own secrets to hide.

With the first payment of her new allowance, she went out to buy fresh bedding and a box of candles. On her way back she found a delicatessen.

They hadn't been able to make an arrangement, never being alone together, but she knew John Farthing would come. At his knock, she opened the door. He stepped in, blinking at the scene she had created, the candles on every surface, the blankets and sheet spread out on the floorboards, the feast of simple food and wine.

He was dressed in the same grey suit he'd been wearing at the meeting, his shirt creased from a long day of work. He looked at her, first with adoration, and then with surprise as he took in the change.

She smiled, turned for him to see her clothes from every side. She had kept the male shirt and trousers she'd been wearing earlier, but unbound her breasts, so that her figure showed through. She had made up her eyes with kohl, and deepened the red of her lips. Her dark hair she had tied back.

The last time they'd had the chance to lie together, she'd wanted him to turn away whilst she stripped from her male clothes. Partly for her own sake. Partly for his. So not to put that image into his mind, of her caught halfway between man and woman.

"Look at me," she said, because he was turning his head away. "Someone once asked me which clothes I'd choose, if it didn't matter what anyone thought, if I could dress either way. I didn't know then. But now I do. When I go out of here, I'll have to dress so that no one sees what I am. I'll be a woman for them or a man. Either way it'll be a disguise. But when I'm with you, when we're alone, I want you to see me as I really am. I can't explain it. I just don't want to hide from you anymore."

He did look, then. Long and slow. Tear tracks on his face reflected the candlelight. "You could have shown me before," he said.

"I couldn't. I'd like to say it was just because I didn't know it myself. But there was more. I don't think I really believed you would want me if you saw me like this. Then I met my brother. For all we came to disagree on, in this they were right. And slowly I came to see it. This is something real."

"I want you above all things," he said. "I was ashamed of it before. That was why I had to turn away when you got changed. It wasn't the manner of your dress. It was knowing I was about to break my vows. I had to look the other way until you embraced me. Only then I could forget."

"Might you break your vows again?" This she asked with a smile, because there seemed no regret in him.

"If you will let me," he said. "It must still be our secret. But I won't be ashamed of what we do."

"I have a new name," she said.

"I'll do my best to remember," he said. "When I whisper in your ear."

He wore a smile now, bright enough to match hers. She opened her arms and he stepped into her embrace.

AFTERWORD

On reading news of her friend's death, Julia had fallen into grief. But three days later, a postcard arrived at her home in New York. On one side was a photograph of Annie Edson Taylor standing next to the barrel in which she had famously plunged over Niagara Falls. On the other side was written a quote from the Bullet Catcher's Handbook: *There is no more complete and satisfying way for a man to disappear than for him to have never existed.*

On reading this, Julia took off her black armband and folded it away in a drawer. She then sought out Tinker, her newly adopted son, and read the message to him. The boy, who had never accepted Elizabeth's death, took the card, sniffed it, then held it to his chest. No words were needed. They both understood.

ACKNOWLEDGEMENTS

I am immensely grateful for the help, advice and support received from many people during the writing of this book. Everyone at Angry Robot has been marvellous. Marc, Penny, Nick, Lottie, Eleanor, Gemma, Paul, Claire: thank you. Thanks also to Sara Codair, the members of LWC, Terri Bradshaw and Ed Wilson, who each contributed invaluable expertise.

As always, my greatest debt is to my family, partly for putting up with me through the whole process. But also for direct help in the form of advice, suggestions and proof reading: Joseph, Anya, Stephanie: thank you.

And finally, a big thank you to the many readers of the previous books who gave me encouragement along the way, by writing reviews, saying hello on social media, responding to my occasional cries of frustration and generally keeping me company as I wrestled the plot of this one into shape.

ABOUT THE AUTHOR

ROD DUNCAN writes alternate history, fantasy and contemporary crime. His novels have been shortlisted for the Philip K Dick Award, the East Midlands Book Award and the John Creasey Dagger of the Crime Writers' Association. A dyslexic with a background in scientific research, he now lectures in creative writing at DeMontfort University. Some might say that he is obsessed with boundary markers, naïve 18th Century gravestones and forming friendships with crows. But he says he is interested in the way things change.

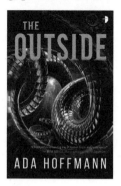